THE CROWNING GLORY OF CALLA LILY PONDER

Rebecca Wells is a novelist, actor and playwright. She is the author of *Little Altars Everywhere*, *Divine Secrets of the Ya-Ya Sisterhood* and the bestselling *Ya-Yas in Bloom*. Wells' books have been translated into twenty-three languages. She grew up on a working plantation in Alexandria, Louisiana, and now lives on an island near Seattle with her husband, their spaniel and their sheep.

For more information about Rebecca Wells and her books, please visit her website, www.ya-ya.com

Praise for *Ya-Yas in Bloom*:

'Welcome back to the original Ya-Ya Sisterhood, *Sex and the City* girls of the fifties!' *Daily Mail*

'Uplifting, uproarious, saucy and smart, the Ya-Ya sisterhood sequel lives up to the highest expectations' *Booklist*

'Essential for Ya-Ya fans' *Heat*

'This is a glorious read that takes you into the heart of small-town America' *Good Book Guide*

'Continuing the tradition of feisty American girlfriends who pull together in a crisis – Thelma and Louise, The Steel Magnolias – this is a beauty of a read' *Good Housekeeping*

Also by Rebecca Wells

Little Altars Everywhere
Divine Secrets of the Ya-Ya Sisterhood
Ya-Yas in Bloom

REBECCA WELLS

The Crowning Glory of Calla Lily Ponder

This novel is entirely a work of fiction.
The names, characters and incidents portrayed in it are the work of the author's imagination. Any resemblance to actual persons, living or dead, events or localities is entirely coincidental.

Harper
An imprint of HarperCollins*Publishers*
77–85 Fulham Palace Road,
Hammersmith, London W6 8JB

www.harpercollins.co.uk

A Paperback Original 2009
1

A catalogue record for this book is available from the British Library

978 0 00 731903 9

Printed and bound in Great Britain by
Clays Ltd, St Ives plc

Mixed Sources
Product group from well-managed forests and other controlled sources
www.fsc.org Cert no. SW-COC-1806
© 1996 Forest Stewardship Council

FSC is a non-profit international organisation established to promote the responsible management of the world's forests. Products carrying the FSC label are independently certified to assure consumers that they come from forests that are managed to meet the social, economic and ecological needs of present and future generations.

Find out more about HarperCollins and the environment at
www.harpercollins.co.uk/green

This book is for Tom,
who ran many marathons,
with the many changing finish lines.

This book is for Tom,
to rest.

The glory is not in never falling,
but in rising every time you fall.

—CHINESE PROVERB

PROLOGUE

The Moon Lady

I know the moon and the moon knows me. I am the moon and the moon is me. I am life itself. I am not who they think I am, that old white man with the long white hair whose judging eyes try to force fear into their very pores. I am the moon mother, and I hold my children on my lap, night and day, in the heat and in the shade. When they wake and when they sleep, I whisper to them: Don't be afraid, don't be afraid. The ones who feel my lunar light pause before they walk out into the day. They take a deep breath, greet the morning with love, and invite grace to enter them at every moment. All have pain, but not all suffer. The body might ache, loss might occur. But for those who embrace my light, there is dancing.

There is a hamlet named La Luna in the center of Louisiana, on the banks of a river with the same name. It is a piney-wood river town of 1,734 souls. I watch them as they try their best to live each moment in their little town named after the river, on this fragile spinning planet. This world is made up of stories—every person's story, those that are hidden, and those that are outright and clear. This is the story of one named for a flower.

I danced with her mother on an old wooden floor where rhythm was queen. I danced with her father as he held her mother. I danced with her mother when her belly was big, a sail blown full with the wind. I held her mother as she let go of the earth's pull, as her family did its best to let the sweet dancing mother come home to me.

The sun shines hard and bright on my people. The air hangs heavy and humid in this swampy state where the quiet La Luna River flows into the Mississippi. That wide, robust river carries life and dreams, commerce and poisons out into the Gulf of Mexico. There I watch the Louisiana coast recede, losing a football-field piece of land every twenty minutes. Saltwater rushes in through canals cut by the oil companies into the fragile, freshwater marshes that struggle to nurture life. I see crazy flames dot the coast from gas and oil rigs that extract from deep in the earth what, eons ago, were once living plants. All that oil provides energy, and carries a cost. It both gives and takes life.

Whether or not they see me, moonlight bathes my raggedy, tender people. Sometimes they are capable of unimaginable kindness. Other times they are filled with near-paralyzing fear. Even when it is dark, though, when all light seems to be eclipsed, there is light on them. Light in them. I see it. I see it every day under the sun, every night under my lunar glow.

Oh yes, I know the moon and the moon knows me. I watch my children as they dance in La Luna, the hamlet named for me, in the beating of the heart of the crazy, holy state of Louisiana.

THE

Crowning Glory

OF

Calla Lily Ponder

Part I

Chapter 1

My name is Calla Lily Ponder. I was born in 1953 in La Luna, Louisiana, on the banks of the La Luna River. That is where my mother cut and curled hair, and my father and mother together taught tango, waltz, and the Cajun two-step. They said they named me for their favorite flower because they wanted me to spiral open into radiant beauty, inside and out. Even when I was born, a red, tiny, hollering thing, they claimed they could see the beautiful, creamy-colored, velvety bloom of a calla lily.

My eyes are blue like my mother's—I call her M'Dear—and my complexion is olive like Papa's. I guess the only thing that resembles the flower I'm named for is my long, strong legs. They've served me well so far, and I'm grateful for that. I was taught not to care much what other people thought, unless someone said you were mean to them, and it was true. Then you better pay attention. My big brothers and I learned this at an early age: That it is kindness that makes you rich.

❧

I also learned very early that I loved my mother's hair. Family stories have it that when I was young, nothing soothed me more than being held in M'Dear's arms, playing with her long, shiny chestnut-colored hair. It fell down to her waist, but photos of her at that time show how she held it back in combs so only part of it fell forward. I'd reach up, let it fall over me, then part it, pat it, and curl my fingers in it. I'd play with it the way other children did with new toys, only my mother's hair was new to me over and over again. After a spell of playing with it, I would settle in and just gaze up at her. She would look back, and when she did, she let me see myself reflected in her eyes. It was as if she held this little mirror inside her, just for me, to see me, to know who I was.

M'Dear was the owner and sole practitioner at the Crowning Glory Beauty Porch. The name of her business came from two sources. First, the Bible. Second, the fact that we had a porch that ran all the way around our house.

M'Dear taught me about the Bible early on. "'A woman's hair is her crowning glory,' the Bible says. It's a beautiful quote. Along with the Beatitudes and the Commandments, it's one of the teachings I hope you and your brothers will learn. And don't just learn them, let them into your heart."

Papa said, "Just be kind. Period."

When M'Dear and Papa first moved into our house, M'Dear had the big side porch enclosed and turned into a beauty parlor. It was there that she washed, dried, curled, dyed, bleached, permed, and gave manicures—but not pedicures, and I don't blame her. Down off the porch was the Beauty Patio, with a fountain that had a lady with mermaids swimming under her like they were holding her up. The Crowning Glory Beauty Porch was where most all the La Luna ladies came to catch up on the latest news. Even ladies without appointments stopped by in the afternoons for coffee, bringing some sweet baked goods to share with everybody. As Papa put it, "Lenora has made her beauty porch the Crowning Glory Gathering Place!" I always got goosebumps and felt slightly disoriented when I heard my mother called by her name. It reminded me of her life that was separate from being my mother. As close as M'Dear and I were, it was good to be reminded. It kept things in balance. In their classes, I watched her at Will and Lenora's Swing 'N Sway, Papa and M'Dear's dance studio. I'd see her cha-cha, swirl and dip, waltz, fox trot, and samba with other men on a regular basis. She had two chiffon skirts, and when she dressed up in one of them, she looked so different from the M'Dear I knew in her cotton dresses, or shorts and a starched white blouse. On the nights when she was demonstrating dances and teaching certain moves, I was both proud and a little jealous. When I told her that, she hugged me, and said, "Oh, little Calla, there's enough of me to go around. I have enough love for you, and other people too."

On the days that M'Dear washed her hair, she called them "Days of Beauty." She spent the whole day pampering herself, and she taught me how to pamper myself as well.

"If cleanliness is next to Godliness," M'Dear said, "then pampering is next to Goddessness." My mother would say those kinds of things and then give a little laugh and a wink like we had a secret club.

On Days of Beauty, we had fans made of vetiver root so that when we fanned ourselves we smelled the wonderful, spicy, of-the-earth smell that is the vetiver plant, grown on the Clareux plantation not far from La Luna. M'Dear made it a game for us to create facials from ingredients out of the kitchen and the garden. This was all before I started school, and was graced to spend days on end with my mother, so rich and private that even now I can close my eyes and relive them. I do not mean to say that those days were perfect. Even at that age, I heard the edge in M'Dear's voice when she and Papa sat at the kitchen table, at night, talking about money. Sometimes we had very little, and that was scary, although I didn't know then what it all meant. It was just as well, since it all worked out. In the world of La Luna, my parents were too creative to go broke.

During the wet, cold months that make up a Louisiana winter, M'Dear's hair was so long and thick that drying it could take all day. On those days we'd stay inside, cleaning, ironing, and cooking up huge pots of gumbo. I'd climb up onto the big soft chair next to the fireplace in the kitchen, and shine shoes or sew on buttons or do the other tasks she was teaching me. I'd sit there and watch her work, watch her go in and out of the washroom like a breeze was blowing her in.

On hot Days of Beauty, we'd put on our swimsuits and stand outside on the wooden platform of the outdoor shower. It was my happy job to scrub clean buckets and other containers and set them outside to gather rainwater to wash our hair. M'Dear would undo my braid, pour the rainwater on my head, put on a little Breck shampoo, and wash my hair. The sun shone down, my mother's hands touched my head, and her fingers lathered love into me. Never has my hair been so soft. Sometimes I still wash my hair in rainwater, to remember.

After our hair was clean, M'Dear would leave hers down, and, still in our swimsuits, we'd hang clean clothes outside to dry on the line, with me handing her clothespins out of a small apron she had sewn for me out of flower sacks. I have a photo of us by the clothesline, doing this very thing. We were working and smiling, squinting slightly in the sunlight. I was just about to enter first grade, just about to leave behind those mother-daughter days of intimacy, of little maternal baptisms. M'Dear prepared me for that leaving so that it was smooth and felt natural. Not all leavings are that easily prepared for.

After finishing chores and when our hair was dry, M'Dear and I would go down to our pier, just before sunset. These memories are so vivid to me that I don't need a photograph to see them. I carry them inside me.

In one memory, it is growing toward twilight. We are sitting on the pier with the La Luna River flowing by.

"M'Dear," I ask, "can I brush your hair with the hundred magical strokes?"

"Of course," she says.

And as the sun sparkled off the cocoa-red water and the wind stirred in the tall pines, I stood behind my mother, my legs on either side of her, and brushed her hair. I lifted her long chestnut hair up off her neck, twirled it up on top of her head, then let it fall, watching its weight settle back down around her shoulders. Then I'd lean my face into her hair and smell it. I can close my eyes and smell it now: sun and vanilla.

What I first learned about love, I learned on that dock with M'Dear. The La Luna River flowing by with its river sounds, the riverbanks with their lovely sweet citrus scent of jasmine, the scent of M'Dear's hair, the oils of her scalp, the fullness of her thick, long curls against my hands, our breathing together, the closeness, her love for me—all of this knit my soul together. When the fading sunlight hit the river, it bounced up to form iridescence, like a halo, around M'Dear's head. *She is the most beautiful person in the universe.*

On clear nights when the moon was out, we'd return to our pier. On the way, she'd point out fireflies. I'd hear a screech; M'Dear would stroke my hair, and say, "Calla, that's just a barn owl, and nothing to be afraid of. Oh, she's a beauty of an owl, with a white, heart-shaped face."

I remember the first time she introduced me to the one who would keep me company forever. She must have told me even earlier, because my big brother Will later told me that as a toddler I used to waddle around in diapers, saying "Moolay, Moolay." And Mama told me, "Your Papa and I held you up in the moonlight when you were barely six months old. Everyone else in La Luna takes their one-year-olds to dip their toes in the river. But we held you up to the moon as well."

That night M'Dear said, "Calla, now look at the moon!" Her voice was filled with love for me and delight in what she was witnessing. "You see how beautiful She is?" M'Dear always called the moon "She." "See how bright She shines! See Her light on the water? Here, let me hold you while we look. Tell me, Calla, what do you see up there?"

"I see a lady."

"I do too, little darling." Then M'Dear wrapped her arms around me and whispered in my ear, "She's the Moon Lady."

We were quiet as we watched the Moon Lady's reflection dance on the river.

"Remember this," M'Dear said. "When the sky and everything around you looks dark, and you feel lost and alone, the Moon Lady is still there, watching over you, whispering: 'What do you need from me now, little darling, what do you need from me now?' "

Then M'Dear lightly touched the crown of my head. "The moon is our mother, sweet daughter of mine. Call on her when you need her. Call on her."

All my life I've remembered those words. Or tried to.

I miss seeing myself reflected in M'Dear's eyes. I thought I'd lost the reflection when she died. But then I learned that it is not permanently lost. That if you wait, like she told me, then you can lift the gauze, lift the veil, and see her eyes again.

I see her now as she held me above the La Luna River, her long hair lit by a waxing moon. I see my mother as she held my baby body up to the lady in the moon.

Chapter 2

Sometimes at night, lying in my bed, I could hear the sounds of the La Luna and picture all that water and where it went. I'd get goosebumps just thinking that I lived on a river that mixed with waters from worlds far, far away. In Louisiana, the town of La Luna is thought of as having a little cuckoo magic to it. Papa says that calling La Luna cuckoo is saying a lot, since Louisiana itself is pretty out of the ordinary. I lived an enchanted childhood in our cuckoo magical little town, but my childhood ended sooner than any of us thought it would.

My parents were Lenora and Will Ponder, and they taught dance at their studio: Will and Lenora's Swing 'N Sway. We were a family of five. Papa was tall, with dark wavy hair and hands that were so beautiful. He played fiddle and squeezebox accordion for Cajun tunes, and trumpet for his 1940s music. It's no wonder he was such a great musician, with fingers like his. Long, tapered fingers.

My mother, with her long hair and blue eyes, seemed to be dancing even when she was still, like there was a dance always going on inside her. My oldest brother was Sonny Boy, who was big, loud, and happy. From the time he was little, his favorite thing to do was building things. He was never happier than when he had a hammer, a nail, and a piece of wood. Will, my other brother, was just a year older than me. He was slender, with beautiful hands like Papa's. He could play just about every kind of instrument, and he was always at Papa's side, learning something new about playing. When Will was six, Papa gave him a fiddle made by one of Papa's buddies, and he was screeching along in his room for what seemed like an eternity, but in a year he was playing in front of Papa's band, the other musicians clapping him on and teaching him more.

My parents taught ballroom, swing, jitterbug, tango, and every other style of dance you can imagine. Grown-ups and children alike came to Swing 'N Sway. Little kids got taught the Cajun two-step, since contrary to some folks' belief, kids in this part of Louisiana are *not* born knowing it from birth. Wednesday nights were Ladies' Nights, and not even Papa was allowed in sight. The most popular was the first Saturday of the month, which was family time at the dance studio, when we'd open as early as nine in the morning. M'Dear and Papa and all our friends made a big pot of gumbo that they cooked in a big cast-iron kettle over a fire that Sonny Boy helped tend. Big ones, little ones, mamas, papas, grandmas, grandpas, uncles, aunts, nieces, nephews, cousins, or friends visiting from out of town—everybody was welcome. Papa's band, Willy and the La Lunatics, played Cajun music on and off, all day long, with different fiddlers, accordion players, and other musicians from all around sitting in. My brother Will loved when these Saturdays would roll around, because he had the chance to sit in with the older Cajun musicians.

Dancing didn't just mean "lady and gentleman" couple-type dancing. It meant any combination of people that wanted to happen. Grandpas dancing with their little grandchildren, old people dancing together, little kids running around causing trouble. People brought picnic blankets and lawn chairs. I always liked seeing the little babies taking naps in their mothers' laps, right under the live oaks outside. I'd go over and visit, and end up holding the baby so the mother could get up and dance—that is, if she didn't want to dance and hold her baby on her hip at the same time, which was a sight you always saw on Saturday mornings. At the Swing 'N Sway nobody felt left out.

No matter what kind of music or people or group, everybody was influenced by my mother's belief in dance. She called it dancing "from the bottom of your heart," or *De plus profond de ton coeur.* Both my parents taught that everything in the world dances, in its own way. Trees dance, stones dance, hats and dogs and candles dance. Pencils dance, flowers dance, telephones and peaches dance. And if we listen, we can dance to the same music.

It was because of M'Dear and Papa that people in La Luna danced so much—not just on those Saturdays, or at a *fais do-do*, our Cajun country dances. Much more than that! People in La Luna danced on their way to the post office if the spirit moved them, and it was not rare to see bankers lock their money drawers and then do the Watusi. Mister Chauvin, the barber, tap-danced regularly in front of his barbershop. He was asked by Mister Bordelon, the druggist, simply not to tap-dance *while* he was giving haircuts. But Mister Chauvin insisted that's how he got his exercise. Pregnant mothers danced, and old people danced with their canes. And everyone knew that the biggest dancer was the river herself.

❧

Some of my happiest moments were during dance lessons. I was content to lie, head in hands, on the edge of the perfectly polished dance floor, studying my parents as they danced by, illustrating different types of dances. My mother's strength and beauty captivated me as she swirled across the dance floor in my father's arms. Her long, flowing hair, her wide open eyes, her power as she swung out and back in, the muscles of her upper arms like no muscles I saw on the arms of the other women in this country town. Her back, so tanned and muscled like the swimmer she was. Above all were the times my parents waltzed together. Watching them waltz made me feel that nothing in the world could ever go wrong. I was so young when I thought that. Yet, it is how I see my mother now—still dancing with strength, power, and grace.

When they weren't teaching at the studio, Papa taught music at La Luna River School, and M'Dear ran her beauty salon, the Crowning Glory Beauty Porch, which was on the side porch of our house. Papa and M'Dear planted a wisteria vine there, and in the spring those cascading clusters of pale lavender blossoms made the whole porch feel like a giant, sweet-scented bouquet.

Aunt Helen was M'Dear's older sister, and the town seamstress. She was married to my uncle Richard, and they lived two blocks from us. Aunt Helen was a big part of our lives. She was not as tall as M'Dear, but almost as pretty, and the two of them loved to cut up.

Aunt Helen had to work after my uncle Richard came back from World War II. M'Dear said he looked just as handsome as when he left, but his mind was still at war. He screamed at night; he could never sleep. Sometimes he cried. We'd often all be eating supper together when Uncle Richard would start to cry. Through his tears, he would say, "Won't you all excuse me, please?" And then he'd go out on the porch alone. Olivia, who came to help Mama sometimes, would come carry his food and ice tea out to him. Olivia was taller than anyone else I knew. And her skin was the color of ice tea once the tea bags had been sitting in there for two whole days. We all loved Olivia and her husband, Pana. Olivia helped M'Dear with cooking and cleaning twice a week. She worked next door at the Tuckers' pretty much all the time. Pana sometimes helped Papa with yard work and fixing gates, hauling brush, and things Sonny Boy and Will couldn't do. Pana was Mister Tucker's right-hand man.

Uncle Richard always carried a book with him everywhere he went. He said it was the best drug he knew of to ease pain. With his full head of thick reddish-blond hair, nobody would have guessed that he was so banged up inside. I suppose that's the way it was with everyone, really, that line between what's inside and what's out.

When I was six, a little bit older, I started asking people if I could fix their hair. I loved to touch it and smell it and feel it. It *soothed* me. It also fascinated me, this line between our insides and our outsides. We have to take very special care I thought, or people's heads could just crack open like eggshells, and everything would come spilling out. So M'Dear's work was important work, like being a nurse, maybe.

M'Dear said the first time I saw a bald man, I thought the world was coming to an end. I must have been around four or five years old. I had never seen anyone who had no hair on their head. It looked like a full moon on top of a man's body.

We were at Kress's Five and Dime Store, where M'Dear was buying me a Coke at the soda fountain, when that bald-headed gentleman walked in. M'Dear said I took one look at him and grabbed her arm so hard she thought I'd break it. "M'Dear," I cried out, "that man hasn't got any *hair*!"

When M'Dear finally calmed me down, the man was standing over by the gumball machine, and I could not take my eyes off him.

M'Dear said, "Excuse me, sir, but my little girl hasn't ever seen a bald-headed gentleman before. Would you mind if she looks at you?"

"Go on ahead and look, honey," he said.

I saw the light glinting off his shiny scalp and asked, "Can I touch your head please, sir?"

I looked at M'Dear.

"It's all right, baby doll," she said. "If it's all right with the gentleman, it's okay with me."

He just squatted down and leaned his head over to me. I rubbed my palm across his bald head, which was smooth and cool. I never realized that there was something like that underneath people's hair.

"Thank you, sir," I said. "Thank you for letting me touch your pretty head."

The man grinned at me. "Thank *you,*" he said, "for calling my head 'pretty.' Been many a moon since I heard that word having anything to do with me."

After that, I saw people differently. Their hairdos protected their delicate skulls! I wanted to be part of making hairdos that might help protect the full moon that sits on top of each person's body.

M'Dear once told me, "Calla, every day, you have to try to improve your angel-eyesight." She always taught me to believe in angels.

Well, to this day, I think that man was an angel. A bald-headed angel.

Sometimes I wondered if my mother was an angel herself. Well, except when I misbehaved. Then she gave me the eye and yelled, and banished me to my room. An hour away like that seemed like an eternity. When I'd get home from school, the first thing I would do was go out to the side porch to see if M'Dear was fixing someone's hair.

When she turned our side porch into a one-chair beauty shop, the ladies started lining up with their pocketbooks dangling from their wrists and scarves on their heads, just waiting for a cut, color, and curl. Papa had put in a beauty parlor sink and a little counter too. The Crowning Glory Beauty Porch was screened in and faced a pretty patio where the ladies could go down during good weather and sit and visit. M'Dear always liked to set out pitchers of ice tea and lemonade, and I took care of that. Louisiana never gets a snowy winter, but it does get bone-chilling cold and wet that calls more for hats than hairdos. But that didn't stop the traffic at the Beauty Porch. Papa would bring in the big heater from the fishing camp that kept the Crowning Glory open and comfortable all year long. During those times, I made big pots of hot chocolate in the kitchen and brought it out to the ladies. I'd stand there smiling, waiting for a tip, until M'Dear shooshed me.

One day, M'Dear was giving Miz Lizbeth a curl. Miz Lizbeth was married to Bernard Tucker, and they were our family's dearest friends. He ran the cotton gin, where farmers took their cotton crop to have it removed from the seedpods and baled. This made him a pretty important man around our neck of the woods, which was full of cotton farmers. Papa knew a lot of them too because everyone danced at the Swing 'N Sway, even farmers on Friday evenings, still using their pocket knives to clean the dirt from under their nails. We called him Uncle Tucker because our families were so close.

One day I asked M'Dear if I could watch her with Miz Lizbeth up close. I was spellbound the whole time. M'Dear was putting Miz Lizbeth's hair into pin curls, and she explained what she was doing as she went along.

The pin curl method is not as easy as you might think. You've got to divide out square sections of the hair with a comb. Then you have to place the curls in *exact* rows, so that one curl covers up the part made by the comb before the next curl.

Well, Miz Lizbeth looked just lovely when M'Dear finished. Her white hair looked full, all thick and fluffy. Now, not a lot of ladies in La Luna had silver hair. They all came to M'Dear to color it on a regular basis.

When M'Dear was all done with Miz Lizbeth, I asked if I could come back and watch her make someone else beautiful. M'Dear tapped her fingers lightly against her lips and said, "Well, all right, Calla. You can watch me this Thursday after school."

So Thursday I got to watch a session with Mrs. Gaudet. Poor Mrs. Gaudet. Her husband, Mister Gaudet, had died three or four months ago, just before school started.

When Mrs. Gaudet came into the Crowning Glory, M'Dear went over and gave her a big hug. "Angie, how are you, sweetheart? Come on in, let me get you a Coke. Go on over there and have yourself a seat."

I said, "Good afternoon, Mrs. Gaudet," then stepped back out of the way and peeked in like a church mouse. Looking back, I would have to say her hair was washed-out gray. If I had to name her hair color like on the color bottles, it would be Exhausted Gray, or Grieving Gray. She was still sad, you could tell. She had that sort of extra-tired look, like there wasn't any amount of sleep that would make things better. I wondered what it would be like to have your husband die. I didn't like to think about it. It was too scary. So I just concentrated on her hair.

M'Dear came back with a Coke and said, "Let's just start with a basic wash today." Then she gently walked Mrs. Gaudet over to the chair at the sink.

"I feel like every single hair is sad, you know what I mean?" Mrs. Gaudet asked my mother.

"Then we're just going to take it hair by hair, okay, Angie?" M'Dear laid her hands on Mrs. Gaudet's shoulder, then very briefly touched her on the forehead. I got the feeling that today's session was one M'Dear wanted me to watch closely. I'd never seen such a sad person have their hair washed before. And then she reached over to get the shampoo, and I watched M'Dear close her eyes first and take a deep breath. Then she leaned Mrs. Gaudet's head back, gently, and got it wet and sudsed it up. "Is that water warm enough?" M'Dear said.

"Well, it could be a little warmer."

"You tell me, Angie. You tell me if everything's all right, okay?" And M'Dear started washing her hair. I could see M'Dear's hands just working up against the back of Mrs. Gaudet's neck, up the sides of her temples, and around her head. And then M'Dear opened her eyes. It was not as if she was looking at the different bottles of hair color on the shelf, Copper Penny or Sparkling Champagne, or as if she was looking at me, or as if I was even there anymore. M'Dear was there but she was also somewhere else. She stared in front of her as she continued to rub Mrs. Gaudet's hair.

She looked down at Mrs. Gaudet's hair, and I sensed that something was traveling from Mrs. Gaudet's heart to M'Dear's. And it was happening through my mother's hands. I didn't really know how long it took, I just know that it happened. I saw M'Dear frown for a moment and tilt her head slightly down, and I could see her take a deep breath. M'Dear kept rubbing and then finally she said, "Ready for a rinse?"

"Yes," Mrs. Gaudet said.

As M'Dear rinsed, I could see her watch closely as the water from Mrs. Gaudet's hair became more and more clear until finally it looked clean enough to drink. The frown passed from my mother's face, and a small smile replaced it. M'Dear began to hum, very lightly, something that I'd never heard before, just a little tune that she'd made up. And then she softly whispered, "How're you doing, Angie?"

Mrs. Gaudet said, "I'm doing a little better, Lenora. I'm feeling washed clean."

"Good." And M'Dear wrapped up Mrs. Gaudet's head with a towel, up into a turban, and she carefully helped her up and into the beauty chair in front of the mirror and towel-dried her hair, and said, "All right, what should we do with your beautiful mane of hair?"

"How about this?" M'Dear said, when Mrs. Gaudet didn't answer. "I've got a fresh new batch of pink sponge rollers. Haven't even tried them out on anybody, so they're not dented in."

"Those sound good," Mrs. Gaudet said.

"Well, while I do it, how about I get you another Coke?"

"Oh Lenora, you're fussing over me too much."

"No, I'm not."

And so I got up without M'Dear asking me and I brought Mrs. Gaudet a Coke in a small bottle, icy on the outside because it had been in the Frigidaire in the back.

She took a sip. "Thank you, Calla."

I watched M'Dear as she began to roll Mrs. Gaudet's hair in a perfect roll all the way back and then on the sides. All the while M'Dear kept humming until Mrs. Gaudet began to talk, just a little bit, very softly.

"The other side of the bed just feels so empty, Lenora," she said, her voice all quavery. "Why did they build beds so big?"

M'Dear just nodded and said, "They do, they build them just too big, don't they? You would think that they'd just automatically shrink to fit to your size so you wouldn't have to keep reaching over so much." That made Mrs. Gaudet laugh. And M'Dear said, "I think we could make a living doing that. Because Angie, just think of it. How many people have people they love die, and when they reach over to the other side of the bed, it's empty." She paused. "You're not alone, Angie. You remember Jolene?"

"Yes, I do."

"That was five years ago, you remember?"

"I do."

"Jolene comes to the Swing 'N Sway on Saturday mornings, she's one of the ones that helps us cook gumbo. And she dances up a storm with her nieces and nephews. Time passes, and it heals like nothing else, except for maybe a new hairdo."

And M'Dear was right. The new style looked very elegant on Mrs. Gaudet, and when she saw herself in the mirror she actually smiled so big it lit up her whole face. She didn't look quite as tired and sad any-more, she actually looked pretty.

M'Dear was usually worn out after sessions like that. She would go and sit down on the swing on our family porch and just swing, back and forth, back and forth, and I could hear her breathing, in and out, her feet sore, barely touching the floorboards. Sometimes she would reach her hand out and I would go and sit on the swing with her. And we would hold hands. I could always feel the heat in her hands then. And I knew that something was passing, not just from Mrs. Gaudet to M'Dear, but something from M'Dear to me.

When little girls say they want to be like their mothers, I was definitely one of them. I saw that M'Dear's hands were doing much more than just washing dirt out of a person's hair. Much, much more. I saw that washing and setting a person's hair could sometimes change her world. That was something I never lost.

Chapter 3

MARCH 1961

My friend Sukey had thick, short, straight black hair. And the largest jewelry collection of any girl I knew. I met her when we were in the third grade at La Luna River School.

M'Dear and Aunt Helen had taken me and my best friend, Renée, to see *Voyage to the Bottom of the Sea* at the Moon Palace Theater. Renée and I have known each other almost since we were born. We played together every day and had both discovered Nancy Drew. We had secret codes and we knew things that nobody else did. We were so close that each of us had pajamas and toothbrushes at each other's house.

Before the show Renée and I went to the ladies' powder room off the lobby, and there was a petite little girl with black hair and very blue eyes standing next to the sink. Her hair was cut short and she had this very cute turquoise satin purse with mysterious things inside, and I couldn't see what all. There were two other girls standing next to her.

"That's it," the short-haired girl said. "Your time for looking at my royal jewels is over." One of the other two girls said, "Please let us look some more."

The girl smiled at Renée and me, and we smiled back. I was glad to have her smile at me, but I would've liked it better if her turquoise purse was mine.

"No, I'm sorry," she said to the little girls. "I have to go. I have people all over town waiting for me."

I washed my hands, then I edged myself over and stared inside the turquoise purse. All I could see before that girl shut it so fast was that it had a velveteen lining and a little place inside where ladies put their compacts. But she just snapped it shut like that! Right in my face. Not one iota of courtesy in that girl's body.

"You could've snapped my nose off," I told her.

"Well, don't put it so close into my pocketbook."

If I had that pocketbook, I would call it a "purse." Someone who didn't even know what to call it should not even have that little turquoise purse.

I just took Renée's hand, and we went back into the dark theater where M'Dear and Aunt Helen were sitting. We didn't even give that purse girl a good-bye.

Voyage to the Bottom of the Sea is about a submarine named the *Seaview* that's supposed to save the world after a meteor starts a fire in the sky. The fire is making the earth really hot, and everyone will die if the fire can't be put out. Well, that's the way it is here in La Luna every summer! Everybody thinks they will die of the heat, but they never do. After a while Renée and I got tired of listening to the movie people talk about the heat, so we slipped out of our seats again and we went back to see if that girl was still in the ladies' room. She was, and this time she was taking a younger girl's hard-earned allowance money.

I whispered to Renée, "Nancy Drew!" which was our private code for needing to do something brave. I pushed the ladies' room door all the way open and said, "Hey! What do you think you're doing?"

The purse girl didn't even look at me.

"Shut up," she said. "If you shut your big mouth, I'll show you my treasures."

She charged us a nickel to open her purse and let us try on her jewels. She had a plastic ring, three Mardi Gras necklaces, a silver dollar, a charm bracelet that was very heavy and smelled like iron, a purple ring with purple and green rare gems, and another ring that was 24-karat gold. "In case you didn't know," she said.

Then she pointed to a ring with a big white clear stone. "That diamond used to belong to Elizabeth Taylor," she told us. When I asked her where she got her hands on all those jewels, she just looked at me and said, "That's none of your beeswax. I am doing you a big favor just by letting you look at them."

Renée pulled on my elbow and whispered, "I think we better leave her alone."

But I said, "How do we know that those jewels don't belong to someone else? How do we know she didn't steal that ring from Elizabeth Taylor?"

The girl said, "If you know what's good for you, you'll leave this ladies' room on the double!"

So we left and went back into the theater. But I was bored with *Voyage to the Bottom of the Sea*. I thought there'd be more sea monsters, but the only thing exciting was when the giant octopus attacked the *Seaview*. I whispered to Renée, "Let's go back to the ladies' room again."

Sure enough, that short-haired girl was still there, and this time she was wrestling with a bigger girl. "Help!" she said, "help me! This girl is stealing my royal jewels!" "Nancy Drew!" I said, and jumped in and helped push the bigger girl away. "Leave her alone! Those are her jewels," I said.

That other girl asked me, "Are you two in cahoots?"

"No," I told her. I didn't know what the word *cahoots* meant, but I wasn't saying so.

Then that bigger girl pointed to this little green bracelet that the short-haired girl was clutching. "I just got that bracelet out of the machine with my own quarter!" she said. "And this little pipsqueak jumped up and grabbed it out of my hands. Do y'all know how long I had to work to get that quarter?"

She took another big swipe to try to grab the green bracelet, but the short-haired girl jumped up on the sink, just *jumped* right up there before you could blink! Ping! Easy as that, like a bunny.

"No!" she was saying, "it's mine! This is my emerald bracelet! Mine! Help me, please, these are my special treasures. Mine and mine alone." She was almost crying then.

"How do I know you are telling the truth?" I asked the bigger girl.

Just then, the short-haired girl jumped down from the sink and skittered out the door.

"Do you know her?" the big girl asked me.

"No, I don't," I said.

"Well, she is a dirty rotten thief!" she said, and headed out the door. Renée and I were right behind her, wondering who the girl with the jewels really was.

One warm afternoon a week later, M'Dear stopped at the library to pick up a record that she was going to use in our next recital. As she and Aunt Helen chatted with some friends, Renée and I checked out some more Nancy Drew books. Then we walked on home, went into the backyard, and sat down under our old chinaberry tree to read them. Little daffodils and crocuses had sprouted up and dotted the grass around us with bright yellow and purple, and all the air smelled sweet. Suddenly, a girl dropped down on us, right out of the tree! Like a coconut!

It was the short-haired purse girl. "Thank you for helping save my rare treasures," she said. She was wearing a little green top and shorts. You could just tell she was pretending to be Peter Pan.

"Well, I just hope that really *was* your green bracelet and that you didn't steal it."

"I did not steal a single thing. I only came here today to show you my jewels. If you're going to accuse me of stealing, I will just leave right now."

"No, please. Show us what you have."

"Okay," she said. "Because y'all were so nice to me, y'all can try them on for two cents. I won't charge you my normal price of a nickel. You get to view them for only two cents! A very big savings and bargain to y'all for one and only one day only."

She opened her turquoise purse, pulled out a handkerchief, and laid everything out on it. She told us that the bracelet the big girl was trying to get was truly a ceremony bracelet, found only on small islands far away.

"The only reason that I even have it," she said, "is because my father was a prince, but he died. He left my mother the jewels of his kingdom to show his love, and my mother allowed me to keep some as my very own."

"What's your name?" I asked her.

She rolled her eyes up. Her eyes were huge. You could skip rope inside them. "Sukey," she said. "My name is Sukey."

"I have never heard that name before. Where does it come from?"

"From a kingdom far away and long ago."

Renée was reaching back and straightening her ponytail, taking it in and out of its barrette, something she always does when she is nervous. "Renée, that's not good for your hair," I told her. "You're going to break off that outside part and have short hairs all over your head."

"You sure act like you know a lot about hair," Sukey said.

"M'Dear—that's my mother—is the beautician at the Crowning Glory Beauty Porch, and she knows everything there is to know about hair, that's a known fact." I reached out to touch Sukey's shiny black hair, but she jumped away.

"Sukey, what's your last name? Where did you come from?" I asked. "Where do you go to school? Who are your parents? Why haven't we ever met you before?"

"You better stop asking me all those questions or I'll take away my jewels and you'll never see them again. Then I'll hit you on the head."

Well, I figured she was bluffing, like Sonny Boy does when somebody tries to make him afraid. And besides, I was bigger than she was.

"I was just *asking*," I told her.

"My royal mother, whose name is Queen Sally, and me came here from another town, and we live in a very big castle over there."

She pointed in the direction of Pearl Street, toward the part of town where most of the Negroes live.

"There's no castle over there," I said.

Sukey started closing up her little turquoise pouch of jewels, and she began to cry real tears, not alligator fake ones.

"Welcome to our town," Renée said quickly, trying to distract her. "My name is Renée Jeansonne. I am in third grade at La Luna River School. My daddy is the pharmacist at the La Luna Drugstore. His name is Mister James Jeansonne, and my mother's name is Mrs. Anita Jeansonne. I like welcoming new people such as you to town. We don't get a lot."

Sukey looked at her like she was shocked that Renée was being so nice. All she could say was "Oh."

I felt so bad for asking Sukey all those questions when I should have been nice like Renée. So I told her, "I am Calla Lily Ponder. M'Dear's name is Lenora Ponder, and my papa's name is Will Senior, and they have Will and Lenora's Swing 'N Sway Dance Studio. You can come and dance with us sometime."

"Well," she said, "my name is Sukey Signette and my mother's name is Sally, and we just moved here from Shreveport, and Hot Springs, Arkansas, before that, and Beaumont, Texas, before that. But La Luna is where Mama grew up. Where she and—um, well, he wasn't my real father, but my mama's first husband—they both grew up here."

"I guess that makes you a princess, huh?" I said. "But your real father was the prince, right?"

Sukey started rubbing her face in her hands. "Kind of," she said, so softly I could hardly hear her.

"Well, we're glad you came to live here with us," Renée told her.

"Okay," Sukey said to Renée, and she lifted her hands from her face. Her face was all blotchy. I watched her as she gathered her jewels piece by piece, the ones that really looked like Mardi Gras necklaces, the emerald bracelet, her silver dollar, the rings of purple and green rare gems, the solid gold one, and the big white Elizabeth Taylor diamond that glinted in the light coming in through the canopy of the chinaberry tree.

Back at home, helping M'Dear peel and chop up potatoes to boil, I told her about the emeralds and rubies in the ladies' room, and about Sukey. "Scrub those potatoes good, you hear," she said to me.

I asked her, "With all those jewels, why do you think Queen Sally and Sukey live over there in that part of town?"

M'Dear turned to me and told me she knew Sally, Sukey's mother, from when they were little girls through the middle of high school, when Sally left La Luna.

"So is it true, M'Dear? Was Sukey's father a prince, and are Sukey and her mother royal?" To think that I had a new friend who was a princess!

M'Dear told me, "Sukey is royal. I'm not so sure the jewels are real, but all people are royal, Calla. They don't need to own jewels. That's better, really, because then nobody can steal them." M'Dear plopped our bowl of peeled potatoes into the pot of boiling water. Then she reached over and caressed my cheek.

I could hardly get to sleep that night. How could I sleep after just finding out that we are all kings and queens, princes and princesses?

Chapter 4

1962

Every summer morning I woke up early, pulled on my swimsuit, and ran down the piney path to the river. Swimming in the La Luna River, watching that sunrise, was my way of praying.

And I loved climbing trees. I loved discovering branches that would hold me up while I looked out on the ground. I would put my head close to the bark and I could hear the tree breathing, and I would kiss the trees.

I imagined that the trees and I were dancing. After all, M'Dear taught me that everything danced. In my closet up on a shelf where I kept my special things—feathers, marbles that my brothers didn't like because they were chipped—I kept branches from trees I loved. I was known for being a scrambler up trees, so I could reach the tiny ones.

"It's your long legs," my brothers would say. "You have the longest legs on a girl that we've ever seen."

One particular morning, when I was nine years old, I had a little extra time after my swim and it just felt too early to be climbing trees, so I walked around town. I liked seeing La Luna before it woke up. It made me feel like my town was a baby sleeping, all sweet and good.

I loved to visit the La Luna Garden Café where Leon was up at four every morning making the French bread to go with the gumbo or red beans and rice or cold shrimp dumped out on newspaper. Some people like Saltines, but my family and me like French bread on the side to balance out the zing of the cocktail sauce. Leon was one of my buddies. He was going to join the Marines soon, something that made me sad. Why do people have to go off to war, leaving us back home never knowing if they'll come back? But he promised he'd be back. He didn't talk much, but whenever I showed up, he smiled and gave me big hunks of fresh bread on a paper plate, with fresh butter on the side. I would put the butter on and quickly eat the fresh bread, letting the butter drip down the front of my swimming suit, knowing I could quickly rinse off under the outdoor shower when I got home.

We didn't have a Greyhound bus station in La Luna, so the bus just stopped behind the Garden Café. There I was, all dripping with butter, when the bus pulled up that morning. Nobody from around here was getting on, so I watched to see if anybody got off. Almost always it would be someone I knew: Mrs. Matthews coming back from Shreveport, where her son Michael had a job. Or Janie Gerard coming back from seeing her boyfriend, who was stationed at Fort Polk.

The Greyhound bus door swung open, and I wondered who might be coming home from a trip this time. Eating my French bread, concentrating on each bite—oh, it tasted so good that I called out, "I'm telling you, Leon, you have outdone yourself. This bread is perfect!"

And that's when I saw the stranger! He was a kid about my age. I kept waiting for some adults to get off with him, but he was the only person to get off the bus. All by himself. With blond hair sticking up all over the place, scruffy-looking all over. I watched the bus pull away, the sound of that big engine and the smell of those fumes. Who could be out here this early in the morning?

He caught my eye and then he turned away. Leon was back inside the shop, so it was only this scruffy-looking boy and me. He carried a suitcase in his arms. The handle on the suitcase was broken, and something about him seemed broken too. His eyes darted around like he was trying to get his bearings, but didn't want me to see him doing it. But I did see. There I was, standing there barefoot, with a towel wrapped around my waist.

I wiped some butter off my chin and walked over to the stranger.

"Hey," I said. "What are you looking for?"

"None of your business," he said, and then started walking away from me in the direction of the River School.

"Where're you headed?"

"*None* of your business."

"I'm Calla Lily Ponder," I said, stepping in front of him. "You want some French bread?"

"I could step on your toe if I wanted to."

"Why do you want to do that?" I asked.

Finally he looked at me. "Just leave me alone."

"Okay, I can take a hint," I said, and started in the direction of home.

When I was about a block away, the stranger yelled, "Where's the Tuckers' house?"

"I'm headed in that direction. You can just follow me."

"No," he said. "I was just curious."

Sheesh. "Okay, it's down this way," I said, and kept on walking. I wasn't going to stand around while someone treated me like I had a bad case of cooties. But I couldn't help turning around just once to look at him.

Later at lunch, M'Dear told us that the Tuckers' grandson had come to live with them. "I want y'all to be very nice and welcome him to La Luna," she said.

We all answered, "Yes, ma'am."

We had to wait an hour after lunch before we could go back down to the river and swim.

That afternoon, Sonny Boy, Will, Renée, Sukey, me, and our friend Eddie were laying on the beach. I can remember the swimming suit I had that year. It was a racer-back, showing almost nothing, and my legs stuck out so long and skinny. Renée wore a one-piece with a strap around the neck and strawberries on the front, with a little ruffle down the side, all modest. Her hair was almost white-blond in the summers. And Sukey wore a little yellow two-piece. Sukey was a tiny thing.

Eddie already had a little crush on Renée; I knew because he had given her a blue box with watermelon candy in it. And she liked him back. Sukey and I could tell by how her white, white complexion blushed. There was no doubt. But she had to turn it down, she said. "Calla, I just couldn't take that watermelon candy. Just one bite of it, and it would have made Eddie feel like . . . well, like I liked him special."

"Well, don't you?" I asked, and Sukey said, "Yeah, don't you?"

"Well," she said, "yes, I do like him. But I can't let him know it."

I couldn't even *picture* liking a boy, let alone liking him special, watermelon candy or not.

We were all a gang, a La Luna, Louisiana, gang. Oh, how we played! How we practiced dives! We did cannonballs, over and over and over again, and spitfires, with one leg held up so that the water kind of swished out to the side. Cannonballs were considered a boy's sport and Sonny Boy was the best. But I decided that I could join the competition myself, and so I did. None of the boys really knew how to swim. They'd flail those arms up and over, splashing and making a mess. They could kick hard, I'll give them that much. But the whole time I could keep up with them because I knew how to breathe, and to match it to my strokes as I cut my hands into the water. Papa's the one who taught us how to swim. And because I'm the one who stuck with it, he taught me how to turn my head from side to side when I breathed and to kick hard, using my leg muscles and keeping my ankles low as I kicked, but hardly splashing at all. Papa had to learn to swim real good when he was in the war. He was lucky. M'Dear says the Moon Lady was with him to get him home safe.

I was known for being able to hold my breath the longest underwater. Just as Sonny Boy was the king of cannonballs, I was the queen of holding my breath. And I was the queen of cannonballs, even if no one would admit it. Papa always said, "If you're good at something, don't be afraid to say it." "I'm the cannonball queen!" I'd call out. But they would only grant me queen of breath-holding, and I guess that was good enough.

I'd dive in and swim till I was out a ways. Then I'd take a deep breath. Just as I began to exhale, I would put my head down under so that no one could see me. I'd let my breath out in little bursts, very, very slowly. And at the same time I'd be kicking as hard as I could, so that by the time anyone would look for me, I'd already be a far ways off, underneath. No one could see me. And when I'd finally raise my head, everyone would clap and cheer. "Oh, God, Calla! You had us really stumped that time!" everybody would say.

Besides doing cannonballs off the pier, there were also three rope swings on trees that you could climb to swing out over the river. First, there was the little kid's rope swing. Then there was the intermediate rope swing, which I was just starting to use. And then there was the high, high rope swing farther down the riverbank that only the adult men used. Papa was always warning that he better not catch any of us down there, because there were snakes down around the overgrown bushes and logs. That was all I needed to hear to stay clear! We called that area "The Scary Swamp."

❧

So all of us were just sitting around on our beach, a wonderful little beach that the La Luna River gave us. Renée, Sukey, and I laid out our towels and rubbed Coppertone on each other. Eddie had brought his father's cooler, the one he used on his fishing trips, and that's where we stored our bottles of Coke and 7-Up and ham and cheese sandwiches. And there we spent our afternoons, just playing and swimming—especially me, because I wanted to become a very strong swimmer. I swam all over every single area that we were allowed to go.

While I was straightening my towel, I looked up and saw that boy who got off the bus. "Hey!" I said. "Hey, I'm the one that tried to be nice to you this morning."

He just ignored me, standing there in front of us. I said, "I'd introduce you, but I don't really know your name."

"Well, you don't really have to know my name," he said. "I'm here to swim." Boy, talk about snooty!

"Do your grandparents know you're down here at the river?" I asked him.

The new boy answered, "Nobody needs to know what I do. I do what I want."

I decided to be polite anyway. That is just the way I was raised. "Let me introduce you to my brothers and our friends."

"I don't want to meet anybody related to you or who you know."

Well, I was ready to hit him with a fishing pole when Sonny Boy walked up and put out his hand and didn't drop it. Just looked him in the eye until the new boy couldn't help but shake hands. He said, "My name is Tucker LeBlanc." And I thought, *Way to go, Sonny Boy.* And then Sonny Boy began to explain where you could swim and where you couldn't. He said, "All those are good places. But don't go over there. Don't do it. Every single one of our fathers—"

"And our mothers too," I chimed in.

"Anyway, don't swim over there in the La Luna Swamp," he said, and pointed to a part of the river near us where some logs had fallen and stopped up the flow a little bit. "That's what we call it. They got snakes down there and ever since we were little, everyone has warned us not to swim down there. And not a one of us has. Right?"

And everybody went, "Right." And Eddie nodded his head. You could tell that Eddie wished he was the one talking to this new boy. And already Sukey was trying out her flirting skills.

So this new boy got in the water and swam. I could tell he had a strong flutter kick, but he didn't know how to dig his arms into the water or turn his head to breathe either. He was not a strong swimmer. He wasn't even what I'd call a *real* swimmer. Just like my brothers, he lifted his neck straight up out of the water like a turtle and gasped for air. He stopped and was just floating for a minute. Then he said, "Is that y'all's rope swing way down there?"

And Sonny Boy said, "Yeah."

"Y'all jump off that?" that boy Tucker said.

"That's for adults only—the old Danger Swing. And Papa says it needs a new rope this year. It can land you right in a snake pit if you're not careful; you can fall where the snakes are," Sonny Boy said.

"You're just scared to do it," Tucker LeBlanc said.

"I am not scared to do it," Sonny told him.

"Well, I'm gonna go do it. And I dare you to—unless you're chicken."

Suddenly everything was silent as we all turned and stared at Sonny Boy.

After a long minute, Sonny Boy said, "All right, *new boy*, I'll do it. I'll go first, to show you how, so you don't get yourself killed."

Just as he was getting up, Sonny Boy leaned over and whispered to Will and me, "Keep your eyes peeled out for M'Dear, will you?"

"Sonny Boy," I said, "are you crazy? *You're* the one who's gonna get killed if M'Dear sees you out there."

"Just give me the whistle if you see any sign of her, okay?"

"No, I'm not giving y'all any whistle," I said. "I'm coming with y'all."

So we all started our adventure.

Eddie started talking. "Many times grown men have been bit by snakes there. Oh yeah. Many times it has happened."

You could see that Eddie was trying to scare this new boy Tucker.

Next thing I knew, Sonny Boy was leading us through the bushes over to the rope swing, and Eddie kept on talking.

"Once, during World War II, a soldier from Fort Polk was messing around down there and died from *multiple* snake bites. They couldn't even recover the body. All they ever found was one boot and his helmet. My father was part of the search party. I heard the story myself."

"You're making that up," Tucker said, trying to laugh it off. But you could tell Eddie's story was getting to him a little.

Then that Tucker said, "Somebody told me something like that, I wouldn't believe him for jack-shit."

Well, all of us were kind of taken aback when he said "jack-shit." Not that we are goody-goody, but we just don't go around saying "jack-shit." We know the expression, but it has to be saved for special occasions.

Sonny Boy tried to strut down the trail, but all the vines and thorns that had grown in over the trail kept slowing him down. I looked back once or twice to see if anybody was watching us, while the rest of the gang trailed behind us. The last part of the trail you had to hang back a little, because it's a little steep to climb up on an old root, and then you have to reach up and grab the rope.

There it was. That big old thick brown rope with four knots tied in it so you could climb up. The riverbank was about six feet high there. Tucker leaned over and looked at the tangle of roots and grasses at the bottom. Still acting tough, he asked Sonny Boy, "I don't guess y'all have any alligators in this part of the woods, do you?"

"About five of them," Sonny Boy said. "Right down there. One is blind and especially dangerous."

"Well, we've got them up where I came from," Tucker turned to all of us and said. "Where I used to swim we had seventeen of them. And they don't bother me at all."

I looked at him and thought to myself, *He is lying through his teeth.* But I didn't say anything. Seventeen alligators. Brother.

Sonny Boy grabbed the rope first and showed Tucker how to get on. Sonny Boy was kind of showing off, hanging on to the rope with only one arm.

He said, "You climb up to the second knot, then you push off from the tree with your feet to get going. If you don't push out far enough, you could land in those roots and you'd be a mess, man. You'd be cut up and have a big old snake and a blind alligator over you in two seconds." Sonny Boy winked over at me when he said the blind alligator part.

Then my brother pushed off the tree like he'd done it a thousand times and swung out over the water. At the last moment he let go, and everybody clapped and hollered. He made a big splash and then he swam out a few feet and yelled back, "You have to swim out here far enough to be away from the bushes and then swim back over to the sandy beach." He started to swim back himself, but then he stopped and dog-paddled out to the middle of the river to watch and see if Tucker would really do it.

So Tucker climbed up there, and he grabbed the rope. He swung back to the tree, kicked his feet, and pushed off. Then he let go and did a big cannonball that made a huge splash, a much bigger splash than Sonny Boy, even though he was smaller. Then he started swimming out to the river, and they swam back together.

Everybody said, "That was really great." And Sonny said, "I can do better than that." So he climbed up there again—this time to the *third* knot—and said, "I'm going backwards this time." And he did a big old cannonball backwards!

And so Tucker went up there too, grabbed the rope, and *he* climbed up to the third knot and he pushed off. He went out there over the water, but he didn't let go. He swung back again and pushed off even higher—but just as he was swinging out, the rope broke! He went straight down and glanced off the roots and fell into the water right under the roots!

Dear Lord, there must've been a moccasin nest right where he fell, because suddenly there were ten or so little light-colored baby water moccasins all around him! And I couldn't believe it, he was hollering and we were all screaming and then, quick as lightning, he grabbed up onto a root and pulled himself up halfway and—I swear to God—this new boy *walked on water.* I mean it. He walked on water about four feet to climb a log, and he just climbed and scrambled up those roots and brambles and crawled up the bank. He had trouble right at the top when the big root he was holding onto started to break. I ran over and grabbed his arm that was reaching up and pulled as hard as I could. I could feel him kicking and scrambling to get back on the top of the bank. I kept pulling for all I was worth and then suddenly he was over and I tumbled backwards and he kind of landed on top of me and then rolled over on his back. He was breathing hard and I thought, he's *got* to be snake-bit. I didn't know if I should help him or run back to the house and find M'Dear so we could get a doctor. Tucker LeBlanc was pale as a ghost and his eyes were kind of wild-looking. But he was cool as a cucumber. When he could finally catch his breath, he looked at me and mumbled, "Thanks." Then he started checking over his body.

All the others were still frozen in their tracks with their mouths hanging wide open. None of us could believe how he had pulled himself up and got out of there.

"You better sit back down while we go get help," I told him.

"Nah, these are just scratches," he replied in between breaths. "I didn't get bit."

Not a single snake bit him!

In half an hour the whole town had heard the story about the new boy Tucker, and of course, every time the story got told it grew bigger and bigger. How he had grabbed three of the snakes and threw them into the bushes. And how he had walked on water for about twelve feet to get up out of the river.

The next morning I actually heard somebody say he took one snake in his hand and just flung it around above his head like a lasso. Just threw it out through the trees, out into the water. He banged it up against the tree itself and said, "I'll show you." Can you imagine?

Sonny Boy and Tucker got punished big-time. But when I asked Sonny Boy if it was worth it, he just smiled his wide smile and said, "Oh yeah." But then he quickly added, "Don't tell Papa I said that, though."

For all our growing up, Tucker was known as Snake Boy. And that's how people thought of him until he became a football star in high school, and then people kind of forgot about the snake business. But even on the football team his nickname was Snake, just to intimidate the other teams. We made sure all the other schools heard the story of Snake Boy, who killed thirty water moccasins with his bare hands and wrestled an old blind alligator to his death.

You'd think that after I had saved his life, Tucker would act like a decent human being. But no. He went and picked a fight.

I went over to the Tuckers' the next day, and there he was, just lording it around the stables like he was king of the universe. So I ignored him and went in the stable to get the Shetland pony, Ricko, that I always rode. Uncle Tucker had been letting us use his stables and ride his ponies forever. I was putting the bridle on him when Tucker walked in and said, "What are you doing?"

"Well, what does it look like I'm doing? I'm putting the bridle on Ricko."

"Who told you you could do that?"

"What do you mean, who told me I could do it? I don't have to ask anybody. Uncle Tucker lets me ride Ricko any time I want."

"Who gave you the right to call him Uncle Tucker?"

"Because that's what I have called him ever since I was born! It's what you grow up calling someone who is very close to your family. I bet we even knew him before you did."

That's when he hit me, hard, on the shoulder! What could I do? I hit him back. I was so mad that I couldn't finish bridling Ricko. So I walked outside, and Tucker followed me.

"Where do you come from," I turned around and asked him, "that you think you can just start off hitting a girl, a girl you hardly even know? I'm sorry, but that's not the way we act around here."

He said, "What do you mean, where do I come from? And what do you mean, you knew my grandfather before I did?"

"Well, it's true!" I said. "You've hardly ever been out here. You weren't even born here."

Then he hit me again—in the leg! I couldn't believe it.

So I just went over to him and grabbed his blond hair, pulling it as hard as I could. I'm as tall as Tucker. In fact, I'm taller, by about four and a half inches.

Then he grabbed my hair back. Well, I don't like people grabbing my hair. So I just pushed him till he fell on the ground.

"Ha, ha-ha-ha!" I said. "I don't know where you come from, but I bet girls there can't beat you up like this, can they?"

He got up real quick and shoved me right down on the ground. Before I knew it, we were wrestling like crazy.

Then I heard Miz Lizbeth saying, "Tucker! Tucker LeBlanc! Don't you dare! Get in here—get in here right now!"

We turned to see Miz Lizbeth and Olivia standing on the porch. Though she is Miz Lizbeth's maid, Olivia is at our house enough to know what M'Dear and Papa's rules are. Whenever any of us did something bad, it seemed like Olivia was the one to catch us. She said M'Dear had eyes in the back of her head, and so did she.

I gave Tucker's hair one last pull. "Ouch!" he said. As far as I was concerned, getting an "ouch" is as good as winning the fight. So I burst out laughing. "Hah!" I laughed. "Hah! Hah! Hah!"

"Calla? Stop that laughing," Miz Lizbeth said. "Now you get up, both of you, and come over here. Y'all are filthy dirty!"

As Olivia picked us up by the collar, Miz Lizbeth told her, "Olivia, take these two children into the house and wash them up right now."

Olivia made us stand in the kitchen while she cleaned us both up. I tried to kick Tucker one more time, but Olivia stopped me. When we were presentable, she marched us into the parlor, where Miz Lizbeth was standing.

Miz Lizbeth told us, "Calla and Tucker, you look at me. I want the two of you, right now, to say you're sorry and then shake hands with each other."

Tucker said, "Are you kidding? She's so ugly with that long pigtail! And that's what she is—a pig! She's a pig!"

"Tucker! Don't you *dare* talk about Calla that way."

I said, "Huh." Just kind of giving a little laugh and a smile so Tucker could see that I had not only won—hands down—by getting the "ouch," but also by getting a little laugh in while Miz Lizbeth was facing him.

Miz Lizbeth then turned around and said, "Calla, don't think you can get away with that little laugh and that smile. I can feel it behind my back—I'm like your mama. Now shake hands."

Neither one of us put our hands up.

"I will not repeat myself one more time."

Well, I had never heard Miz Lizbeth talk like this. But she was just so nice, with all her soft white curls, and I had loved her since forever.

And she was one of M'Dear's best friends. I didn't want to hurt her feelings.

Besides, if I put my hand out, that would make it look even more like I won the fight. Because who puts their hand out first? Certainly not the loser. Even I know that's how the game is played.

So I put my hand out to shake, but Tucker didn't even move his arm. He just stood there. I couldn't believe it.

"Tucker, can't you hear what I keep telling you to do?" Miz Lizbeth said.

Finally, Tucker put up his hand and we shook. His hands were still so dusty and grimy that I had to wipe mine on my shorts afterward.

"Now, say you're sorry, both of you."

"He's going to have to say sorry first," I said, "because he's the one who started it."

"I am not! She's the one who started it. She went out there without asking and saddled him. She was putting a bridle on him—my horse, the horse I wanted to ride."

"Ricko?" Miz Lizbeth asked. "Tucker, that is the pony that Calla has always ridden. There are plenty of other ponies, any one that you can make your own."

"Well, I'm not saying I'm sorry."

"Do I have to go through this all again? Do you want me to have to go in and get Papa Tucker? Because he will handle this a little bit differently."

"No, no, ma'am," Tucker said quickly. Then he said, "I'm sorry."

First he was so tough, and then he acted downright scared when he heard Uncle Tucker's name, like Uncle Tucker would beat him up or something—when everyone knows that Uncle Tucker is gentle as can be. I apologized, too, and started to walk off, but just then I decided to turn around for a second and whisper, "I'm still taller than you."

Chapter 5

JULY 1964

On the day it happened, I swam in the river first thing in the morning, like any other summer day. I dove in off the pier and swam the Australian crawl, like Papa had taught me. Then I turned on my back and floated for a while, looking for figures in the clouds above.

I walked back home along the path, making sure not to step on any stickers—those things that stick in your feet when you're barefoot. After I changed into my shorts, I stuck my head into the Crowning Glory and asked M'Dear if I could go to the Shop 'N Skate. She gave me a kiss and a quarter, and I headed out.

One of the things I have always loved about our town is there are all these paths that you can walk without having to go into the streets with the cars. Once I crossed the street in front of our house, I could go all the way to Nelle's Shop 'N Skate without ever having to walk on another road! Some are just sandy paths, but some are covered with pine straw, which smells so good on a hot day. When you walk on the paths, you pass other people's backyards and vegetable gardens. And if they're outside I always wave and they wave back and we talk and visit a while. That's how it is in La Luna.

I had my mind set on a cold Orange Crush when I pushed open the screen door to the Shop 'N Skate. Orange Crushes were the onliest cold drinks I would touch because I'd read in *Teen* magazine that anything brown in a bottle gives you pimples.

And there was Nelle. I can still remember the way she looked that day, beautiful like always, sitting on her swivel stool behind the counter, wearing a blue cotton short-sleeve shirt tied up over a pair of faded yellow shorts. She loved color, and it showed all over. She had a deep tan all year and pretty light brown hair that she cut very short with fingernail scissors. It looked kind of sophisticated in what M'Dear calls a Bohemian way. That hair had a mind of its own, and so did Nelle. She was an original, what everyone called "a character." She and I took to each other the first time we met, which would have been when I was three months old. M'Dear was about six years older than Nelle, and had watched her grow up.

"Nelle," I said, "if it was any hotter, I'd have to crawl up under the porch with the yard dogs!"

"Well, come on in, girl," she told me. "You're smart to have your hair up in pigtails like that—keeps your head from getting too hot. Get yourself a cold drink out of the cooler."

The heat never did seem to bother Nelle like it did the rest of us. She was always cool and slow, like she and the store's old ceiling fan were on the same speed.

Nelle was the proprietor of Nelle's Shop 'N Skate roller-skating rink. After her daddy died and left her the family place and some good-size acreage, Nelle shocked everyone by up and buying the old La Luna grocery and fixing it up.

She fixed herself up a little apartment to live in behind it. Everyone had just assumed she would settle down and get married, but now folks said she was "not the marrying kind." Sukey, Renée, and I suspected Nelle had a secret boyfriend who she went to see when she went away for three or four days every month and closed the store but we never told anyone, because we didn't have evidence that Nancy Drew would approve of.

Besides the grocery and roller rink, Nelle kept horses in her own barn, and gave lessons to Renée and me, along with a few other girls. Both M'Dear and Papa loved Nelle. Sonny Boy said he wanted to be like her because "she comes when she wants to come, and goes when she wants to go. She's got her business set up good, and she has time to go fishing." I guess that described Nelle pretty well. That, along with the fact that, along with M'Dear and Papa, she was one of the best dancers in La Luna. Folks just liked it when Nelle liked them, because she sure didn't like everybody. When Nelle decided she liked someone, M'Dear called it a "Nelle Endorsement." Mama knew who liked who because of being in the position she was in, both a dance teacher and beautician. A whole lot of town "information" came to my mother, but you'd have to put bamboo shoots under M'Dear's fingernails to get it out of her.

Nelle added the skating rink about two years after she took over the grocery. Papa says he remembers coming in and seeing her in there hammering right along with the builders. Even back then she had a sign in the grocery like she does now, that read, "Help yourself. Leave your money on the counter. Honor system."

Nelle was petite, maybe about five-feet-one at the most, and what little there was of her was muscle. She was a fine horse lady, and I only wished I could someday be as good as she was. She taught me how to ride, and from the minute I got my own horse, she helped me learn good horsemanship. She was good to our town, too. Always donating canned goods for our Christmas food drives and opening up the skating rink for special causes. I looked up to her—well, I actually looked *down* to her, since I was already taller than she was. But I was still a kid, and she was a grown-up. She could have been my mother, age-wise. But no one else in the universe could be my mother but M'Dear, the brightest star in La Luna.

I hopped up on the big red Coke cooler, which is where I liked to sit, to sip my Orange Crush and watch Nelle zero in on a fruit fly. Nelle was still as a turtle for a second or two and then she *whomped* that flyswatter down so fast it made my head spin. Then she reached for a clean rag and slowly wiped her counter clean. Nelle always had that old wooden counter polished to a shine.

I loved to just sit and look around the Shop 'N Skate. The store had wide old pine plank floors that Nelle kept gleaming. On one side of the store Nelle had her food aisles—mostly canned goods and what have you. Then there were the stacks of empty soda bottles in wooden racks and Nelle's big shiner box for folks who liked to use live bait. I mean, that shiner box had some of the biggest worms you'd ever see in your life! Next to that was a big bright yellow display card of all kinds of fancy fishing lures. On the walls were old painted metal signs to advertise things like Holsum bread, Viceroy cigarettes, and Coca-Cola. Nelle also had this great rack of used paperbacks. They cost a nickel, but if you brought in a paperback to exchange, they were free!

I would have to say, though, that my favorite part of the Shop 'N Skate—besides the rink, of course—was the magazine rack. Nelle had all these magazines from all over the place, always displayed so nice and neat. She let me look through them if I was real careful not to bend them up.

To get to the rink you had to go beyond Nelle's counter, sitting first at a long wooden bench to put your roller skates on. There was a small room there where the skates were stored, in all sizes—black for boys, white for girls, and little bitty red ones, cute as could be, for the small kids. Rows and rows of skates on plywood shelves, skates with wooden wheels. Nelle paid me a nickel a pair for polishing those skates every month or so. She had an old carpenter tray filled with tubs of shoe polish and brushes and Texana heat powder to sprinkle inside so the skates wouldn't stink. Skaters had to provide their own socks, but Nelle always had a few clean pairs lying around for people who forgot and came in barefoot.

I was staring at the cover of the new *Life* magazine that had a lady with a swirly hairdo swept high on her head when Nelle broke me out of my daydreaming.

"Calla, girl," she said, "Ruth Ellen Ronson came in here yesterday after you did her hair. Looked like movie star hair—even on Ruth. I suspect you have the gift of beauty, honey. Anyone that can make Ruth Ellen Ronson look that good has *got* to have the divine grace. You ought to get yourself some training, sweetheart. Start up a *career.* A career's an important thing. That's what kept me going when I first opened the store. I thought, 'Nelle, you get to call the shots now. You got your own place and your own possibilities.' A career's something to hold on to, Calla. Look at your mama. She's got a career, and I suspect that she gets almost as much as she gives."

Well, it was true. I *was* getting pretty well known around La Luna for doing hair.

When Mariane Trichelle got married—a huge wedding, every single soul in the parish of Tallabena was there—I helped M'Dear do the entire bridal party's hair. After that, word just spread that I was good with hair. And I *was.* I had flips down cold by the end of that wedding, and I could tease a head into a smooth bubble in nothing flat. Later, I told M'Dear that I wanted to learn a French twist, and she said, "Calla, I think you might just be what we call a beauty prodigy."

But until that day, talking to Nelle in the shop, I had never thought about beauty as a career. I was still thinking about beauty as a career when the screen door squeaked open and in walked Cleveland Bonton.

Now, Cleveland's mother was Bertha Bonton, Olivia's daughter, who had been ironing over at Aunt Helen's house forever since I could remember. Cleveland must have been a few years younger than me, maybe nine. Sometimes he mowed our yard when my brothers couldn't get to it. I will never forget one time M'Dear had me take him some ice tea out to the yard, and when I went back out there to get the pitcher, he was sitting under the pecan tree just singing like you never heard! He sang so sweet it made me want to cry—some gospel song, I can't remember exactly what, but it was something like, "Over my head, I see glory in the air." Beautiful, high, sweet little-boy voice. I stood there listening to Cleveland, just amazed. When he finished, I told him, "Hey, you are *good.* You could be the Little Stevie Wonder of La Luna, Louisiana."

He smiled at me and laughed. "Onliest thing is, I ain't blind!"

"Still," I said, "you are a boy musical genius like Little Stevie Wonder."

"Thank you, Miss Calla," he said. "I sings in the choir at St. Claude AME Baptist." Then he finished up the rest of that ice tea in one gulp.

Miss Calla, that's what he called me. Even though we weren't nothing but kids, both of us.

When I went back in the house, I told M'Dear about Cleveland's singing. She said, "Lord, yes, Negro people are blessed with a good ear. You should have heard Cleveland's grandfather sing! Played guitar, too."

M'Dear and Papa taught us to always say "Negro" because they thought it was more polite than "colored." And we *knew* it was better than "nigger." That word was not permitted in our household.

Anyway, so in came Cleveland to the Shop 'N Skate. Pair of long black skinny legs sticking out from under his cutoffs, his head hanging down, staring at the floor.

"Afternoon, Cleveland," Nelle said. "How's your mama doing?"

"My mama doing just fine. How you, Miss Nelle? Miss Calla?"

Then he kept on standing there. His eyes were glued to the floor like it was going to look up and tell him what to do next.

"What can I do for you today?" Nelle asked him.

Cleveland didn't say a thing. We waited and we waited and we waited some more, but Cleveland didn't say a word.

Finally, he said, "Miss Nelle, I wants to skate."

Whoa! Negro people had never skated in Nelle's place. Oh, Nelle served them, sold them bread, shiners, Coca-Colas, and all. But they didn't use the bathroom there, they didn't drink from the fountain, and they didn't—*couldn't*—skate in the rink. But there was Cleveland Bonton, standing there and asking if he could skate!

I'd known Bertha and her boys all my life, and I never thought that one of them would up and do something like this. It was wild. It was sticky. *It was against the law.*

I had been seeing so much on TV. In Birmingham, hundreds of Negro people out in the street, and huge police dogs with mean, sharp teeth. Dogs trained to kill, taking down little boys, girls, and old women. Fire hoses forcing regular everyday Negro people down on the ground, up against trees, with force so strong that M'Dear said, with tears in her eyes, "You know it must have ruptured kidneys and torn-apart spleens." Oh, it was ugly business. The Sunday those four little girls were killed by a bomb, little girls in their best Sunday dresses. Papa cried when he saw the news with Walter Cronkite. Will, Sonny

Boy, and me, we were all so sad and confused. M'Dear lit a sanctuary candle that day, and everyone was asked to join in prayers. For months, my dreams were all full of those little girls, the whiteness of their church dresses flying apart like burned feathers.

But we hadn't ever seen anything like that around La Luna. The danger seemed far away. But when Cleveland asked to skate, though, it made my stomach start to hurt. What kind of mess was Cleveland fixing to get into? Did he want to skate so bad that he was willing to take this chance? Or was he just a little kid who wasn't stopping to think?

Nelle didn't answer Cleveland right away. The longer she didn't say anything, the hotter it got, like that ceiling fan was somehow slowing down. Cleveland stood there, his knobby knees shaking like he was cold, even though sweat was dripping off his forehead.

Finally Nelle said, "Cleveland, it costs fifty cents to rent you a pair of skates. Two quarters."

A big old grin spilled across his face. "Yas'm," he said, "I got me the money."

Then he reached down into his pockets, pulled out a handful of nickels and pennies, and plunked all the change down on the counter.

It seemed like time just stopped then. Nobody moved a muscle—not me, not Nelle, not Cleveland. I could still hear fruit flies buzzing over by the bait stand, the hum of the big red Coca-Cola cooler below me, the ticking of the clock with the Dr Pepper boy on it behind the counter.

All these things were flying through my mind: *What harm is it going to do, letting him skate on the empty rink?* I wanted Cleveland to skate, and at the same time I didn't.

What did I see but Nelle picking up the change from the counter! She put it all in the register and asked, "What size skate you take, Cleveland?" She said it like she rented skates to colored people every day.

Cleveland said, "I take a size nine, please, ma'am."

Negroes, people say, all of them, got big feet. That was what was running through my mind.

"Go on over to the rink side," Nelle told Cleveland. She went to the little room and brought out the skates, and I watched while Cleveland sat on the long wooden bench and bent over to lace them up over his bare feet. He didn't ask for socks, and Nelle didn't offer. It took him a long time to get them laced up because his hands were shaking.

But I could not take my eyes away from his hair. So black and kinky but soft-looking, like lamb's wool. How does it stay so tight like that, I wondered, those curls like little springs ready to pop out at you? The Bible says every one of our hairs is numbered, that God knows every single thing about us, whether we're black or white.

Cleveland finally got his skates on and headed out to the rink. He fell down twice even before getting there. I thought, *Well, where's all that natural rhythm they are supposed to have?*

Nelle got out the broom without a word and started sweeping the floor of the grocery. Oh, she sure got busy all of a sudden. But every once in a while, I could see her steal a look at the rink.

Cleveland had not let go of the railing. Matter of fact, he was holding on to it with the grip of death while slowly walking himself around the circle. But just when I was thinking he'd stay glued to that railing forever, he shoved off. Just a little ways, but still, he got moving. He got about five, six feet out onto the rink floor, then started to lose his balance. He almost fell down, but he caught himself.

Watching him, it seemed like I could feel every move he made in my *own* body, like something in me was leaning out to him, like my muscles were straining to help him stay up on those skates.

He stopped for a minute to get his balance, then he pushed off again. One wobbly leg in front of the other, the blackness of his skin blending with the black of the leather, so that those skates looked like extensions of his legs. He sailed for just a minute. And I knew that feeling—that a little minute of flying is worth almost anything.

But then he fell, and fell hard, like the floor suddenly yanked him down.

"Cleve!" I yelled out. "I don't care how hot it is, you don't get out on a roller rink your first time in cutoffs! You need you some long pants!"

His knees were bleeding. He brushed himself off and worked his way back to the railing. Then he just stood there, looking out at the rink like a sailor looking out to sea. Or a bull rider who'd just been bucked.

Nelle stepped back into the rink from the grocery.

"Nelle," I said, "he is gonna bust himself wide open."

"Naw," she said, flipping the switch on the jukebox like only she knew how to do, to make music play without even putting in a dime. "Boy's been dreaming about this. Been coming in here all summer, acting like he just wants to buy a Coca-Cola, but eyeing that rink like it was Christmas. Let him go."

"Ramblin' Rose" came on the jukebox and flooded the rink with Nat King Cole, that old silky voice of his making the hot air feel softer.

"Go over there and turn on the big fan," Nelle said, surprising me. She never turned on the huge industrial fan at the end of the rink for just one person. It cost too much money. When you're in business for yourself, you watch your expenses, she told me.

I did like she said, then followed her back into the grocery. I took a sip of my Crush and asked, "Nelle, aren't you a little scared of what might happen?"

Nelle leaned on the broom handle, lit a Pall Mall with one of her kitchen matches, and told me, "Calla, girl, comes a time when you run your own business, you got to make your own decisions. This grocery, this rink—they're my career. A career's a whole lot bigger than nickel-and-diming your whole life long. And you're damn right, I am scared."

I looked at her for a minute, wishing I understood everything she was saying. "Well," I said, "this makes me scared, too."

"Go on home now. Go see if your M'Dear needs you." She walked back over to watch Cleveland skate.

I stood in the doorway between the grocery and the rink. The light coming in through the doors and windows was hot—ugly, mid-afternoon Louisiana hot. I had a jangled, snaky kind of feeling winding tight up in my body.

Then, out of the blue, Burr Jenkins sashayed in to the grocery, looking like King Kong. Burr was one of the older kids, must have been around seventeen or eighteen. He acted like he was ruler of the rink for the last three summers. Taking girls in his arms, skating backwards, sneering at kids who couldn't skate as good as him, acting like he owned the whole entire place. You could tell by Burr's face that he didn't know that brown cold drinks cause pimples.

He stopped cold when he saw Cleveland. "Nelle know that nigger is out on the rink?" Burr yelled at me.

I ignored him.

"I asked you a question," Burr said, and lit himself a cigarette. "Nelle rent the nigger those skates?"

"Why don't you go crawl back under your rock?" I told him.

He looked at me under those hooded eyes of his, like some lizard. I never knew how so many girls found him sexy with that old greasy ducktail of his. Then he stared out at Cleveland, who didn't seem to be aware of either one of us.

Burr finished his cigarette and ground it out on the floor. He threw me one last sneer, then turned around and stomped out the door.

Out on the rink, Cleveland was getting the hang of it. Still falling down, but not taking as long to get back up and start again. Those long legs coming out of those cutoffs made him look like a wobbly baby deer out on a gravel road. He skated to my end of the rink, and

I could see the sweat on his skin. That's when I noticed that his skin wasn't exactly black. It was more like dark roast coffee with a tiny bit of evaporated milk in it, just a few drops. I just drifted into a trance, watching that boy skate for the first time. I looked at his hair. Earlier, I had thought it was true black, but then I saw that it had some dark brown and maybe even some auburn in there. It was beautiful.

When he finally circled the entire rink without falling down once, Cleveland threw his head back and let out a little whoop. I couldn't stop my hands from clapping. But Cleveland wasn't paying me any attention. He was smiling to himself, pleased with the day. Just putting one foot in front of the other, happy skating boy, his mama's son, sweat glistening on his skin, singing Fats Domino's "Ain't That a Shame" right along with the jukebox.

I turned for a second to look at Nelle, who was back in front of the grocery fan, blowing down the front of her blouse to cool herself off. She looked pretty pleased with herself.

But just then Sheriff Ezneck's car roared into the parking lot, spinning dust and gravel everywhere, lights flashing and siren blaring, breaking up this quiet, lazy afternoon. We hardly ever hear a siren in La Luna. When we do, we make the sign of the cross and we run to the window. But not today. He must have been in La Luna, rather than at the jail in Dry Creek or across the river up near Claiborne. Otherwise, he could never have reached us that quick, being a parish sheriff not from La Luna.

At first I thought, *There must be a car wreck out on the road.*

Sheriff Ezneck busted through the skating rink entrance. He was a big heavy man, strong as an ox, with a scalp-close crew cut. I don't think he even saw me standing in between the rink and the grocery. He did see Cleveland. And the second he did, I knew that we were in trouble.

"Cleveland, look out!" I shouted. Sheriff Ezneck charged out onto the rink floor, dead-set for Cleveland, moving awful fast for a fat man. I turned to run into the grocery, but before I could even call out Nelle's name, she came sprinting out of there. She didn't throw me a glance, just raced straight across the rink after the sheriff.

Sheriff Ezneck ran up behind Cleveland, grabbed him by the waist of his cutoffs, and bulldozed him down to the floor. Cleveland never even saw Ezneck coming. His head hit the floor first—I could hear it, like a pumpkin thrown against a wall. I could see blood along his scalp line, blood oozing onto those tight black curls. I wanted to run out there, hold his head. Then Ezneck was kicking Cleveland in the ribs and head with his cowboy boots. I hated those boots: pointy-toed, snakeskin, black and shiny, with little swirls tooled along the instep. The cruelty of the kick, the pointed toe against his skull.

Cleveland curled his body into a ball, trying to cover his head with his hands. His knees, already raw from his earlier skating falls, were bleeding onto the rink floor.

"Boy!" Sheriff Ezneck barked. "What in hell you doing on a white rink?"

Nelle planted herself between them, but Ezneck didn't stop kicking. His boot hit her calf, then her bare ankle, then up higher under her knee, which took her down.

"Stop it! Stop it!" I screamed, terrified, running over to Nelle, who got back up in an instant.

"Grab the boy," she whispered to me. "Grab Cleveland."

I could smell him. I could feel the dust on his skin, see the tears on his face, and feel the heaving of his body as he sobbed. But it was the blood on his hair that I couldn't take my eyes away from. Blood flowed from his head in every direction onto the dusty wooden floor. It mixed with the dust to form a strange reddish brown pudding. I screamed,

"Stop it!" There was so much blood, and it kept on coming out, Cleveland's blood flowing. Stop it! He needs that blood. The blood he needs, wasted for nothing on the floor.

Ezneck lunged for Cleveland and me, out of control at this point. But Nelle stepped in front of him again, blocking him, shunting from side to side. "For God's sake, Ezneck," she said. "He is a little boy! This is a *child*."

"Get out of my way, woman!" he shouted, his breath snorting in and out like a hog.

"Ezneck," she said, "I rented the boy the skates. You got a bone to pick, you pick it with me."

"You're obstructing justice. This is against the law, and you damn well know it."

"Well," Nelle said, talking real slow, like she had all the time in the world, "just what do you plan on doing about it, Ezneck?"

I saw his eyes get real small, and his jaw was clenched so tight he could hardly talk. "*Get outta my way.*"

"You are the one on private property!" Nelle said, sounding almost as mad as he was. Then she stopped herself. "Look, Roy, it's a hot afternoon. Why don't we just calm down here? Go on in the grocery, have a Coke, and talk this thing over? What you say?"

"Nelle," he told her, "I always knowed you was a odd kinda woman." Then he reached his hand down to his crotch and hitched himself up. "But I never knowed you was also a nigger lover."

"Get out, Ezneck. Get off my property," Nelle said. Not loud. Just final.

"You don't talk to me like that, woman. I'm a sworn officer of the law. You either step aside or I run you in with the jigaboo."

"I ain't got nothing better to do. Business is slow this afternoon."

Drops of blood were starting to clot on Cleveland's left eyebrow. I knelt by him and pulled a Kleenex out of my back pocket and tried to soak the blood up. Oh, how delicate his head was, a little shell holding his dreams. And his hopes. What did Cleveland hope for, and how will this change everything? God, I see it—the blood, the thin line between our heads and the world, Cleveland's head, Cleveland's world, split open for nothing there on the floor where we all skated, white hand in white hand.

"Goddamnit, girl," Sheriff Ezneck shouted at me. "I wouldn't touch that bleeding nigger with a meat hook."

And I couldn't help it, I started to cry. *Meat hook. He wouldn't touch Cleveland with a meat hook.*

Ezneck eventually put handcuffs on Nelle and Cleveland and dragged them both out toward the sheriff car. Those skates must've hung pretty heavy on Cleveland's skinny legs. I followed them out to the parking lot and watched him stuff Nelle in the front seat, Cleveland in the back.

"Ezneck," I heard Nelle say, "how stupid can you be? How *stupid* can you be?"

I ran to Nelle's side of the car. I could hardly talk, I was crying so hard. "What should I do, Nelle? What should I do?"

"Call your mother to come and get you," Nelle said. Then she took a deep breath and whispered to me: "*See* what's in front of you. Don't let those tears cloud your eyes, Calla."

Then the blue-and-white sheriff car screeched out of the parking lot, and I could feel the dust it stirred settle on my face, mixing with my tears, making my face feel gritty. When I rubbed my eyes, it felt like sandpaper.

They kept Nelle overnight in the parish jail over in the ugly town of Dry Creek. Not La Luna. When Cleveland got out of jail a couple days later, he looked like somebody had beat him over every inch of his body with a baseball bat. You could not recognize his face. He could not walk by himself, his mama had to help him. I know because I rode with M'Dear when she drove Olivia and Bertha over to the jail to pick him up. Nelle didn't come. She said she couldn't bear it. To see Cleveland like that shocked me to my core. I could hardly breathe when I saw him. For a long time after that when I closed my eyes I still saw him.

At the end of that summer, the licensing board gave Nelle a lot of trouble about renewing her business license. When she finally got that cleared up, they gave her trouble about the rink meeting fire code. Finally, some agency told her if she didn't air-condition the entire rink, they'd close the whole place down. So she put four window air conditioners on the rink side, and another one in the grocery.

Nelle had to start charging a dime more to rent roller skates. Somebody had to pay to run those air conditioners. But those things didn't put out like the old fan did. Matter of fact, it felt a whole lot hotter in there than it ever was before.

I think that maybe we all have a calling. I got mine in a tiny instant when I blinked and saw the blood on Cleveland's hair.

There are doctors who sew up cuts. There are people who know how to lead marches. There are leaders who sometimes do what is right. I want to be a beautician. I want to heal hair that's wounded or maybe on people who are wounded. And bring out some beauty in a world that can sometimes seem ugly. Because we are one family, really. Like M'Dear says, We are all brothers and sisters under La Luna's sweet healing light.

Chapter 6

SUMMER 1965

I remember the day that I began to feel that Tuck was okay. It happened one day when we were playing on the cotton truck, jumping down into the high truck bed full of cotton, and Tuck said, "Look! Look, Calla, this boll of cotton feels like a Christmas tree."

I said, "Tucker, what do you mean? That does not feel anything like a Christmas tree."

"I think it's what country people put under their trees. But we never really had Christmas, so I'm pretty dumb to even talk about it."

"Then you haven't ever had a Christmas tree," I told him.

He didn't say anything for a while, but just as I was fixing to shimmy up the wooden side of the truck to jump down again, Tuck said, "We never had a Christmas tree when I was growing up."

That made me feel bad. "I promise you can come to our house and see my tree decorated and all."

"Don't tell me you promise," Tuck said. "People who say *promise* are always just lying."

"Who told you that?"

"Didn't need anybody to tell me that."

Then I knew he'd had buckets full of things promised to him that just never came true.

"Well, now you're in La Luna," I told him, "and none of us are gonna lie to you."

Again, Tuck got real quiet, then finally said, "Well, okay."

I decided that was good enough and threw a handful of cotton at him. I just wanted the puffy whiteness of cotton to touch him, to make Tuck see that at least cotton didn't lie.

After that we became friends.

Sonny Boy and Will were so different. Sonny Boy had kind of reddish blond hair, and he was strong and muscular. He could still lift me up, just lift me right up. And M'Dear—he could lift her up too! We'd be dancing, all of us just kind of hanging around in the kitchen, and he'd just pick M'Dear up at the sink and lift her right up in the air.

And Sonny Boy would do anything, anywhere! One day he got in trouble for riding his Stingray bike off the flatbed cotton truck at Papa Tucker's. He just rode his bike *with himself on it* straight off onto a gravel road, rolled over, and got brush burns all up and down his body. M'Dear had to put Mercurochrome and Band-Aids all over him. And I told him he was an idiot.

When I went to his bedroom, M'Dear had a fan blowing up on him. I said, "Sonny Boy, how are you doing, you crazy thing?"

He said, "Well, it hurts, but it was worth it."

That's just the kind of boy he was.

And Will, he was so quiet and sweet. He always dressed nice. I don't know how he came up with his clothes, but he'd find things at the swap shop like a white linen jacket and a little cotton vest that cracked us up whenever he wore it. And his music playing was getting to be known even outside our parish. He was happy to dance with the rest of us but didn't get wild.

Sonny Boy would sing and dance like James Brown, and his routine was pretty darn good. Now, it turned out that Tuck didn't mind pulling out the stops. He got so carried away his loafers barely stayed on his feet. So he kicked them off and danced in his bare feet to polish off the number! We all clapped and stomped. He was so shy afterward. It was two people inside of him. Now, Eddie *tried* to dance like James Brown, and he did give it his all. But his all wasn't very much as far as I was concerned. But Renée clapped and said, "Oh! You're just like James Brown—except you're white!"

Then Sukey said, "Renée! Gosh! That was a stupid thing to say."

Well, I guess Renée could be really kind of sissy and slightly dumb at times. That's just Renée. My brothers and my friends can be goofballs sometimes, but I still love them.

Anyway, we all hung out together. Of course, we went to Nelle's Shop 'N Skate.

It was so much fun to skate there! I became a better and better skater all the time. In fact, I was so smooth that if they had a roller-skate Olympics down here, I would have been in it.

Tuck turned out to be a pretty good skater. I mean, right off the bat—that shocked me. He put on a pair of skates, and he was around and around that rink before I knew it!

"Hey, Tuck!" I said. "How'd you get so good?"

"I don't know. I guess it just comes natural to me."

Well, everything comes natural for you, I thought. "Well, goody-goody for you."

Then Nelle came and chimed in, "I don't want to just see y'all drinking Coke without having a bite to eat."

So she went back to her kitchen and threw something together—some good fresh Holsum bread, mayonnaise, a little mustard, if you wanted it, and ham. Maybe some tomatoes if she had them. You'd cut that thing in half—mmmm! It was so good! "If you eat this with your Orange Crush," Sonny Boy said to Renée, "it is a full meal."

Renée looked horrified. "Well, I don't know. For me a full meal is supposed to be hot, like shrimp and rice with salad or something like that."

"Renée," Eddie said, "that's just what I like to eat!"

Brother. Those two lovebirds should just go out of my ear's reach for a while.

"I think that just Cokes are full meals," Sukey said. "They're filled with everything. Mama doesn't care if I have a Coke for breakfast. In fact, whenever I wake up and it's hot outside, I drink a Coke. My mother's got the whole refrigerator just filled with Cokes."

I started drinking Cokes, just a little. M'Dear allowed us to have one Coke a day. But Cokes for breakfast?

But we were allowed to have belly-wash, which is what we called the drink you make out of these big bottles. You'd pour the liquid inside into water, and it made it all orange, which was called "orange belly-wash." Or you could get it in different flavors like raspberry, depending on what Nelle ordered.

Grape was my favorite. The grape drink in the purple bottles it came in—I loved to see it! It was like grape bubblegum, it was so dark. And then once Nelle mixed it with water and poured it over ice, it was perfect! She used it straight for her snow cones.

Sonny Boy and Will and Tuck would skate with their arms touching each other at the waist. They just skated all the way around the rink as a trio, and none of them fell. Then they spun away from each other and started skating alone, practicing skating backwards.

They were taking over the whole rink. I hated it. So I got in there and said, "I'm skating too."

"No," Sonny Boy said, and Tuck backed him up. "Come on, Calla. This is for boys."

"What do you mean, it's for boys?"

Tuck piped up, "We mean *it's for boys*, not for girls."

And then I couldn't help it. I kicked him in the leg. He grabbed on to the rail, or he would have fallen.

And the next day was when Nelle made Tuck and me start selling snow cones together. We had to stand together at the end of the rink where the snow cone machine was and pour different flavors over the shaved ice. For hours and hours at a time Tuck and me had to stand there and take kids' and big teenagers' money, make change, go back and forth between the shaved ice, the little paper cones, different flavors, and that whole time, not kick each other.

After a while, we couldn't help it, in order to bear it, we started cracking jokes till finally I was laughing so hard at something Tuck said, I accidentally dropped some shaved ice on my bare feet, which felt very good. So, I threw some ice on Tuck's feet and we stood there with our hot feet all cooled off, looking out at the other kids skating, something we could not do. He looked at me and said, "Ponder? You're not a bad snow cone maker."

"Neither are you," I said, and smiled.

"Maybe we could ask Nelle if we could borrow this machine and set it up and travel all over the state of Louisiana with it."

I laughed. "You are crazy!"

He looked at me and winked. "Yeah, I know."

After that, I did not want to kick him in the leg anymore.

Wouldn't you just know that it was Sukey who came up with the idea of playing Spin the Bottle?

Me, Tuck, and Renée were at Sukey's house, and then Eddie joined us. If you could have seen the look on Eddie's face, you would of just gotten sick. All he cares about is being a boyfriend. What is the big idea?

So we all sat down in the garage and Sukey got an empty Coke bottle. She was just about to do the first spin when I remembered that Renée had never played Spin the Bottle before. I hadn't either, but I heard about it from my brothers.

"Wait a minute, Sukey," I said. "Let's explain to Renée how you play."

And everybody started to kind of laugh.

"C'mon, y'all," I said. "Not everybody has played every game in the universe. So, here's how it goes. You take an empty Coke bottle, okay? You put it down on a flat surface, like here on the garage floor, and you twirl it with your hands—right there in the middle of the bottle. And you just spin it around. Now, the person who spins it has to go and *kiss* the person who the bottle lands on. And it's just up to Fate, as to where the bottle will land. So, *no faking* it. Some people have been known to fake it, so the bottle will land on a certain person."

"Right," said Sukey.

Renée said, "Thank you, Calla. I appreciate you for telling me the rules."

"It wasn't just for you, Renée. I wanted to sort of, well, clean up the rules for all of us."

Everybody started to laugh. I told them, "Oh, hush up, y'all!"

Renée sometimes doesn't hear if people are laughing at her, or else she doesn't care, which is the same thing.

Tuck spun the bottle next and it pointed right at me! Oh, God! I got up and started to walk right off.

"Calla!" Sukey grabbed me by the shorts and pulled me down. "If the Coke bottle points at you, you don't walk off, you stay and get kissed. People don't just walk away. That's the rule, and you can't break it."

"Oh, I'm going to *get* you one of these days, Sukey!"

"Just try!" she said.

So I sat back down, and Tuck was just standing there. "Now I've sat down," I said. "Do I have to stand up again to get this stupid thing over with?"

Then Tuck knelt down and looked at me, and I could tell he was thinking the same thing I was. *Cooties*, that's what he was thinking, *cooties*. But he gave me a kiss, then he jerked back, and I jerked back too. I was dying to tell him, "Get out of here! Don't you ever try that again."

But I got a sense, for that second, that maybe he liked it. And maybe I wanted him to.

The next day after school, Sukey taught me how to kiss—really kiss, and not jerk back like I did with Tuck.

"You have to *practice* kissing," she told me. "When you start kissing, you don't want to be a dumbo."

So we went to Sukey's house because her mama was at work. Her mama had to go to work. She'd get all dressed up every day, and always wore her hair, which was black like Sukey's, teased up into a beehive. I couldn't believe that could be good for her hair, so I asked M'Dear about it.

"Well, the beehive's hard on the hair shaft," she told me. "But a lot of women think it's a sophisticated style these days."

Sukey's mama always left food for us, peanut butter sandwiches wrapped up in wax paper in the refrigerator. We each ate a sandwich and then went to Sukey's room to practice. Sukey said, "I've got an idea. Let's go put on some of my mama's lipstick."

So we got into her mama's lipstick. She had probably sixteen different colors, all lined up in a plastic divider in her drawer. We pulled out different colors, and Sukey went, "Here, Calla, you take Mocha."

I said, "Mmm—I like that! That's good."

Then she said, "I'm going to take Dreamgirl."

We each put lipstick on our lips and started practice-kissing on the inside of our arms.

Sukey said, "I don't think that's good enough, Calla; I think you need to press harder."

So I kissed my arm harder till Sukey said, "Maybe that's good enough. But we need more lipstick."

We put on more lipstick and went into the bathroom to do the mirror kiss. *"Mmmmm,"* Sukey said, as her lips touched the mirror.

"Nooo, Sukey! That's not a kiss! That looks more like a smear. Try it again. Look, watch me. *Mmmmwah!"*

"Mmmmwah!" Sukey said. "Better. That is a little better." I was faking it, but I was tired of Sukey bossing me around. I couldn't really tell if her kiss was better than mine, but Sukey knew a lot of things that I didn't know. We kissed the mirror a few more times till Sukey went, "Okay. Now, put on some more lipstick."

We both did, and then Sukey told me, "Now we're going to practice on each other."

"What?"

And she said, "Yes, that's the next step. There is no other way."

Then Sukey leaned over and gave me a big kiss. She didn't even give me a moment to prepare. She just upped and kissed me!

"There," she said. "How does that feel?"

"I don't know."

"Okay, well, I'm going to do it again. Sit down!"

"All right. But let's put on more lipstick and blot a whole lot." I sat down on the bathroom stool, and then Sukey gave me another kiss on the lips and just stayed there for a while.

"Now, how does *that* feel?" she asked.

"That was pretty good, Sukey."

"Good. Now you try kissing me."

I gave her a kiss on the lips. Sukey said, "Calla, I don't think you will ever, *ever* become a good kisser. That was a '*mmm*' kiss, not a '*mmmwah!*'"

Oh, God, what if I can't become a good kisser?

"Put on more lipstick," Sukey said, "and give me a real kiss. Give me a 'mmmwah.'"

So I kissed Sukey hard on the lips. Then I thought, What the heck Calla! I kissed so hard that I just bent her backwards over the sink. We kissed like you see in the movies. We kissed until it kind of felt good. Then we cracked up laughing.

Sukey looked at me, and I looked at Sukey.

"I think we kiss boys now," I said.

"I think we can kiss *all* the boys!" Sukey said.

"Yes, dahlink," I said, imitating the old movies, "once you have graduated from the 'Calla & Sukey Kissing Academy,' your lips are the only badge you need!"

Chapter 7

1967

In summertime, I had to wake up early. In Louisiana, if you're not up by 6:30 or so, you miss the whole day, because it gets so hot that you have to do indoors stuff, trying to stay cool until evening, when you can go out again. Of course, it's not so awfully bad to go out in the evening, because La Luna doesn't have many mosquitoes that suck you to death and leave you itching and scratching for weeks. We're blessed. It's like some kind of huge mosquito net hangs over our little town, protecting us not only from the insects themselves but also from the DDT truck that comes and sprays in Claiborne across the river. M'Dear says that truck is full of poison, spraying ugly chemicals onto little children who ride their bikes behind it, trying to get covered by the spray so they can play outdoors without getting bit.

One summer morning I woke up, smelling coffee brewing and

bacon frying. Pulling on a T-shirt and jeans, I ran down the stairs to the sight of M'Dear and Papa in the breakfast nook.

I sat down with them and ate quickly because I was meeting Tuck for a ride before the heat got too heavy for us and our horses. I gave M'Dear and Papa each a hug before I headed out, lingering with my M'Dear, breathing in her scent.

I love horses. They are not "essential to the very essence of my soul," like Renée said about her horse, but I do dream about them sometimes. I dream about being on a horse and flying. I remember the magical day when I was old enough to stop riding Ricko, the Tuckers' Shetland pony, and get on a real horse. It was my tenth birthday, and I woke to find a large red bow tied to the end of my bed. Next thing I knew, M'Dear, Papa, the boys, and I were tramping over to the Tuckers' barn. There stood a palomino with red ribbons strung from her bridle! Her flax mane and tail were so beautiful that tears came to my eyes. "Happy Birthday, Calla Lily," my family said.

I stepped forward and pressed my nose into her soft neck. "Golden Princess," I whispered, as she and I met.

Since I was little I've been tantalized by the smell of horses and wet bridle leather. Once, before Golden Princess came into my life, I found a piece of broken rein in a pasture and brought it home to keep in my room so I could smell it at night. I kept it up on a shelf in my closet, along with special rocks and feathers that I collected from around our yard. Then, of course, I fell in love with Ricko. But I'd never loved anything—except for my family, of course—as much as I loved Golden Princess.

The morning had already begun to steam as I headed from our house to the barn. The sun was a couple of hours above the horizon when I got to the pasture gate, with carrots in my pocket. Golden Princess greeted me by nickering as she trotted over to take the treats from my hand. I was petting her and talking to her when Tuck came into the barn. Tuck's horse, Sable Star, was following him across the clover, eager for a ride.

Tuck was wearing a worn white shirt with the sleeves rolled up. He was growing up—we both were. I noticed the muscles of his chest under his shirt, and the muscles of his upper arms pushing out, making the shirt a little tight. The shirt was tucked loosely into an old pair of jeans that looked like he'd grown out of them a bit, so the muscles of his thighs—*Stop looking at him like that.* I didn't even know exactly what I was feeling about the boy who was practically a part of our household. I only knew that it was territory I hadn't walked, ridden in, or swam in.

"Mornin'," Tuck said, looking at me, then turning away, like he had been doing lately—like he was afraid of me or something.

"Hey," I said, giving him a little smile.

"Hey, you." He gave me a little smile back, then looked down at his boots. His right foot was tapping, the way it did when he was nervous, the way it had since I met him when we were kids.

"Gonna be ninety-six degrees," I told him.

"That's a little high for early June."

"Papa had on the *Farm Report* at breakfast," I said. "And it's going to be humid, 91 percent. Chance of rain, but not till this afternoon."

"Whew," Tuck said.

Temperature and precipitation didn't just mean inconvenience or a hot ride. Every change in the weather affected the crops, as we all knew. My parents were dancers and musicians, but we lived in a farming community. When harvest time came, Papa, Sonny Boy, and Will helped Uncle Tucker in any way needed. Tuck helped out in the fields every day after school. The land and her gifts were close to us, just like the river was close.

"Well, we're standing around here talking," I said, "and we've got two horses here who want some attention."

"Yeah, look who knows he's so handsome," Tuck said, stroking Sable Star's forelock. The gleam of the brown gelding's coat, all flashy with white socks and a star, was a beautiful contrast to my horse.

"Well, look who knows she's the most beautiful horse in La Luna," I told him, rubbing Golden Princess along her neck, making the cooing sounds she loves to hear from me, telling her that I am just loving up on her.

Tuck came over and gently chucked Golden Princess under her chin. "Sometimes," he said, "when Sable Star breaks into a full gallop, I feel like I'm riding a wave."

I extended my hand and fed some of the leftover carrots to Sable Star, admiring the dark brown beauty of his coat.

"You know something, Calla Lily? One of the things I like about you is that you're beautiful, but you don't go around acting like it. You're beautiful like our horses are beautiful. They don't know it, they just are."

I loved hearing him say that, but I didn't know how to answer.

"Sable Star's a pretty good contrast to my palomino, don't you think?" I said. It was getting hot, and I lifted my hair up off my shoulders.

"That's for sure," Tuck said. "That is one good thing for sure."

I could feel his eyes on me as I reached in the rear pocket of my jeans and pulled out an elastic band. I pulled my hair back and slipped the elastic over it.

"Let's go," Tuck said. "But it's too hot to saddle up our horses." So we bridled and mounted and headed out bareback along the grassy strip next to the cotton field behind the Tuckers' barn. A light morning breeze riffled the rows of cotton plants, tender, green, and young. I looked at them in their newness and somehow felt a kinship. Right then, the cotton plants were so fresh, so different from how they'd look in that late-summer push to blossoms and, eventually, at the harvest that came with the bonfires and gumbo and dancing.

I could feel Golden Princess's muscles, strong and rippling under my thighs as we walked and trotted along for a half hour. Even at that pace, we were already sweating, and the horses were in a lather. My T-shirt and jeans were sticky and clinging to my body. Having been born in Louisiana, I loved that feeling—at least I did in June. And I could see patches of sweat forming under Tuck's arms and at the back of his shirt.

When we reached the other side of the cotton field, a wide dirt road skirted a big pecan orchard before reaching the horse trail along the raised bayou levee. The levee was like a flat-topped hill, high enough to contain the waters of Bayou Semer, even during the spring flood season—at least in most years. Papa told me that the bayou connected our pastures and pecan orchards to the La Luna River, where steamboats had traveled from the 1800s up to when he was a boy, carrying loads of cotton down to the Mississippi River and into New Orleans for export. Eventually the river traffic stopped when the La Luna silted up. Now the river gave us the gift of rich, black soil that it dropped along its banks, making our farmland rich and fertile.

I'd always loved riding along the levee, fourteen feet above the riverbanks. There was so much wildlife to see. Sometimes I'd spot a kingfisher cruising for breakfast, a bunny in the brush, or mourning doves feeding on seeds in the grass. And it was cooler on the levee, so when we got there, Tuck and I broke into a trot and then into an easy canter. It felt like our horses were relieved to get the chance to cut loose.

So Tuck and I raced, just letting Sable Star and Golden Princess run as fast as they wanted. I looked back and saw that, behind us, the sky was getting dark, the sign of a Louisiana thunderstorm moving our way. My T-shirt and jeans were soaked now, from my own sweat and Golden Princess's, but she just kept running. I think she could smell the coming storm before I could.

"Tuck, look," I called out. "Look at the sky!"

"Whoa," he said. "I smell the rain now."

Sweat was soaking his hair, and I could see the darkening at his thighs and the crotch of his jeans, where he'd picked up Sable Star's sweat.

Sable Star whinnied, smelling the storm too. He broke out ahead, with hooves pounding, and before I knew it, we were barreling at full speed along the levee back toward Uncle Tucker's barn.

"Easy, Golden Princess," I said, knowing it was better to hold a horse back than to let her run at will. But she and Sable Star had no plan to stop. They wanted to beat the thunder and lightning.

Then the rain started. Heavy drops hit me in the face as we galloped, stinging my eyes, sopping my hair. I looked down and saw that my white T-shirt was completely soaked, and that the nipples of my new breasts, which I wasn't yet used to, were sticking out. I tucked my chin down to my chest to keep the rain from pounding my eyes and face.

Finally, we reached the pecan orchard. The pecan branches were swaying in the wind. Only the mighty live oaks at the edge of the pasture seemed solid and unshakable.

We raced toward them, those ancient trees with their huge limbs dipping down to the ground. I screamed out, "Yahoo!" as we rounded the stand of them and pushed hard around the edge of the cotton field.

"Yahoo!" Tuck called back.

Golden Princess and I were like one animal, racing and bucking together. I could feel her energy was mine, firing me up as I bent down over her neck. "Here we come!" I shouted.

Just as we made it to the barn, lightning cracked through the sky. I was afraid of the storm that would follow. Luckily, Tuck and I pulled into the shelter before it struck.

I slid off Golden Princess and began to dry her off with a towel.

Tuck was toweling down Sable Star, and he came over to me. The smell of wet horses and the smell of us hung in the air.

Tuck looked at my face and my budding breasts poking through my sopping shirt. I could smell his sweat, a man's sweat, mixed with the smell of Sable Star. It was a smell I'd never noticed before.

Suddenly he pulled me to him and pressed his lips on mine. The softness of his lips, the smell of him, amazed me. I felt faint, as if the center of my body had suddenly dropped down to between my legs, where I had a strange feeling.

Tuck licked his tongue along my lips, and I breathed in his breath. The softness of his tongue was like nothing I'd ever felt. Some memory of being a baby—of touching with my tongue, of sucking—came to mind. But I didn't know what to do with that feeling.

Then I felt Tuck's tongue inside my mouth. I could feel the sweat on his back, my own hair and clothes soaking with rain and sweat and horse sweat, the water running down my back. My breasts pressed against his wet chest. I was confused. I could feel Tuck's heart beating under my hand.

Just as suddenly as the moment had begun, it was over. We pulled apart and quickly busied ourselves with currying our horses, cooling them off, leading them back into the pasture, and going separately about our chores.

Chapter 8

1967

A few hot weeks later, I was sitting with Tuck on the Tuckers' porch. Their porch was something like ours—a deep, big porch so there was plenty of room to visit, with fresh-painted light blue floors, a ceiling fan, a swing at one end, a table and chairs at the other, and little wicker end tables. But our porch was messier, with Sonny Boy's *Popular Mechanics* magazines on the chairs and stacks of library books everywhere since Will was always reading, and my books were there, too.

The Tuckers' yard was prettier than ours too, because Miz Lizbeth was a fabulous gardener. Much of it was shaded by big old live oaks and pine trees high as you could see, but there was a big sunny spot filled with all different types of roses, which Miz Lizbeth was famous for. Our yard had so many old, thick magnolia trees that you could stand under them and not even get wet when it rained. M'Dear liked a garden that just goes wild. She didn't know why people got so upset about weeds. M'Dear said a garden should be a circus, filled with everything from Louisiana irises to impatiens to four-leaf clovers.

M'Dear and Miz Lizbeth were out shopping, and Papa and Uncle Tucker were at work. Olivia was cleaning upstairs, but it was just Tuck and me sitting in the swing on the porch, eating slices of Miz Lizbeth's lemon pie.

Neither one of us could think of a word to say. I wasn't sure whether this felt good or not. Then Tuck set down his empty plate, reached for my hand, and twined his fingers through mine. My stomach leaped, I let out a little breath, and we just kept rocking, both of us staring straight ahead. The feeling of his body next to mine was so exciting! Finally we both turned to each other and started to say something, but instead we just burst out laughing. "Did you know what you were going to say?" I asked him.

He didn't answer. "I just want to look at you," he said, finally.

I could feel a blush starting at the roots of my hair and sweeping down my whole body. Let Tuck just look at me? But he squeezed my hand and smiled so sweetly that I said, "Okay, if you want to." He looked at my hair, then at my face, my eyes, my lips, and he just lifted his hand and took his finger and touched my lips. I couldn't move a muscle.

"Can I look at your body just sitting there like I was painting you?" he asked, and I realized how much I wanted him to look. "Yes," I said. "Yes," I said again.

Tuck stared into my eyes until I couldn't take it anymore. I had to look away.

He gazed at my shoulder blades and at my breasts and my belly and down my legs to my toes, the heels of my feet, the soles of my feet, and then he gave a little sigh. "I wish I could eat you up," he said. "You're sweeter than that lemon pie."

I never had felt the way I felt right then, and my mouth was stuck wide open.

"Your mouth won't close," he told me. "Flies are going to fly into your mouth."

So he reached up and gently closed my mouth with his fingers, and we both burst out laughing again.

Then we heard out of nowhere the sound of an old truck with no muffler. I knew that sound. There were so many trucks like that, Negro men coming in from the fields who couldn't afford a muffler job. I wondered if it was some of Olivia's people coming to get something. But no, I didn't recognize this truck. And it was going fast, passing the Tuckers' house, then it cut into reverse and screeched to a halt right in front, tearing up the lawn.

That made me mad. Couldn't they see that this was a fine yard, a real lawn with pine straw at the edges, which had been well tended and mowed? Was this someone who couldn't see, or who didn't care?

A man jumped out of the truck, and I could feel Tuck's body stiffen next to mine.

The man came strutting up to the house like he was the king of everything and God's gift to the world, when really he was dirty-haired and greasy.

"Get outta here, you no-count of a man!" Olivia hollered, sticking her head out of a window upstairs, like she knew he was coming, like she had recognized the sound of his truck.

"Shut your mouth, nigger woman," he said. I winced at the sound of him calling Olivia "nigger woman." He *was* no-count. And he was wearing this blue Banlon shirt that was too tight even on his thin body, over tight dirty jeans and scuffed-up white patent leather shoes. This Mister No-Count had anger in him so strong that I could feel it up on the porch. My body shot up a shield like M'Dear had taught me to do, a strong shield circling my body so none of this man's anger could touch me. I tried to stay calm by breathing through my nose, the way she told me to, in and out, real slow.

Behind the man was a lady, petite, with burned-out blond hair, dark roots showing, wearing a printed shift that hung on her like a dish cloth on a rack. But the dress was clean. Her hair was clean. She was trying, this lady. I could see all this before they even made it up to the porch.

"Hey, Tuck, my boy," the man said.

Tuck was on his feet watching them, his legs spread like he was on the football field, ready for whatever might come his way.

"I'm not your boy," he said to the man.

"Come on, Tuck, it's your old man. I've come to take you home."

I cannot believe that the Tuck I knew was the son of this man.

"Tuck!" the lady said, rushing over to hug him, and he hugged her back.

I was stunned and thought, *That must be his mother.* She seemed so small against him, and Tuck was only fifteen. "Oh, you've grown so fast! You're so big, you're so healthy. Oh Tuck, I'm so glad—"

She was right, Tuck was so tall, so healthy—so different than when he stepped into La Luna.

"Go on and get your things," the man told Tuck. "Oh—and see if they don't want to give you some going-away money."

"What do you think you're talking about?" Tuck said.

"We're talking about how your mama begged me to come down here and bring your sorry ass back to Foret City. That's what we're talking about."

"No, no," said Tuck's mother, "your father, he doesn't mean it that way. We've come to get you, Tuck. I'm sorry it took so long for us to come find you. Things have changed. We're all cleaned up now. I'm sober. I've missed you so much. Oh Tuck, baby, I love you."

Tuck looked at his mother, closed his eyes, then opened them again wide, quick, like if he blinked a certain way, his mother would look different and his father would disappear.

Mister No-Count sleazed his way toward the open front door and leaned in to look at the living room. "Where's the old man and the old lady, anyway?" he said. "They leave you alone with a pretty little thing like this?" His tongue came slightly out of the side of his lip. "Mmm," he said, "you're looking good, sweet thing."

Miz Lizbeth had gone shopping with M'Dear in Claiborne. I knew Uncle Tucker was out in his fields taking a look at the cotton. How could they all be out of reach? I couldn't believe it. Daddy was still at school, teaching band, but would Olivia think to go get him? And where was Olivia?

"Leave her alone!" Tuck shouted and moved toward his father.

"What do you think you're gonna do, little boy?" his father said, like he was teasing. "Now get your stuff and get your ass in the truck."

He shoved Tuck toward the living room. Tuck shoved back. I was shaking.

Tuck's mother was crying now. I could see how delicate her features were. How her nose was slightly turned up, and her eyes were the same startling blue as Miz Lizbeth's. Her hands were fine, but her polish was chipped and her nails were chewed to the quick.

"You made your mama cry," No-Count said to Tuck.

"You're the one who makes my mama cry," Tuck said, "you sorry excuse for a man."

No-Count punched Tuck on his shoulder, and I thought, *Danger!* Should I run for help? I didn't know what to do. I didn't want to leave Tuck alone with these people. I moved to Tuck's side, scared out of my wits, but thinking I should help.

The cigarette Tuck's father had stuck behind his ear was on the floor. I stepped in front of him, and I said, "Excuse me, sir, but your cigarette is—"

Tuck's mother grabbed me, yanking me to her just before No-Count punched Tuck in the face. Blood spurted out of Tuck's nose, and No-Count knocked him against the wall.

"No!" Tuck's mother called out, "Please, Sam, don't!"

She let go of me and reached out for Tuck. No-Count shoved her, and she crashed against the door, falling so hard her elbow tore through the screen.

Tuck came back from the wall, punched his father in the stomach, and No-Count fell backwards to the floor.

Then he got up, yelling, and lunged at Tuck, then hit him hard in the stomach. Poor Tuck made a scary gasping sound and crumpled to the floor, doubled over in pain. I started screaming.

"Shut up, bitch," the man said to me. I pressed myself up against the wall, frozen with fear. Blood was spattered all over the porch boards, Tuck's face was covered in blood, and I could feel the wetness where Tuck's blood had hit my leg.

No-Count gave Tuck a kick, saying, "Oh, come on, little girl, get up. We was just starting to have fun."

"That's enough. Stop it, please stop. That's enough. You hurt him bad. Please, Sam," Tuck's mother said.

"I said GET UP!" No-Count shouted and went to kick Tuck harder. But Tuck grabbed his foot and jerked it, making his father fall back and hit his head hard on the floor.

Just then I saw Miz Lizbeth's big Buick coming up the street. "M'Dear! Miz Lizbeth!" I screamed at the top of my lungs.

Suddenly there was a huge explosion, and everyone froze. Olivia was standing in the doorway pointing a pistol straight at the father's head. The gunshot had left a splintered hole in the porch ceiling.

"You move and I'll blow your head off," she said to No-Count.

Tuck was sitting up, still holding his father's foot. Olivia didn't move a muscle or take her eyes off the father as she said, "Tuck, you done won the fight. Now let him go, and I want you to back up against the wall."

Tuck was kind of frozen and started to shake. Olivia told him, "Now do as I say, Tuck."

Tuck did, and he was starting to cry in small sobs. I saw M'Dear and Miz Lizbeth jump out of the car and come running across the lawn.

Olivia's voice was calm and cold as she told No-Count, "You piece of trash, you do one move wrong and I'll kill you so help me God. Now stayin' on your back, you drag yourself off this porch and down the stairs. Do it SLOW! Then you better run for your truck, 'cause I already done called the police."

M'Dear and Miz Lizbeth stood to the side as Tuck's father slid himself out of the screen door. He got up slow and swaggered back to his truck. M'Dear ran to me and threw her arms around me. I could feel her pulling me tight, her chest against mine, her arms strong around my back, her hands touching my hair. And she whispered to me, "Breathe, Calla. Breathe with me."

I felt M'Dear's deep breath as she inhaled and let it out. I breathed in slowly with my mama. I let my breath fill my body. I felt it go down to my toes, and then up, until I could feel it at the top of my head!

"Remember," M'Dear said, "you're a baby whale."

I remembered. This is what M'Dear taught me in the mornings when we sat quietly next to each other, not talking. I breathed in, breathed the clean air into my body, circled it around, and then blew it out of my baby-whale head. My mama held me, and I remembered that so long as she was there, my world was safe.

But poor Miz Lizbeth! She grabbed Tuck's mama and said, "Stay here please, Charlotte. Please don't go. You don't have to live like you're doing. Your papa and I want you here with us, where you'll be safe. Tuck needs you here. Don't go off with that man."

Tuck's mama clung to Miz Lizbeth for a minute, but then she broke free. "I'm sorry, Mama," she cried. "I'm sorry." Then she rushed down the steps to her husband. Olivia kept the gun pointed right at them until they got in the truck and peeled out, with chunks of lawn shooting out from under those spinning tires.

Miz Lizbeth broke down in tears, and she looked like she was going to faint.

"Miz Lenora, it look like Miz Lizbeth ain't gonna be good for comforting herself, let alone Tuck," Olivia said.

"Tuck can come home with us," M'Dear said.

M'Dear went over to Tuck, who was sitting on the steps with his head between his knees, dripping blood. He was shaking and rocking slightly from side to side.

"Tuck," M'Dear said, sitting down next to him and stroking his hair. "Tuck, please look up. I'd like to see you."

Tuck didn't move.

"Come on, sweetie. It's okay," M'Dear went on. "You were so brave, Tuck. You defended your mother, defended Calla, defended yourself. You did a fine job. Tuck, listen, you're safe now. He's gone. You're with people who love you."

M'Dear kept stroking Tuck's head until, slowly, he lifted it from between his knees. His face was caked in blood, and bruises were starting to form all over his face.

M'Dear didn't seem to mind that Tuck's blood was now on her hands. She reached out to him. Her arms were wide open. "Tuck?" she said. He leaned his head on her shoulder, so she put her arms around him, and he began to sob.

"It's all right, Tuck. It's all right."

Miz Lizbeth was still crying.

"Tuck, why don't you come on home with us for a little while?" M'Dear asked him. "Lizbeth, I'll call our husbands and ask them to come home right away. Now you go on inside and try to get a hold of yourself."

Then M'Dear followed Miz Lizbeth inside so she could use the phone before she took Tuck and me over to our house.

❧

Tuck had the first bath, and then Olivia filled the tub for me, throwing in some of M'Dear's bath salts. It felt so good just to soak that I was turning into a prune when Olivia knocked. "Come on out, Miss Calla," she said. "Time to get dried off. Tuck done gone home for supper, and it's getting on time for you to eat too. I'm fixing to go home."

"Olivia, you probably want to get more cleaned up."

"Oh," she said, "I cleaned up enough. Things don't stick to me like they do some of y'all. My skin is thicker. Blood don't stick on me. Now you go on downstairs. I done fixed y'all a pan of cornbread."

"Hey, my baby," Papa said when I went downstairs, and he gave me a big hug. "You going to be okay?"

"Yes, sir," I said, breathing in Papa's scent. "I think I'm going to be okay."

And we sat down at the kitchen table, Papa and me, and ate Olivia's cornbread with tall glasses of cold milk. When we were finished, I said, "I want to go tell M'Dear good night."

"Calla," Papa said, "your mama is already asleep."

"But I wanted to see her," I said. Papa gave me a hug and said, "You'll see her in the morning. She was just real tired tonight." And he hugged me tighter and gave me a kiss on the forehead.

"You know we all love you, don't you?" he said. "You know we'll always be here to protect you?"

"Yes sir. Yes, Papa," I said. And I looked at him and could tell that he was ready to go to bed, too.

Sonny Boy and Will came into the kitchen then and finished up the cornbread and milk.

"Baby sister," Sonny Boy said, "you know you always got us by your side. If anybody wants to fool with you—"

"They'll have to deal with us, first," Will said.

Just before I turned off my light, my brothers gently opened the bedroom door. "We're just checking on you," Will said.

"I'm fine, y'all."

"Just holler if you need anything," Sonny Boy said. And I went to sleep knowing that I lived in a house full of people who would care for me, no matter what.

A month or so later, Tuck asked me to go down to the pier with him after supper. We just lay back and listened to the river, looking up at the stars and the moon. The moon was a thin crescent, so I told Tuck, "That's what I call a fingernail moon."

Then I explained to Tuck what M'Dear had taught me about the Moon Lady in the moon, who watches over us and who we can ask for help.

"Your mama is so wonderful," he said. "I mean, I love Papa Tucker and Grandma Lizbeth, but I have never known anyone like your mama."

Then his voice got soft, and he told me about what had gone on in his family—the drunken fights, the beatings, and what finally made him run away to La Luna. I just listened to him as he talked until Papa started calling me to come inside.

M'Dear was alone in the kitchen, kneading dough for our breakfast biscuits. I sat down and told her everything Tuck said.

"Tuck never told anyone—not even Uncle Tucker and Miz Lizbeth—because he was afraid that it would cause trouble and his father would hurt his mother."

M'Dear was quiet. She kept on working the biscuit dough.

"Calla," she said, and put down the dough like it was all of a sudden too heavy. "Let's you and me go sit out on the porch." So we went out and sat together on the glider.

M'Dear stroked my hair. She said, "Calla, baby, some people are just born with more evil locked up inside them. And then there are some people who get bent that way. I suspect that Tuck's father is a little bit of both."

"Well, M'Dear, what about his mother?"

"Oh. I don't know, Calla. I don't pretend to know all what happened to Charlotte LeBlanc. But alcohol, I do think that's something that runs in the blood. Still, it's hard for me to understand how she could let her precious son get hurt by it.

"But you don't have to understand somebody, Calla, in order to stop from judging them."

That night, for the first time since I was a little girl, M'Dear slept with me in the big old four-poster bed that had been in our family for decades.

"Let's dream of the Moon Lady, Calla," M'Dear said. She held my hand across the bed, and I could smell her light lavender scent. I looked over to see her long, thick hair as it fell over the clean cotton sheets.

"All right, M'Dear," I said.

"Picture this bed as a boat, Calla, that can carry us anywhere, that can carry us through time, through sadness, and through joy.

"What do you see?" she asked.

I closed my eyes and felt my head heavy against the pillow, my body clean.

"I see us with you at the helm, M'Dear."

"And are you paddling?" she asked.

"No."

"You must paddle. I cannot move this boat without your help, Calla Lily."

"All right," I said. "I'm paddling, M'Dear."

"Good," she said, and squeezed my hand. "The Moon Lady will shine, and I will do as much as I can, but you must paddle. Because we are in a small boat, sweet one," she said, and threaded her fingers through my hair.

"Now, we're safe. We're clean, we're sleepy," she said, and squeezed my hand. We fell asleep that way.

And I dreamed of screaming and blood on blue floors, and my mother's nightgown cleaning it all up. She was naked as she leaned over the river, washing her gown. Her arms had grown heavy. Her arms were so heavy.

Chapter 9

1968

They told us it was stage-four cancer. It was why she'd been so tired lately. The doctors operated on M'Dear right away. She went across the river to Claiborne Parish Hospital, and they cut my mother's breasts off. After that, I felt dizzy, I couldn't get my balance. But M'Dear is the one who helped me understand that this was what she chose—this was what she decided to do to try to stop the cancer. If M'Dear decided something, then it was right by me. The surgery, though, was so much more serious than we thought it would be, and M'Dear was in the hospital for three weeks.

She had to go back for radiation every two months, and after that, her skin looked more and more like it had been burned in a bad fire. Thank goodness the radiation burns didn't affect her whole body. Her face still looked beautiful, but the burns began on the right side of her neck, where the skin had little bubbles of red on it. Sonny Boy got sick the first time he saw it. Will just sat and held her right hand. I had to fight to keep my eyes open to the full reality of my mother, body and soul.

When she got home, she was in and out of a wheelchair. When she could stand, it was only for short periods, and with great care from the person who was helping her. But she was so happy and excited about everything—the new birdfeeder Papa made and hung outside her window, the smell of the cheese biscuits I'd cook for Papa in the morning—except for the days when the radiation treatments made her so sick. She was grateful when she could walk around the yard again and out to the pier. When friends visited, she contentedly chatted with them, catching up on the news of our little town.

Aunt Helen took over the running of the Crowning Glory. I helped one day a week after school, but mostly M'Dear had me keep up with my school activities so that things could stay as normal as possible.

Miz Lizbeth changed Olivia's schedule so that Olivia could be at our house almost all the time. M'Dear would tell her, "Olivia, go home. Take a rest."

But Olivia would say, "Miz Ponder, I'm gone stay and take care of you. And don't you be going telling me what to do. I'll leave when I want to leave. So don't you go be bossing me around."

When I'd get home from school, with Tuck with me most of the time, as soon as I opened the door, I'd check to see if M'Dear was in the living room. If she was, that meant she was having a strong day. If she wasn't, Olivia would be in the kitchen, asking, "What you two want? I know you hungry."

"I'm not hungry, Olivia, I just need to go check on—"

Then she'd stop me. "Your mama don't want you starving. You done already lost enough weight off that tall long-legged body of yours." Then she'd give me a hug.

"And Tuck," she'd say, with a smile, "I know you eat both Miz Lizbeth and Papa Bernard outta they house and home, so we need to pick up the slack."

Then Olivia would fix us some good after-school snack like leftover biscuits, toasted, with butter and honey dripping off them.

After that, we'd go to M'Dear's room. I was so used to her saying, "Hey, y'all!" when I got home, but when she didn't have the strength anymore, I became the one to say, "Hey, y'all!" I would go to the edge of the door and peek in and said, "M'Dear?" If she didn't raise her head right away, Tuck and I would just hang around the house or go outside on the porch. He never pushed me about going somewhere and doing something else. He knew I needed to be around M'Dear.

"I love her too," he told me. "Your mother has been kind to me. In fact, she has always been dear to me."

The day I fully realized that I would never be able to hug my mother again, it felt like the breath had been knocked out of me. I sat in my room and put my fist in my mouth. I didn't want her to hear me cry. I stared at the Peace poster on my wall, with the flowers on it. And I began to sob. *What will it be like, the world without M'Dear? Will I remember her scent? The touch of her hand? How she cradled and washed me? Will I remember how she moved?*

I took my fist out of my mouth. *What if I forget?* And then I held myself.

I always tried to make sure that M'Dear felt clean and pretty. Olivia usually took care of her sheets, but I'd do special things. For instance, Olivia would iron the pillowcases really pretty, but I'd sometimes go ahead and iron the sheets, too, so they'd be all nice and crisp for M'Dear. Soft old cotton sheets like she likes. Pretty, not wrinkled. And sometimes I would tuck lavender from Miz Lizbeth's garden inside M'Dear's pillowcase.

I made sure that M'Dear's hair got washed. When she was too weak to shower, I'd wash her hair in bed. I'd get a little shampoo on a washcloth, wet it, and then drape a plastic beauty cape from the Crowning Glory over M'Dear. I'd just take the cloth and, real gently, rub it over her head and around her scalp. Then I'd rinse out the cloth and do it again.

"M'Dear," I'd say, "do you want any cream rinse or anything?"

"No, Calla, this is just fine. Thank you."

I could tell how tired she was, so I'd say, "Let me put a towel underneath your head so you don't get those pillows wet, okay?"

Then I'd give her a kiss on the forehead and take the pail outside to empty it in the garden. Any part of my mother that went into the ground was like a blessing.

I looked down at M'Dear one day and thought, *Oh, no. I haven't done anything about M'Dear's fingernails!* They'd grown long and had ridges in them. When I was little, M'Dear told me, "Watch out if you get ridges; it's a sign from your body that something's wrong."

Now the ridges were so thick, and her cuticles needed cutting. I said, "M'Dear? I want to give you a manicure."

"Oh, Calla, I'm too weak for a manicure. Plus, who's going to look at it?"

"Well, Papa's going to look at it, and *you're* going to look at it."

"Let's do it another day when I'm stronger," she said.

"Yes, ma'am. You just let me know, and I'll put on my manicurist jacket."

She smiled and closed her eyes. Her hand reached out for me, and I held on to it for a moment.

"Thank you, Calla Lily. I can feel love in the touch of your hands. I can feel the healing in them, *bébé.* There's room in your heart for so many kinds of love. Everyone has a unique path, and you're already walking yours.

"Calla, without a doubt, you have the gift of touching someone and them touching you. But you have so much to learn, Calla, so much to learn in the world outside of the Crowning Glory and La Luna. You have people to meet, experiences outside of your life here, things you can't imagine, and I want you to have them. Come back if you want to, but go out into the world, and bring back the best and leave the rest. Do the same with La Luna as you leave it. Take the best and leave the rest."

Then she took a deep breath and rolled her head from side to side.

Some days, when she was feeling up to it, M'Dear would call out for Will to come in and play the mandolin for her. And M'Dear would sing the old songs, the words that few people knew anymore.

"It's a shame," I told Tuck, "a shame that the words to the old songs will go out with M'Dear's generation unless someone cares to learn them."

"Why not us?"

I looked at him, thinking about it.

"You and your brothers could sing with your mother, and I could do my best to transcribe."

Sonny Boy, Tuck, and I set out to join Will in Mama's room at every opportunity, singing our hearts out till she grew weak for the day.

Finally an afternoon came when M'Dear called me to her. She was propped up in the bed with the fluffy linen-covered pillows that Aunt Helen had made. "I want you to see something," she said, and reached up to her head. As she touched the crown of her head, her hair began to fall out. She brought her hand down beside her, the hair still in her palm.

I began to cry.

"Don't be afraid," she said. "Don't be afraid, *bébé.* Take a deep breath. Let it blow out the top of your head. Now look. It's even easier for me to breathe out, now that I am going bald! You just remember the bald-headed man from when you were little. Everything will be fine.

"Come on. Let's do my hands. You know that tin I use to wash butter beans in? Go ahead and get that. Fill it with some warm water, then put some Palmolive in there. And go get my manicure kit."

I said, "M'Dear, you don't have to tell me how to do it."

She answered, "I know. But I'm still your mother."

It made me feel so good to hear M'Dear say that.

I ran upstairs to get the manicure kit Papa gave M'Dear for Christmas one year. It's white leather, real leather, and inside it had beautiful cream-colored velvet, with all of the instruments laid in there perfectly. Two types of fingernail files, some nail clippers, a cuticle pusher, some orange sticks. I took the kit and just held it to my breast, like it was a part of my mother. Then I came back downstairs.

I started by clipping and filing M'Dear's nails, round at the edges, just the way she liked them. Then I filled the butter bean tin with warm water and Palmolive, so M'Dear could soak her hands.

I very gently pushed back each of her cuticles, one by one. I started out using the little cuticle pusher, but then realized that M'Dear's skin was so fragile that I should just use my thumb.

"You want me to rub some of your lotion on?" I asked.

"Oh, that would be lovely," she said. "Get my Jergens."

I took some Jergens lotion and massaged it into each hand. M'Dear closed her eyes and smiled. I could tell that I was soothing her. Just as I was finishing her second hand, she stopped and turned my hands up in her palms and looked at my hands, at my fingers. "Oh, Calla Lily," she said. "Your fingers used to be so tiny."

"Let me finish up your manicure," I told her. I had some very pale pink polish, so pale it was like a pink gloss. After I painted each nail, I blew on it to dry the polish.

Then M'Dear held out her hands to admire my work. She smiled at me and said, "Go on out there and see if your papa's home yet. And if he is, ask him won't he come in here to visit for a minute and see how pretty you've made me."

"Yes, ma'am," I said. And I thought of all the different kinds of love M'Dear had in her heart.

Of course, I wasn't the only one taking care of M'Dear. Along with Olivia, Aunt Helen was always around. One day she came in with a big paper sack, and inside was a beautiful quilt she'd made for M'Dear. It had a huge tree on it—limbs going out with leaves on them, reaching to the top of the quilt, and then roots stretching down to the bottom. It looked like a Louisiana live oak, but you couldn't tell for sure. On the limbs were little baby birds, and there were little bitty squirrels on the trunk, and a little wasps' nest—all the things that live in a tree.

When Aunt Helen gave it to M'Dear, she unfolded it *very* slowly across the bed. "It's the tree of life!" she said. "Look, this tree has got so much life in it. It's like you, Lenora. You've got so much life, so many roots that hold you, and that wonderful strong trunk. Now look real close. Tell me what you spy with your little eye."

M'Dear looked and looked until she finally spotted a tiny little pink ribbon holding a tiny little pouch. She said, "Sister, what is that little pouch thing?"

Aunt Helen smiled, and said, "That pouch holds all the secrets you and I ever kept from each other. See how tiny it is?"

M'Dear's eyes began to glisten. "Thank you," she said. Their eyes met, and they held their gaze for a long time.

"Do you think that pouch is tiny enough?" Aunt Helen asked.

"Sister of mine, I am trying to let go of the things that bind me to this earth, but oh, I will miss our laughter together."

Aunt Helen lightly put her hand against the side of M'Dear's head. M'Dear looked up at her, and they smiled at each other for a long time.

I thought about the two of them, really thought for the first time—about sisters and what they gave—about how they came up together, were girls together, had done most everything together. I'd always just taken their closeness for granted. I never had a sister. Maybe that's why I latched on to Sukey and Renée and why they latched on to me. Because we all need sisters. My M'Dear and Aunt Helen had been so lucky to have each other. But now they would have to let each other go.

Day after day, my girlfriends held my hand as I tried to let my mother go.

Chapter 10

WINTER 1969–1970

I had been so worried about M'Dear. I kept waiting for her to start getting well, but as the months went by she didn't seem to be getting any better. I knew she was fading away when she was too weak to celebrate much over the holidays. She had always enjoyed Christmas the most and had always worked to make it special for us. Now she barely noticed its arrival. And when I thought about that, my throat closed up and my stomach felt twisted inside.

One night M'Dear and Papa knocked on my door to ask me to join them in the studio to dance. I looked at my alarm clock and it was three in the morning. We danced all the time as a family, but even for *us*, starting at 3:00 a.m. was a bit surprising.

We went to the boys' room and said, "Y'all, wake up! We're going to the studio." The boys looked at us like we were crazy, M'Dear in her nightgown, and even in January, with no shoes on. I looked at her bare feet and wanted to cover them up immediately. I didn't want any inch of her body to get cold or be in any way stressed. M'Dear must have read my mind because she looked at me and said, "I want to feel my bare feet touch the floor, to touch the ground."

Sonny Boy and Will got up out of bed in their striped pajamas and followed us through the hallway that connects the house to the dance studio. Papa turned on the big industrial heater, and M'Dear slowly walked over to the stereo player and put on "Clair de Lune." I knew that song because we danced to it in a summer concert that M'Dear planned when we were little. She held it outside in the park under a full moon because we lived in the moon's hometown. That was what she told us.

Now M'Dear took my hand and Papa's hand, and Sonny Boy and Will linked theirs with ours. We stood there in silence, nobody moving, all of us waiting for M'Dear to start. M'Dear who we loved so much, who looked so tiny now, but who had all her radiance shining through. M'Dear squeezed my hand, and I stood there with my eyes closed until I absorbed all the energy I could from her squeeze.

Then M'Dear dropped our hands and began to move by herself. "This is a dance to honor the Moon Lady." Then her body changed, like it was charged somehow with new energy, and she went to Will and pulled him close to dance with her. Fluidly moving his thin muscular body, Will kept his eyes on M'Dear the whole time, not imitating her but moving his hands to the beautiful music that was like moonlight, like turquoise water flowing over white rocks. Then M'Dear stepped up to Sonny Boy and took his hand. Sonny Boy, over six feet, towered over M'Dear and looked down at her like he wanted to remember this moment forever. Then she stumbled and held on to his shoulders. She stood there for a moment. We could see her taking a deep breath, seemingly to get some strength back.

I watched them, and I had to hush the voice in my mind that said:

"Me, M'Dear, now *me*! Me, please!" Finally, she took my hands and she looked me in the eyes, smiling, shaking her head like she was so happy at what she saw. Her eyes told me, "Calla, you are all that I hoped." Then we moved together. I reached my arms up to the sky and M'Dear raised her arms as much as she could. We reached our hands out, went low, down to the ground, and then turned our bodies in slow circles that ended in light steps of stillness. M'Dear came toward me, touching my arms lightly, and whispered, "Remember to look up now and then and throw me a kiss, baby, and I'll send one back to you. Remember the stars, Calla." We looked at each other, tears rolling down both our faces.

Then it was Papa's turn. To see M'Dear and Papa together was like watching butterflies. They smiled at each other so deeply that they seemed lost for a few moments. "My Lenora," I heard him whisper. Then the smile cut loose into movement. At first, I thought their dance was too intimate to watch, my father in his pajamas, his eyes all red from lack of sleep, my beautiful mother's face drawn and tired—both of them dancing themselves out of pain. I could see that it wasn't easy for M'Dear and Papa to move like this when they hurt so much. I watched as she leaned into him for strength. I saw that pain is part of beauty—that inside of all that music, all that love, all the moonlight and sunlight, are shafts of pain, and we are meant to bear it all.

Then M'Dear and Papa reached out to the three of us. We all stepped together and wrapped our arms around each other.

I did not want my mother to leave me. But I knew she must.

After our night of dancing, M'Dear was so weak that she rarely left her bed. Olivia and Aunt Helen were always by her side. Often as not, when I got home from school, M'Dear would be sleeping, so I started spending the hours between school and dinnertime over at the Tuckers'.

And that's how it happened that Miz Lizbeth wound up buying me shoes for the Valentine's Day Ball.

I had been telling her about the dress that Aunt Helen was making me for the ball, with Tuck as my date. We had picked out the fabric together, and I showed Miz Lizbeth a swatch I had in my purse. It was white, with little red hearts all over it.

She said, "I can just picture you wearing that with a pair of red shoes."

Now, I was so excited about the dress—the ball was still a month off—that I hadn't even thought about my shoes. "Tell you what," Miz Lizbeth offered. "We have plenty of time to ride over to Claiborne and see if we can't find you something nice."

So the two of us got into her Buick and headed out for Richardson's Department Store. And, wouldn't you know it, there was a whole display of pumps and platforms. "Get out that swatch," Miz Lizbeth told me. We held it up to the shoes, and sure enough, a pair of *red* platforms looked perfect.

"I'll have to talk to Papa about these," I said. "I don't have enough money of my own to buy them today."

"I didn't mean for you to buy them, Calla. It would make me very happy if you just let me get these shoes for you as a gift."

"Oh, Miz Lizbeth," I said, "I could never impose on you that way!"

"You're not imposing. I offered to get these shoes for you, and I mean to do it."

When we got home with the shoes, Miz Lizbeth dropped in to see if M'Dear was awake. She was indeed sitting up, and she seemed a little more energetic than usual.

We both kissed her, then sat down at her bedside to tell her all about our shoe-shopping adventure.

I got out my swatch and held it up to the shoes. "Look, M'Dear, isn't this a perfect combination? Can't you just see this with my dress?

And I have to give Miz Lizbeth all the credit. She just imagined exactly the kind of shoes I needed."

"Well," M'Dear said, lifting a shoe from the box, "the color is perfect. Reds are hard to match. Lizbeth"—she smiled at her—"has always had great fashion sense. But you're only sixteen years old. I think you're going to break your neck trying to dance in these."

"Oh, M'Dear," I told her, "Sukey gets to wear even higher than these, and so do other girls. Watch how well I can walk in them. And they do make me feel sooo glamorous."

I put on the shoes and paraded around the bedroom, proud that my ankles didn't even wobble. "You see?" I asked her. "Everybody's going to love these shoes."

"Now, just where did you get the money to buy them?" M'Dear said.

"Lenora, I insisted on buying them for her," Miz Lizbeth said. "I practically had to press the gift on her. It was just something I wanted to do for Calla."

"Hmmph," said M'Dear.

I heard the anger in M'Dear's voice—M'Dear, who never snapped at anyone, whose heart was full of love.

M'Dear said, "Lizbeth, Calla is not *your* daughter. She's mine. And it's not my fault if your own daughter left!"

Miz Lizbeth couldn't even look at her.

I saw M'Dear gripping the sheets, trying not to cry. She was that tired and spent. I didn't understand what had just happened, but it scared me. "M'Dear, are you okay?" I asked.

She didn't answer.

"Lenora, don't even think about this," Miz Lizbeth said. "I'm going to let you rest now. I promised Bernard that I would have his supper early tonight because he has a Rotary Club meeting." She kissed both M'Dear and me lightly on the forehead, saying, "Good-bye, I'll see you tomorrow."

M'Dear grabbed at her hands and said, "Wait!"

She held Miz Lizbeth's hands between her own and said, "Lizbeth, I was unkind. It hurts me that you bought Calla her first pair of grown-up dress shoes. I am laid up here, unable to do that for her. And it hurts me that you'll get to watch her become a woman and I will not be here."

"M'Dear, don't say that," I protested.

But Miz Lizbeth was telling her, softly, "I understand. But I also know that no one could ever take your place in Calla's heart—or in mine."

M'Dear sank back on her pillows, tears spilling down her cheeks, exhausted.

Miz Lizbeth kissed her again and left to go home.

I reached out for M'Dear's hand. "M'Dear, I'm sorry I'm spending so much time with Miz Lizbeth. It just happens, you know, because Tuck and me—"

M'Dear said, "You don't need to say you're sorry. She's a woman I want you to count on. And you can."

The next day was typical January weather, dark and gloomy. I usually woke up on Saturdays feeling excited about the weekend, but that morning Sukey and I were at Renée's, and Sukey sensed my mood. "What's wrong, Calla?" she asked.

"It just feels like there's so much *weight* on me! Sukey, I feel like there's this heavy black coat on me, just weighing me down to the ground, and I don't know how to take it off."

Sukey hugged me and said, "We'll help you, Calla."

"Yeah," Renée said. "Let's just cut that coat right off." She went and got two pairs of scissors and an old sheet, which she draped over me.

"Now, Calla," she said, "this sheet is that heavy coat. Close your eyes. Do you feel it?"

"I do. It feels horribly heavy. I can barely walk in it. I can barely put one foot in front of the other."

"Don't even try to walk," Sukey told me. "Just wait till we cut you free."

Then they each took a pair of scissors, and with Sukey in the back and Renée in the front, they cut the sheet into strips, starting at the bottom. When their scissors met at my shoulders, they'd give one last snip, and that strip of the sheet would fall to the ground. I watched the strips puddle at my feet, and it did feel like I was slowly shedding that black and heavy weight. And at that moment, I realized that I had two sisters so strong and so smart that I would never be crushed by even the deepest darkness.

It was the night of the Valentine's Day Ball. M'Dear watched me get dressed with dark, shiny eyes, sharing my excitement. She even helped me with my hair, sweeping it up and creating little ringlets in the back. She asked me to turn around and around so she could see me from all angles, as if she was memorizing me. When Tuck arrived, she made us pose for pictures, which Papa snapped. As I was leaving, she smiled and said, "You know, those shoes do make the outfit."

When I got home that night, she was waiting up, hoping to hear all about the ball. I told her about the music and the dancing and tried to make her feel like she'd been there herself. She couldn't get enough of each detail.

Later that night, after cookies and milk, Papa and I both fell asleep in the bed with M'Dear. The bedside table light was still on. In the middle of the night, I thought I heard something and woke up for a moment. But everything seemed still. I could see the moonlight on the windowsill, and I could hear Papa breathing. He always had a little snore, nothing too bad, just a sort of whiffle. M'Dear hardly made a sound when she slept. I heard a hoot owl in the trees near the river.

Then it was silent. Papa stopped snoring. The refrigerator downstairs in the kitchen stopped its old comfortable hum. There was only silence.

Then I knew. I couldn't hear her heartbeat. Since I was alive in her womb, I'd been hearing that old, comforting sound. I reached out to touch M'Dear, and I felt it. Her heart had stopped beating.

Papa woke up, seeming to sense this, and he kissed my forehead. *He knew too.* Oh, how much my Papa loved me and how brave he was to do that, before he leaned down and kissed M'Dear's lips and hands. Did Papa want to feel any warmth of M'Dear that was left? Or to try to give her some of his? Or had he already set her free?

There was so much I didn't know about what lay underneath M'Dear and Papa's strong love. You could see it the way they touched all day long, the way Papa would come up behind M'Dear when she was stirring a pot on the gas stove, kiss her neck, turn down the gas, then pull her around to start dancing, making us laugh.

I stepped back to the doorway of the room and watched them. Outside the window, I could see the trees were bare. The room started to spin. *M'Dear, you told me this would happen—that you would die.* How I hated it when she took me and showed me the spot under the live oak where she would be buried, in the little graveyard near her mother and father. "To be near a tree is a wonderful thing," M'Dear said. She told me to think of the roots of the tree, to think of the limbs and the branches and the thick leaves and how the tree reached up to the moon and stars. "Think of the stars, Calla," she told me, "and imagine that they're just other towns, and I've moved to them."

I started to cry, and that's when I felt a hand on my shoulder. I knew who it was. I could smell her, that lingering scent of bacon from her breakfast and the scent of Ivory soap so faint you might not smell it if you weren't me. Olivia. She stroked my shoulder, then my hair.

"Everything all right, baby," she whispered. I didn't realize that my hands were freezing until Olivia took them in her own warm hands, the strong black hands with the pink palms. "Every single little thing gone be all right."

Olivia is the one who understood why I wanted to do it. Before the men came to take Mama's body away, I trimmed off some of the white feathers of her remaining hair. "I'm going to put this in a locket so I can have it the rest of my life," I said, sobbing. Will came in then, and put his arms around me.

"I have known y'all since you were little babies," Olivia said to us, "and I have never lied to you."

Then I saw Sonny Boy in the hallway, leaning in closer.

Olivia continued, "Listen to me, and believe me when I say now: everything gonna be all right."

I took a deep breath, and I tried to believe her.

Chapter 11

1970

The day of the funeral I could barely get dressed, my hands were shaking so bad. Will and Sonny Boy each held one of my arms as they helped me into the church and sat on either side of me.

How could this happen? M'Dear in all her beauty and dancing and laughing and greatness, how could she just be lying there in that coffin? How dare they put her there where people could just file past and look at her! I prayed with everyone during the Rosary, but couldn't believe how they acted like this was just a regular prayer session—even with M'Dear lying right there in front of them. If it hadn't been for my brothers and Tuck, I would have run through Our Lady of the River and jerked the rosaries out of their hands, yelling "Pray for yourselves! She doesn't need it! Pray for those of us who don't have her anymore, you rosary-clinking fools!"

Goddamn them! Goddamn breast cancer! I still couldn't accept that the cancer ate up my mother through her breasts, the breasts that fed me and my brothers so lovingly.

And goddamn Aunt Helen. "Lenora, we love you," she had said to M'Dear. But she didn't listen to her! She broke her trust. M'Dear had told both Papa and me that she wanted to be laid out in a nude-colored leotard. "I want to show them what breast cancer does to the body. I don't want to hide it or seem ashamed in anyway. I am going to show them my flat, boy-breasted body."

But Aunt Helen betrayed her. In the funeral home, before the wake or visitation, as we Catholics call it, I confronted Aunt Helen. "How dare you! How dare you let them put her in a dress, and make it look like she still had breasts!" I screamed, unable to stop in my anger and grief. "You knew what she wanted, Aunt Helen!"

"I didn't know," Aunt Helen said quietly, Uncle Richard standing next to her.

"Yes, you did," I said, feeling so enraged I wanted to slap her.

"Calla," Aunt Helen told me, "things change once people move on. I couldn't stop them. I'm sorry. I'm so sorry, Calla."

It was then that I realized Aunt Helen was going through her own sadness of losing M'Dear. We all had to share this. We all had to carry our own load. When Aunt Helen reached her hands out to me, I took them in mine. We were a family.

I was sixteen. M'Dear was thirty-nine. I was in her body for nine months of her life. For almost a year I lived inside her. And now she would live inside me forever.

When we got back from the funeral home, our house was full of pound cakes and casseroles. Even Mrs. Sally, Sukey's mama, brought her string bean, mushroom soup, and onion ring casserole. She must have baked it right after she got home from work. Seeing Mrs. Sally was like seeing her for the first time. She had so much understanding in her eyes that I reached out for her and she held me in her arms, Sukey's mama, who had only ever touched the top of my head before Sukey and me went to sleep. Sukey's mama holding me in her arms.

The rest of the day, all of it, was a blur. Miz Lizbeth finally got me to eat something at some point, but the taste of it came back up.

Eventually I had to get away from everyone, and Tuck came out to the pier with me. I couldn't even speak till we got down there. We sat down together, and Tuck put his arm around me. That made me cry. When I started to speak, I felt like I was choking.

"Oh, Tuck, I knew M'Dear was sick, but I still kind of believed that her heart would go on and she would live forever. Why couldn't she? Why did M'Dear have to die?"

I was sobbing so hard that I could hardly get the words out. "She never did anything wrong. She never hurt anybody in her life! Tell me, damnit, tell me! Tell me why!"

I started pounding my fist on my leg, and then I began to slap my face, *slap my own face*. Tuck pulled me to him, wrapping his arms around me even further. I raised my fists and tried to shove him away.

"Goddamnit!" I cried, pounding on his chest. "Damnit, damnit to goddamn hell! How did that cancer get into M'Dear?" Then I started to beg, "God, please take M'Dear and make her alive again. Make it before the cancer got into her!"

I stopped pounding on Tuck and buried my face in his chest, running my fingers through my hair and pulling at it for comfort.

"Calla, I'm gonna hold your hands now, okay? You're pulling your hair too hard. I'm just gonna hold your hands like we always hold hands. Just hold them in my lap."

I tried to pull my hands out of his, but he held on tight. I yelled at him: "I hate all those people and all that food and flowers! How can any of that make us feel better? Nothing can make me feel better."

I collapsed in tears again, and Tuck cradled my head in his lap, stroking my hair. That calmed me a little, and after a moment, he said, "Calla, you oughta look up at the sky. The moon is what you always call a fingernail moon, a little tiny sliver, but still so bright."

I lifted my head to look at Tuck. "I need for her to come back, Tuck."

Very gently, he said, "I know. I know, Calla. I do know."

I stared at him hard until I remembered that he *did know*. I remembered the face of Tuck's mother as she left him on the Tuckers' porch. He kept stroking my hair as he dropped his head, and his own tears began to fall, for the pain I was suffering and for the pain he hid so well for the mother he had lost.

Then he continued to hold me as I murmured for both of us: "M'Dear, you weren't supposed to die. I know you said all those words about living and dying and living again right away and not ever really even leaving. But you were wrong, M'Dear. You have gone and left and I am so angry that I can't find anything big enough to hold my tears."

I am big enough to hold your tears.

I slowly lifted my head from Tuck's lap. I looked out at the river our little town is built on. I looked up at the sliver of a moon. A river, a moon. They could not replace M'Dear. But they did give me comfort.

The river and me, La Luna—together we can hold your tears. Go ahead and cry.

The day after M'Dear's funeral, Papa brought an envelope over to show us. In it was a letter in M'Dear's handwriting, written in heavy black ink and in her own way of talking. It was her final letter to all of us. We taped it to the refrigerator door, and we each couldn't help but read part of it every day.

Dear All of Y'all,

You might get tired of reading this, but I made Papa promise this letter was going to always be here so you can remember The Rules of Life According to M'Dear.

1. Sleep with the windows open. (Window screens are fine, when necessary.)

2. Whistle in the dark. Calla Lily, your attempt at whistling is good enough.

3. Good enough is good enough. Perfect will make you a big fat mess every time.

4. Sing anytime you feel like it, and even more when you don't feel like it. Sonny Boy, this does not mean in math class, although you have my permission to sing in all other classes. Will, all your silent singing is good, and also try to sing out loud at least once a day.

5. Am I going to have to haunt y'all to keep everybody laughing? If I have to, you know I will.

6. New visitors are going to come join y'all. Welcome them with open arms.

7. Make new friends, keep the old ones. Get a new dog or cat as soon as you can, and always let one keep you.

8. Let love slip underneath closed doors, through tiny cracks in the wall, through your pores.

9. Remember: Y'all are so dear, each and every one of you make it so easy to love you, as if anybody needed a reason.

10. Don't push the La Luna. You do not push a river.

11. Do not, and I repeat, DO NOT, wash my seasoned cast iron skillet in soapy water. It MUST simply be wiped clean with an oiled paper towel. We have got to respect things that help bring us good food from the Louisiana earth.

12. MOST IMPORTANT: KEEP ON DANCING. Dance while you're brushing your teeth, dance while the sun shines, dance under the moon. Oh, please be sure to dance under the moon, Calla. Remember, La Luna waits for us to dance in her light, so dance in the streets. When life is happy, dance in the kitchen, and when life is roughest, dance in the kitchen. My dear holy family, dance for the good of the world.

Love,

M'Dear

Chapter 12

1970

Everybody knew we were going through a lot with M'Dear's passing, and chipped in wherever they could. But it was Nelle who was most persistent. She was part of a rotating group of lady-friends who had organized themselves to help with groceries, cooking, and cleaning, working alongside of Olivia and staying when it was time for Olivia to go home to her *own* family. But besides those chores, Nelle often stayed after supper. Just sort of hung out, visiting whoever in our family needed visiting the most. While Renée and Sukey were my best friends, like sisters, Nelle I could talk to, well, not like a mother—nobody could be a mother but M'Dear. But I could share stuff with her that I somehow couldn't share with my girlfriend sisters, Tuck, or Aunt Helen. School stuff, stuff I was so embarrassed about—like my mile-long legs, or how tall I was.

"You look like a model," she'd say. "Girls would *kill* to be tall like you—the way clothes drape on you like a runway model. You're no Twiggy, although you're gonna get too skinny if you don't start eating. No, you're an original; you are CALLA LILY. Tuck sure seems to know it. He's a cutie-pie," she said, trying to get me to smile. "Isn't he?" I didn't answer. "He certainly is one helluva cutie-pie." I turned away.

"That olive complexion of yours can't hide the fact that I know you are blushing inside, if not on the outside." She paused. "Like so many things, huh, Calla?"

"Yeah," I said. "How'd you get so smart?"

"On-the-job experience," she answered and gave a little laugh, then leaned over and gave me a kiss on my forehead.

For a week or so, Nelle stopped her long visits and only came by for a short "good night." It didn't seem to bother Papa or my brothers. But it bothered me. I missed her. I'd gotten used to her being there every night. But I knew she had duties at the Shop 'N Skate.

Then one afternoon, Nelle came up to my room where I was listening to Simon & Garfunkel. She was wearing a Hawaiian shirt, tied at the waist over a pair of baggy khaki shorts, the waist cinched in so tiny, she looked cooler than most girls my age.

"Come on!" she said, lifting the needle off the LP. "Get dressed! No more mournful music!"

Next thing I knew, she was driving me to the Shop 'N Skate, which had a new sign out front. "Shop, Snack 'N Skate," it read. If that wasn't enough, there was a red ribbon going across the skating rink door, which had been widened and repainted. Everybody in town was there, it seemed, including the gang—Sukey, all dressed up in a yellow minidress, Renée, and the boys. Even the grown-ups had taken off work, including Papa, who had the La Luna band there, playing a lively tune.

"Here," Nelle said, and handed me a shiny pair of scissors. I looked at her and at the whole crowd, and decided to laugh and have fun. I cut the red ribbon and walked through the threshold into a place that I didn't recognize at first. Tuck came up behind me and hugged me. I looked over at Nelle, who stood on the other side of the crowd and just gave me a wink.

It turned out that, as Nelle put it, "Y'all are around this joint so much, doing nothing but drinking Coca-Colas and eating peanut butter crackers, that I thought I ought to bring some decent *food* into this joint. Besides, a good businesswoman has got to have a sense of timing."

She had put in three diner-style booths between the grocery items and the skating rink. And she had hired her a cook, Bertha Bonton, Cleveland's mama and Olivia's daughter, and one of the best you could ever find. Oh, just the smell of her homemade French fries! She also hired Cleveland to wash dishes, and to help with all sorts of chores.

"Just let old fat-ass Sheriff Ezneck fool with having Negroes on the premises now," Nelle said.

I said to Nelle, "I can't believe you didn't think of serving food before."

I kept telling myself that I was lucky. Because everyone showed me so much love. Miz Lizbeth and Uncle Tucker invited me in their home like I was one of the family. And I already felt like family with Tuck. The way he held me, looked at me, told me that he'd never leave—he'd say it out of the blue like a chant or something, and I'd realize that it was just what I wanted to hear.

Sukey and Renée were the best friends a girl could have. They were by my side all the time. There were, of course, many days when I had to stay home from school because I was just too sad. On those days, my brothers were champs. They brought me hamburgers and fries and *Seventeen* magazines from Nelle's. Then Will would sit and play songs that he called "Calla Tunes" on his little guitar. M'Dear must have been looking down on us then, keeping an eye on us and smiling.

I loved my friends' mamas, too. One day, Renée's mama, Mrs. Jeansonne, thought it would be nice to take Sukey and me shopping for school clothes at Richardson's Department Store in Claiborne, since Sukey's mama was busy at work. Now, I'm sorry to say this, but I just kept wishing and wishing that it was M'Dear who could have taken us.

First of all, Renée's mama liked clothes for us teenage girls that made your body feel boxed in. M'Dear always said that clothes were meant to make your body want to dance. Renée's mother liked clothes that make you want to sit down and fold your hands. You could tell by her hair how formal she was—it was always up in a super tight French twist. I never saw Renée's mother with her hair down in my whole life.

Still, she was dear to take us, and mostly, I just missed M'Dear. She had just been so much more fun than any other mother. When she took us to Richardson's, I loved how she would dance around the store—and oh, how she loved the scarf department! M'Dear would pick a scarf and she'd twirl and twirl around and finally whirl the scarf in the air! She knew Miss Betty, the lady behind the counter, and Miss Betty would just shake her head and smile as she and the other salesgirls watched. She'd say, "Oh, you just go ahead, Lenora. Just play with any scarf you want."

Then M'Dear would hand some scarves to me and say, "What do you think?"

I'd say, "Oh, M'Dear! I can't decide—I love them all."

Then M'Dear would say, "You know which one speaks to you, Calla."

M'Dear was right. I did know the scarf that spoke to me. It was light purple with blue swirls in it, like the ocean, and we bought it right there on the spot.

Renée's mama was different. When we got to the store she told us, "Girls, I want you to find outfits that match the clothes you already have. Always try to mix and match. It's the way to build a wardrobe that can serve you without breaking the bank. Bring a little list of skirts that need new blouses to match them, or blouses that could use a little sprucing up with an accessory—a little pin, or just the right scarf, for instance. There is really nothing like an accessory for stretching the dollar!

"Accessories make the girl, wouldn't you agree?" Mrs. Jeansonne said, and gave me a smile.

It took me a moment to realize she was talking to me. My mind was still picturing M'Dear dancing with the scarves.

"No, ma'am, I don't agree. Accessories don't make the girl."

"It was just a figure of speech, sweetie," she said, apologetic. I knew she was trying her best to be nice to me now that M'Dear had passed.

"I suggest you start with three items of clothing apiece," Mrs. Jeansonne went on. "That way you won't get the clothes mixed up."

I nodded and smiled, but then piled on about twenty different items and walked into the big dressing room with three mirrors, urging Sukey and Renée to join me.

Once we were all in there, I took off my miniskirt and tights and started dancing around. "Come on, y'all," I said. "We've never had this many mirrors before. Let's do our Supremes number!"

Sukey peeled off her bell-bottoms and turtleneck and then her panties, and swayed there, almost nude. I was a little shocked, but I just started loosening up my shoulders and warming up, like it's good to do before you dance. Then I took off my blouse.

"Come on, now, Renée," Sukey was saying, "don't be a fuddy-duddy."

"I don't *want* to take off my clothes," Renée said, looking at the door, her eyes peeled to see if her mother was going to step in. "I'll get undressed if Sukey at least puts her lingerie back on."

"Oh, brother," Sukey said, crossing her eyes. "All right. Y'all are no fun! I'm only putting my panties back on because you called them *lingerie*. Anyway, I hate my boobs. I can't even take my bra off in front of y'all because they're so tiny. They look like mosquito bites!"

"No, they don't," I said.

"Yeah," said Renée.

"Look," I said, "I'll take off my bra, and you can look at mine. They're not *big*." I took off my bra, which I never would have done if I didn't need to make Sukey feel better.

"See?" I said, then mouthed to Renée to join me. Renée slipped her blue wool jumper over her blond hair, then took off her bra, even though I could tell that she was mortified.

"Look at our boobs, Sukey," I said, reaching for Renée's hands.

"Yeah, do," Renée said, keeping her hands firmly covering her breasts.

"See?" I sighed. "Boobs are simply the size we need to fit our own bodies. You're really petite—" I started to say.

"—so you have petite boobs!" said Renée, finally uttering an intelligent phrase.

"Okay, girls," I said. "Bras back on. We are the most famous girl group in the world! Hit it!"

We had done our "Stop! In the Name of Love!" number countless times at the Swing 'N Sway, standing in front of the long mirrors and copying the Supremes' dance movements. We each had our own verse tied to our own movement, and we put as much emotion as we could pack into those lines. Sukey sang first, jumping in front of her mirror, her hand held out in a stop signal. I sang my verse next and leaped in front of my mirror, with my hand held over my heart.

Then there was a little pause. "Come on, Renée!" I whispered. She looked at me, and I nodded. Finally our Renée jumped in front of her own mirror, put her hand up, and made circles around down from her head and sang about thinking it oooover!

We did the whole song, with all the moves we'd made up. After we finished, we all cracked up laughing, squealing together, "Oh, we all are *so* good!"

"Maybe we're the La Luna Supremes," Renée exclaimed.

"No!" I said. "We are the Lunettes!"

"No, no, *non*," Sukey said. "We are the La Lunettes! Calla, you were perfect! You get to be Diana for now unto eterrrrnity!"

"And Renée," I said, "girl, you are learning to shake it."

"Maybe big old boy Eddie done stirred up the honeypot," Sukey said.

"Will you stop that!" Renée was blushing.

"Okay, okay, we'll stop," I told her. "But let's be sure to get some outfits today for our magic performance nights."

"Yes!" Renée said.

We were all still dancing around in our panties and bras when we heard, "Girls, yoo-hoo, anybody in there?"

Mrs. Jeansonne stuck her head in the door. She looked down at the clothes that we'd just left lying there in piles, then up at us in our underwear. I thought that for sure we were in for some stern correction, but people will surprise you sometimes.

"Y'all been having fun in here?" she asked.

"Yes, ma'am!" we said.

Then she looked at me, almost a little shy. "I got you something, Calla." She stepped into the dressing room carefully, and handed me a Richardson's box. When I pulled back the lid and tissue paper and peeked inside, there was a scarf I knew that M'Dear and I would have wanted. It was big and blue, silk, with soft, almost undetectable white swirls. Pulling it out of the box, I held it up. I could see Sukey's eyes open wide, and Renée smiling at her mother. They all watched as I swirled the scarf around, like M'Dear used to do in the dance studio, moving with the scarf, barefoot, hearing the rhythm of the cloth, as she would say.

"Thank you, Mrs. Jeansonne! This is gorgeous. It's so, so—" And I couldn't find the right word. "It's just so right, somehow. Know what I mean?"

Mrs. Jeansonne closed her eyes for a second and smiled. "I do, Calla," she said. "Do you think you might be able to work it in with your other outfits?"

"Yes, ma'am, I do. Absolutely."

"Good!" she said. "Well, y'all keep on having fun and meet me in women's shoes in thirty minutes."

"Okay," we said.

After Mrs. Jeansonne left, Sukey and I saw that Renée was holding up an orange crêpe blouse that I picked out.

"I like this," she said. "Maybe we could wear something like this to perform."

"Yeah," Sukey said. "Wild paisley blouse, tied at the waist, and these!" From under a deep pile of her clothes, she pulled out a pair of brown suede hot pants with butterflies on the sides.

"Those are mine!" I said.

"Well, can't I get a pair too?" Sukey asked.

I thought for a minute and said, "Let's all of us get the same outfit! We can triple-date and surprise the boys!" And I swished my scarf around.

"We can get dressed at my house," Renée said, "and walk down the stairs wearing our coats. When we get into the living room, we'll say 'Hey, y'all.'"

I swished my scarf again like a punctuation mark.

"And then, and then," Sukey said, "and then we'll swing open our coats, and *Voila!* Tuck, Eddie, and—well, whoever my date is—will fall out on the floor!"

"On the floor!" I said with a *swish* of my scarf.

We were cracking up laughing, and with each idea we had, we struck different poses in front of the mirror like we were fashion models. Then, all of a sudden, a dark wave of sadness came under the door of the dressing room. My sadness seemed so sudden and so private that I'm not sure what made Sukey drop what she was doing and put her arms around me before my sob was even fully there. Renée put her arms around both of us. None of us had to say a word.

Sadness can find you anywhere, anytime, so you better have fun when you can.

After a while, Sukey took the blue scarf from my hand and swirled it through the space above our heads. Then she lightly wiped away my tears with it and held its cool silkiness to my hot, blotched face. "We're the La Lunettes," she said. "We'll always take care of each other." That made me cry again, and Renée held the silk scarf as I blew my nose into it. "It was supposed to stay pretty and curl through the air," I said. "Oh, I have ruined it."

"No, no, you don't understand," Renée said. "Mama gave you that scarf for you to do what you wanted with it. Mama doesn't think you are an accessory. She knows you are Calla Lily Ponder, and she knows M'Dear would have wanted you to have it."

"Yeah," Sukey said, "she wanted you to have the perfect accessory, what every girl needs: a big beautiful blue silk scarf to soak up her tears."

Chapter 13

1970

One time, for World History class, we had to write a paper on trends that shaped civilization. I thought and thought about ideas like democracy and world wars. They all seemed too dull to me. Then it struck me how big a role hair has played in human life. I went back as far as I knew for my research, to the Bible and to Greek mythology and stuff. I was thrilled by what I learned.

I started my paper with the Bible, where God threatens to punish snooty women by making them bald. I wrote about the ancient Greeks, who thought up the chignon, still a good style today. About Lady Godiva, who rode naked through the streets, hidden only by her hair, to make her mean husband let up on his subjects; and about Saint Barbara, whose father dragged her by her hair because she was Christian. I described the hairdos of the eighteenth century, which were padded with horsehair till they were mile-high and then decorated with toy sailing ships and birds' nests. I can't imagine how those women slept in them! Then I covered the bobs of the so-called flappers—the wild women of the 1920s—marcel waves, which introduced curling irons; ratting, which led to beehives; and the trend toward long hair for both men and women today. What I discovered about hair was amazing—or at least I thought so.

Mister Mason, my teacher, did not agree. "Calla," he said, "this paper has nothing to do with the growth of civilization or the wars that made it possible or the march of progress—it's about hair!"

"Yes, sir. It is."

"Well, we are not in beauty school," he said with a laugh. "We are studying the history of the world."

"Yes, sir, and hair is a part of the history of the world."

"Calla, hair is just fashion. Fashions come and go."

"Isn't fashion part of civilization?"

"Well, it is," Mister Mason answered, "but it hasn't changed history like the rise of Christianity or the Industrial Revolution or the world wars."

He gave me a C.

That upset me. I asked Papa about it. He was in the South Pacific at the end of World War II.

"Why is war more important than regular people's lives and the way they want to look or feel? Why is war more important than things people care about in peacetime?"

He looked at me and said, "Calla, for some reason there are a lot of people who find war more exciting than just about anything you can name."

Chapter 14

1970

It was our senior year, early autumn, and still hot. Tuck and I were walking out of school when we saw a beat-up pickup truck parked down the street. A woman got out and started walking toward us. At first I hardly recognized her, but then I realized it was Tuck's mother. She looked so much older. Tuck looked at me and said, "I'll be back in a minute, Calla." Then he just dropped his books on the ground and went over to meet her.

She took his hands and led him around the corner of the school, away from the pickup truck and almost out of my sight. I followed, watching from a distance. From where I stood I could still see the two of them, as well as the pickup. As Tuck's mother talked, I could sense her urgency and watched as Tuck's head began to slowly drop all the way down until it rested on his chest. Then he raised it and looked at her; he seemed to be pleading with her.

Then the driver's-side door of the truck lurched open, and Tuck's father got out and made his way toward them. He was weaving so bad as he walked that it was clear he was very drunk.

"I told you to go get him, not have a talk with him," I heard him bellow. "Now get both your asses in the truck."

Tuck hesitated for a moment, then they all walked toward the truck, got in, and drove away. My heart was pounding as I picked Tuck's books up off the ground. Then I ran all the way to the Tuckers' house. I was terrified at what was happening.

"Miz Lizbeth! Uncle Tucker!" I called out, hardly able to breathe. "Miss Charlotte and her husband came looking for Tuck, and he went off with them in their pickup."

"Oh, Lord!" Miz Lizbeth said, meeting me at the door. Uncle Tucker ran down the steps and over to his car without a word to head out to find them. I set Tuck's books down and said, "Miz Lizbeth, is there anything I can do?"

Miz Lizbeth looked up at me, trying to clear the worried look from her face. "Everything's going to be fine, and Olivia's here with me. It's going to be okay, Calla. Uncle Tuck is already on his way over there. I want you to head right home right now."

So I got myself on home. As I walked down the path to our house, I tried to steady myself and take deep breaths.

Papa was just hanging up the phone when I got home. He came over and gave me a hug and a kiss. "Come on in now and help me finish making this crawfish étouffée, what you say?"

"What's this? Something special?"

"Naw, I just let the horn section go early and thought we might have ourselves a real special supper. You gotta admit—I'm a pretty good cook for a man."

"Papa," I said, "you sure are." I gave him a kiss on the cheek, and then I sat down and told him what I'd seen.

❧

Tuck called me later that evening and told me how Uncle Tucker had jumped in his truck and gone looking for them. Turns out he didn't have to look far, as Tuck's father had put their truck in a ditch less than two blocks from the school.

"Tuck, are you all right?" I asked.

"Yeah. The asshole was so plastered he couldn't even get the truck out of first gear."

"What happened, Tuck? Why did they come for you?"

"Calla, I can't really talk right now. Papa Tucker is waiting for me in his study. You know what that means. I shouldn't even be using the phone right now, but I didn't want you to worry. I have to go."

The next day after school Tuck told me the whole story. When Papa Tucker reached them, his father—his no-count father—had threatened both of them with a pistol. He'd threatened to kill Tuck if he ever tried to take Miss Charlotte away from him again. "He was out of his mind," Tuck said. Luckily, his father was so drunk that Papa Tucker quickly got the pistol away from him.

Then Papa Tucker and Miss Charlotte got into it. They were screaming and yelling at each other. She wanted Tuck to come home after he graduated and get a job in Bossier City. Papa Tucker had told her she no longer had any claim to her son. He'd said, "Charlotte, you broke your mama's heart, and now you're trying to pull your son down in the gutter with you. I will not let that happen. My grandson is going to *be* somebody. So I'm telling you now, if you ever come around here again, I will go to court and get a protective order to keep you away from Tuck. You have never been a mother. You have never been *anything* but trouble to him."

Tuck took a deep breath and let it out.

"Papa Tucker put his arm around me and walked me away from that truck. Calla, I could feel his whole body shaking. He looked straight ahead and his face was like stone, but tears were streaming down his cheeks. He didn't say another word until we drove home and got inside the house. By then he had composed himself and you'd never have known what had just happened by looking at him."

Then I asked Tuck what had happened in his grandfather's study. He just looked down. I asked him again. He stood up and looked off toward the river and held out his hand. I took it in mine and we walked home in silence.

He never answered my question.

After that, Tuck wasn't the same. I mean, we still went out together, just not as much. He studied for hours every day, and I hardly ever saw him. He started applying for every scholarship there was. He was with a guidance counselor at least twice a week, and you better believe it wasn't because Tuck was in trouble. He was asking her for advice about schools and how to apply.

"Aw, no," he'd say, "I can't go with y'all to the Shop 'N Skate, I've gotta study tonight. See y'all tomorrow, okay?" Then he'd kiss me on the cheek, and walk on home alone to study.

Sukey was the one who said it first. "Goddamn, there isn't a thing wrong with studying, but Tuck, you're taking this thing too far. Where you want to go to, Harvard or something?"

"Yeah," Tuck said. "That's one place I want to go."

We all laughed. "Yeah! 'La Luna Graduate Heads to Harvard!'" Tuck laughed along with us, but I knew it wasn't a real laugh. And he kept mentioning little things to me, such as what I planned to do about college. Where had I applied?

"Nowhere," I said. And I sat quiet. Since M'Dear had died, I hadn't really known how to talk about the future. I still felt like I needed M'Dear to be around to make any plans. And somehow, I thought

Tuck and I would plan everything together. The past and the present and the future were all mixed up in my mind since M'Dear died. But he got me thinking.

Soon after the semester ended, and finals came. As I expected, Tuck didn't just do okay on his finals, he aced them.

I asked him, "You happy with your grades and everything?"

He said, "I got what I went for. Got just what I went for." And then he smiled.

One day around Christmas time, Renée, Sukey, and I were driving around in Renée's mother's car when Sukey made an announcement. "I decided what I'm going to do after we graduate. I'm moving to New Orleans. I'm going to dance; I'm going to sing. I'm going to meet thousands of boys—and I'm going to kiss them all! I think I'm going to get me some kind of job that's really fun—something that's not really work, but you still get paid money."

"I'm going to marry Eddie," Renée said. "He's going to be a policeman. And I want to have children. I already have names for them."

Sukey said, "Ohhhh, you never know! You might meet somebody else."

"No," Renée insisted. "I'm going to marry Eddie. Just y'all wait and see! And what about you, Calla?"

"Well, I'm going to do what I've always wanted to do—become a beautician! I've been looking into different beauty colleges, and have been corresponding with L'Académie de Beauté de Crescent in New Orleans. Anyway, that's my dream."

Sukey said, "Calla, maybe we'll end up in New Orleans at the same time!" She took both my hands. "I love your dream. Sometimes I used to see you and M'Dear out on the pier at sunset, and you would be brushing her hair. That was something so beautiful; I used to hide out sometimes, just to watch y'all."

That night, lying in bed, after Sonny Boy cooked us pork chops for supper, I closed my eyes and pictured all those moments on the pier with M'Dear. I remembered when she said I had healing hands. I thought back to the conversation with Renée and Sukey in the car, and started to see my plan forming. I would get a job and save up some money. Then I'd go down to New Orleans and go to beauty school. I was going to become a professional and have a career. I was excited.

Tuck wasn't all that happy about my decision. He wanted me to go to college.

"Have I said one word," I asked him as we walked around town, looking at the Christmas decorations, "one single word against you going to college?"

He shrugged. He knew that I hadn't.

"So you can do whatever you want, and I can't? I want to know why you are all hot and bothered about me not going to college."

"Calla, you're so smart. Look at the scores on your college entrance exams. You only took them on a lark, and you were in the top ten percentile. You could get into a school just as good as Stanford, where I'm hoping to go."

"Well, whoo-wee." I wiggled my finger in the air. "Big deal."

"Do you know how many people would kill to have your kind of scores?"

"No, not really. Eleven? Maybe eleven people give a poot about it?"

"Stop it, Calla," he said, raising his voice. "I just don't see why someone as smart as you would be dead set on going to *beauty school*, of all things."

"Don't say 'beauty school' like it's something idiotic to do."

"Well, it's something an idiot woman *could* do. You know how Papa Tucker is always saying that we're supposed to aim high. Well, this is your chance to aim high, Calla."

My jaw dropped. Tuck had been bugging me about the college thing for a while, but this was the first time he had up and told me why.

"Look, I'm sorry I said that. I take it back."

I just stared at him.

"Please. Let me take it back. All I meant, Calla, is that you could rise up in the world, make something of yourself."

"Don't give me that! You're the one all worried about *making something of yourself*."

"That's right, *I am*."

"Why, Tuck? You have already made something of yourself. You *are* somebody."

"Maybe I need to do more," he said, so softly that I could hardly hear him.

"We said a lot of things this year, didn't we?"

Tuck looked at me and rubbed his left hand under his eye. He didn't answer, so I did it for him. "Yeah, we said we loved each other."

Tuck didn't say anything for a while. He just closed his eyes and lowered his head.

Then, "This year was not the first time I felt I loved you, Calla. I started loving you that time in the barn."

"If you've been loving me that long," I said, "then why are you going so far away? Why are you making my dream sound like it's stupid? This is about the most cowardly way of breaking up I have ever heard of."

"Who said anything about breaking up?"

"I did."

"Calla, I didn't mean we should break up. I never wanted that."

"Oh, there is a lot you didn't mean, isn't there, Tuck? Like maybe you didn't mean a thing when you said, 'I gave you my heart.'"

"Calla, please, let's don't do this. Let's don't talk like—"

"You started it, Tuck, by not letting up on how I needed to go to college to meet your standards. Go to California, go wherever you want. Just don't expect your idiot girlfriend to be waiting for you."

Tuck folded his arms across his chest. "Well, then, go ahead," he said, "go ahead and be a beautician. Take a job even my mother could get if she could ever scrape her alcoholic self up off the floor. Somebody in my family has to make something of themselves. My mother sure didn't."

I clenched my jaw so tight my teeth could have cracked. "Don't put this on your mother, Tuck. This is your life, not hers. And this is goodbye as far as I'm concerned."

Then I turned and walked away, past the pharmacy, past Our Lady of the River Catholic Church, down to the path that led across Uncle Tucker's land and onto our place.

I waited until I got upstairs and into my bedroom before I started to cry. This is an important tip for my future customers: Don't believe them when they tell you that mascara is waterproof, because it's not. And that's a tip that is not idiotic.

Chapter 15

1971

The class of 1971 was getting ready to graduate! So much had already happened since Christmas. For one thing, Tuck and I had made up on Valentine's Day. I had refused to talk to him, though it was hard to avoid him since he lived next door. But when he showed up on Saint Valentine's Day with a big bouquet of roses and a little gold bracelet, dropping to his knees and saying, "Calla, I beg your forgiveness," my heart melted. I had missed him so much!

But before graduation, of course, there was the senior prom. This one will go down as the first time in La Luna history that one girl went to the prom with two boys. And you can guess who that was: Sukey. As she explained it, "Well, I dated them both, so why not go with them both? I didn't want to turn one down for the other."

So it was Sukey and Peter Robertson and John LaCroix. She wore a black dress that was cut on a slant and had a single white ruffle down the back. And it was short. Even I couldn't believe it. Sukey wore a *short* gown to the prom.

I said, "Sukey, did you see this dress in a magazine or something?"

She sniffed and turned up her nose. "Are you kidding? They wouldn't think of having *this* in *Seventeen* magazine."

Sukey had designed the dress herself, and Aunt Helen had made it. Again and again, Aunt Helen asked Sukey, "Why don't we just make it a *long* dress, with the ruffle running down to the ground?"

And Sukey kept saying, "Because I want a short dress."

Aunt Helen had bought the extra yardage anyway. "By the time I'm through fitting this," she said, "I'll break her down. It's going to be a long dress."

Sukey won that fight, of course.

Renée, who was the opposite of Sukey in so many ways, wore white. Her dress was organza, with an empire waist, with long sleeves that you could see through and little pink flowers here and there. It was such a sweet dress, for a sweet girl.

And my dress—oh! I will love it till the day I die. My inspiration was the beautiful flowing dresses that M'Dear used to dance in, and I showed Aunt Helen a picture of my favorite one. "Remember this dress?" I asked.

"Ohhhh! Oh, yes, I do," she said.

So she copied it in lavender chiffon. The delicate top came down in little scallops to just below my collar-bone. Then there was lavender chiffon to my waist and, below that, a lavender skirt with purple chiffon flounces.

I did my hair myself. I just brushed it out, then leaned over, put a rubber band around it, and wound it into a bun. Then I pulled out some strands and curled them so they would billow around my face.

Tuck was talking to Papa when I came down the stairs. He looked up at me where I stood on the landing.

"Wow! Calla," he said, "you're beautiful. It seems like each year you're becoming more and more beautiful. What will we do, Mister Will? She'll have the other guys knocking me over to get a dance with her."

"Gotta be brave, son," Papa said. "But you knew that a while ago, didn't you?"

I smiled to hear them talk like that. It helped ease the pain of M'Dear not being there.

Tuck leaned in to kiss me. "I love your scent," he said.

We all met before the dance to head over together, and wouldn't you know it, Sukey pulled out a bottle of bourbon. She was always the one to provide the booze for almost every event we'd go to. We all mixed it with Coke except Sukey, who drank hers straight in little sips. I couldn't believe that she could stand the taste. By the time we got to the prom, we were all pretty giddy, especially Sukey, who was already screaming and having a ball.

The Get Down Boys, our band for the night, knew all the songs we loved, like the Youngbloods' "Get Together" and Janis Joplin's "Piece of My Heart." It was a woman's song, but the band was all men. It wasn't the same with a guy singing it.

We all headed out to the dance floor, and I loved seeing my best friends moving around Tuck and me as we danced. I had done both of their hairdos, so I checked to see how they held up. Renée's hairdo worried me, and a trip to the ladies' room for some extra Aqua Net seemed to be in order.

My sweet Renée with her dainty fine features. I gave her a feminine style to enhance her Dresden loveliness: long Victorian ringlets, slightly undefined and loose, not anything too tight, with wispy tendrils on her face. I pinned the tendrils back with a perfect little dainty flower pin to go with her scalloped lace organza dress with the pink roses on it. Oh, she looked so sweet and beautiful.

And then there was my Sukey, moving like a madwoman. I was really glad that they were playing Janis Joplin because it allowed her to dance as crazy as she wanted. The straps of her flouncy dress had already fallen off the side so that her shoulders and her back were showing even more.

With her hair, I gave myself a challenge—how to build on her Sassoon and make a more dressy look. I tried to capture a 1930s look with a provocative design. I wanted to revive the classic pageboy by making it very wavy and full, so that it swirled onto her cheek really elegantly. Graceful giant waves that I wove into one fluid line to go with her big eyes and her full lips and perky nose. Oh, she looked beautiful. With that tiny short little dress with ruffles going down the back.

"Suke!" I called out. "Maybe you won't want to dance so wild if you think about your hairdo."

Then she looked at me and said, "Hairdo, smairdo." I could hear her voice starting to slur a little bit.

"I love what you did with your hair, Calla," Tuck said. "The top almost looks like a princess, the way you pulled it back."

I was so glad he noticed because I had worked very hard to sweep it back so that it looked like a crown at the top. *Princess* was the very word I thought of. Then I let the rest of my hair fall down so that I had two layers.

Next, the band played "When a Man Loves a Woman," and it didn't matter to me that the lead singer didn't sing it as well as Percy Sledge. I was dancing with Tuck, and every once in a while, he would lean over and kiss me on the back of my neck. I would look up into his eyes, and he'd smile down at me. He had his arms around me, and I could feel his strength as he held the back of my waist.

"I love you, Calla Lily," he said. "I'll always love you. No matter what happens, I'll always love you."

Reaching up, I wrapped my arms around his neck as we swayed together, so tender and close. "I love you too, Tuck," I whispered. "I will love you forever, no matter what happens, no matter what you do. I will always love you."

We stayed up all that night, fooling around and making out. We had plenty of beer to fuel us, courtesy of Sukey and her two dates. Sukey definitely had more to drink than the rest of us, but that was nothing new. But then Sukey tried to take off her dress while she was dancing on top of one of the cars. I said, "Sukey, just keep the dress on. Keep the dress on. You can dance on any car you want. Just don't take off the dress."

"Come on!" she said. "You're no fun!"

"And you're a little *too* fun," I told her.

"All right, all right, all right," she said and climbed down from the car and put her short prom dress back on.

Just before five in the morning, we all met at Renée's to fix our hair and gargle, because we were invited to the Tuckers' house for an after-prom breakfast with our families.

And what a breakfast it was! Fresh orange juice with champagne, eggs with hollandaise sauce, bacon, tons of homemade ham biscuits, and Miz Lizbeth's perfect cinnamon toast, which was always crisp and cut into triangles. She had also made her famous cinnamon buns from scratch. And French toast too—she had really outdone herself! Plus, there was coffee, chicory dark roast with cream and two sugars—who could ask for more?

So we all sat down at the long table, ready to eat, except for Sukey. Papa looked over at her and said, "Sukey! You're looking a little green around the gills, girl. Do you think you'll survive this breakfast?"

Sukey's mother looked a little embarrassed. She said, "Um, would it be all right, Miz Lizbeth, if my daughter and I had a cup of black coffee and sat out on the porch for a little while?"

"That would be just fine," Miz Lizbeth said, like she was sort of relieved.

When everyone was almost finished eating, Uncle Tucker stood up and, gently tapping his fork against an antique champagne flute, said, "Hear! Hear! It's time for the clique of 1971 to reveal your plans for the future!"

My heart did a flip. Sure, I'd been discussing my plans, but I wasn't sure if I was ready to make them final by announcing them widely. Plus, I wasn't sure that the others would understand that Tuck and I had planned to keep our love alive and remain a couple even though we had different plans. We knew in our hearts and minds that eventually we'd be together again.

I looked over at Renée, who looked especially lovely this morning. Her skin was milky, and her white-blond hair was tumbling down now, loosened from the updo I'd fixed for her before the prom, what seemed like a week ago. She must have felt me looking at her, because she looked my way and gave me one of her sweet-eyed smiles. Eddie had his arm around her like she was the most precious thing in the world to him.

"Well," Uncle Tucker said, "who wants to go first?"

Eddie stood up and looked at everyone with exhausted eyes that might have seen a little too much bourbon. With his glass in his hand, he said, "I'm here to—," and then Renée tugged at the sleeve of his rumpled tuxedo jacket. He turned to her, and then pretended to knock himself in the head with the palm of his hand. "Oh, excuse me," he said, "I wasn't supposed to do this yet. Sorry."

Just when I thought that this moment couldn't be saved, Renée stood up, looked down the table, and said, "Mama and Daddy, would you mind if Eddie continued what he was about to say?"

Well, what could they do?

Mrs. Jeansonne just sat there shaking her head and smiling. I had the feeling that, after so many years, she had made peace with who Eddie was—a happy playful fellow who didn't stand as much on custom as she did.

"Certainly," she said.

"I'm all for it," Renée's father said.

So Eddie announced that they were going to be married, and we all clapped and wished them well. Papa acted like he was shocked at the news, which made me laugh. Nobody was at all surprised by their plans, and I could feel their happiness circle around the table in the Tuckers' porch.

"You next," I said, pointing to Tuck. I was so proud of him.

"I'm going away to college," Tuck said. "I got accepted at one of the universities I applied for."

Everyone started clapping again. I could hear folks say, "Great." "Way to go, Snake Boy," Eddie said. "You done good," Sonny Boy added.

"Where to?" was the question that folks didn't realize they weren't ready for.

"I'll be going to Stanford University," Tuck said.

"Where?" everybody asked. "Where is that?"

"I thought you were shooting for University of Virginia," Will said. Will had been offered a scholarship there, but had turned it down to study with the old Cajun musicians in Louisiana. He said universities would always be there, but that the musical geniuses of our homeland wouldn't.

"I *was* shooting for Virginia," Tuck said, "but—"

"Okay, okay," Sonny Boy said, "pardon me, I'm just a dumb old country boy, but where is Stanford?"

"It's in California," Tuck said.

"California?" Eddie said.

"Near San Francisco."

"I hear that's a beautiful city," Sukey said. "On a big bay. Oh, to go to school so near a big bay! A big *California* bay."

"California," Eddie said, "man, that is where people go and never return."

That's exactly what I feared.

"Yeah, right," Sonny Boy said in a scary-sounding voice, "and they are never heard from again." Everyone laughed.

"Come on, y'all," Sukey said, looking at me. "It's not like it's Europe."

No, but it might as well be.

I was so caught up in that thought that I barely heard Uncle Tucker say, "And Calla Lily, the flower among us, how will you step out into the world?"

Tuck squeezed my hand before I stood up and said, "I'm going to beauty school."

At first there was this awful silence. Like Tuck had announced he'd won the Nobel Prize and I'd just said I was in the last rounds of the Louisiana State Spelling Bee. I sat down, and I breathed like M'Dear taught me. *I can get through anything if I just keep breathing.* I looked over at my father, who gave me a wink.

It was Miss Lizbeth who broke the awkward pause. "Tell us more, won't you, Calla?" she asked, smiling at me with love.

"I have researched beauty training academies across the South and have decided that I do not need to travel any farther than New Orleans for my training. Just as soon as I have enough saved, I'm going to head to New Orleans, home of L'Académie de Beauté de Crescent, the best in the state."

Sukey said, "All right, Calla!" Then everyone clapped and Papa raised his glass and said, "To the class of 1971!" And we all raised our glasses in a toast.

I looked at Tuck. He put his arms around me and gave me a big smile. I looked at Renée and Eddie and thought, *They're so happy!* I couldn't help but feel a little envious.

After everyone had left, and the sun was rising, Tuck and I walked down to the river, to our pier. We kissed for a while, then just lay back on the dock, our legs dangling over the edge. We watched the thin dancing wisps of clouds change from peach to pale yellow and eventually to white in the soft early-morning sky. Tuck's arm was under my neck, making a perfect little pillow, and he had his tux jacket rolled up under his head.

"When I come home at Christmas," he said, "we can come right back to this spot. It might be a little bit cooler, so you might need a sweater. Or I could give you my coat, Calla. If you were cold, I'd give you my coat. If you ever need anything, I'll give it to you." He paused, then said, "This Christmas, and every one after that. If you want, Calla Lily."

"Yes, I do want that."

"I'll write you every day, Calla. We'll be together on holidays, and every summer. I promise."

A little breeze rippled across the water and broke the still air. Tuck noticed it too and said, "As a matter of fact, I think I better give you my jacket right now."

"No," I told him, "I don't need your jacket, it's not that chilly." Then I sat up, gave him a mischievous little smile, and said, "Give me your shirt, though. Your shirt would be just right." That made him throw back his head and laugh. Then he unhooked his cummerbund, took off his tux shirt, and wrapped it around my shoulders.

Then we lay back down and stared up at the sky again, and I could feel it protect us. The rays of the morning sun worked their way over the trees behind us and lit us up with warm gold light. I leaned in close to Tuck and watched his bare chest rise and fall with each breath. I was happy, and I knew it. Knowing that I had someone who loved me, someone who might be leaving but who would come back to me, seemed as beautiful as the La Luna sunrise.

Chapter 16

1971

June 4, 1971
La Luna, Louisiana

Dear Tuck,

You're off! Summer school at Stanford. Seeing you off this morning as you got on the bus, I remembered the first time I saw you arrive in La Luna. When the bus pushed off today and I smelled the Greyhound smells, I saw you as a little kid again. It's funny, huh? Memories, I mean.

By now, you are in the air to San Francisco, California! I can't wait to hear all about it. Flying across the country and everything.

I'll mail this first thing in the morning and look forward to receiving your letter.

Your girl,

Calla

P.S. I put a surprise in your duffel bag, so look! xo

Right after graduation, I got a job as a waitress at Melonçon's Café in Claiborne. I figured it would take me a year to save up the money for three months of living expenses in New Orleans, the car that I'd need there, and my beauty school tuition.

M'Dear and Papa first took me to Melonçon's Café, and I always loved it. Its double doors are old, varnished wood with heavy, wavy glass in them, and the floors are shiny black and white tiles—a traditional Louisiana place where you feel comfortable right away. It was not a big restaurant—people sometimes had to wait in line—but it was elegant, with real linen tablecloths and sterling silverware.

And the food! We served all kinds of Louisiana seafood, like shrimp, oysters, crabs, and catfish, but our specialty was crawfish. We made them any way you'd want—spicy-boiled or in étouffée, in boulettes, boudin, bisque, casseroles, and cornbread—but our crawfish pie was famous. I mean, it was written up in the *Times-Picayune*. People from all over Louisiana came to Melonçon's for the crawfish pie.

I took a lot of pride in making sure that my tables were clean, that the baskets of Saltine crackers were full, and that my napkins were folded just right. I liked to fold them into a fan shape to suggest a scallop shell. The owners, the Melonçons, who made me part of their family, loved this idea. It was a little extra effort, but I felt that our customers should enjoy every bit of their dining experience, right down to the napkins.

June 5, 1971
La Luna, Louisiana

Dear Tuck,

I bet you are there, now—Stanford! I try to picture where your dorm might be, but the brochure you gave me doesn't say much. So I'm going to just imagine it all. I know you said there was an early orientation for honor students. I just wish I could be there cheering you on!

My job at Melonçon's Café is going to be even better than I'd thought. The Melonçons are going out of their way to welcome me.

Well, I better go now. Just know that I'm loving you from La Luna!

Love,

Calla

Since I felt that I represented Melonçon's Café, I always made sure that my nails were short and painted with a light pink polish—something that looked neat but didn't stand out while I was serving the food. My uniform was always perfectly ironed and starched. It was a shirtwaist dress, blue-and-white checked, and over it I wore a cotton pinafore—a real apron, not those plain nylon jobs that the other places made you wear.

I got some very good shoes, too, thanks to Aunt Helen. But my hardest decision was how to wear my hair, which was halfway down my back. People told me it was beautiful when I let it flow loose with its waves cascading down my shoulders. Most of the time I wore it in a long braid, but I felt Melonçon's called for something more fluffy. So I ended up wearing it in a high ponytail. It's funny, I always thought about other people's hair but I rarely thought about mine, even though folks told me that it was lovely. I took my hair for granted most of the time except when I looked at it in the mirror and thought of M'Dear.

Anyway, since we were near the courthouse in Claiborne, I'd gotten to know a lot of lawyers who came for lunch. They'd call over, "Calla Lily! How are you blooming today?" I'd go on over there, and often it would be Randall S. Beaumont III. "Hey, the Third!" I'd call him. "How're you doing?"

"Miss Calla Lily, I'm doing fine. Why don't you bring me two of those good crawfish sandwiches? Tell Mister Melonçon that his grandson will be okay. He wasn't driving under the influence; he was just driving fast. And I'm going to get him off before you know it."

One Sunday the café was closed so that the Melonçons could celebrate their thirtieth anniversary. I helped serve, and there was so much laughter and kissing and hugging between Mister and Mrs. Melonçon and their seven children and all their grandchildren. It was so inspiring to see such history and family in one room.

Renée and Eddie came in a few times to visit while I worked there. One night they came just for cocktails. Just to look at them you could tell they were married, the way they easily held hands. "Calla," they said, "tomorrow night, on your day off, could you come over for dinner?"

"Sure," I said. Now, I didn't know why they were making this dinner so special. I was at their house all the time, a darling little house that Renée was fixing up in the most colorful way. They had saved money for it by skipping a big wedding and getting married at city hall.

So the next night we had dinner in the small breakfast room that Renée painted so pretty with buttery tan walls, to match the kitchen. She had cooked a great meal, and for dessert we had carrot cake. I was already on my second cup of coffee and piece of carrot cake.

"Calla," they said, "we wanted you to be the first to know, after our family."

"Know what?" I said.

They held hands, and Renée gave me a big smile and bit her lips for a moment, just like she always did when she was about to burst out with something. And she said, "We're going to have a baby!"

"Oh!" I said, getting up and giving Renée a kiss. "That's so wonderful!"

"Hey," Eddie said, smiling, "don't I get a kiss? I did have a small part in this, you know."

I turned to Eddie. He suddenly seemed so much more—oh, I don't know how to put it—*substantial*. They both seemed so grown-up.

"Of course you deserve a kiss," I said, and gave him a peck on the cheek.

He smiled at me. "Renée's lucky to have a friend like you."

"Oh, I'm the lucky one," I replied. "I'm lucky to have both of you."

We all finished our desserts and chatted about the baby. That was the evening when I missed Tuck the most.

June 7, 1971
La Luna, Louisiana

Dear Tuck,

You will simply NOT believe this! Get ready, 1–2–3! Renée is pregnant! They had me over for dinner last night to tell me. Here you and me are, just starting out after graduating—you at Stanford University, and me still getting ready for beauty school. I guess it's different strokes for different folks, right?!

You are probably as bowled over as me, so sit down, drink a Coke, and start studying!

You are my sweetheart!

Calla

On my days off from Melonçon's, I would do hair. I knew I would miss the customers once I moved, so I was greatly relieved that Aunt Helen and a friend of hers had agreed to keep the Crowning Glory open and alive. This made it so much easier for me to follow M'Dear's wishes for me to go out into the world. After she died, people had started going to Claiborne to get their hair done, but there were some older people who couldn't make the trip. So, that first Saturday after Tuck left, I had Miss Mildred, who lived across the road from us, out on the Crowning Glory Beauty Porch as my first customer. Miss Mildred had never married and had retired from her job as a social worker in Claiborne, working with the mentally ill.

She needed a wash and set. So I sat her down in the chair, tipped her head back, and began to drizzle her hair with warm water. I put some shampoo in my hands and then began to massage it into her scalp. I could feel the tension, but as I rubbed the shampoo in, I felt her scalp relax.

Then I felt it. Suddenly there was a warmth under my palms. I felt a strong wave of tenderness toward Miss Mildred, and I realized how lonely she had been since retiring. I kept my hands in place, massaging, until the warmth moved down her scalp.

"Ohhh, Calla, honey, this feels so good, to be touched like this right now. Oh, I just can't tell you."

I lifted my palms up off her head, but the warmth was still there. I could feel it moving under my hands, down her neck, over her shoulders, then down her back. As my hands moved, I was overcome with visions of the feelings Miss Mildred was releasing—missing her clients but also feeling exhausted from all those years of giving. I was shocked by the power of these revelations and by the fact that my hands could sense and soothe the way they were doing, entirely on their own. It was a strange and intimate connection that was kind of frightening.

Then, as suddenly as it came, the warmth passed. Soon I was just standing there with shampoo on my hands, ready to give Miss Mildred a rinse like nothing happened.

It struck me that this was what M'Dear meant by my having healing hands. Somehow she knew. But I'd never felt that kind of power within me before, and I wasn't sure if I wanted it to come back.

June 15, 1971
La Luna, Louisiana

Dear Tuck,

How are you, sweetie pie? I thought we were going to write every day, but for now, I'll just keep writing you until you've had time to settle in. We are all doing well down here. I am busy with my job at Melonçon's, but the really important changes are happening while I do hair. It's like M'Dear is *with* me sometimes, do you know what I mean?

It's humid as can be. The figs are getting larger. As soon as it's time to pick them, I'll can fruit like M'Dear taught me. Then when you come home, you'll taste summer at Christmas.

You must be very, very busy not to write me. If you'd just drop a short note in the mail, it would put my mind at ease.

Your Calla Lily

I didn't know how to describe the strange warmth, so I didn't tell anyone about it—not even Sukey, when she came from New Orleans to visit. She had moved right after graduation, and had already gotten a job. I just about fell on the floor when my girlfriend since the third grade told me that she had become a Playboy Bunny.

She never told us this was what she was planning. While we were still seniors she actually sent away for a Playboy Bunny kit! She had passed the test, so now she was an actual Bunny.

Luckily, there was a Bunny Mother at the club to make sure that the girls were treated properly and that the men didn't touch them. But knowing Sukey, if some of them bothered her, she'd have liked it. Sukey said that I could live with her when I moved to New Orleans. But I didn't think that would be good for our friendship, since she could get wild. I really needed my own apartment.

The first time Sukey came home with her Bunny outfit, my jaw just about hit the floor. So did Renée's. You could have put the entire thing into your purse—and still had room left over. That's how tiny it was. I mean, the biggest part of the whole outfit was the bunny ears! The rest was just a skimpy satin leotard, white cuffs with cufflinks, and a bunny tail on the butt.

"Sukey," I said, "couldn't you just be an airline stewardess?"

"Yeah, Sukey," Renée said. "The life of an airline stewardess would be so adventurous. Just think, a stewardess flying high in the sky!"

"Calla, Renée," she said, "you just don't understand. Being a stewardess is just like being a waitress, except you're in the sky, and I don't want to be a waitress. Being a Bunny is a whole way of life! So much more *now*."

"Oh," I said. "Well, *now* is just *now*, Sukey."

"Oh, God," she said, rolling her eyes. Then, as she'd always done when she was upset or when she thought you were being stupid, she crossed her eyes. "Look, I just wanted you to see my costume. If you don't like it, tough.

"Now come help me pull it up a little bit. And see if we can stuff a little Kleenex in there to make it look . . . not so baggy at the top."

"All right," I said.

And Renée started pulling out Kleenexes. She looked up at Sukey at one point and said, "Well, Sukey, are you sure we can get by with just one box?"

"Okay, Renée, let's not be snippy about this."

Then Renée started laughing, and I started stuffing Kleenex under Sukey's boobs, trying to lift them up and make them look fuller. When I pulled them up as much as I could, I said, "Now Sukey, you know, these Kleenexes could come out at any point."

"Hmm. That's right," Sukey said. "I don't want to serve drinks and have a Kleenex fall right into a cocktail."

Renée and I both started laughing.

"All right, y'all, cut it out!" Then she said, "Well, Aunt Helen is such a great seamstress. Do you think that maybe she could—you know, help make it so it pushes my bosom up higher?"

"Oh, Sukey," I said, "I really don't know if Aunt Helen would work on that Bunny outfit. You know, she is wide-minded—of all the people in La Luna, she is wide-minded—but I don't know if she is wide-minded enough for this."

"Maybe I'll ask her. But in the meantime, let's just see what we can do."

So I reached down in the Bunny outfit and carefully tried to pull her bosom up a little more, knowing that my face was turning beet red.

Then Sukey looked at herself in the mirror. "Well, that's a little better," she said.

None of this Playboy Bunny stuff should have surprised me; Sukey had always been a character. Even though I didn't agree with everything she did, I wanted to go visit her and see New Orleans. But it was hard without a car, and weekends, when I was off work, happened to be Sukey's busiest time. She came home to La Luna often to see her mother, though, and we'd tell each other, "Girl, we'll be together soon. It's just a matter of time."

Time passed, and Tuck never wrote. Not once. I couldn't stop my mind from going back to the last time he kissed me, right as he was about to board that Greyhound bus. "I'm going to call you as soon as I get settled," he promised. "I'll write you as soon as I get there." But he didn't write. And he didn't call.

I still wrote to Tuck every single week. I even tried to call. But I stopped after a few times, not wanting to hear the guy call out down the hall, "It's Calla Lily for Tuck—again."

I could see how someone like Tuck could get caught up with school, but I still missed him. I looked at the pictures of us on my dresser, with my dried corsage from the senior prom hanging off one of them. I thought about his smell and his hair, and how I loved to run my hands through his hair when it was clean. It was just amazing, the way it was so blond, and so thick that when he moved, it shook from side to side.

Every time the phone rang, my heart leaped and I ran downstairs, even though I knew that Papa could see me acting like a schoolgirl. I answered the phone, "Hi—hi, this is Calla Lily—" But then it would just be Renée.

Then we'd have some conversation about how she was feeling with the pregnancy and about how my feet hurt after my waitress shifts. And she'd ask, "How's Tuck doing?"

I'd say, "Oh, just fine."

I was too embarrassed to tell anyone that Tuck hadn't been in contact. Finally I got so fed up one night that I threw his football trophy across the room. *Damn it! He said he would call! If Tuck was in the room right now, I'd say, "You liar! I hate you!"*

After supper one evening, Papa and I were sitting on the porch swing and we could hear classical music coming from the Tuckers' house. We often spent evenings alone since Will was away studying music and Sonny Boy was spending more and more time with his new girlfriend, Melise.

"How you getting along with all this, Calla Lily?" Papa asked, patting my hand.

"Not so good."

Right then, as though it was planned, which I don't think it was, Miz Lizbeth came over.

"I was wondering if y'all could do with some figs and homemade ice cream. I made the ice cream for the Garden Club meeting on Friday and had some extra."

I couldn't bring myself to say anything, and I knew Papa knew why.

"Thank you, Miz Lizbeth," Papa said. "Won't you join us?"

"No, but thank you very much."

"So, how's that boy doing?" Papa asked, like it was no big deal.

"He's doing just fine. Studying hard, making friends." Then she paused.

By that point I had left the porch without excusing myself and was in the kitchen, hearing them only faintly, as I dumped her dessert offering in the trash.

September 23, 1971
La Luna, Louisiana

Tuck,

I did not take you for a liar. We made a promise that we would write every day. I have not received one single, solitary note, letter, or phone call since you got on that bus. And I was left there, smelling the fumes. Who do you think I am? What do you expect me to think of you? Well, let me tell you. I think you are a shallow, plastic excuse of a man, with no dignity, respect, or anything left. You are a nothing. You are a nothing to me, as you have made it clear I am to you.

So this is it.

When it was almost Thanksgiving, I thought, Well, some kind of plans ought to be made by now! So even given my last nasty letter to Tuck, I went over to the Tuckers' and knocked on the door.

"Good morning," I said. "I brought you some mayhaw jelly that I put up myself."

"Calla," Miz Lizbeth said, as she opened the door. "How lovely to see you. And how sweet. Would you care for a cup of tea, or coffee?"

"Well, some coffee would be lovely," I told her.

"Okay," she said. "Come on in. Have a seat at the kitchen table, and I'll make you some coffee. I know how you like it, with cream and sugar."

So she brought two mugs of coffee, sat down, and we talked about this and that until I finally said, "Um, how's Tuck?"

"Well . . ." She paused and looked down into her coffee. "He's doing real well out there, Calla."

I tried to make it sound like it was just small talk. "How're his grades?"

"Fine," she answered. "Up at the top of his class."

Then Miz Lizbeth got up from the table and busied herself with washing dishes.

"Is he coming home for Christmas?"

She turned around and looked at me with kindness in her eyes. "I'm sorry, Calla, he's not. He's going to spend Christmas in California this year."

I tried to keep breathing. "California?" I said.

"Yes, sweetheart. He's made a good friend who's from San Francisco, whose family has a place in Big Sur."

"Place?" I asked. "Big Sur?"

"It's a beautiful town on thc Pacific Ocean."

I didn't say anything. I didn't want her to know how sad all this made me feel. "Well," I said, "I guess that just leaves us turkeys here at home," and tried to make a little laugh.

Miz Lizbeth looked away for a moment, then said softly, "We'll be flying out to California to join him."

"Oh," I said, and then I could not stop from crying.

Miz Lizbeth put her arms around me. "I'm so sorry, Calla. I wish it were different."

"I do, too," I said, my voice hoarse.

❧

After that, I started feeling really low. Tuck had erased me. I couldn't even get mad because I was too low. I guess people would say I was depressed, but I wouldn't talk to anyone about Tuck—not Sukey and Renée, and not even Papa.

December 2, 1971
La Luna, Louisiana

Dear Tuck,

How nice that your friend's family has invited Miz Lizbeth and Papa Tucker to California for Christmas. I guess you have a whole other life out there now. There was a time when I thought you would turn around and finally write back. But you have not just left the town that welcomed you when you were alone, but also me.

I will not be writing to you again. Or thinking of you, or hoping that we could in any way come back together. I gave you my heart that night on the pier. I thought you gave me yours. I was wrong. Hearts are not so easy to give and take away. They are not like money or something. I would like to hurt yours badly, but I won't. I was raised to always take the high road. If or when you do come home, do not expect to find me here. At least not for you.

Calla Lily Ponder

When Christmas came, it was hard. For the first time in as long as I could remember, Papa and I walked down along the river, just the two of us.

"You doing okay?" I asked him.

"Yeah. Might be sad every Christmas for a while."

"Oh, Papa, I'm sad, too!"

He gave me a big hug, and I could tell he was trying not to cry. My heart just broke for him. His sadness was so deep, all I could think about was cheering him up. I said, "Papa, remember M'Dear's Refrigerator Rules? How she said she was going to haunt us to keep us laughing? I believe she meant that, don't you? It's Christmastime. We should go inside. I got some presents I haven't wrapped. You want to help me?"

"Yes, I do." Papa seemed to take heart a little, and he said, "You know what? I got some eggnog in the fridge that Miz Lizbeth dropped off before she left for California. Let's put a little bourbon in there and have us some."

So Papa and I went back to the kitchen, and we laid out our tissue paper, the special kind with the glitter on it. We found our extra shoeboxes that we'd saved for wrapping gifts. I'd gotten two albums for Sonny Boy and two books for Will. Will would probably know what his gifts were, but I didn't want Sonny Boy to guess, since he was such a trickster.

Then Papa had a great idea. He told me, "Hey, I got me one really long, flat box that my rifle came in. You know, the one I got a couple years ago?"

"You saved that box, Papa?"

"Oh, you never know when something's going to come in handy."

So Papa brought in this long box. The albums would fit in there for sure.

I laughed and started to ball up some newspaper to cushion the albums. But Papa said, "No, let's not use newspaper. We're going to pop some popcorn."

So we did. And that popcorn smelled so good that we just started eating some right out of the pot.

"Calla," he said, "I have a special little gift that I'd like to give you, you know. When you were born, your mama and I took out a savings bond for you. We did that for each one of you kids. Yours matured around Thanksgiving. It's earned a good little bit of interest. So here you go," he said, and handed me an envelope.

I opened it and looked inside, and felt so touched.

"It's from your mama and me, you know. I thought maybe it would help you go on down to New Orleans for your beauty shop training earlier than you planned."

"Oh, Papa," I said, "thank you. Thank you and M'Dear, all those years ago, for thinking of your daughter."

Then, all of a sudden, we were having fun, Papa and me. We even put on some music and started dancing. But after a few songs, my tears came so quick that I didn't have a second to bite them back. Papa put his arms around me.

"I miss Tuck, Papa," I told him.

"I know. How 'bout I be your date for tonight?"

"I would love the pleasure of having you as my date."

"All right then," he said.

We turned out all the lights in the house except for the Christmas tree. Then we just sat there, drinking eggnog, eating popcorn, and watching those lights sparkle and fade.

It was not the Christmas I thought it would be. You don't always get all the things you want. I thought I had learned that already, but here I was learning it all over again, and it hurt. But my papa was sitting on the sofa with me, and the lights were twinkling. If there's one thing that can make you feel like the girl you were before the big hurts began, it's staring at a Christmas tree, all lit up, with your papa. A sparkling tree growing up from a circle of gifts.

Chapter 17

1972

The next day, when I went back to work, I let Mrs. and Mrs. Melonçon know my decision to leave for beauty school earlier than I'd planned.

"I don't want to leave you in the lurch, though, so how about if I work for a couple more months to give you time to replace me," I said.

"Calla," they said, giving me a hug, "there's no replacing you. But we will have to find someone else to serve our food! You're a part of the family now, and you'll have a hard time shaking us."

Once I gave notice at my job, I knew there would be no turning back on making the big leap out of La Luna. But I was feeling nervous about it all. It made me wish Sukey was living closer, because she wouldn't be so afraid. She'd just pack her bags and go.

January 3, 1972
La Luna, Louisiana

Dear Sukey,

I know you are busy as a bee doing the work of the devil down there in Sin City, but I need you here. It is finally clear to me that you were right. Tuck, who was my angel boy, is a little shit.

I am so angry with him I could hire some of those scary boys from deep in Nabedaux Parish to drive out to California and make him sorry he ever lived! I would have phoned you, but I am saving my money for my big move. So would you please get back home right away because I need you?

Love and xoxo,

Calla

So Sukey got the weekend off and came for a visit. Saturday night, Eddie was out to play bourrée, leaving Renée free, so I gathered with my girlfriends to try and help me get Tuck out of my heart. Renée showed up with soft new T-shirts and panties for the three of us.

"It seems every time we get together, we end up in our T-shirts and panties. So I decided to give us new ones."

"Ooh, goody!" Sukey said. "I love uniforms."

It was a T-shirt Louisiana early January. In the eighties, and humid as all get-out. "He didn't even bother to send a damn Christmas card," I said. They knew who I was referring to.

"Well, you did send him a letter telling him you would never speak to him again. You're just not over it, are you?" Sukey asked.

Renée looked at me, then at Sukey, and said, "I have an idea! We'll just 'wash that man right out of your hair!'"

And so the three of us headed to the outdoor shower behind our house, in the middle of the thick trees where nobody could see. We all took off all our clothes. I had never in my life known Renée to be so open about her body. She always had been so modest, but with the pregnancy, that had changed.

"Wow!" said Sukey, "You are some kind of *pregnant*! And your *boobs*!"

Renée looked down at her big belly, and smiled. "Yep," she said.

They then took turns trying to wash my hair. I said, "Please stop, y'all. I don't like other people washing my hair! I'll wash it myself!"

And so I scrubbed and scrubbed, and all the while we were singing at the top of our lungs, "I'm gonna wash that man right out of my hair!"

It was a good thing we had the house to ourselves. Papa was off at the fishing camp, Will was playing music in South Louisiana, and Sonny was at the movies with Melise. The showers kind of got us worked up, so we came inside, dried off, put on our new T-shirts and panties, and poured ourselves some Cokes.

"Hey, y'all, I've got an idea!" Sukey said. "Let's get out the yearbook, and start tearing his pictures out!"

"That's great!" I said, "y'all come on up to my bedroom." We all piled up on the big old four-poster bed that had been in my father's family for decades. I grabbed my copy of the yearbook from the bookshelf.

"Okay!" I said.

"Here," I said to Renée, "Open this sack from the grocery, sweetie." I handed her a huge sack filled with M&Ms.

"Great girlfriends-grill-the-son-of-a-bitch food!" Sukey said.

Renée started ripping the bags open to pour the candy into a bowl. "Rip! Oh, I like that sound," Sukey said. "That is a very good sound for the business at hand."

"Y'all wait a minute now," I said. "I don't want to destroy the whole yearbook. Let's just rip out his football picture, and sit here and eat M&Ms."

After we finished downing several hundred M&Ms, I leaned back and said, "Y'all, this has been fun. Well, more than fun, but I'm kind of tired."

Renée said, "I am too. This is the latest I've been up since I got pregnant."

"I'll only go," Sukey said, "if you'll lift up your T-shirt and let me feel your belly."

"Sure," Renée said, and lifted her shirt.

Sukey put her hand on Renée's big belly.

"Me too?" I said, looking at Renée.

"Yep."

And so Sukey and I both pressed our hands and felt a little baby kicking.

"Wow!" Sukey said.

"Yeah, wow!" said Renée.

"Wow," I said, then turned my head away so they could not see that I was crying.

After they were gone I reached up on the shelf in my closet, in the back where I had stored the tux shirt that Tuck had given me that early morning on the pier.

I went down the stairs and out the back door. I walked out to the fire pit, an open area that lay far from the heavily treed area on our property, and put kindling under a couple of thin logs. On top of that I laid the white tuxedo shirt. With it I laid the part of my heart that had been wounded by Tucker LeBlanc. Wounds can be healed, I thought, but I doubted if this one would. Then I let it all go as I watched the flames turn the shirt into cinders that rose up into the January night sky.

The next morning, I woke up and went to M'Dear's desk, which Papa had offered to move into my room. I sat down with a hot cup of coffee and, no longer needing to write to Tuck, decided to send M'Dear a little message.

Dear M'Dear,

I know that you have probably been wanting to kick me out of town by now. Well, that Savings Bond helps.

I have decided:

1. To live my life without waiting for the postman or the phone to ring.

2. To pack up and get out of La Luna and get myself a career.

Love,

Your Calla Lily

As I was saving my last dollars and planning my move, Renée's due date was getting closer. I started spending a lot more of my free time with Renée. Each time I saw her I'd think, Well, her belly can't get any bigger that this. But it would!

Then, at 5:30 in the morning on February 16, 1972, a sweet little gift arrived in La Luna. Calla Rose Gremillion was born! I went over to Eddie and Renée's house the night after they got home from the hospital. I couldn't help but notice how Eddie looked at Renée and Calla Rose, who lay in her lap. The love in the eyes of this muscular man, now a police officer, touched me to see.

"I love my baby," he said.

"Our baby," Renée corrected.

"I'm sorry, sweetie," he said, and kissed Renée on the mouth. "I keep forgetting."

"Right, baby," Renée said. "Now, go on to bed."

"Yes, ma'am," he smiled. "Good night, little mama. Good night, little baby. Good night, Calla Lily. Good to see you again." Then he headed toward their bedroom.

Renée and I sat and whispered as Calla Rose slept. One moment the baby was completely silent, then the next thing I knew, she was wailing and squealing.

"Right on time," Renée said, smiling as she unbuttoned her soft white cotton nightgown that Aunt Helen had made for her. She opened one side of the yoke, unhooked her nursing bra, and plopped out her full, swollen breast. My goddaughter knew exactly what to do. I heard gurgling, sucking sounds as her tiny fingers found their way around her mother.

"How many times a day do you need to do that?" I asked.

"Oh, about a million."

I watched in silence and marveled that my girlfriend carried within her all the nutrients that my goddaughter needed to survive.

Awe. That's the word, that's what I feel. That, and a tangle of other emotions. After Renée finished feeding and Calla Rose had given a very unladylike burp, Renée held her in her arms and looked at me.

"Want to hold her?" she asked.

At first I was afraid, afraid of the longing in me that might rush forth.

"Yes, I'd love to." I sat close to Renée on the sofa as she handed Calla Rose to me. The longing did rush forth. But the beauty of the creature in my arms pulled me back to the present moment. I lightly touched the little tufts of hair on her head, which reminded me of M'Dear's hair after radiation began to take its toll. *Oh, M'Dear. You would be so happy to see this!*

As I held the baby, I felt the weight of her head in my hands. How vulnerable the skull of this little one, so newly arrived from the heavens that the baby powder on her body might as well be the dusting of angels.

"I'm so happy," I said, biting back the tears. "Here," I said, carefully handing Calla Rose back to her mother. "I'm just so happy for y'all. This is just how you wanted it. To have a house and a baby, and you did it, not even a year after you graduated!"

"What's wrong, Calla?"

I couldn't answer her.

"Come on, Calla. What's wrong?"

"Oh, it's just that I've hardly done anything."

"That's simply not true. You have enough money for beauty school now. And you've been accepted to L'Académie de Beauté de Crescent. Your mama's old friend has offered you a place to stay until you find an apartment. You'll be in a big city and meet tons more people than I'll ever meet in my life."

"Yes, but will I have friends?"

"Of course you'll have friends." And she put her hand on top of mine.

"It's just . . . I miss M'Dear. Just when I thought I was really over her death, Tuck has left me. What is it? Why do people leave me? Do I make them leave?" Then I was crying.

"You know that's not true. And Tuck is not everybody," she said. "You've made your decision to go, Calla. Everything's lined up. It's time to finally do it."

"Well, I don't feel excited," I said, forcing myself to lower my voice. "They all leave."

So there was my oldest girlfriend, Renée, holding my infant goddaughter in her arms. And there I was, crying on her shoulder. As I wept, I thought about how many kinds of love the heart can hold: mother and child, child and mother, girlfriend to girlfriend.

I gazed down at Calla Rose for a very long time. I let my tears fall, though not on her. Finally I breathed in and let it circle around my body until it blew out of the blowhole at the top of my head. *I will not be a godmother who hides because of a broken heart. I will be a godmother who holds her broken heart in her hands and walks with it without shame. Just holding that broken heart to the next place the river takes her. I will hold my broken heart for you, Calla Rose. For you, the beautiful blue-eyed wonder in front of me.*

❧

CONGRATULATIONS, CALLA, the banner read. When I came over to help clean up Our Lady of the River's parish hall, I had no idea that I'd be walking into a surprise party—for me! I was leaving for New Orleans in just a few days.

Everybody was there, including all my friends from Melonçon's Café. Papa was playing the trumpet with his little combo, and as soon as I came through the door they started playing "For She's a Jolly Good Fellow." Sukey had come up from New Orleans, and she gave me a big hug. She looked tired, her eyes a little blurry. Nelle blew me a kiss from across the room. Miz Lizbeth was there, and apologized that Uncle Tucker couldn't be there because of a cold. My brothers were singing at the top of their lungs. Melise was there with Sonny Boy, and Will brought a friend of his from Ville Platte who makes fiddles. And I was so happy to see Cleveland and Bertha standing next to Olivia.

"Oh, Olivia!" I said walking over to them, "I'm going to miss you so much."

Both Olivia and Miz Lizbeth had become just like mothers to me ever since M'Dear's death. And just then, I could feel M'Dear's presence at the party. Papa hugged me during one of the music breaks, and I whispered, "She's here, isn't she?"

"Oh, you better believe it!" he said, and kissed my cheek before the band started up again.

When they finished playing, I got another big surprise. Aunt Helen whipped a sheet off from a clothesline strung across the back of the hall—and on it were brand-new outfits she'd made for me to wear in New Orleans.

"Aunt Helen! I can't believe this!" I'm on the tall side, and with my long legs and short torso, Aunt Helen's creations always fit me better than store-bought clothes.

"Calla," she said, "we can't send you off to the big city not looking up-to-date."

Then Miz Lizbeth and Renée's mother announced that it was time to eat. Oh, the food! There was shrimp gumbo, chicken gumbo, crawfish étouffée, red beans and rice, cornbread, French bread—you name it. And that's not even mentioning the desserts!

I said, "Y'all! You didn't have to go to so much trouble! It's not like I'm going away to Paris, France!"

"Well, what do you expect?" Miz Lizbeth said. "This is a party in La Luna, Louisiana."

For drinks, they served punch and Cokes and 7-Ups. But Sukey, of course, had a little flask of something and took a few nips now and then, as did Sonny Boy and Will. Drinking wasn't exactly encouraged in the parish hall, so they had to sneak outside for little breaks.

I got a little bit of everything on two paper plates and went to sit with Renée, who was nursing Calla Rose.

I gave Renée a hug and told her, "I'm going to miss you."

"I know," she said. "You and Sukey were always the closest, and sometimes I felt left out. It's been really good to have you just to myself."

Then Renée started crying, dabbing her eyes with a little lace-trimmed handkerchief.

"Now, you stop that," I said. "This is a happy occasion. And don't you worry—no matter where I am, we'll always be best friends."

Then Papa came over and put his arm around me. He said, "There aren't any notes I can blow that could tell you how much I love you, Calla girl."

The combo was tuning up again, so Papa left to join them. Will, who was holding his fiddle, said, "This old Cajun waltz is for my little sister who's flying the coop." He played a waltz that started sweet and sad, then moved into something more lively, the band kicking into gear. Then we all started dancing, me with Sonny Boy as my partner. Even Renée tried it, bumping up against Eddie with Calla Rose in her arms. Nelle made Sukey dance with her.

When the song ended, Nelle came over and gave me a hug. "Take all the love that's in this room with you to New Orleans. Study. Play. Become a businesswoman. Remember M'Dear's Refrigerator Rules. Let yourself become a fine hairdresser so you can do that healing hair work your mama was queen of. Then, if you want to come back here and set up shop, we're here with open arms, on the river you know so well.

"I am so proud of you," she said.

I'm going away, and I have no idea what kinds of adventures await. I'm setting sail down the Mississippi to the city of New Orleans, in pursuit of my career*!*

"Keep your heart open, keep your head on your shoulders, and don't be afraid," I heard M'Dear say.

I felt the Moon Lady jump into my heart, into my suitcases. You could travel the seven seas and still, she'd be with you.

Part II

The Moon Lady

The best way to travel from the tiny, sleepy hamlet of La Luna down to the bustling city of New Orleans is to float among a few high, scattered clouds along the waterways that wind their way south toward the great dark expanse of the Gulf of Mexico.

Floating to the west, my light is a silvery white beacon tracing the undulations of the La Luna River, a tiny shimmering thread that gives herself out into the Red River. I sparkle on the waters of the Red as it makes a short run southeast to the Lower Old River, which empties into the great, majestic Mississippi herself. So wide and mighty, the muscular Mississippi lazily winds her way south in huge sinuous arcs and bends. As she traverses the flat delta farmland, the yellow and orange glow of lights from farms and small towns accents my quicksilver glistening.

My rays fall on the oil refineries, steam, smoke, and bridges of Baton Rouge before dipping again into the inky darkness of swamp, bayou, woods, and fields. I gleam down on little towns like Carville, Darrow, and Convent before touching the raven bodies of Lake Maurepas and Lac des Allemands.

Up ahead, I unite my light with the shimmering glow of the city that care forgot. The river is now a black snake cutting through the sprawling, gleaming mass of diamonds, emeralds, sapphires, and blinking rubies, spilling all the way to the edge of the ebony vastness of Lake Ponchartrain.

I shine down through a few thin hazy clouds, and the apricot-tinted diamonds gradually become streetlights, the blinking rubies transform into the taillights of cars and neon signs. Then my rays leave the peaceful quiet of the cool heavens for the raucous realm of restless humanity in all its forms, honking and shouting, singing and sax playing in an alley beneath the window where Calla Lily Ponder sleeps her first night after her long journey.

Chapter 18

1972

In 1972, as far as I knew, you could have traveled to Paris, France, and you would not have found any finer beauty training than you could get right in uptown New Orleans at L'Académie de Beauté de Crescent. It was one of the finest beauty academies in the South, bar none.

When I first got to the Crescent City, driving up in the used Mustang I had bought, you could have knocked me over with a feather. I thought that, at nineteen, I was a grown woman, but I quickly discovered that there was so much I didn't know.

First of all, New Orleans is so much *bigger* than La Luna. You could walk down the street here and see people you might not ever see again in your whole life. When I first got to New Orleans, I smiled and said hello to everybody I passed on the street, just like at home. But after a while, I quit doing that. It just wore me out.

And I couldn't help but stare at all the different kinds of people out here! Black people who were every color, from sort of a brown paper bag color to jet-black. Beautiful black men and women with blue or green eyes. And hippies. And men that prissed when they walked. And there were people in New Orleans from places like Cuba and Guatemala. I just loved watching people stream by on Canal Street. In New Orleans, if you have a nose, eyes, and ears, there's no way you can ever be bored.

New Orleans has streetcars—and don't you dare call them "trolleys" either, or people will think you're a hick. And the Mississippi River—whoa! She's the Mother of Rivers, so huge and mighty. The Mississippi in New Orleans has real ships that sail the seven seas and all the oceans of the world. And the river—it's higher than the city. She sits up above us and flows on behind the levees while we just live our lives down below.

My home river, the La Luna, flows into the Mississippi, so during my homesick moments I just looked at the river and saw the place I came from flowing into where I had just arrived.

The smells are all different, too. There's this musty smell that saturates everything in the city. It's a smell soup of damp acorns, oak leaves, and muddy water. Everywhere you go, that river smell trails you and makes your hair smell like the river. In the French Quarter, you get a sour and putrid odor in the warm months, which means almost all year long. I think it's a combination of mule's pee from those poor, tired carriage-pulling mules and that beer the bar owners pour on the hot pavement. And there is also—not to be rude—the odor of upchuck from tourists who just eat and drink themselves into oblivion when they come here to visit. One time I heard a lady on the bus say, "New Orleans is where the rest of America comes to urp." I betcha that is not something the Chamber of Commerce likes to talk about.

Oh, but then there's the scent of Luzianne coffee roasting in the warehouse district. It's like burned toast but still delicious. And the smell of those fried and baked Hubig's Pies coming out of their factory. Sometimes if the wind is right, you can get a whole snack in just one whiff!

And they have coffee places here that stay open the whole night long. People just sit outside at Café du Monde and smoke cigarettes and eat hot beignets covered with confectioner's sugar at any hour of the day or night. People in New Orleans are like people in La Luna: we adore anything that we can do with our mouths—eating, drinking, smoking, talking, or singing.

When I first got to New Orleans, I stayed in an apartment owned by Mrs. Josie LaBourde, M'Dear's childhood friend, who would later help me find my own permanent apartment. So it was just a sublet for a while, but it was mine.

After moving in, I got a part-time job at the Camellia Grill, which had the best pecan pies in the state of Louisiana. I'm not kidding you, those pies would just slide down your throat like baby food. The cooks also whipped up pillowy omelets and chili cheese dogs that people stood in lines for, right out the door. Between the money I'd saved in La Luna and the money I made at the grill as a split-shift cashier, I got by fine. I'm not talking Cadillac, but I'm talking just fine.

I like school, and I am good at it. I am working very hard to develop a professional manner. It's important that you achieve a kind of charm to become a success in the beauty culture profession. I am trying my best to learn how to guide the conversation and not be argumentative. To be a good listener and, above all, not to pry into personal affairs. These are among the many things that they test you on in the Standard Book of Cosmetology.

One of the things we learn early on is that each type of face demands a certain coiffure that is rightly proportioned to that face. There are many types of faces: oval, round, square, pear-shaped. You need to be good at first recognizing these different shapes and characteristics and features, then coming up with a hairdo that will help bring out those features. Because really, all features are beautiful.

Thing is, you got to have a whole lot more than just a flair for hair to get a beauty career up and going. There are lots of other kinds of responsibilities. For example, you need to listen to people and know what they want, even when they don't know themselves. But thankfully, L'Académie has the very best teachers. They teach you everything from cutting hair and dealing with people to coloring and rescuing even the most damaged head of hair.

After only two weeks one of my teachers, Vicky Varnado, had to be replaced because she was as pregnant as a cow—I'm not kidding. Every time she'd turn around, that big belly of hers would knock something off the manicure cart. And to tell the truth, I didn't think all that Aqua Net she was breathing in was good for that baby growing in her belly. When Vicky left to have her baby, who do you think took her place? *Ricky Chalon*. As in La Clinique des Cheveux, which is French for "Hair Care Clinic," down in the French Quarter. The man was a capital-H Hairdresser. Ricky knew Mister Phil, the owner of L'Académie, who had begged him to come and take Vicky's place. Ricky was in the middle of making plans to open a new salon of his own, but he agreed.

Ricky Chalon was a true stylist. He had studied with teachers in Houston and Dallas, and for a while he gave seminars across the South on "Cosmetology: The New Approach." I was lucky enough to have five classes with him: Cutting, Finger Wave, Setting with Rollers, Color Basics, and Repair.

Many people don't know it, but a beauty shop is sometimes an emergency room. Suppose a woman goes and bleaches the living daylights out of her hair, then she decides she doesn't like it. So she puts on another color on top of it—say, Pretty Penny. Well, that combination is going to turn her hair *green*. Yes, I mean *green*. And most likely, the spot where she did her patch test strip is going to be green and *orange*. That's just what happens when an amateur fools around with hair chemicals. It's the same thing as when people take drugs that aren't prescribed and they end up in the emergency room. In my Hair Repair class, we learned to handle a beauty casualty just like a doctor takes care of a drug overdose.

And Ricky Chalon was the King of Beauty Casualties. One day just after I started classes at L'Académie, a student beauty operator put color on a woman without giving her a patch test. For a patch test, all you do is put a little of the color on a Q-tip and dab it behind an ear—that's to tell whether the person will have a reaction to the chemical. Ricky happened to be in the shop, and he could just *smell* that something was wrong. He took a look at that woman's roots, and sure enough, she was having a hypersensitive reaction to the dye! He managed to get that dye out of the woman's hair in the nick of time without her even panicking. That is how cool an operator Ricky Chalon was.

Now, I want you to know that that woman's head would have *swole up* and she would've *died* if Ricky hadn't had the sixth sense that something was wrong. I'm not kidding, people die from dye reactions. Ricky saved that woman's life! It was a beauty miracle.

Ricky said in class one day that the mark of a true beautician is that you don't even have to *like* the head that's in your hands to take care of it. You see, a beautician's hands have to feel things that other people's can't. It's like taking a pulse. And Ricky said that to be a true practitioner of beauty, you need to learn to feel several pulses, deeper than just the first pulse, just like the Chinese doctors practicing Eastern medicine.

He also talked about how healthy thoughts can be cultivated, and they can create beauty that can stimulate the functions of the body. Strong negative emotions, he told us, like worry and fear, have a harmful effect on the heart and the arteries and the glands. So you should do everything you can to improve the quality of your thoughts. These were things M'Dear had taught me, too; sometimes I felt like Ricky and M'Dear had met somehow.

One of the first things I noticed about Ricky was the shape of his hands. His wrists were narrow and elegant, and his long fingers were so refined. When he was working—say, wrapping perm rods—those hands moved around so fast that you could swear he was a sleight-of-hand artist. But when he slowed down to demonstrate something to us, you could see that each one of his fingers was doing its individual job, just as graceful as could be. The only other men who have Ricky Chalon's kind of hands are piano players and brain surgeons.

Yes, Ricky Chalon's hands were magic.

I always thought I wanted my own shop. I'm like my M'Dear was, I don't like taking orders from other people. But it isn't easy to open up and maintain your own beauty salon, and this was the kind of academy that would train me to do that. Yes, I was still miserable from missing Tuck, but I was already beginning to wonder if maybe I shouldn't start thinking about a different kind of man—a man who shared my dreams. A man like Ricky Chalon.

So, one morning in Repair class, Ricky asked for a volunteer so he could show how to administer an emergency Nutra-Kit. I said, "Do me! Do me!" Ricky invented Nutra-Kitting, and I was just dying to be his Nutra Kit–ee.

First of all, he washed my hair. But this was not a regular wash. When my hair was wet and sudsy, he began to massage my head. He took those beautiful hands of his with the long piano-player fingers, and he rubbed my head straight into heaven. I was so relaxed that I worried I might be drooling out the side of my mouth. I actually started to pray, "Dear Jesus, please don't let this end. I'll give up everything else, just don't let him stop touching my head."

Then Ricky rinsed my hair and rubbed in a combination of warm olive oil and some kind of placenta stuff. After the placenta worked its way down to the very base of my hair shafts, Ricky rinsed off the Nutra-Kit. The touch of his hands made my whole body tingle. As that Nutra-Kit swirled down the drain, every one of my worries rinsed away, too. And, well, let's just say that every *tissue* in my body felt pretty darn good.

Then I knew that Ricky had healing hands, too.

I tried to imagine it: Ricky and I would get to know each other a little better, get married, and then open up our own shop together. Budgeting and licensing and shop permits—Ricky could help me do all that! We'd call the place La Ric and La Lily's or U.S. Hair Force or the Curl Couple. We'd wake up and eat our breakfast, then go to our shop, where our customers would love us and the wonderful hairstyles we would create.

My thoughts got interrupted when Ricky towel-dried my hair after the Nutra-Kit. When he did, I felt the touch of his hands again, this time all the way down to my—well, my special spot. I couldn't believe it. No one but Tuck had ever made me feel that way.

I wanted his hands in my life.

From then on, I just couldn't get Ricky out of my mind. Sitting at the Dollar Day matinee on my day off from the Camellia Grill, all I could see on the screen was Ricky. Swimming my laps at the YMCA every evening, all I could picture was Ricky. Walking through Audubon Park and looking at those live oaks, so old and deep, Ricky was still on my mind. Every time I took a breath and looked at the sky, I thought, "Ricky, Ricky, Ricky." I fantasized about introducing him to Tuck, triumphantly, after we were married—with me just looking at Tuck like he'd never mattered in my life at all.

I was lying in bed one Saturday morning when it hit me: Ricky probably loved me too! A man wouldn't Nutra-Kit a woman the way he did unless he had very special feelings! *I bet Ricky is just too shy to admit it. Well, I learned the hard way that a girl cannot afford to sit around and wait when she likes a guy. I am going to have to tell him, that's all there is to it.*

The perfect moment seemed to come when I was in the laundry room at L'Académie, helping Ricky fold the clean towels just out of the dryer. We were talking and joking around, and just on a whim, Ricky took one of the white, fluffy towels with "L'Académie de Beauté de Crescent" stamped on them and wrapped me up in it. I could feel the softness of the towel, still warm from the dryer, and Ricky's hands on my shoulder. When he unwrapped me, I decided to spill the beans.

"Ricky," I said. "I think I'm in love with you."

He started to say something, but I told him, "No, please. Just let me talk and you listen."

I took a deep breath and the words started pouring out of my heart. "I felt the way you touched me when you did the Nutra-Kit, Ricky. And I think you feel something for me, too. So, I was thinking that after I graduate and pass the state certification test, I could be your teaching assistant. Just till I'm—well—good enough to teach. And then, you know—and then we could, well, we could sort of see what happens next between us, as a man and a woman."

Ricky folded up a few more towels before he spoke. "Calla, honey, I think you need to know that I think of women as—well, as friends."

"Well, I know that! What I mean is that we could become *more than friends*."

"No, darling," he said, "what I'm trying to tell you is that I prefer men."

My mouth dropped open so wide that a jillion fat june bugs could have flown right in. But just as quickly I thought, *Ricky believes this because he has not met the right girl*. I figured that there were hundreds of men thinking they liked other men—especially in New Orleans—because the right girl had not yet stepped into their lives.

So I might be in a whole new situation with Ricky, but a gal has gotta go for what she wants! In this case, a sweet, handsome, funny man who knows everything there is to know about hair, and who has hands that can heal. And who can teach me everything he knows about beauty. He is the one for me in so, so many ways.

A man with strong, tender hands who could banish my loss and sadness and share a life filled with beauty! I realized that he had been sent to me for a reason. He may not know it yet, but I do. Those eyes, those lips. Those hands that can do just about anything to people's heads and many other parts of their body, I am quite sure.

So I told myself, *Go, Calla. Bat those eyelashes!*

I looked at Ricky across the stack of warm towels and said, "I think I'm going to love being *friends* with you, Ricky."

I started making plans. First things first: the right perfume. A gal's first subtle move. I heard that Ricky loved gardenias, so I bought a big bottle of Jungle Gardenia, and every day on the streetcar to L'Académie, I sprayed on a little extra.

I liked to get to L'Académie early in the morning, before anyone else. Ricky was always in the back, fixing a pot of coffee and reading the new issue of *Modern Hair.* I'd walk up behind him and waft the perfume his way, but he didn't seem to notice.

So I got me one of those lace body stockings that looked like you could see through it. Twice over by the hair dryers I *accidentally* bumped into Ricky and lingered there for a minute before saying, "Oh, pardon me!"

See, I planned to try one new thing every day. *Calla,* I told myself, *if you want something, you've got to be willing to work for it.*

But nothing was working. I mean, zilch. Ricky just kept looking at me like I was a little *neuter.* Something just had to be done.

Chapter 19

1972

I was at Godchaux's semiannual shoe sale when I learned about Madame Marie, Modern Voodoo Queen. I was trying on a pair of pink *peau de soie* pumps with clear Lucite heels when my eye caught a flyer on the chair next to me. It had a picture of a woman on it, wearing a headdress. She was staring with what looked like lightning bolts shooting out of her eyes. Underneath the picture was a slogan: "Can Bewitch Even the Most Stubborn Beloved."

Now, I would not normally ever need or try something like this. But tough times call for tough measures. So I decided to call up Madame Marie and make an appointment for the following Tuesday.

On that Tuesday, I rode over to Tremé, the neighborhood where Madame Marie lived, right outside the French Quarter. She had what they call a "Creole cottage," with four rooms set two in back, two in front. There was no bell, no knocker, no nothing on her front door.

Just French doors opening from the front rooms straight to the banquette, which was what they call sidewalks in the Crescent City.

Through the French doors, I saw a figure sitting up in an armchair. I cleared my throat and said, "'Scuse me, Madame Marie, I'm Calla, the one that called about the Love Enchantment appointment."

Her house smelled like the fires Papa built in the fall to burn off brush. It was the middle of the day, but the curtains were pulled, and the only light came from a TV set and an old fish aquarium set up against the wall. I never imagined that voodoo queens watched *Days of Our Lives*. Well, I guess they have got to fill up their slack time, too. The room was tight and close, with low ceilings. Ladies with tall beehives would have to stoop to stay in the room, I imagined.

Madame Marie had wrinkles so deep you could stick a dime in them, but with those green eyes and that hair hanging down her back, you knew she'd driven men crazy in her day. Her hands were all gnarled and big-knuckled and full of rings, with skin the color of café au lait. And she had on a *tignon*, a big scarf wrapped around her head. Her earrings were so big and heavy that I couldn't see how human ears could support them. Her mouth was large and set off by deep ruby lipstick.

"What you want, girly?"

"I got love problems, Madame Marie. I got this man, he's my teacher over at L'Académie de Beauté. And I want him to love me. I want us to get married and open up a beauty shop together. Because, you see, he has magic hands. Only, he thinks of women as friends."

Madame Marie let out a laugh. "He like the sweet boys, yeah?"

"Yes, ma'am, that is correct. He says he prefers men. So he won't give me the time of day!"

"Does he do you mean?"

"Oh, no, no! He's not mean at all. He's the best beauty teacher a girl could have. Only he doesn't see that I could help him with his problem."

"Uh-huh!" Madame Marie said. "Girly, I got your answer. You take dried newt and burdock root, grind to a fine powder, and sprinkle it in this man's food. You make sure he gets at least two ounces. Less than two ounces, no good."

"Where can I get newt and burdock root?"

Madame Marie got up and went through a beaded curtain. I waited and watched while Hope on *Days of Our Lives* came back from having amnesia, only to find that her husband had married another woman, who was a cripple. Her heart was broken, but Hope was kind and hated to steal her husband away from a woman in a wheelchair. And there was something about malaria and a brain tumor that got just too involved for me to follow.

Madame Marie finally came back. She handed me a little paper sack full of powder. "This is potent, girly. You'll get him good."

"This stuff sure does smell strong. Nasty too."

"Listen to Madame Marie. If the food sprinkle don't work, you take another two ounces, mix with talc, and sprinkle it all over his clothes and person, you hear?"

"That's not going to be very easy," I said.

"Look, you want this man or not?"

"Yes, ma'am, I do want him. I'll figure out a way."

"How much cash you got?"

"Well, I got twenty-seven dollars, but I could get more if I absolutely had to."

"Well, Madame Marie Love Powder will be twenty-seven dollar even. A onetime special for you, today only."

I ran straight home, thinking: Now I'm all set! Ricky will be *mine for life*!

I had my dried newt and burdock root. So next I decided to invite Ricky over to my apartment for dinner. That way I could mix the powder into his food, and he'd never know.

A couple days later, I finally got up the nerve to invite Ricky, and his answer was yes! Yes, Ricky Chalon would have dinner at my apartment that Friday. I spent my nights after class planning the menu. After much thought and study, I ruled out chili bean macaroni, because this was not an evening for anything but the most seductive of smells. Definitely said no to wild duck in a Crock-Pot, because I didn't know where to get wild duck in New Orleans, and besides, I didn't own a Crock-Pot. Finally, I called up Aunt Helen to get her ideas.

"Calla, hon," said Aunt Helen, "you can always win a man's heart with TNC—you know, tuna noodle casserole. I will light a candle on Friday night at eight to make your romance come true. And be sure you get Noah's, not Lay's, potato chips to crumble on top."

I wanted my special dinner to be elegant but easy. For hors d'oeuvres, I rolled a cheese log in pecans to serve with Ritz crackers. Then I made a Sunshine Salad—shredded carrots with raisins and mayonnaise and a little sugar, with some dried newt and burdock root. Then I fixed my casserole, so all I had to do was slip it in the oven. I actually got a tad bit nervous when I went to mix more of the dried newt and burdock with my melted butter for the tuna noodle casserole. That Madame Marie Love Powder stank to high heaven. But I knew if I threw in enough garlic, it would disguise any odor. That man would never know what hit him!

I planned to serve English peas with the casserole, the little LeSueur Petit Pois, not the big fat squishy ones. Then, for my garnish, I'd serve Del Monte pineapple rings on a bed of lettuce, with a cherry on top of each one. I knew Ricky would appreciate that little touch of color.

For dessert, I made strawberry shortcake. I had to go to three different stores to find those little sponge shells, but I finally got them at Langenstein's. I thawed out the strawberries, which I planned to put in the sponge shells at the last minute, so they wouldn't get all soggy. Then I'd squirt on the Reddi-wip.

At seven minutes after eight, the doorbell rang and there he was!

"Good evening, Calla. Thank you again for having me over." Ricky looked so stylish in his baby blue Nehru jacket and matching socks.

"Well, I'm just so thrilled you could come." *Be still, my beating heart!* "Could I get you something to drink? I've got wine from Martin's Wine Cellar and beer and Cokes, too."

"I'd love a Coke."

Damnit! This would be so much easier if only he would drink. But it doesn't matter. Liquor might be quicker, but voodoo is pronto.

As I fixed him a Coke over ice, all words fled my brain.

"Sure is different seeing you outside the salon," I finally said.

"Yes, it's always different outside of the workplace."

"How about some cheese log rolled in pecans?"

"I'd love to, Calla, but I don't eat pecans. I am allergic to them."

"Well, I guess if the good Lord meant cheese logs to have pecans on them, He would've made cows with nuts all over them!"

Then I broke up laughing at my own joke, but unfortunately my laugh turned into a snort. *Not good.* Ricky just gave a tiny polite laugh, and I tried to calm myself down. It's no fun to sit at your dinner party and laugh at jokes you make all by yourself.

"What a sweet little place you've got here, Calla."

"Thank you, Ricky. It's just a sublet until I find my own place, but it's home."

"I really like all the houseplants."

"Maybe I could send you home with a cutting from one of them."

Oh, I would've cut off anything of mine and given it to him, I thought. Then I glanced down at my watch and excused myself to get the casserole out of the oven.

"Tuna noodle casserole!" I announced, bringing it to the table. "Old family recipe. Have all you want. I made two. I could even wrap some up in aluminum foil—or put it in one of my Tupperwares for you to take home. You could just return the Tupperware the *next time* you come over."

"It looks like a real feast," Ricky said, ignoring my rambling and unfolding his napkin carefully.

"Be sure to have a little Sunshine Salad, too. And here, can I butter a hot roll for you? I like my butter *dripping* off a roll, not stuck on there like a hard little plastic pat, you know what I mean?"

"Calla, I never knew you were such a good cook as well as a career woman."

"There's a whole lot you don't know about me, Ricky." Then I gave him a long, slow smile.

"What is that special seasoning in this casserole, Calla? I can't quite put my finger on what it is."

"Oh, that's just my little secret seasoning. My aunt Helen would kill me if I told. That secret seasoning is what makes her recipe so special."

He touched his hand to his chest. Good Lord, I thought, that is a sign—that is definitely a sign the newt is working.

"So what are your plans, Calla?"

"My plans?" I was stunned. *Oh sweet Jesus, he knows I've asked him here for a reason.* "My plans for what?"

"Your plans for after graduation."

"Oh, after graduation," I said, and laughed like I had never even given it a second thought. "Graduation's not for a whole six months. You never know what could happen in six months, do you? By the way, Ricky, do you by any chance like strawberries?"

"I love strawberries." He smiled at me.

"I knew it! I said to myself: 'Self, Ricky Chalon is a strawberry man.' That is very, very good because I just so happen to have made you a strawberry shortcake for dessert. But I need your help, Ricky. Could you do the honors later by squirting on the Reddi-wip?"

"You've got a deal."

"And do the Supremes happen to strike a chord in your heart, Ricky?"

I stood up to put on the record, and then he actually asked me to dance with him. Hot dog! I thought. This newt stuff is working for sure.

Being in his arms felt as good as I imagined. I floated in his arms like chiffon, like the Reddi-wip on the berries. I could smell Ricky's good clean scent topped with a touch of English Leather cologne. And I was getting warm and runny myself, just like the Reddi-wip.

"Calla, I hate to eat and run, but I really have to go."

"Go? Now?"

"Yes, I'm really sorry," he said, backing up. "But I didn't realize it was so late. I have to meet some friends down in the French Quarter."

"Oh, I see. Yeah, I guess things are just getting started down there about now."

"Thank you for going to so much trouble with dinner," he said, getting ready to leave. "It was wonderful."

"Oh, don't mention it. Well, I guess I'll just see you on Monday, then." I felt defeated as I opened the door for him to let him out.

"You bet you will."

"Okay. Well, bye-bye."

I shut the door and just stood there, staring at the table, at the cherry on top of my garnish. Ricky didn't even touch them, let alone comment on how red and perky they looked.

I could hardly sleep that night. I couldn't believe that Madame Marie's magic powder had failed. I was going to have to take the rest of that powder and sprinkle it all over Ricky's body somehow, just as Madame Marie instructed. I'd do it if it killed me.

The next morning I remembered Ricky saying that he was giving a cut to a friend on Sunday afternoon. Probably a man-friend, but I didn't care because I was determined: this was for the good of both of us!

Sunday afternoon I got to L'Académie and sneaked in through the back, working my way quietly into the laundry room. Then I climbed on top of the dryer to peek through the vent into the training salon. Sure enough, there was Ricky, kneeling in front of a man in one of the chairs! My heart was pounding out of my chest, but I knew what I had to do. As quietly as I could, I reached down behind the dryer and jerked the dryer hose out of the wall, then ripped open the love powder packet. Standing on that dryer, I cursed myself for wearing platform heels instead of more practical shoes. Then, with the dryer hose in one hand and holding the open love powder packet in my mouth, I reached down and turned on that industrial dryer to high—and whoa! The hose assumed a life of its own. It blew my hairdo to pieces and even blasted off an earring.

Not a minute to waste! I regained control of the dryer hose by holding it under my arm, turned it down to low, stood up on tiptoe on the back edge of the dryer, and started to blow out the love powder onto Ricky through the vent.

In struggling to get the dryer hose higher and pressed against the vent, my platform shoe slipped and my right leg plunged into the crack between the wall and the dryer. The dryer hose got loose again and started blowing up my dress. Desperately I tried pulling my leg out of the crack, but *it would not budge*! I tried again. No luck. I took a deep breath and gathered all my strength for one last attempt. No way.

I tried to calm myself and somehow managed to turn off the dryer. This stopped the dryer hose in its tracks. But there was no getting around the fact that I was stuck.

I'm going to have to call out for help.

"Ricky?" I called out real softly. Nothing. Then, a little louder: "Ricky!"

Still nothing.

Eventually Ricky and the man would leave. I'd just stay trapped with my leg against the wall, my magic love powder covering my face, my hairdo blown to smithereens, and count my blessings. M'Dear always said, "What matters today, won't matter tomorrow. Count your blessings instead of your sorrow."

I could be stuck the whole night, and Ricky would be the one to come and find me first thing Monday morning. By then my leg could have gangrene. My right leg would have to be cut off! A one-legged beautician. Well, at least then maybe he would notice me.

Snap out of it, Calla! I told myself. I yelled at the top of my lungs: "Riiiiiiiicky!!!!!!!!! Help!!"

Ricky finally ran back to the laundry room and pulled me up from the crack. I had bruised my leg a horrible blue, tore my brand new lime-green pantyhose, and ripped off the strap on my platform shoe. I couldn't stop crying and all the mascara gooched up under my eyes. Once again, don't you ever believe it when they tell you it's waterproof, because it is not.

Then the old man came in and put his shoes back on. "Can't thank you enough, Rick," he said in an old Cajun voice. "If it wasn't for you, them old toenails of mine would still be cutting into my feet. You get so old and stiff, you can't bend over and cut them yourself, *non*."

Ricky was cutting that old man's toenails. And there I was, trying to blow a spell over Ricky while he was performing an act of kindness.

When the old man left, Ricky said, "What do you want from me, Calla?" He handed me some Kleenex.

What does a girl have to lose, after being pulled out from behind a dryer with the yuck-o smell of newt and burdock hanging in the air? "I want for you to fall in love with me," I told him, "and I want us to get married and open up a shop together. Ricky, it'd be real fun, because you've already got the experience and you know all the finances and city codes and all the beauty ins and outs. I'm a real hard worker, and

I'm very, very good with people and—oh, shit." I tried my best to stop crying, but I couldn't. "What I mean is, Ricky, you are the one with the magic hands."

Ricky lifted my hands up in his. "Calla, dear young girl, you don't need me. You have all the magic in your hands that I've got in mine."

I couldn't believe that he was turning me down flat. I stood there, too numb to move, then I ran to the ladies' room and locked myself in the stall. I just sat there, so ashamed I didn't think I could even open the door. What was Ricky going to think of me—a girl who tried to seduce him but instead fell into the crack between a dryer and a wall, covered in stinky voodoo powder?

I don't know how long I was in there, dying of embarrassment, before Ricky called out, "Are you okay, Calla?"

There was no way to escape. "Yes, yes," I blubbered. "I'll be right out."

I tried to get the mascara and burdock root off my face and fixed my blown-away hair as best I could. Then, feeling like I was under a death sentence, I opened the door.

Ricky was standing there with kindness on his face. Though I'd made a fool of myself, he seemed concerned.

I took a deep breath. "Ricky, I'm so embarrassed. I hate myself for doing this."

"Don't ever say you hate yourself. It's like jabbing your heart with a sharp stick. And besides, I don't imagine you were raised to hate yourself, or else you wouldn't be able to touch people the way you do."

I couldn't say anything for a minute. *This is a person to trust*, I heard M'Dear say. Raising my eyes to meet his, I said, "I apologize."

He looked at me, smiling. "No need to," he said, as he straightened my hair. "C'mon, let's go grab some lunch."

Ricky took me uptown on the Charles Avenue streetcar to the Bluebird Grill. While we waited for our burgers, I tried to let Ricky know how much I enjoyed school. "Every day, I learn more and more. I love that you build a world that I can step into, so that now I can actually envision being a cosmetologist. I love that word 'cosmetology' because it is like 'cosmologist.' And yes, I am a girl who loves the cosmos. I love the heavens, the stars, the constellations, and hair. My mother first opened the door, and now the universe of cosmetology is opening up for me."

It was only by the time our food came that I worked up the courage to say, "Ricky, I want to apologize. You know, you're so handsome and all, and your fingers are so beautiful. I don't know if I should tell you about my life before New Orleans. But I think it has something to do with me going after you like I did."

"Calla, go ahead and tell me. I want to hear about you." And Ricky seemed like he really meant it.

So I told him about Tuck, and about M'Dear and her dying.

"Calla, I'm sorry that your M'Dear died when you were so young."

"She had breast cancer."

"Oh, I'm so awfully sorry, Calla! You know, I have a special friend named Steve. His cousin Louise died of breast cancer. He visited her every week, and he took me sometimes, so I know a little bit about it. I am so sorry, Calla."

I said, "I'd like to meet your friend, because meeting somebody else who knows—well, it would go a long way."

"Yes," Ricky said. "Steve and I are very close."

There was silence for a while. I thought for a minute. "He's your love, isn't he?" I asked.

"Yep," Ricky said as he picked up a French fry. "He's my guy."

"I've never thought about it much," I said, "two men together. But my parents had a dance studio—maybe you've heard of it—Will and Lenora's Swing 'N Sway?"

Ricky took a sip of his ice tea. "No, I don't believe I have."

"On the first Saturday of every month, we threw open the doors to music, dancing, and gumbo, and M'Dear and Papa didn't care one bit about two men dancing together. So nobody else gave it a second thought. Anyway, I'm glad you have someone close. I thought I did. But Tuck left, went off to college, and never called or wrote or came home, even though he promised he would."

"He never contacted you at all?"

"Never," I said. "Not one bit."

"Oh, Calla, it just breaks my heart to hear that happened to you."

"I waited and waited while I was working for a year to get the money and the nerve to move to New Orleans. He broke my heart—and then I met you! You were teaching, you were just so handsome, and you just had such a way with your hands. When you gave me the Nutra-Kit, the way your hands touched me, it seemed like you weren't just teaching me, but you were doing something else."

"Well, I was, Calla."

I said, "You were? I mean, because it seemed like, well, I'm kind of embarrassed to say it . . . but it seemed like you were trying to turn me on."

I could feel my face turning beet red. I had to put my hamburger down.

"Oh, Calla," Ricky said. "I understand. In fact, I'm flattered!"

"You are?"

"Yes," he said. "I'm flattered that somebody as lovely as you felt that, somebody who knows about the healing that a beautician can do. Not everybody gets that.

"Calla, what I was trying to do wasn't to turn you on, but to calm you down. I was trying to let my hands send a message to you. A message that everything was good between us. You can do that through your hands, you know."

"You see, I was afraid I might never fall in love that way again, and then when I felt your magic hands—"

"It's okay, Calla, I really do understand."

"Well, I'm afraid there's more to the story." I took a sip of my Coke and told him about Madame Marie and her potion.

"Calla! Honey!" Ricky reached for my hands and looked at my palms. Then he said, "I want you to take a vow right now to put your past behind you. Become friends with me, and open up to your new life in this city. Can you make that vow?"

I thought for a moment, remembering how sad I'd been. Then I said, "Yes, I, Calla Lily Ponder, do vow that I will let go of the past. And I vow to let this lunch be the beginning of our friendship. To launch it like a rocket!"

Then Ricky was dead serious. "And now I want you to do something else," he said. "Remember I said you have the same magic in your hands as I do in mine?"

"Ricky, it's true, I've been wanting to tell someone. One time, I got this great sense of warmth when I was doing hair. I felt that I was moving energy around. I thought that I could read emotions. My mother, M'Dear, is the one who taught me that I had healing hands."

"I believe it, Calla," he said. "That's the highest gift. The challenge is to learn how to use your healing hands. The Bible says, 'Study to be quiet and do your work with your own hands.' Look at your hands, Calla. I mean, really look."

I looked hard and saw my hands—really *saw* them—for the first time. The lines on my palms, my fingers, my thumbs, my strong wrists. I thought of how much my hands did for me, how many different things they could do.

Just then an image of M'Dear came to me. She was saying good night to her ballroom dancing students. One of the men said something about how he didn't know where she found the energy to work so hard. M'Dear smiled at him and replied, "Oh, my body loves to work!"

Calla, my hands whispered to me, *we love to work*.

"You see?" Ricky said. "I believe that you have the gift of beauty."

"Ricky." I smiled. "I have healing hands. I got them from my mother."

September 10, 1972
New Orleans

Dear Papa,

Oh, how it did my soul good to spend the weekend with you! Friday night, you outdid yourself with that trout almondine. Any man I end up with is going to have to be a good cook to measure up. Sitting down, just you and me, was so nice. I needed that.

Riding over to Pana and Olivia's house on Saturday morning put me in a great mood. I'm glad I used M'Dear's satchel bag to swing over Golden Princess to carry back those good fresh collards. And you were right to make me take them up on their offer to go back into their "hidden" garden to pick sweet potatoes to take back to New Orleans. You tell Pana that he is right: Mister Pana LaVergne's sweet potatoes are famous here in the big city! Please thank him again for me.

And thank you, Papa, for such a wonderful weekend back home.

I love you!

Calla

Chapter 20

1973

I was so excited to see Sukey, I waited for half an hour on the steps to my new apartment for her to arrive. "Sukey!" I said, when she walked up, like a one-person welcome wagon. "I couldn't wait for you to get here."

I'd left Mrs. LaBourde's place and moved about twenty blocks to my new apartment a month ago, but Sukey hadn't seen it yet. Our schedules were just so different, with her work at the Playboy Club and my going to school and working at the Camellia Grill, that it was almost like we lived in different worlds in New Orleans. I had only visited her apartment once so far. So it was so good when she finally got a Saturday off and called me to just hang out. I had missed her!

My new place was a darling little one-bedroom place in uptown New Orleans, right above a vintage clothing store called JoAnn's Vintage Palace. My rent was $150 a month—which seemed like a fortune, but Mrs. LaBourde told me it was a pretty good deal. My apartment was clean and pretty with new harvest gold appliances and a pink bathroom with little one-inch octagonal floor tiles New Orleans people call a "drugstore floor." I had French doors opening onto a skinny little balcony facing the street—well, really, it was more like a balconette. But it was all mine! Right there on the river side of St. Charles, on Magazine Street.

Walking to and from my apartment to the streetcar everyday, I went by the St. Elizabeth's Home. St. Elizabeth's is this huge orphanage that's been in New Orleans since before the Civil War. It's a three-story, U-shaped building with a courtyard in the middle that takes up an entire block, with Prytania Street on one side and Napoleon on the other. It's still run by the nuns. I always think about all those girls who got sent there, back when the yellow fever used to hit New Orleans like a long, slow hurricane, killing many parents. So many children were left behind.

I often say a prayer for them when I look out my bedroom window, watching a wisteria vine and tuberoses growing up the back stairs by my kitchen.

"Well, Calla Lily, I really think you're cutting loose a little bit. I saw you from down the block, sitting there with your legs crossed like we were raised never to do."

We laughed as we hugged each other tight.

"I'm dying for you to see my apartment. I've spent so much time—"

"Wait a minute! You didn't tell me that you lived above JoAnn's Vintage Palace! I can't believe that you live right upstairs!"

I said, "Maybe we can come back down after—"

Sukey interrupted me. "It's famous!"

"Yeah, I'm lucky." As I followed Sukey into JoAnn's, I could hear the familiar sound of the bells tinkling. I introduced Sukey to JoAnn.

JoAnn seemed to know everyone in New Orleans, or at least in our neighborhood. Since I'd moved there, she'd been kind and funny, and I felt safe knowing we lived together—she on the floor above the shop, and me up another flight of stairs. Today, she held forth wearing a paisley caftan over her head of wild, curly hair.

"Well, Sukey, it's a pleasure to have you," JoAnn said. "Are you new here in New Orleans too?"

"Oh, no," Sukey said. "I've been here working at the Playboy Club for a year."

"Oh, really!" JoAnn said. "Then you must know Dick!"

"Yes, I do."

"Oh, wonderful! Dick has been a great doorman for that place, and the fact that his name is *Dick* just makes it all the better. Wouldn't you agree?"

We all laughed.

"Absolutely!" Sukey said. "I couldn't believe that was his real name. I thought he'd made it up."

"Well, he *did*," JoAnn said. "His actual name is Douglas Francis Pritchard."

"Oh, I'm going to tease him with that," Sukey told her. "I love to tease every boy in that club."

"Yeah," JoAnn said. "That's what they go for, to be *teased*." She winked. "Well, y'all just look around now. I've got plenty of work to do. Holler if you need anything. And Calla, I understand you've had a little dripping with your faucet. I'll get somebody over there as soon as I can."

"What a great landlady!" Sukey said. She was heading straight for the hats. Sukey loved hats because they looked so good with her short shiny jet-black Sassoon haircut. She's worn her hair like that ever since *I* gave her a Sassoon cut when we were teenagers—the first that had ever been seen in La Luna. Nothing made Sukey happier than being original.

We started trying on all the vintage hats. None of them fit over my thick, almost waist-length hair. JoAnn, who'd come over to see how we were doing, said to me, "Sweetie, what you need is a *man's* fedora. Don't worry, Barbara Stanwyck wore them all the time, and Hepburn too. You know, Hepburn had thick hair like yours, and it was about the same color, though she dyed it red."

Then JoAnn whipped out a fedora, which fit me perfectly.

"I keep my men's things over here because it's basically a women's shop. But some of the men come in for ladies' clothes, too."

"Why?" I asked. "Why would the men come in for ladies' clothes?"

JoAnn laughed. "Oh, Calla, you really haven't been in New Orleans for long. Let me just say that there are men in this town who like to dress up in women's clothes and strut around. And if you go down to Godchaux's Department Store on Canal Street, you'll notice that they stock the latest ladies' platform shoes up to size thirteen."

"Oh," was all I could say.

Sukey told me, "Calla, don't worry. You're going to do okay here in New Orleans."

After the hats, we started working through the racks. So far I'd only bought some vintage jewelry from JoAnn, one or two skirts, and a cute little jacket with a peplum skirt and wide shoulders, which I loved. I wore it with slacks, and it sort of made them look more feminine.

But today I was in the mood to splurge. A girl always has to keep Mardi Gras in mind, and I had been asked out on a few dates. Sukey was pulling out all kinds of wild clothes for me. One was a mauve silk full-length dress that looked like a nightgown, with ecru lace on its hem and at the bodice. "You've got to try this on," she insisted. "This is just too glamorous to pass up."

"Good eye, Suke." The skirt was cut on the bias, and it hugged my bottom like it was made for me.

I twirled, and the way that silk moved was like a wave. "Wow," I said, rubbing my thighs. "This feels so good against my legs."

"Oh," Sukey said. "That is fabulous!"

"I love the way the dress is open down to the waist with lace, giving the illusion that it's see-through."

"And look, there's a little peignoir sort of jacket you can wear over it if you feel shy. That dress is *you*, all the way. Look in the mirror. Now, undo that braid."

"I can't undo it right here in the store."

"Yes, you can."

Sukey got up on a stool inside the dressing room. She quickly undid my braid and ran her fingers down my hair.

JoAnn came over and examined me. "You fill that dress out divinely, Calla! Hmm, you really look like a movie star. There's just one more thing you need. Take off that jacket."

She waved her hand at me, bossy as could be. She went to the mannequin in the display case at the front of the store and brought back a long white feather boa. We cracked up laughing as she swept it around my neck.

Though it did look good, I said, "No, I cannot wear this. Where would I ever *go* in a feather boa?!"

"You'll find a place in New Orleans. I promise you," Sukey said.

No one could ever win an argument with Sukey. "Okay, I'll get it. But what about you? Aren't you going to get anything?"

"Nope," Sukey said, "this is *your* day to splurge. But I do want to try this on."

She held up an outrageous olive green dress with dolman sleeves. "Look at these winged sleeves. They're lined with leopard skin! JoAnn, is this real leopard skin?"

"Of course," JoAnn told her. "This is from the 1930s."

So Sukey put on the dress, and I had to admit it was a very gorgeous idea on Sukey. The stand-up collar was lined with leopard skin, too, which was just meant to go with Sukey's jet-black hair. The dress had a zipper down the front, a leopard-skin belt, and a swirly skirt with leopard-skin trim. It was too long on Sukey, and kind of baggy in the chest, but otherwise it fit perfectly.

"What do you think?" Sukey asked JoAnn, doing a Loretta Young twirl.

JoAnn studied Sukey. "It needs to be shortened, which I'd be happy to do for you. I can raise the hem and stitch the leopard skin back on. And you need to wear more of a push-up bra under it."

"I know about that. It's my tiny boobs, right?" Sukey said. "I need push-up bras because my breasts are smaller than every other Bunny."

"You have beautiful breasts," JoAnn told her. "You have nothing to worry about."

And I could see for the first time that Sukey truly worried about the size of her breasts. She used to kid about them in high school, but now she was noticeably relieved to have someone like JoAnn tell her that they were the perfect size.

After JoAnn finished pinning Sukey's hem, we paid for our new outfits.

"Okay," Sukey said. "Now, let's go see your apartment."

We climbed the twenty-eight hardwood steps up from the first floor. The first thing I wanted Sukey to see in the apartment was the balcony. As soon as we walked in I raised the nine-foot double hung windows that led to it, and Sukey stepped out. "Oh, my! This is lovely, Calla!" she said.

When she came back in, I gave her the full tour.

"Ohh, Calla! Your ceilings!"

"They're *ten feet* high," I told her.

"And your bathroom—it's huge! You could park a Volkswagen bug in there. I love your four-poster bed, too."

"I bought it on Magazine Street when I got here. It was a steal, though I had to clean it up. I rubbed Vaseline on it from head to toe."

"It's beautiful. And look at your great duvet!"

"Aunt Helen made it. I picked out the fabric."

"Gosh," Sukey said, "this is like a real New Orleans apartment. It kind of makes me wish I'd gotten real furniture, instead of beanbags. I like them because they're 'mod,' but they basically mean you're always sitting on the floor."

"I like your beanbags and throw pillows," I told her. "Now, would you like something to eat?"

"No, thanks," Sukey said. She walked into my kitchen and opened the fridge. "But would you mind if I had a beer?"

"No, help yourself."

Sukey opened a beer and took a big gulp.

"How's your job going?" I asked.

"Well, I feel like I know a lot of valuable information now, like all about wines and liquors and about the psychology of customers. And our 'Bunny Mother' has taught me a lot about hairstyling and makeup and that kind of thing. You know, if I wanted to, I could ask to transfer to another club. There are clubs all over the country. They have one in *Jamaica*."

"Jamaica!" I said. "That's amazing."

"Calla, I got my one-year raise, and you won't believe what I'm making now. I mean, I don't want to make you feel bad or anything, but I make almost three hundred a week!"

"A *week*? You make three hundred dollars a week?!"

"Well, almost," Sukey said, "almost three hundred dollars a week."

"Still, Suke! That's just—girl, if you're saving that money, you're not going to have to work for the rest of your life!"

"Calla, I have to tell you, I love my job. It's exciting. I'm never bored! And I get to meet international and famous people. Guess who came in two weeks ago? *Tony Curtis*. You know, it's an elite club, so you need a key to get in, and Tony Curtis is a key holder! And the atmosphere of the club—oh, it's just like walking into another world. It's designed to feel like you are at a cocktail party with fine food and drink and entertainment, and us—the Bunnies! It's not sleazy because we have *members*—not just anybody off the street. They have to wear dinner suits, or at least sports jackets, they must treat us with respect, and they are told that they cannot *ever* touch the Bunnies."

Sukey popped up and got another beer.

"I've met several girls there that I like very much," she told me when she came back. "Bunny Ginger and Bunny Lou are the best. One of them is from Iowa, and the other is from Indiana. They applied and became Bunnies right out of high school, like I did, but some of the Bunnies have actually been fashion models.

"So, Calla, my world is fulfilled. Every time I go to work, I look forward to it."

"Really?"

"Yes. I really feel like I'm part of the sexual revolution. Like I am representing the fact that we have a whole new freedom about sex that would blow those pointy red hats off the Vatican cardinals."

I got up and walked to the refrigerator. Sukey seemed like someone had wound her up, and she couldn't stop talking. "How about something to eat?" I offered, setting out a platter of cheese and crackers that I'd prepared for her visit.

"No, thanks," she said with a little laugh. "I'm on the New Orleans Liquid Diet."

When I didn't laugh, she said, "Oh, my God, Calla Lily, don't start jumping down my throat."

"What do you mean, Sukey?"

"I mean, be a good hostess and please get me another beer," she said, imitating the voice of our Home Ec teacher. When I went and got her the beer, she continued talking.

"And I feel that I've gained so much grace and poise being a Bunny, like when I do the 'Bunny Dip,' which is the way you have to put one foot forward and lean back on the other while you're holding your tray. It's very important to learn, because if you bend down to serve drinks, your boobies can just fall right out of that uniform. Well," she said, "in my case, the brassiere pads!

"And then there's the 'Bunny Perch,'" Sukey continued. "That's when you sit down on the edge of a chair or on the edge of a booth, just barely touching with your butt, and holding on with your hands, so that you don't fall. And you've got one leg down and one leg up, because that's the most attractive way to present your legs."

While she was opening the beer, I thought, I hope she doesn't ask for another one.

Sukey came back and said, "You really have to come to the club sometime."

"Well, sure. Yeah. Sometime." But I thought, Please. No.

"So," Sukey said, "now tell me all about you and what you've been up to."

I had to hesitate a minute because suddenly it seemed like there was no way I could talk to Sukey about what I'd been "up to."

Closing my eyes for a moment, I thought about my life. "I'm beginning to grow into what M'Dear had been teaching me all along—to touch people in a way that doesn't shut them out. To let them in. And I'm surrounded by good people, who are helping me learn my craft. Good, kind people."

"And *boobs*," she said. "God forbid if your boobs are small."

I wasn't sure Sukey and I were occupying the same place. I was just there in my apartment, and she was—I don't know exactly where Sukey was, but I sure missed her.

Chapter 21

1973

A day came when a huge beauty lesson just fell in my lap. Ricky and I were starting to become good friends, and we could laugh about my little infatuation phase. I was cutting and doing hair as a training student with him out on the "floor," as we called the public part of L'Académie's salon.

One evening I was staying late to clean up the little kitchenette in the back that we all shared, while Ricky was still out front. Well, I heard the tinkling of the bell on the front door, followed by some sounds of sobbing. Then Ricky came through the pink-and-white-striped curtain that divided the rooms and said, "Oh, Calla, I'm so glad you're still here. We have a woman whose hair is seriously damaged, and I really need your help."

"Well, of course, Ricky!"

"She has almost *total* hair breakage. Almost the worst I've ever seen." He parted the curtain just enough to show me.

"Oh, my God, Ricky," I whispered.

Now I had seen some pictures in our textbook that you wouldn't believe, but this sight made my stomach turn. Even from a distance, I could see that the poor thing had had an awful bleach job and that most of her hair had broken off, leaving just a few long, very weak strands hanging here and there. I decided to go out on a limb with Ricky, so I said in my best doctor voice, "Bad bleach job followed by a permanent wave with tension; didn't get the solution off in time, so her hair broke off where the rubber bands went across the perm rods."

"Right on, Calla."

"Ricky, was this done at home? I mean, surely this is not the work of a professional?"

"Calla, I cannot bring myself to use the word 'professional' in the same sentence with the name of the person who did this. I'm sorry to report that this *was* done by a beautician—a very, very bad beautician. It's enough to make my blood boil."

Ricky Chalon was the very definition of cool and calm under pressure in any beauty situation, but his face had turned a dark shade of red.

"Dear Lord, Ricky!"

Ricky just put up his hand and continued, "I will not name the person, but I will say that he is known for damage. 'Hair Hurricane' is what many of us call him, the baddest of the bad, the Cruella De Vil of the cosmetology world. But enough on that. We have a beauty emergency on our hands. It will keep us here a couple of hours, but Calla, you can learn a lot this evening. And afterward, I'll buy us muffulettas. Are you in?"

"I'm ready, Ricky."

"Good! Now, you and I have begun the conversation of *healing* in beauty. It is essential that our client leave here tonight feeling good about herself and how she looks, and ready to follow her hair recovery regimen every day. It is part of our job to make her feel whole again."

Then Ricky swept through the curtain back onto the floor with a flourish and confidence that only Ricky Chalon could muster.

Ricky said, "Erbolene, you are so fortunate that you have a face that looks fantastic with short hair. I was just browsing through this month's *Vogue*, and I saw Mia Farrow with her short cut, and you are her *spitting image*. Now, one of our finest here at L'Académie will be assisting me this evening. This is Calla Lily Ponder. Calla Lily will begin by applying a special deep moisturizing treatment that I have developed especially for this type of situation."

"Do you think you can really help?" Erbolene asked. You could just tell by her voice that she had been making bad hair choices her whole life.

"Help?" Ricky said. "Baby, we're gonna have you looking like you stepped off the plane from Paris."

Ricky kept on talking to Erbolene as he went over to a special locked cabinet to get some ingredients. The cabinet was a source of great gossip and speculation at L'Académie, with everyone just dying to know what all was in there. Ricky came back over and mixed into the basic moisturizer I prepared a couple of his "proprietary potions," as he referred to them, and then I applied the mixture to her hair. *Whooee!* It had a pretty strong earthy, herbal smell that was new to me. Then Ricky put on some soft, soothing music and had me just hold Erbolene's head in my hands for a minute or two, as he'd taught me. Since I'd told him about the warmth coming from my hands, he had been coaching me on how to "move energy," as he called it, whenever I wanted. I began by lightly holding Erbolene's head, then breathing deeply and evenly as I drew my palms away. That drew her energy into my hands. Basically what I was doing was washing her energy. When I hold a client's head in my hands, their energy comes into me and then moves up from me to the Moon Lady, where she washes it in her river of love and goodness and sends it back down through me and back into the client in all its cleanliness. Erbolene's deep sigh and the look of peace on her face let me know that M'Dear's and Ricky's teachings were at work through my hands.

Then I carefully rinsed out the treatment. I looked at Ricky and mouthed the words, "Filler next?"

He gave me back an approving nod. The general public doesn't know about fillers. They're hair colors without peroxide, which you put on first to fill in the damaged part of the hair shaft. After the fillers, you can put on the regular color that you want to use.

Ricky took out some color charts and showed me what he was thinking. He then explained the color choices to our client, talking about her complexion and asking her about her favorite colors to wear. He didn't turn her toward the mirror to look at herself, which is something Ricky usually does while he is working on a damaged case like this one.

We got the color done, and then Ricky gave the woman the cutest, smartest little cut—he really was as brilliant a cutter as everybody in New Orleans always said. When he got his special made-in-Germany cutting shears in his hands, he could move over a head of hair like greased lightning! And the soft strawberry blond tint he chose was so natural on the woman and so perfect with her skin and her little spray of freckles.

Ricky waited until he was all done to turn the woman around to the mirror. She put her hands to her cheeks and started crying again. Except this time, they were tears of joy.

Ricky was as good as his word, and he took me out for muffulettas at a little place down the street. We were laughing and joking the whole time—in part, to relieve the tension of the last couple of hours. When we got back to the salon I turned the conversation back to beauty. "Ricky, I would never have thought that you could make that woman look so good."

"We did it together, Calla. It was a team effort. And I saw once again what I have been suspecting for some time. You've got the touch to be not only superior at the craft of cosmetology, but also a true and sensitive practitioner who can raise the craft to be a healing art."

"Oh, *Ricky*—"

"After you graduate, I'd like to invite you to work with me. You could finally quit working at the Camellia Grill and do hair full-time. Because I think that you have the hands—not only the hands, but the heart—to help heal damaged hair, to really help people."

"It's what M'Dear—my mother—began teaching me when I was a teenager. She taught me that the heart and the head are cousins to each other. How *hair* is right there at the spot where the head meets the world, so it's important for things other than looking pretty—although *that* is always a healing aspect all its own."

"Tell me about her," Ricky said. How sweet for him to care.

I closed my eyes, and saw M'Dear's face.

"She had her own shop, the Crowning Glory Beauty Porch, and I could have just taken it over when she died, but she wanted me to experience the world outside of La Luna, to learn more about doing hair as a healing, happy thing—to really learn my craft well."

And here I was, with a great opportunity. Well, I was just beside myself. "Ricky, it would be an *honor* to work with you."

Ricky gave me a hug. "I'm your guy," he said, twirling around a pair of scissors like a cowboy.

"And I'm your girl," I said, grabbing a blow dryer and, in an attempt to twirl it, knocking a few items off the counter.

"Right," Ricky said, chuckling at my clumsiness. "Okay, so now you'll be working directly with me as an apprentice for about a year after you pass your state boards. We will be going into areas unknown by the standard beautician.

"To work together in this way, I'll need to show you some things—trade secrets that you must hold in utter confidence. There are hairdressers in this town who would do just about anything to get at the cosmetological discoveries I have made over the years."

"Ricky, you can trust me two hundred percent!"

"Calla, lean close," Ricky said. "I'm referring to the ingredients in the locked cabinet. We've talked flower essences; we've talked vetiver root, we've talked dried orchids from the bayou. But, Calla, there is an ancient woman in Bayou Gaudet whose only clients are voodoo practitioners except for one—me, Ricky Chalon, the *only* hairdresser to go there.

"And that's where I get my secret, secret ingredients. Calla, here in New Orleans, spells are still a commonplace occurrence. Think of my secret potions like protective spells. Did you know that in the colder climates, ninety percent of the body's heat is lost from the head? Well, the reverse is true with spells. Ninety percent of the spell goes in through your hair and your head."

I was getting the chills, listening to Ricky talk.

"A true hairdresser pushes the bad energy out and knows how to replace it with good energy. And also when to walk away from certain energy, because a good hairdresser must know how to protect him or herself as well. The inspiration that a beautician—a true beautician—can bring to a person, that person in turn can bring into the world.

"Calla, it is no accident that beautician and magician sound so similar."

I thought and thought about that. I was so grateful for Erbolene's emergency that drew me closer to Ricky, and so thankful that he was sharing his gifts with me. I'd given up on loving him romantically, but I felt that he was teaching me a different kind of love and healing. I knew that I was lucky to have his attention, so I continued to stay late at the Académie now and then, just in case another lesson came my way.

So I was there late after class, sweeping out the work stations, on the night Sukey came by for a visit.

"Sukey!" I said, "what are you doing here?"

"Well, you've been here for months now. I wanted to see where you work," she said.

But then her eyes fell on Ricky, and she strutted right past me.

"Oh, you must be Ricky!" she said, pecking him on the cheek. "I've heard so much about you."

All I could think was, *Ugh! Sukey, you don't even know him!*

But there she was, just standing there in her knee-high white patent-leather boots and a little outfit that showed her belly—a tight little top and totally red vinyl hot pants.

"Sukey," I said, "this is Ricky, my teacher. And Ricky, this is my girlfriend, Sukey, whom I've known all my life."

Ricky said, "Sukey, how fabulous to meet an old friend of Calla's. Who has been cutting your hair?"

"Julia."

"Oh, Julia," Ricky said. "Hmm. Well, turn around."

And so she did.

"I like it," Ricky said, tapping his finger to his lip. "I like the look on you."

"It could be tapered a little bit more toward the neckline," I said.

And Sukey just kept on flirting with him—God! All she'd ever done was flirt, flirt, flirt, since the day she was born, I swear.

Then Sukey complained to Ricky that he was working me so hard that she hardly ever got to see me.

"Well," Ricky told her, "let's just the three of us go out right now. What do you say? Let's grab some cocktails in the Quarter."

So we took the streetcar down as far as it went and then walked on over to the Napoleon House, one of my favorite places. When you walk in, you can just feel how ancient it is, with its peeling paint walls and floors, small rooms and little tables, and bartenders who've been there forever. I mean, I wouldn't know, since I'd never been, but you could almost think you were in Europe!

"Ah!" Ricky said, seeming to catch the European idea in my mind. "Isn't it a shame that they outlawed pure absinthe?"

Sukey said, "Oh, yes! It is."

And I thought, I'm not sure I like the two of them together.

To change the subject, I piped up with, "Now, Ricky, we need to talk about that woman who's coming over from Natchez to discuss those antebellum ringlets."

"Uh-oh, shop talk," Sukey said. "That's my cue to go to the bar." She came back and listened to us for a while, then said, "Excuse me just a minute, I have to go to the bathroom." She came back with yet another drink, and then all three of us chatted some more.

Then Ricky said, "Hey, the two of you are something else. I can tell that you've known each other forever, just the way you look at each other."

I laughed, but then I looked at Sukey and suddenly noticed a kind of tiredness and fragility around her eyes. "Suke," I said, "Ricky's right. Even though we have different schedules, we've somehow got to get together more."

Sukey answered me with a little slur in her voice. "Calla—" but then she stopped herself. She just took my hand and gave me a short kiss on the cheek and a long one on the lips, right there in the middle of everyone. And I could smell bourbon on her, so strong!

Sukey must have seen me grimace, since she said, "I met a friend earlier today, and we had a little quick nip of bourbon—you know, just a shot. This guy, Skip, I swear he's crazy. He said, 'Bring my girlfriend a jigger of bourbon.' So I drank it to make him feel good."

Ricky raised a questioning eyebrow at me as Sukey continued, "But I had to say, 'Look, Skip, I'm a working girl. I have to go to work tonight.' And I do, y'all. So I've got to go now."

"Hey, wait a minute," Ricky said. "Calla, I've been wanting to have you over. Why don't the two of y'all come for brunch in the New Year. Calla, it's time for you to meet Steve, my man of five years now. You two will love each other. What do you say?"

Sukey said, "We would love to!" And all I could think was: Wow, I can't believe he's been with Steve for five years.

"Well, I'm off," Sukey said. "Calla, it was real good to see you. I love you, baby." She gave me a big hug, and it struck me again how tiny she was.

She whispered, "I feel like a squirt next to your long-legged self."

I whispered back, "You make me feel ten feet tall. What else is new?"

We've said this for years.

Then she went, "Ta!" and was out of the room before I knew it, leaving me with my worry.

Chapter 22

1974

On Fat Tuesday, the last day of the Mardi Gras season and the highest of its festivities, Sukey and I headed over for brunch to meet Steve, Ricky's boyfriend, for the first time. Ricky and Steve lived in an upstairs apartment in an old building with high ceilings and slow-turning ceiling fans. Steve was so gracious and kind from the moment he opened the door and gave Sukey and me big welcoming hugs. He won my heart right off the bat.

And their place was beautiful. The floors were old cypress planks, and as you looked around the living room you could see places where the old wallpaper of magnolia flowers and leaves showed through the paint, highlighted by lamps with tiny lights behind crystal teardrops.

"Oh, Ricky, I love this!" I said. "What do you call how this apartment is fixed up?"

"Well, Calla," Ricky explained, "it's Old Louisiana meets Cubana meets Parisian."

"Wow," I said.

"Yeah, wow," Sukey said. Then she asked, "Can I use your bathroom?"

"But of course," Steve said, and led us down the hallway. The bathroom had old fixtures and an extra-long claw-foot tub. Once we were alone in there, I couldn't help but jump around and say, "Isn't this just wild?"

"Yeah," Sukey said, putting a pill in her mouth and swallowing it. "I have a headache." She gave me a wink. You just had to wonder.

Ricky and Steve's kitchen was much larger than mine, so we had plenty of room to stand around and talk while they were cooking. I took the time to take a good look at Steve.

Steve's complexion was as olive as Ricky's was fair. Ricky was the taller of the two, and while he was lithe and sleek, like a tawny cat, Steve was more muscular in build. And unlike Ricky, the flamboyant one always dressed in the latest style, Steve's navy slacks and blue polo shirt were subdued, though no less impeccable. I liked the two of them together.

Ricky got out a big copper skillet and placed it on the stove. "That's gorgeous," I told him.

"You won't believe it, but I got this for five bucks at a garage sale."

Ricky then uncorked a bottle of olive oil, poured just a splash in the skillet, then added a pat of butter. He quickly peeled and chopped a few cloves of garlic, tested the oil by flicking in a drop of water, then added the garlic to the pan.

"Ricky, you're just like a ballet dancer, only with kitchen utensils," Sukey said, and we all laughed.

Then Ricky grabbed two little chili peppers, split them down the middle, removed the seeds, and tossed the pepper halves into the oil, along with the garlic. Next he threw open the icebox door to see what the food gods had left him. In short order he pulled out a carton of eggs and a hunk of sharp, hard cheese that he called Asiago, which he handed to me along with an antique-looking grater.

"That was my dead aunt Bettye Kaye's," he said. "My dad always called her 'a piece of work,' said that she was addicted to Hollywood. But I loved Aunt Bettye Kaye, and I think of her every time I use this grater." Ricky was full of colorful stories.

He instructed me to grate the cheese while he finely diced a little stubble of leftover chorizo sausage, along with a red bell pepper. I was used to being Ricky's helper.

On the counter was an odd-looking mixing bowl. It was cream colored on the inside, but the dark reddish brown outside looked like someone had tapped it all over with a ball-peen hammer, making little round indents. I turned it over and saw "Kla Ham'rd" stamped on the bottom. "Is that bad or just poetic spelling?" I asked.

"Another Aunt Bettye Kaye relic," Ricky said. "She was known in three parishes for her cooking."

When I set down the bowl, Ricky broke eight eggs into it, using only one hand. Then he just *whipped* up the eggs with his wire whisk, adding a touch of cold water and fresh-ground white pepper. Then he plucked the little chili peppers out of the skillet and poured in the eggs. In no time, the deliciously sweet and savory smell of peppered oil, egg, and garlic filled the room. After swirling the eggs around the pan for a minute, Ricky added the chorizo, the grated cheese, and the diced red pepper.

"Now, Steve, my secret ingredient," he announced. Steve picked a shiny little apple from the fruit bowl and tossed it to Ricky.

Ricky pulled the skillet off the fire. He cored, peeled, and quartered the apple in the blink of an eye, then diced it and tossed the tiny pieces into the omelet. After thrusting the skillet back onto the burner he sprinkled the top of the omelet with dried dill. When the egg started to firm up and the mixture could easily slide around in the pan, he slipped an extra long spatula under it, tilting the pan slightly, and flipped one half of the omelet on top of the other. Then letting the folded omelet cook for another minute, he flipped it in the air, catching it back in the pan.

"Bravo!" we all said, clapping.

Steve had started setting the table with plates, forks, coffee cups—all wonderfully mismatched—and linen napkins embroidered with the name of some restaurant. Sukey and I sat down and started tearing off big pieces of crusty French bread, as Steve splashed some red wine into our juice glasses. By then the omelet was done. Ricky topped it off with a dollop of sour cream and fresh dill. It arrived at the table like a starlet pulling up to the theater for a movie premiere, camera flashbulbs flashing, on the arm of Ricky, the leading man. We all oohed and aahed.

"That just smells so delicious," I told Ricky, "but it's way too pretty to eat."

"Not for me," Sukey said. "I'm starved!"

Ricky cut the omelet into four portions and slid them onto our plates. Then I raised my glass of wine and said, "A toast! To Ricky, the master chef."

After we finished eating brunch, Ricky put on some Neville Brothers and I started to boogey. I couldn't help dancing whenever I heard my favorite band. The music got going, and so did I.

"Come on, y'all!"

And soon the four of us were dancing all together, our hips swaying, and our arms high up in the air.

Then Ricky went to the other room and came back with four gorgeous Mardi Gras masks with blue feathers that I couldn't believe were for us.

"Look! Look, look!" Sukey said, as she put hers on. "Please, a mirror, please."

"Mystical blue, just beautiful," I said, turning toward Steve, who was beaming with pride. "You made these, didn't you?"

Ricky jumped in. "Yes, he did! My lawyer, the mask maker!"

"It's a lot more fun than writing briefs," Steve said, grinning at Ricky.

I looked at them and saw two happy people, and my idea of perfect love changed completely in that moment.

We all clinked glasses, and then Ricky stood up to make a toast of his own. "To us!" he said. "To the four of us!"

"To us!" Steve sang forth.

"To us!" Sukey said, swallowing her wine in one gulp, "to us, the Quartet That Care Forgot!"

"To us!" I said. But in fact, I cared about so much.

Then Sukey said, "To the big party!" And we headed out on to the streets for the biggest party in the country.

We stepped into a sea of thousands of people, parties of every kind and stripe and gender—people in costumes, people on stilts with painted faces, men elaborately dressed as women, dogs dressed as kings. The city became one giant party, one giant bar. Before long the crowd began to move like one giant body of music, drumming, bright feathers, sequins, rhinestones, and jewels of every color. I found myself being pushed along by the crowd of people until I could hardly make a decision about where I wanted to go. I didn't like this feeling. When it comes to Mardi Gras I like feathers and rhinestones, but just on Main Street where kids can run alongside the floats and catch beads and candy while their parents sit in lawn chairs visiting and keeping an eye on their little ones.

Chapter 23

1974

A few weeks after Mardi Gras, Sukey and I were over at Ricky and Steve's for the evening. I had been going back and forth about whether to go up to La Luna for my birthday. The three of them were encouraging me to stay in New Orleans to celebrate this year, and as they were suggesting places in town they might take me, the conversation turned to the most unusual bars in New Orleans. I swear, I could not believe some of the things they were describing! At one bar there was a live monkey, they said, and at another, a stuffed alligator as big as the *entire* length of the bar. Then Ricky said something about a carousel bar, and I asked, "What's that mean?" All three of them turned to me, and Steve said, "Calla, have you not been to the Carousel Bar in the Monteleone Hotel?" Ricky chimed in, "That does it, Calla. That's where we're taking you for your birthday." So the four of us made a date.

Because the Monteleone is a famous old hotel, I decided to wear the ice blue linen halter dress that Aunt Helen made for me. It was elegant, not too dressy, and not quite as short as a miniskirt, but still sexy. I had platform shoes that would go with the dress just fine, and some spangly earrings. For a bit of flair, and just to keep that Sukey girl on her toes, I decided to wear the fall I had gotten at a discount through L'Académie. So I put my hair up, weaving in the fall, and ended up using quite a bit of Aqua Net. My hair was long and thick to begin with, so I didn't really need a fall like someone who had thin hair or wanted their hair to look longer. As I stared in the mirror I worried that I looked like a Dairy Queen triple soft ice cream cone. But hey, I was the birthday girl, after all!

JoAnn's shop downstairs was closed, but I could see that she was still there, having a glass of wine with a friend, so I knocked on the window and she waved for me to come in. When I did, JoAnn said right off, "A vision has entered my shop. A vision."

"Is my hair too much, JoAnn?" I asked a little sheepishly.

"Where are you off to?"

When I told her, "The Carousel Bar at the Monteleone," JoAnn and her friend looked at each other, nodded, and said in unison, "Perfect."

Then JoAnn had me walk back and forth a couple of times so she could study me.

"Beautiful. Calla, that dress looks like it was just made for your body."

"It *was*, JoAnn. Made by my aunt in La Luna," I told her.

"I have a vintage clutch in that same shade," JoAnn said to her friend. "Marti, don't you think this outfit calls for a clutch?"

"I'm not sure I can afford a clutch on top of drinks at a pricey hotel bar just now. I have my monthly budget to think about," I said.

But JoAnn patted my hand and said, "I'm sending it out with you as a loaner—to advertise."

"Oh, JoAnn, thank you so much. Do you want me to take some business cards to hand out at the bar?"

Both JoAnn and Marti just laughed at that. Then JoAnn said, "Calla, don't you tell *anyone* that I lent this to you. I have a business to run. I'm only doing this because you're my friend—and my very favorite tenant."

"JoAnn, I'm your *only* tenant," I had to point out, and we laughed. It is so good to have friends. Here I was, nervous as a tick when I walked in, and now I was ready to hold my head high—and I do mean high—and strut out into the Big Easy.

Right before I left, JoAnn said, "Calla, sweetie, take a moment to look at yourself in the mirror before you go. You are *so* beautiful."

I got to the Monteleone Hotel a few minutes early, so I walked around the lobby trying to act like I fit in. And I thought about the fact that this was the first birthday in my entire life that I wasn't in La Luna. All of a sudden I felt like a real grown-up. And I was getting some interested looks from people, if I do say so myself. Then I saw Sukey walking across the lobby. She was wearing high black leather zip-up platform boots, a black leather miniskirt that was more mini than skirt, and an aubergine flouncy Qiana blouse with balloon sleeves. To top off her outfit, Sukey had a purple-and-black-checked newsboy cap perched on that Sassoon cut of hers. Of course, the first words out of her mouth were, "Sometimes I just wish I was five-foot-nine, like you."

Then she stood on her tiptoes and I leaned down a bit, and she kissed me right on the lips, like we always do, and said, "Speaking of tall, look at you! I *love* your hair—but you're going to have to duck when you go through doorways! I'm so glad you didn't wear your usual braid, Calla. Oh, you look so gorgeous! You'll be turning heads tonight, girl, let me tell you. Ooh, look over there—you already are."

She was right. This handsome guy gave me quite a long look, so I looked right back and smiled. He was so busy staring, instead of watching where he was going, that he walked smack into one of those stand-up ashtrays.

Oh my, I could not *believe* the Carousel Bar. It looked like a movie set! There were booths and tables all around, of course, but the bar itself was an actual carousel, like the kind kids ride on. Now, I don't mean the ponies with the brass poles, but the center part that's wood with mirrors, all carved and painted and lit up with hundreds of little white lightbulbs. The backs of the barstools circling around were also carved wood, each with its own brightly painted circus animal, lions and zebras and elephants.

Sukey and I grabbed two stools at the bar, and the bartender asked us what we'd have. Sukey said, "Two martinis, Billy. Make them dry doubles, sweetie pie, with olives."

I don't think Sukey actually knew the bartender, but she was very good at glancing at nametags without a person noticing. I had never had a martini before, but I decided if I was going to have a big-city experience, why not do it on my birthday? When Billy set our frosty cold martinis in front of us, we clinked glasses and said, "Cheers." Then Sukey said, "Here's to the best friend a girl could have. Happy, happy birthday, Calla."

I felt so sophisticated. But when I took a sip of my martini, I just about gagged! It was the worst drink I'd ever had in my life, and it burned all the way down my throat. That made Sukey laugh. "Sweetie," she said, "you have to be bolder when you drink a martini and not take tiny sips like that. Here, watch me."

She proceeded to drain about a quarter of her glass, then she slowly crossed her eyes, which got me laughing. I tried taking a bigger gulp, and it burned twice as bad! "Sweet Jesus Sukey, I can't believe you like these!" I said.

I excused myself to go powder my nose, since I wanted to see how my hair was holding up. When I got in front of the mirror I thought, Lord, it *is* tall. But it looks good. It looks *very* good.

By the time I got back to the bar, there was already a guy on either side of Sukey. No surprise, she was flirting her little butt off. I had to say "Excuse me!" twice to one of the gentlemen—I'm using the term loosely—just to get back to my barstool. The guy looked me up and down, but not in a nice way, like the guy in the lobby. I had about four inches on him, even without my hairdo, so I just stared him down until he slunk away and I sat back down next to Sukey. The guy who was standing on the other side of Sukey was making stupid jokes.

I thought I was going to throw up—and not from the martini. I cleared my throat rather loudly and gave kind of a snort, too. Sukey rolled her eyes and then crossed them again as I said to the joker, "We're waiting for our husbands, who are police officers here in New Orleans, but it has just been lovely chatting with you."

Thankfully he took the hint and moved on down the bar. I attempted yet another sip of my martini, but I quickly came to the conclusion that, birthday or no birthday, I was just a wine and beer kind of gal. Sukey saw me wincing and said, "Hang in there, baby. It's *worth* it for the olive. And like I said, take bigger sips. They go down easier." I noticed that Sukey had just polished off her second double martini, so when she wasn't looking, I dumped the last of mine into her glass. She was right about one thing, though—the olive was just about the best-tasting olive I have ever had.

I ordered a glass of white wine from Billy, and out of the corner of my eye I saw two men in tuxedos staring at us. Great, here we go again, I thought. It wasn't until they'd walked almost all the way over to us that I realized it was Ricky and Steve in *tuxedos*!

"Ohhh! Y'all look like Cary Grant! Two Cary Grants, right here in the Carousel Bar. I can't believe it!"

The three of them proceeded to sing me "Happy Birthday." In harmony, to boot. Lots of people in the bar joined in too. Then Steve and Ricky each gave me big hugs, and they presented me with a beautifully wrapped little box.

I had to stop myself from getting up and pawing them, because I loved them both so much and they looked so handsome.

"Where did y'all rent those?" I said. "At Simonsen's rentals?"

Ricky said, "Oh, Calla, shush up."

"No, Calla," Steve said, "though they do an excellent job of custom tailoring there, if you don't mind having straight pins at the back of your pants."

Sukey and I laughed, and she blew a little martini through her nose.

Ricky added, "But it's worth it to look good for you on your birthday, honey."

He ordered a martini too, but Steve asked Billy for a "Vieux Carré."

"What's that?" I asked.

"It's a cocktail created by the head bartender here in 1938. I believe his name was Walter Bergeron. It's equal parts rye, cognac, and vermouth, with a little Benedictine, Peychaud's, and Angostura bitters, on the rocks. A lovely little New Orleans refreshment."

Now, if anyone else was to say something like that, I would think they were pulling my leg. But that was just Steve. His mind was an encyclopedia of New Orleans.

Then we all got to yakking and joking and having a good time before I eventually opened my gift from them. Ricky and Steve gave me a beautiful vintage bracelet. Then Sukey slid a little box over to me. In it was a pair of lovely little pearl earrings.

"Y'all," I said, "your gifts are so wonderful and perfect. Thank you."

I carefully put my gifts into my clutch. As I looked up, I started to feel a little queasy and disoriented, even though I'd only had one glass of wine and half a martini. I excused myself to go to the ladies' room, but it wasn't there anymore! I knew I wasn't drunk, but there was a wall with a painting where I was *certain* the bathroom had been before.

I began to walk around the bar trying to find the ladies' room, but just kept feeling more and more confused. I turned to look back at Steve and Ricky and Sukey, and *they* weren't there. *I must be losing my mind. Ohhh!*

While I was looking back, I ran smack into a big tall man wearing all these gold chains around his neck. "Oh, I am so *sorry*, sir," I said. "Please excuse me."

Luckily, this was New Orleans, so the man just laughed and said, "Don't worry hon, pretty young women don't run into me often *enough*!" He knew where the bathrooms were and pointed me in the right direction. Once I got in there, I saw that my fall was gone!

I rushed back out to the bar to try to find my fall. I was crawling around the floor between potted plants when Ricky and Steve came up to me, looking very concerned. "Calla, are you okay?" Ricky asked.

I started babbling about how I had been looking for the bathroom and it had disappeared on me and—

"Oh, *honey*!" Ricky said, "I guess you didn't know that the Carousel is a revolving bar! The bathroom changes positions!"

"What! What do you mean? Like the earth revolving around the sun? And the moon revolving around the earth? Or the earth revolving around the moon, or however it is?"

I was patting my head. "Ricky," I said, "my fall has vanished!"

And he said, "Yes, honey, it has. But I know that Steve and I can catch up with it. We saw it go by, hanging off the gold neck chains of a rather imposing gentleman over there."

Well, at least that got us all back to laughing, and Sukey came over to hug me and dab at my eyes with a Kleenex.

Back to my first-ever sip of a martini, though. I did love the olive—I always have loved olives. As nasty as that martini tasted, I had said to myself, "Suck it down. Get that olive, just get that olive." But later, as I lay in bed and thought about the night, looking at my beautiful fall—now mangled on the wig stand—I thought to myself, Calla, some olives just aren't worth it.

Chapter 24

1974

One afternoon I was working particularly late on a dye job. It was a challenging case, as the client had come in asking me to fix a bad dye job she'd gotten the week before that had made her miserable. As Ricky had predicted, I was starting to get a couple of these kinds of referrals a month, as well as building my own loyal clientele. Anyway, as I was working that evening, I glanced up to my mirror and—I swear, it was like I had a vision. The most beautiful man I'd ever seen was standing behind me. He looked slightly Cajun, with dark, curly hair, golden skin, and a wiry, muscular body.

What was he doing at L'Académie? I knew everybody's husbands, and he wasn't one of them. He caught me looking at him in the mirror and gave me a little smile. My customer saw that and said, "Calla, now remember that I want my hair a nice soft black—but with just a hint of brown, not like the hair of some kind of woman with her head sticking out of a hovel in Portugal. I want an uptown black that looks good with things like a deep true red satin."

Oh, what these women tell me!

I couldn't stop glancing at the man, though. I had to keep pulling myself back, thinking, "This is your work, concentrate on your work."

The man had on cowboy boots and old jeans that fit him very well. Those jeans looked like they buttoned up the front, instead of zipping. I don't usually notice things like that on men, but there was something about the way those jeans *fit*. I thought maybe the buttons were part of the reason that those jeans looked that way. *That's not it, Calla. It's his body*. The man just wandered around, looking at the hairdo pictures on the opposite wall.

I could just see myself running straight to him, jumping up and wrapping my legs around his waist and my arms around his neck. *Girl, get a hold of yourself! This is your work. You have a reputation to uphold.*

Finally, I finished the dye job, sent my new client happily back out in the world, and went to the ladies' room to clean up. I looked in the mirror and thought, *Hmm, why don't I loosen my hair a little bit around the sides. And you know, I could use another little dab of lipstick and just a little bit of blush.*

But when I came out, the man was gone. I was surprised at how disappointed I felt.

I was cleaning my station a few minutes later when Ricky called out from his office. "Calla, come on back here."

I did, and the man was right there, sitting across from Ricky. "Calla, I want you to meet my cousin," Ricky said. "This is Sweet, Sweet Chalon. His boat is in New Orleans for repairs, so he just dropped by to see me."

"How do you do?" Sweet said, standing. I must have been just staring, because Sweet then offered, "You are Calla?"

"Oh," I said, a little embarrassed. "Yes, my name is Calla Lily Ponder."

"Calla Lily Ponder? Calla Lily." He twirled his tongue around my name, and somehow I could see all the calla lilies lined up, just waiting for his tongue to say their name again. Calla Lily.

I realized that I was staring again, so I made myself choke out, "What brings you to our lovely city?" Then I let go a laugh that was a little too high, and told myself, *Bring it down, Calla.*

He said, "Well, my boat engine. I run my own boat—I ferry the guys out to the oil rigs in the Gulf. I just came in from Cutoff, which is one of my usual stops, and my engine was making a noise I didn't like. So I brought it in, and then I thought I'd drop in to see Ricky."

"Ricky never told me he had a cousin who came to town."

"Well, I don't come in often. I usually see Ricky back in Donaldsonville with the rest of the family."

I reminded myself to scold Ricky later for waiting so long to introduce us. "Well, how do you like it in the Big Easy?"

He said, "I think New Orleans is far out."

I just laughed. I loved the way he said "far out."

"When I come to town, I like to go get myself fed at Felix's with some really good oysters. Just line them oysters up with saltine crackers, a good dipping sauce, some Dixie beer, and I'm in heaven."

Ricky said, "Calla, Sweet's having dinner with Steve and me tonight. Why don't you drop by?"

And I thought, Sweet knows about Steve. That was another good sign, as far as I was concerned. Not every guy could handle his cousin liking men.

I said, "Yes, I would love that. I'll just run home and change after work."

"Don't keep us waiting all night," Ricky joked. "I know how you gals can draw out getting dressed."

"I won't," I promised.

I left them and got my station clean and set up in record time. Then

I ran home, undid my braid, and shook my hair loose. I flung open my closet doors, thinking, What am I going to wear? After rummaging around, I pulled out a pair of black jeans and my three pairs of cowboy boots: the red leather ones, the black ones with purple running up the side, and the brown ones. The brown ones looked too scuffed, the red leather seemed—oh, I don't know. It just felt natural to wear the black with the purple stripes.

That meant I should wear my purple crepe shirt, which had a V-neck and sleeves that came down in big poufs. I loved that shirt. And I'd wear my braided belt with the little tassel.

And underneath—I rummaged through my underwear drawer and came across the lacy black panties Sukey gave me for my birthday a couple years ago. Back then I'd said, "Sukey, they're too fancy! I'm never going to wear them! And look at how they're cut—so low on the hips and high on the legs! I'd feel naked."

But tonight I looked down at those panties and thought, *Oh, you're just going to make me feel so flirty tonight.*

I was almost all the way to Ricky's when I heard bells chiming, even though I was nowhere near a church.

"That's a sign," I told myself, as I walked up Ricky's front steps. "Bells chiming."

Steve opened the door, and I gave him a big kiss on the cheek. Then Ricky called out, "Calla! Come on in! Pop you open a beer."

"Thank you."

And there was Sweet. He'd changed into a plain black T-shirt. You know, not a lot of men in Louisiana wear black. Usually it's just the guys who play music. That black T-shirt looked great to me. It fit him well, and I could see Sweet's muscles at the sides of his stomach.

"Hi, Calla," he said.

And the way he said it was so courteous, but also playful. It shifted me from being nervous and tongue-tied to actually feeling relaxed.

"Y'all go ahead and sit down," Ricky said. "I'll fix you up something to eat. But first I'll bring you a little something to snack on."

Sweet and I sat on the couch together. Not a big man, I thought, but wiry. Maybe a little bow-legged. "Have you ever ridden in a rodeo?" I asked, before realizing that might sound rude.

He said, "It's amazing you'd ask me that. When I was in high school, I used to bull ride until my mother made me quit. You know, just around in small-town rodeos."

"Really!"

"Yeah, and I am flattered that you might have thought that."

I was glad he didn't ride the rodeos anymore. I didn't want this man to get hurt, I wanted his body to stay just as it was. I could feel myself blushing as I felt his body touching mine.

"Yoo-hoo!" Ricky came over with a bowl of spiced cashew nuts.

"Oh, my favorite!" I said. "I can't get enough of these."

Sweet said, "Same here. I just love cashews—spicy, salty, any way I can get them. I could cover the side of a building with all the empty cans of cashews that I've eaten."

"I can just picture that," I told him. "All those cans sticking out. In the middle of each one you could start a plant growing, put something in that really spreads, like ivy."

And he said, "Or honeysuckle."

Then we just looked at each other. The word *honeysuckle* just hung there in the air between us.

I can't even remember what Ricky made for dinner that night. All I could do was look at Sweet, listen to his voice, watch his eyes under those long lashes. Think about reaching out and stroking his golden skin.

Sweet—that was the right name for him.

The thrill of meeting Sweet was all mixed up with the excitement of Ricky's new salon opening. He and Steve had bought an old house on Burgundy Street just outside of the Quarter, on the other side of Esplanade. Their plan was to live in part of it and convert the front rooms for the salon. When they'd first bought the house, the yard in back was a run-over, junk-filled mess, all overgrown and tangled up in weeds. But Ricky and Steve rolled up their sleeves every day after work and gradually transformed that place into the most beautiful and magical garden.

Right in the middle they had discovered a fig tree all covered over in vines that became the centerpiece of the garden. They'd also put in banana and lemon and kumquat trees and all kinds of fragrant flowers. And they'd strung little white lights everywhere and installed *two* fountains—one with the water shooting out of old bowling balls! Then Ricky collected all the broken-up china he could get and called his friends and said, "Okay, it's time for hammering. I'm going to make cement pavers for the garden path and stick that china in it."

Ricky even drove out to Metairie to pick up a bunch of blue and yellow pottery and told his neighbors, "Listen, if you've got any extra pieces of garden decorations, I want them—I don't care how broken they are." Over time they gave him pieces of old fountains and iron gates and little angels with their wings broken off, and the walkway he eventually made was like a little piece of heaven, surrounded by the most beautiful and unusual plants and flowers I'd ever seen. Then one of Ricky's neighbors told him that an antique chandelier of hers had crashed down out of the ceiling and was going to be thrown out. Well, Steve and Ricky got that cracked-up chandelier rewired and rigged it up right in the beautiful flourishing old fig tree at the center of everything.

"The garden still has a ways to go," Ricky said, as he showed me around one day. "But we're getting there!" Ricky and Steve had also gotten themselves a dog, a little cockapoo who they named Ginger Rogers because they claimed she danced when she walked. She loved to prance around their gorgeous garden, in and out of the gardenias.

I loved the way they fixed up that old house. They called the decorating style "Cuban Chinoiserie," with a "Caribbean Fiestaware" kitchen done in turquoise, yellow, orange, and red. You walked from the colorful kitchen through screen doors out onto a porch that had turquoise-painted plank floors and white tables. It was a wonderful place for customers to sit and wait and take in the garden.

I could not wait for the salon to open. Besides Ricky, I would be the only other stylist. We all discussed a bunch of names for the new salon, but he had the confidence to keep it simple. So Ricky's was born.

Finally the big night came—the opening party for Ricky's! It took me ages to decide how to wear my hair, since after all, a cosmetologist's look is her best advertisement. Ricky taught me that. Finally I settled on keeping it long, but curling it into what the latest hairstyle publications called "cocktail-party look," soft and feminine, but romantically coiffed. It would be basically a deep dip of a wave, with long, loose ringlets held in place by a camellia.

I picked a little floaty chiffon dress to wear, with red and white swirls. It was ruffled around the neck and came down low, but not too low. Its waist was cinched in, and then the skirt flowed down. The ruffles around the skirt were just a little bit longer than mid-thigh to keep the lines going.

When I got to the party, the salon couldn't have looked more beautiful. The entire front was decorated with sparkling Christmas lights, cowboy hats, all kinds of feather boas, Mardi Gras beads—you name it! Its French doors were flung wide open, and I could hear Ella Fitzgerald on the stereo.

I got there a little bit early, to help set up.

"I'm here!" I said. "Where's my apron?"

"Ooh, la-la!" Ricky said as he greeted me. "My dear little Calla Lily of the Valley! Turn around. Yes, you look so flirty, sexy, fresh, and innocent—if I weren't into my man a hundred and ten percent, I'd be into you."

"Well, that's a compliment!" I said. "Give me a kiss." And he gave me a kiss on each cheek, like the French do. Then Steve came in and asked, "What are you doing, flirting with my girlfriend?"

Both Ricky and Steve were dressed to the ninety-nines, as they put it. Ricky was wearing a pair of vintage white baggy linen pants with a gold silk shirt, and beige-and-white two-tone shoes. Steve wore a stylish pair of slacks with a light pink oxford cloth shirt.

We were in the kitchen when the first guest to arrive was JoAnn, whom I'd invited. "Don't worry," she told me. "It doesn't hurt me one bit that you are wearing a new dress. I am not offended. Not to worry, doll, my ego was removed surgically years ago."

Then she gave me a big kiss. She had picked up a stunning indigo-colored vase as an opening gift. My own gift was a vintage set of beauty tools—combs, brushes, and a manicure kit.

Then, as I was tying on my apron, who should appear but Sweet, carrying a big heavy pot from which I could smell some good cooking. Ricky hadn't told me his cousin was coming! My heart was racing. I'd just recently started wearing M'Dear's ring on my hand, and now I rubbed it, trying to calm down.

Sweet gave me a big smile as he walked up and said, "Calla Lily, it's good to see you again."

I just melted at that smile. Sweet had on a pair of tight bell-bottom jeans with the most beautiful embroidery down the side, spelling P-E-A-C-E. I liked that he wasn't afraid to wear them. And his shirt was aqua, with rolled-up sleeves that were kept up by little buttoned tabs.

His hair was long—thick, black Cajun hair—and those dark eyebrows set off his blue-blue eyes. Oh! He was gorgeous.

"Did you come early?" I asked him, immediately realizing what a dumb question it was.

"I did. Ricky wanted me to cook up some red beans and rice and bring it over."

Joining us, Ricky said, "Yeah. My cousin is a master of red beans and rice, especially."

"Hey, don't brag too much. Calla hasn't tasted mine yet."

"Oh, I bet I'll like them a lot," I said. *I like any man who cooks.* "I come from a family where men cook good, and I appreciate it." *Oh, brother! Everything I say seems to come out wrong.*

Ricky picked up on my nervousness. "Calla, have a gin and tonic. I think that's what the doctor ordered."

"I think you're right."

He made one for me. I drank it a little quicker than usual, and it did help me feel less self-conscious. But whenever I got near the stove where Sweet was stirring the red beans and rice, my insides started fluttering like the ruffles on my dress.

"What've you been up to?" he asked me. "How's the hair business?"

"It's great. I'm so excited about the salon opening," I told him.

"Well, Ricky sure is lucky to have you coming with him into the shop."

I laughed. "Well, I don't know about that!"

I went out to see how Ricky and Steve had decorated the yard for the party. Then Sweet did the dearest thing. He brought out a little piece of French bread with warm crab dip, one of Steve's specialties.

"Just thought you might want a little bite with that gin and tonic," he said, and popped it in my mouth. "But I have a hard time just spreading this dip on a cracker. I want to dig into it with a spoon."

"I feel the same way," I said, swallowing the delicious dip. "I swear, I could swim in it. I'm a real swimmer, and I ride horses too—although not here in New Orleans, of course." *Oh God, is there anything more idiotic I could say?*

"I wondered how you got such strong arm and back muscles," Sweet said.

I reached behind me and felt my muscled swimmer's back, then I told him, "And here I meant to look feminine in a 'soft cocktail kind of way.'"

"You do," he said. "But you look strong too, and that's beautiful to me."

I started blushing, so it was a good thing Ricky called me just then to help arrange the hors d'oeuvres.

On the way back in, I showed Sweet the walkway with everyone's china embedded. Somehow, remembering all that hammering made me bold.

I said, "Sweet, I've been thinking about you, and I was wondering—" *Oh my God! My mind went blank!*

Sweet didn't seem to notice.

"I've been thinking about you, too," he said. "I would have called, but I work long stretches sometimes, you know, piloting the guys out to the rig. I know it's only been two weeks since I met you, but I find myself thinking of you at the oddest times. Like when I'm shaving. Isn't that crazy?!"

"Oh, *no*," I told him. "That's not crazy at all. When I wake up in the morning and make coffee, I'll be pouring water into the coffeepot—you know the way it sounds, water going over the coffee grounds—and that makes me think of you. Now *that's* weird, huh?"

"No, it's not weird."

We looked at each other. Sweet's eyes were such a deep, dark blue. His lower lip was just a little fuller than the top.

"Sweet," I said. "Boy, that's a name."

"I know, the girls started to call me that in school, and the name stuck. It's a name to live up to. I'm not always sweet, but I try. Now Calla Lily, there's a name with a story, I bet."

"Yeah, but I'm not what you think of when you think of a flower."

"But you really are. You're not a rose or a super-sweet gardenia. You're like, oh, like the note of a song on the stem of a flower."

That gave me butterflies inside.

"I'd better go help Ricky with the hors d'oeuvres," I said, trying to keep my voice from trembling.

By this time, guests were streaming into the salon. The stereo was blaring Ricky's favorite, early Louis Armstrong, though the music was almost drowned out by glasses tinkling and loud squeals of laughter.

Sweet and I pretty much stuck together for the rest of the night, with the party swirling all around us. At sunset, we wound up back in the garden, where I could smell lemon blossoms and see the magenta glow of bougainvillea in the changing light. A young man dressed in a sailor suit with short pants, carrying a tray of champagne flutes, stopped to offer us two. We toasted each other, and then Sweet was holding my hand. I felt that we were alone on a little boat, out there among sparkling lights and garden torches, a little boat adrift in the sea of people.

Then I heard, "Calla, babeeee!" and the sound of glass shattering on the china walkway. "'Scuse me, getoutamywayou, would ya, babe? And oooh—love the look."

It was Sukey, and she was making her way over to us.

At that moment it seemed the fountain stopped gurgling, the music stopped playing, the people stopped laughing.

I got a bad tingling feeling in my hair. The little boat that Sweet and I made was rocking on wild waves.

"Hey you darlin' thing," Sukey was saying to a man whose arm was draped lightly over the woman next to him. "Hey you darlin' thing. I bet I got something you want."

Oh, no. No, Sukey. No!

I wanted to pull Sweet through the crowd and flee from Sukey. What would he think? He barely knew me. I didn't want him to think that I was like her. But Sweet saved me by taking my hand. "Let's go inside for a while, see what Rick and Steve are up to," he said.

"I'm here. Sukey is here. La *Suke* is ready for action." She was shouting now, slurring her words. And I realized just how drunk she was.

"Who is that?" Sweet asked.

"Uh, I think that's my best friend Sukey," I told him, biting my lipstick off as I felt my heart beat faster.

"Are you okay?" Sweet said.

"Yeah, I'm fine."

"Callll-lah! Baby!" I heard Sukey yell, "It's Sukey, it's Su-*kay*!" Then it was like she had some kind of radar. She came straight at me.

"Oooh," she said to Sweet, as soon as she noticed him, "who—are—you?"

And then she just flung her arms around his neck and wrapped her legs around his waist.

"Baby, you are something else!" she said, planting a big, wet kiss on Sweet's cheek. Then she let go of him, and I thought, Oh, God—thank you, thank you. Let her back away, just back away.

But Sukey was just gearing up.

"Yes, you *are* what I want! You *are*! C'mon, baby, let's strip!"

And then she actually started to unzip the back of her dress, let it drop, and was standing there in her tiny bra and panties. I was about to cry.

"Sukey!" I said, "get out of here! Don't even put your dress on. Just pick it up and *drag your drunken ass out of here*! I've had it with your drinking! Now, *get out*!"

"Oh, Calla!" she slurred, "don't be such a goody-goody! That's all you've ever been—a goody-goody."

"Don't you dare talk to me like that!" I said. "I've known you since we were little girls." I was sobbing. *"Now get out!"*

The next thing I knew, Ricky was there, and he had his arm around Sukey.

"Suke, I think it's time for you to go home."

She tried to shove him away, saying, "When I leave is not up to you!"

Steve stepped up and said firmly, "I think it is. It's our party."

I wanted to reach out, grab Sukey myself, and throw her out the door. Steve must have seen the look on my face, because he came over to me and whispered, "Calla, it's okay."

Ricky had hold of Sukey and was walking her out, half carrying her naked little self. I closed my eyes, unable to look at Sweet.

"I'm so sorry," I told him. "I'm just so sorry. I told you that I'm not always a flower. Sometimes I'm not pretty at all!"

Sweet pulled me to him and said, "I don't know anybody who could have continued to be a flower at the sight of her best friend plastered and jumping all over me."

He laughed, and then he held my hand and kissed me really lightly on the lips. Again, it seemed like the party faded, leaving only the tinkling of the fountain, the sparkly lights, and Sweet Chalon holding me in his arms.

That was the opening night party for Ricky's, and the opening night of my love for Sweet.

Chapter 25

1974

Sukey laid low for a while. Ricky guessed that she was embarrassed to death, which I was sure was true. But I missed her, so I decided to break the ice and just go out and have fun with her. I asked Ricky and Steve to come with us.

"Let's make it coffee," Steve suggested. "I think we'll be more likely to see Sukey at her best in the daytime."

So I called Sukey and asked her to meet us at the Café du Monde, down by the river. I rode the streetcar down St. Charles and then walked along Chartres Street, thinking about my friend and her drinking. Sukey and I arrived at the same time, and the boys already had a table. She apologized for her behavior at the party, admitting that she couldn't remember much.

"All I know is that you were mad at me, Calla, and that Ricky and

Steve kicked me out. I want to tell you why I was so out of control that night. I'd lost my job. Bunny Mother Trixie fired me."

"Why?" Ricky asked.

"Well, I don't know," she said. "It was something about how she didn't like the way I was, quote, *behaving* in the club. Like I would do anything wrong! I mean, I was the best in my Bunny training class. Even Bunny Mother Trixie said so. But she said over the past year or so I'd slipped and no longer met the club's high standards. That is just bull. You want to know the real reason? It was jealousy. Bunny Mother Trixie and some of the girls hate the fact that all the key holders love me. I was the best!"

None of us could say anything. So we all just sat there eating hot beignets, waiting for Sukey to go on.

"I even told that to Bunny Mother Trixie," Sukey said. "I said, 'You know, I can't help it if the men like me more than the other girls. How is that my fault? Isn't entertaining the key holders the whole point of the Playboy Club?' But she didn't even answer. She told me I could no longer represent the Playboy Bunnies. She took away my outfit. And"—Sukey started sobbing—"she even took away my little bunny tail!"

I began to think about when I'd talked to Sukey in the evenings. She usually went to work around seven and came home after three in the morning. But there were times when she'd called me at ten or eleven, and it would be hard to understand her because she'd be slurring her words. "Aren't you at work?" I'd ask.

"No," she'd say. "It was a slow night, so they sent some of us home." Or she'd say, "You know how I get bad cramps at that time of the month, so I told the Bunny Mother I had to get in bed with the heating pad."

Then there were the times when Sukey came to visit and just

cleaned out all the beer in my refrigerator. I *always* had a six-pack in the refrigerator—you don't live in New Orleans without that—and when Sukey left, it would always be gone.

I realized I had been very worried about my dear girlfriend.

Sukey was crying hard now, and Ricky and Steve were soothing her. Suddenly, she stood up and said, "I've got to go."

She took off so fast that she forgot her purse, a big burlap bag from India with ivory handles and an elephant on it.

The three of us sat there in silence for a while, just drinking thick coffee out of our heavy, ivory-colored mugs with people swirling around us, boats going by on the river tooting their horns, and the sounds of a saxophone coming from somewhere.

Finally, we all looked at each other. "Poor Sukey," I began. "She loved that job."

"I don't blame her for being upset," Ricky said. "But do I blame her for blaming other people when she screwed up."

"Do you think she did screw up?" I asked, knowing the answer in my heart.

"Well, it seems possible," he told me.

Steve was the one who said it. "Our Sukey is a drunk."

I had to jump to her defense. "Don't say that, Steve! Sukey's always been high-spirited. She likes to be outrageous. And if she got fired, I can understand why she'd drink too much."

Ricky was silent, so I turned to him and said, "Ricky, can't you please tell Steve not to talk about Sukey like that?"

He didn't answer and just looked away.

"Come on, Ricky! We all love Sukey. She's our dear friend," I said.

"Calla Lily." Ricky looked back and gently told me, "I can't ask him to take it back."

"Well, fine," I said, "Y'all just go ahead and think what you want." Then I picked up Sukey's purse and left. I didn't even say good-bye.

When I got home, I put on a Curtis Mayfield album. He always made me feel better with his wonderful, kind, falsetto voice singing to the soul, "Everybody knows that it's all right, whoa, it's all right." And I danced like M'Dear taught me to, because really, dancing was the way I prayed. After a while, I gathered the nerve to open Sukey's purse. Inside was a pint of Smirnoff vodka. She must have bought it before meeting us. *Oh, Suke!* I thought. *Oh, baby. Oh, Suke.*

But I wasn't about to give up on my best friend. I made a date for just the two of us to go listen to jazz at Preservation Hall. It started out late at night with slow music and good blues and then built up to Dixieland.

Sukey was late picking me up. I waited fifteen minutes—no big deal. I waited half an hour. With Sukey, that was nothing special. But then two hours went by, and she didn't show up. I called her. No answer. I kept calling and calling, and still there was no answer.

Something could have happened to her. Anything can happen to you in New Orleans. Anything can happen to you anywhere.

Another hour went by, and I was worried sick, so I called Ricky and Steve. They were already asleep.

"Look," I said, "I'm sorry to wake y'all, but it's late and Sukey hasn't shown up. Will you give me a hand? I mean, can we go look for her?"

"Okay," Ricky said, "just give us a half an hour to get there."

I sat down, and I thought about the times that I went over to Sukey's house. The times I thought she was sleeping really sound because she worked those wild hours. I'd gone over and tried to wake her up. "Hey, Sukey!" I said, "Get up! C'mon, let's have a Coke and go walking outside. There's some nice air—a little breeze is going—and it's not too hot."

I remembered her not waking, not even stirring. And I realized she wasn't sleeping—she was passed out. It was starting to seem like Sukey had a private life, and that her private life was all about drinking.

We drove Steve's VW bug over to Sukey's favorite bar over on Esplanade. I'd never been there, but Ricky and Steve seemed to know it.

In New Orleans, bars are allowed to stay open all night, and this place was jumping. The Hook, Line & Sinker was a small place, only a couple of tables, but every seat at the bar, which had a blue light shining up through it, was filled.

Ricky and Steve walked up to the bar, and I followed. The bar was glass—a big aquarium with real live fish swimming in it, back and forth like snakes. I couldn't help but wonder how those poor fish could breathe, being sealed in that way, and how it was to have drinkers staring down at them all night.

Ricky asked the bartender, "Hey, have you seen my friend Sukey?"

"Yeah, Sukey, the one that likes her vodka. Uh-huh, that Sukey can throw it down! We've got to pick that gal's head up off the bar at least a couple times a week."

"We don't want to hear about it," Steve said. "We just want to know if you've seen her tonight."

"Yeah, I've seen her tonight," the bartender said. "She took off with some guy. Look, I run a good bar here. I don't like young girls laying their head up on my bar. I've told her before, 'I don't like the way you drink, and I don't like serving you.'"

"Do you have any idea where Sukey and this guy went?" Steve asked.

"You might try that bar over by the river, where all the French sailors go. It's called Simmy's."

"Thank you." Steve slipped the bartender a five-dollar bill.

The bartender said, "I hope you find your friend, and I hope you can dry her out. I really don't need her business."

So we went back out into the night, and we found Simmy's. Inside, the music was playing loud, and there were sailors everywhere, and sure enough, there was Sukey at a table with three sailors. But she wasn't really with them. Her face was flat down on the table, and the sailors were ignoring her. They just kept on talking to two other women.

Meanwhile, Sukey's glass had fallen over, and her face was just lying in bourbon.

"Calla," Ricky said, "why don't you wait outside? This is ugly. You don't need to see it."

"It's Sukey," I told him, "so I'm going to help."

Ricky and Steve got Sukey up. They were right—there wasn't a whole lot I could do. It's not easy to carry anybody—even little Sukey—who has passed out. They dragged her out to the car and laid her down on the back seat. We drove her back to Steve and Ricky's place, where they sat her up, put on a pot of coffee, and got her to drink one cup after another. Finally, she came fully awake, looked at us, and started to vomit.

"Jesus Christ!" Ricky said, picking Sukey up and rushing her to the bathroom.

"Help me," he called out. "Steve, can you help me get Sukey under the shower?"

I said, "No, Steve, let me go in there. I'll do it."

I rinsed all the vomit off her, then I soaped her up and I washed her hair. I imagined that rain water was falling down over her, washing her clean. I massaged her head with shampoo and saw all the darkness flow into the La Luna River. "Let it flow into the river," I heard M'Dear saying. "The river can handle it. The river can wash it all away." And I could see that Sukey's life had to change. No way could we go through this again.

I dried her off and helped her into bed. She stirred for a moment, her eyes looking terrified. "You'll make it. Remember: you're a La Lunette," I whispered.

When I came out, Ricky said, "This is not the first time—you need to know that, Calla. Sukey has called us to come get her when she can't even tell us where she is, just crying and begging to be rescued. Then, when we get there, she's passed out. Sometimes she fights us."

"Why didn't y'all tell me?" I demanded.

"Because this is New Orleans, so people act up. And because, unlike a lot of people we know, Sukey wasn't doing drugs. She was just hitting the bottle too hard. We thought it would end. We'd talked to Sukey, and she promised that she'd get a hold of herself. But she kept going back to that Hook, Line & Sinker."

I said, "Oh, the fish, the fish in that horrible bar—" And that's when I started to cry. "We ought to do something, shouldn't we?"

Steve said, "No, we don't have to do anything. It's really Sukey who does."

Ricky and I both stared at him.

"Hear me now. We all love Sukey, but I've had situations like this before, at home, with my family. You have to love enough to let it be hard. If you love Sukey, then you'll let her hit *rock bottom* and *crawl* up as best she can. Don't throw a lifeline. She'll just go back and drink. You have to let her crash."

"Oh, God!" I said. "Steve, you're not saying that we're just going to sit here and watch our Sukey hurt herself?"

Steve said, "Right now, all we can do is let her play this out and be there for her when she wants to straighten up."

We talked and talked all night, Steve, Ricky, and me. We put Sukey to sleep wrapped in a nice duvet on the floor, where she wouldn't do too much damage if she vomited. It must have been close to dawn when I stepped out onto the sleeping porch off Ricky's bedroom. The fingernail moon still hung in the sky.

"Moon Lady," I prayed. "I'm going to put this in your hands. Sukey's like the sister I never had, and I love her so much. Please hold her in your care and guide us about what to do."

I sat there on the porch for a while, smelling the scent of sweet olive in the air. Sukey loved that smell, so intense and pure. It was strange, sometimes, how you could smell it stronger thirty feet away from the tree than right up next to it. Sukey used to put those flowers in little-bitty Gerber baby food jars and put them around her bed so she could breathe in their scent all night.

Then I thought, *Sukey doesn't do that anymore. She probably doesn't even recognize that sweet olive smell. She wakes up in the morning, and she doesn't remember how the person in her bed got there!* Then I thought, *The La Luna is a powerful river, but you have to want to clean up before the water really reaches you.*

I cried and wiped my tears, then I went back inside and said, "Okay, here's my vote. We go ahead and we do hard love. We just let Sukey hit rock bottom."

Ricky gave me a hug and said, "That's my decision, too."

Steve said, "Without Sukey, we're only a trio now. We're not a quartet, but we will be again."

"We will be again," I said.

January 3, 1975
New Orleans

Dear Nelle,

I hope this letter finds you doing just fine. I'm curious to know how your hip is feeling after working all three of our horses so intensely. To work my Golden Princess, then Sable Star, and your Mister Chaz you need to spread it out, don't you think? I can see you right now, saying "Who do you think you are? Telling me what to do?" So I'll stop. Have you been keeping an eye on Papa? He really is spending more time at the fishing camp, isn't he? Teaching music and dance and fishing. I told some of my New

Orleans friends about Papa, and they said he sounds like a character from a movie or something. Hah! I tell them. My whole La Luna is like that.

How is Miz Lizbeth? I bet she is in her garden from dusk to dawn now. I'm going to come home next weekend—or my version of the weekend, with Sundays and Mondays off.

Do you see Renée out with Calla Rose and Little Eddie? That is the hardest thing living here—not being able to see them grow up from scratch, so to speak, and not just from visit to visit.

Here in the Crescent City, Sukey is not doing so well. In fact, she is not doing well at all, Nelle. I'm worried what's going to happen to her if she doesn't slow down.

My work keeps me sane. Like you always told me. Build a career, and you'll have a platform to stand on. I do feel that my career will continue to be the strong place where I can stand, no matter what. I'm only now beginning to understand what you meant, and I thank you for it.

Love,

Calla

Chapter 26

1975

It had been almost a month since I'd seen Sweet at the opening party for the salon. I'd only seen him twice in person, but I found that I was missing him already. He popped into my mind all the time.

He'd called me a couple of times, and we'd talked late into the night, even though he had to be up before dawn. Even though he was beat-tired, he always kept his sense of humor. And he listened on the phone to my worrying about Sukey. He'd make a wise observation here and there, but mainly, he just listened to me. Recently, one of his buddies had to have his boat in dry dock, so Sweet had been working seven days a week to help cover his buddy's route. Two or three times a week, though, I'd get postcards from him, postmarked from places like Barataria, Lafitte, and Ollie. Sweet would write them on his boat and then ask the rig workers he dropped off to mail them for him when they got home.

Then, that dear Sweet! He stopped in New Orleans on his next river trip, and he called to ask me out on an actual date.

"Why don't we go have oysters at Felix's?" he said. "And after that—well, do you like to dance?"

"I love to dance and I don't get to enough. I did tell you that I am the daughter of two dance teachers, didn't I?"

So we had raw oysters for dinner and then went to Tipitina's for some good old rhythm & blues—the kind where every once in a while you get that rolling low bass, Dr. John piano sound. We started out doing a Cajun two-step, and Sweet knew all the little dips. He knew just how to hold me, light as air! You could tell he'd danced like this since he was a little kid, just like me.

Then we started getting down. I thought, *Just play around. Just move it around with your body, Calla.* And I let my body move.

Ohhhh! Just put my foot down—plant that boot on one side, lean over on that hip, and let the rest happen on the other hip. Let my head go down and around, and move my body on that hip, and get that foot up and off the floor. And then I wanted to just lift up, look straight at Sweet, and stick my hand out. Getting so far down, hearing that long snake moan, that when the music stopped my hips were still moving.

Then I opened my eyes, and Sweet was smiling. His mouth was slightly open, which I liked. I had no idea whether he was shocked by me, or whether he really liked me.

As I reached for his hand, I thought, *I don't care if he's shocked! I'm just going to have a good time tonight!* And we did, the two of us, dancing and laughing, cracking each other up. Just playing all kind of games. Just sitting at the table, looking at each other. Just picking up our long-necked beer bottles and putting them to our mouths.

I said, "You know what I like about New Orleans?"

"No, what?"

"Well, I like the way most of my favorite things in this town have to do with your mouth."

He said, "You know, I have always thought that myself. Like singing, right?"

"Uh-huh. Singing."

"Eating."

"Yup."

"Talking."

"Uh-huh."

Then, all of a sudden, I couldn't think of the fourth one. Sweet looked at me and he put his beer to his mouth, holding it there for just an instant too long.

I said, "Singing, eating, talking, and sucking—uh—I mean, sucking crawfish heads. That's the way you can tell real get-down-with-the-seafood kind of people from your sissy seafood-eaters. It's whether we suck the heads or not, right?"

Sweet said, "Exactly! I tell you, in Donaldsonville—man, we get down. At our parties, if they don't suck the heads—they're out on their butts!"

Maybe I'd had too much to drink, but that just got me laughing.

"So, tell me about your boat."

"I'll be proud to," Sweet said. "I went to the university in Lafayette for a couple of years, but all I've ever wanted to do was work on the water. So I worked hard for a couple years, saving every penny for a down payment on a boat. Now I have my own crew boat, and I'm the captain. I'm self-employed, and I pick up contracts with oil-related companies—although to tell you, I'm beginning to wonder about all this oil business. There's nothing pretty about my boat, but it can negotiate almost all the bayous, and the open sea out to the Gulf. I deliver crews and supplies to off-shore and marsh oil rigs. It's not the most glamorous job in the world, but to tell you the truth, I wasn't lookin' for much glamour in my work." He took a sip of beer. He kept the bottle in his hands and gave me a long smile before he put it down. "But maybe now I'm lookin' for a little glamour in my life."

I couldn't help but laugh. "You're a bit of a flirt, aren't you?" I said, taking a sip of my own beer, slowly removing the bottle from my own lips.

"Naw," he said, "just trying to get you to like me. Hell, I'm shooting off at the mouth, aren't I?"

"Well, you could call it that," I said, and smiled.

"But can I tell you just one more thing, the most important thing?"

"Sure." I nodded. "You can tell me as many things as you want."

"The one thing that really gets me when I'm carrying those workers out to the oil rigs. It's those poor guys kissing their wives good-bye, kissing their little babies' heads. And I say, 'Come on, y'all! Ain't gonna be gone but two weeks! You gonna be back before you know it!' You gotta cheer them up a little bit, you know? But I guess even two weeks can be a long time when you love somebody. You know what I mean?"

I thought about the two weeks after M'Dear died. And after Tuck left.

"Yeah, I do, I know what you mean," I said.

And with those words, all the time I'd been missing Tuck, especially that first year when I kept thinking he would come home, just went floating away. I leaned back and stretched my legs out in front of me. I felt like Snow White—like I was just dancing around outside, so happy in a perfect dress, with little birds around me! And I looked at Sweet and thought, *God, could he be my prince? Could he be the one?*

I wanted to know all about this man, and I wanted him to know me. "Tell me about your brothers and sisters," I said.

"Well, I got three sisters and two brothers. Good Catholics, you know. We like to keep on going."

"I know," I told him. "My Papa and M'Dear—that's what I called my mother—always said they weren't quite as blessed as some people. M'Dear would say, 'Well, even though we only have three kids, our Calla makes up for at least four.'"

Sweet laughed. "Two of my sisters are married," he went on. "And the one sister who's single works in the funeral home business run by my mother's side of the family. It's kind of odd to tell people that your family is in the funeral home business. People always think it's weird. But, here I am, talking your ear off while you're sitting there with an empty bottle. You want another beer? Let me get you one."

"Okay."

I watched Sweet as he walked up to the bar. There wasn't anything strutting about him. He just moved with a certain confidence. Then he came on back, holding our beers by the neck, smiling at me.

We took a sip of our beers, then headed back out on the dance floor.

"What a city this is, *non*?" he said. "'The City That Never Sleeps.' Wait—that's New York City, isn't it?" he said, giving a laugh.

"Yeah," I said. "They call New Orleans 'The City That Care Forgot.'"

We sat back down to finish our beers, watching the others on the dance floor. I could feel a strong but gentle connection with this man. When we left Tipitina's to go home, Sweet held the door open for me. He said, "If this is the City That Care Forgot, then maybe I'm in the wrong town." He looked at me for a long time. "Because if I cared for you, I'd never forget."

We went back to my place and stayed up all night talking. I told Sweet about M'Dear dying, about the way she taught me to dance. And I told him about Tuck, who I'd always thought would be my husband, how he'd left and broke my heart.

"Does it still break your heart?" he asked.

"Not really," I told him. "I mean, sometimes it's still there. I don't know if you've ever felt this, but it's like when I had my wisdom teeth pulled. I kept thinking that if I touched my tongue back there, I might still feel them. But of course, they are gone. It's the same with that hurt. I think I might still feel it, but I don't."

"Oh, I'm glad," he said. "I hate to think of you with a broken heart. Hey," he said, changing the subject, "tell me more about your work."

"My mother was a beautician. She knew how to hold people's heads in her hands so that each hair wash she gave was like a little baptism of love and kindness. As she was dying, she encouraged me to see the wider world and to try to find more training—to learn how to touch people in a way they could feel safe enough to lean back into you. Your cousin Ricky is doing that, and I'm so grateful to be learning from him. At some point I plan to return to La Luna and practice, but for now it's the Crescent City.

"Your cousin, besides being one of the most sought-after hair stylists in New Orleans, knows how to bring out the beauty in a person. Just to touch their hair in a way that says, 'I know how beautiful you are. You might not see it yet, but I do.' In fact, that's what I say to clients sometimes. I say to them, 'My gosh! Look at your bones!' 'But I'm embarrassed,' a client will say, 'about that mole on my cheek.' And I say, 'That mole is beautiful! Look how it matches your hair.'

"I just tell them sometimes, 'You're so pretty, you just break my heart!'"

Sweet took my face in his hands and said softly, almost in a whisper, "Calla Lily Ponder, you're so pretty, you just break my heart."

I looked deep into his eyes, and I imagined him saying, *Here's my heart—you can break it. If you want to break my heart, you can. But here it is.*

I felt like I could almost see his heart—this plump, magic organ, so alive and pumping. And yet I knew something could happen to it in an instant—and poof! A heart can get broken in so many ways.

Papa, standing in my bedroom doorway. I'm sobbing on my bed, the year Tuck left me. Without a word. "Calla Lily, believe your old Papa. Tuck is just a boy. He doesn't know anything. There's a man out there, and he's waiting for you. And when he finds you, he's going to see that you're Calla Lily, straight to the heart, you're Calla Lily Ponder."

In that moment with Sweet, I recognized that he was that man.

Sweet closed his hands over mine and said my name again. "Calla Lily Ponder."

He pulled my hands toward him and kissed them.

Then he got up, picked up his hat, and said, "Now I got to go. Time for bed. Thank you." And he walked out of my house. My heart was not the only thing in my body that was turning backflips.

A few months later, even though we hadn't been dating for long, I knew I wanted to take Sweet to La Luna. I'd been going to La Luna every couple months, driving back in my Mustang to check on Papa. So, when Papa's birthday rolled around, and we were planning a big party for him, I thought, Well, this might be the perfect opportunity.

Sweet said, "I would be pleased and proud to come to La Luna with you. Tell me a little bit about your papa, and I'll see if I can't get him a birthday gift."

"Well, Papa is funny but also a little shy. He plays trumpet and the accordion and about twelve other instruments. He teaches music, and he's a great dancer—he loves to dance."

"Hmm, okay," Sweet said. "How tall is he?"

"Why, you going to buy him pants?"

He said, "No, I'm just trying to get a picture of him in my head."

"Let me show you one."

I went back into my bedroom and looked at all the pictures of M'Dear and Papa I had on top of my chest of drawers. I decided to bring out the one of their wedding. I showed it to Sweet, and he asked, "May I hold it?"

He sat down at the table and held it in his hands for the longest time. He looked like he was letting M'Dear and Papa seep into him.

Then he asked, "You dream about M'Dear?"

I was shocked that he knew. "Sometimes," I admitted.

"Well, I hope she comes to you as beautiful as she is—that she just floats her beautiful self all around your bed, Calla Lily."

I paused, and then I told him, "I do this thing at night before I go to bed. I close my eyes, and I try to look outside the window to see the shape of the moon, trying to keep track: the new moon, half-moon, three-quarter moon, and the full moon. Because I do come from La Luna, after all. M'Dear used to take me outside when I was a little girl to show me the Moon Lady. When I look at the moon now, I picture this Moon Lady coming out of the moon, and she mixes together in my mind with M'Dear.

"Then, when I'm in bed, I say, 'Now, cover my bed, Moon Lady. I feel you as you dance at all four points of my bed.' And if I'm quiet enough, I can feel this gossamer bed cover floating over my four-poster bed, protecting me. So I have a sweet sleep almost every night."

"Aw," Sweet said, "Calla, you are something else." And he just kept shaking his head and smiling.

Sweet loved the trip up to La Luna, and the long drive just flew by as we talked and laughed and sang songs. When we pulled up to town, Nelle was there to meet us, and I could tell from the get-go that she was checking Sweet out to see if he was good enough for me. Sweet and Papa hit it off right away. "Son," Papa said, "I have known maybe two other fellows who do what you do. But they never were as young as you when they started. You must have something going for you."

"Well, sir," Sweet said, "I did work pretty hard. I come from hard-working people."

"We do too," Papa said. "But we also celebrate birthdays. Now, I got to tell you that this present from you, Sweet, is fantastic. I'm going to try it on now."

When Papa came back, I like to have died—he was so proud! Sweet had given him a midnight blue polyester shirt, with wide cuffs and a pointed collar. It was so cool—a musician's shirt—and it fit Papa to a tee. He looked so handsome.

"Mmm, son," he said. "You make an old man feel good!"

I loved the sight of Sweet and Papa talking. To give them some time alone, I went into the kitchen and acted like I was still cleaning up after the party. But really I was watching how much kindness came out of Sweet, just talking to my father.

When I rejoined them, Papa told me, "Sweet has just asked me to show him the dance studio."

"Papa," I said, "it's late, I'm sure you're tired. You don't have to."

"I know," he said. "But we got to talking about dancing, and I thought I should see what this boy can do."

Then Papa walked outside and across the lawn to the studio. He unlocked it and flicked on the lights. The room looked a little less vibrant without M'Dear, but it was still filled with magic!

Then Papa made one of the dance moves he used to do with M'Dear. And oh, it made me so happy to see my Papa dance like that. Then he put on some music and said to Sweet, "Okay, let me see you dance with my girl here." The song he chose was "I Got the Sun in the Morning and the Moon at Night."

Sweet and I started dancing, with Papa moving next to us in a slow fox-trot. And I could just imagine him holding my mother, the way his hands held the air in front of him.

When the song ended, Sweet went to choose a new one. Papa started singing as soon as it came on.

"Blue mooon, you saw me standing alooone . . ."

At first, I just felt so embarrassed for my father. But Sweet didn't miss a beat. He just took me in his arms and waited to follow my father's lead until the three of us were in step, my father dancing with my mother in the air and Sweet dancing with me. Then Sweet added his voice to my father's.

Then I joined in and we sang the whole song together, doing the fox-trot. Slowly, the three of us were getting to know each other. Getting to know that we were no longer alone.

Chapter 27

1975

After we'd pulled her out of Simmy's bar that night, Sukey kind of dropped me and Ricky and Steve and mostly hung out with her drinking buddies. We didn't even know who those people were.

I'd go to her apartment to check on her, and I could never tell how many drinks she'd had. Her breath never smelled. Ricky told me that was because when you really get good at being an alcoholic, you start drinking vodka so people can't smell it on your breath.

Sukey would say things like, "Ohh, God! It's so hot today! I've had a glass of ice water in my hand all day long."

I'd think, Does she really expect me to believe that's water in her glass? When she can barely walk? And her words are all slurred?

Or she'd claim to be drinking coffee, but then I'd hear *ice* clinking inside her mug.

The three of us had tried one more time to talk to her about her drinking, saying, "Sukey, we're worried about you. Come on, you've been drinking too much. Things have got to change, Suke. You've got to take care of yourself."

But she didn't listen, and so for a while, we lost her. I kept going over to see her, and each time it hurt me so bad that I would go home and cry.

It didn't help that Sukey wasn't working. She told me that she'd saved enough money from the Playboy Club to take a break and decide what to do with her life. But it seemed that all she had decided to do was drink.

But this was Sukey, my best friend. I had to do something. So one day I tried begging. I took her hands in mine and said, "Suke, this is me, Calla. Sweetie, please don't do it."

"Don't do what?" she said.

"Sukey, you know what I mean. Don't drink anymore. Please don't be an alcoholic."

"I am not an alcoholic," she said, pulling back her hands.

"Sukey, please. I'm not trying to criticize you. I'm just trying to say please come back to us—we love you!"

"I don't want to hear you get all emotional about friendship, okay?" she told me. "I'm tired of that. So you can tell them all—all of you—to stay out of my life. You stay out of my business. I know we've been friends for a long time, but y'all have gone too far. You're sticking your nose where it doesn't belong."

That just about did me in. That night, when I was in bed, I couldn't shake the image of dear little Sukey on the day I met her, dropping out of a tree to show me all her treasures.

Then Sukey stopped answering her phone. And when I'd drop by after that, she was never home. Or else she didn't come to the door.

I didn't hear from Sukey for months, so I was surprised when she called one night and asked me to come over for dinner with Ricky and Steve. I couldn't imagine what we'd find there, and I was terrified.

But when we arrived, we saw that the front steps of her porch were swept, and her flowers had been watered. She must have been watching for us from the window because she called out, "Come on in, y'all. You don't need to knock."

Inside, Sukey's place was spotless. The last time I'd been there it had been filthy, with dried food in plates lying around and every open container stuffed with cigarette butts. But now it had that good smell of lemon oil. There was a glass vase with fresh flowers, and the smells of cooking filled the air.

I looked at our little Sukey, and her hair was shiny. In fact, it was combed and had a great little shape. Her face looked thin and drawn, but she'd done her best to put on makeup. She wasn't wearing a high-fashion Sukey outfit, but her T-shirt and jeans were *clean*.

She said, "Hey, y'all, why not sit down? Don't be strangers. Let's get to eating. I've got a loaf of French bread, and homemade lasagna, and anything you want to drink."

The word *drink* sent chills up my spine.

Sukey had folded the cloth napkins on our plates into flowers, and her table was set simply, but with great care. She brought her pan of lasagna to the table with a cheery "Tah-dah!" She took a spatula and cut out pieces of lasagna to put on our plates, then she had us pass around a big salad she'd made in the hand-carved wooden bowl that her mother gave her when she moved to New Orleans. We filled our plates, but we were all so stunned that we could hardly eat.

She said, "Pulleeease! I don't have two heads. Stop looking at me like I'm crazy. I'd like to say grace."

Sukey closed her eyes, so we all closed our eyes. And I heard my little girlfriend say, "Thank you. Thank you God for this food. Thank you for my friends who have loved me and still love me. Thank you for the fact that through many people's help I am sitting my little butt right here on this chair. Amen."

Then we started eating the lasagna and tearing big chunks of bread off. And as we ate, Sukey spoke. She tried to sound casual as she refilled our glasses of Coca-Cola and lemonade.

She began by saying, "Y'all were right all along, and I know it."

"Sukey, what happened?" I asked.

She paused. "Let me go ahead and spell it out. What happened is . . . I'll start with my hair first, Calla. It didn't look good, and neither did my face. I had bruises on it, right here." And she pointed to underneath her eyes and to the whole right side of her face. "And here. And part of my hair was pulled out. That's why I decided to cut it this short—me and Mia Farrow," and she laughed.

I looked at her and thought, How brave she is being right now.

Sukey continued, "I woke up one morning in a motel room, and I didn't know how I got there. I had been beaten up, and I saw that my wallet was gone. I didn't know what part of town I was in, and when I stepped outside the door, the sun almost knocked me down, I was so hung over. Then I saw that I wasn't even in New Orleans. I was somewhere out on the old highway.

"I didn't have any money. So I went to the front desk—the motel was so cheap that there were no phones in the rooms. A thin woman with blond hair whose roots were showing was working at the check-in place. You could see where she might have been pretty if she wasn't so run-down. I could have imagined it, but she looked familiar.

"I said, 'Excuse me, ma'am.' I could see her wince when she saw my face. 'Um, could you please let me use your phone?'

"She said, 'Yes. Who you gonna call?'

"I realized that I didn't know. I couldn't call Mama because she is in La Luna, and I was too ashamed to have her see me like that. I didn't know if I could call y'all anymore, since I'd pushed you away and told you to get out of my life. So I told her, 'I don't know who to call. Where am I?'

"And this lady said, 'Where you are, girl, is in hell. I've seen people like you come and go out of here. I know that you're in hell, and I'll tell you what you need. You need Alcoholics Anonymous, and you need to go today. There ain't no other road that will lead you out of this hell, sister.'

"I said, 'No, no, that's not what I need! That's for old guys lying in the alley, you know? With spit going down their lips.'

"'Well, look at *you*,' she told me. 'You got a busted-up eye, and bruises and blood on your face, and I can tell where spit was dripping out of your mouth while you were passed out.'

"And I was thinking, How can this woman be so mean to me? I said, 'I only asked to use your phone!'

"'Okay,' she replied, 'go ahead and use my phone. But you didn't even know who to call. Do you know now?'

"That's when I broke down crying.

"'I'll tell you what,' the woman said. 'I'll drive you over to AA. I know where the meeting is, and I know it's held on Wednesday nights. You go on back to your room—I'm not going to charge you anything—but I want you to clean up. I want you to take a shower and give me your clothes, I'll throw them through the wash.'"

The whole time Sukey was talking, I clutched my fork so tight that it left red marks on my fingers. I could not eat a bite, I just watched Sukey's face as she told her story.

Sukey went on. "So I cleaned up, laid down, and took a nap. When I woke up, I had had a dream of some fluttery little figures around me, just all around me, like they were butterflies.

"I walked down to the office and told the woman, 'I'm ready.'

"She drove a big green Dodge that looked like an FBI car. It turns out we were down near Mandeville. She dropped me off at her church. And so I got out and I went downstairs. There, in the basement, was the AA meeting."

Then Sukey leaned closer to us. "Please go ahead and eat your lasagna. I've got some wine if you want it, but—ahhhh, I'm not sure I'm quite ready to serve wine in my house just yet. I haven't gotten to that step yet."

"What?" I asked.

"Well, there's twelve steps to Alcoholics Anonymous. I'll explain them later.

"Anyway, I got to the meeting, and I just sat down and listened to people tell their stories. One by one, they would stand up and say, 'My name is Germaine, and I'm an alcoholic.' And then the person would say what had been going on for the last week. Then someone else would stand up and say, 'My name is Arlene, and I'm an alcoholic.' They went around the room so everyone got to speak.

"Nobody looked at me. Nobody waited for me to put out my cigarette. I puffed on it until it was right down to the filter. Then I stubbed it out, and I stood up. I said, 'My name is Sukey, and I'm an alcoholic.'"

I was in tears again. I got up from the table and went to give Sukey a hug.

"Sukey," I said, "nothing you've ever done in your life has made me more proud."

"Come on, don't get all corny about this, for heaven's sake! It's not like I'm going to change the outfits I wear, y'all! I'm just going to try not to drink. One day at a time. Okay?"

"Okay," we said.

"That sounds really good, Sukey," Ricky said.

"Sukey," Steve said, "any help you need, just give a holler."

"Exactly," I said.

Sukey paused for a minute, and said, "Oh, there's another thing I need to tell y'all. The real reason I got my Bunny ass fired was that I was showing up for my shifts drunk. I thought I was hiding it okay and that the Bunny Mother wouldn't notice—it is a club, after all. They gave me a couple warnings, and some of my close friends there, Bunny Ginger and Bunny Lou, tried talking to me. Even Bunny Mother Trixie suggested that I get some counseling, but I just blew them off."

Then Sukey said, "Well, look at the bright side. Now I have a whole new social life. I can go to a meeting every night of the week if I want. Talk about being booked, huh? The only trouble is, I can't date any of the guys. It's just clear as the nose on my face that I shouldn't try to hook up with anybody right now. It's not a good idea to date, frankly, because for me, dating means drinking. And it has since I was fifteen years old."

I nodded my head and thought, Why didn't I catch this sooner?

It was like Sukey could read my mind when she said, "There is not a thing that any of you could have done to make me not drink. I did it myself.

"And I want to tell you all that I'm sorry. I'm sorry for hurting you. I'm sorry for my drinking and the way it jeopardized our friendship. And I ask you please to forgive me."

She looked back at me first, and tears were in both our eyes as Sukey watched me, waiting, her eyes pleading. And I said, "Oh, Sukey, of course I forgive you." I reached out to hold her hand. We sat there while the boys waited and the lasagna got cold, and together we cried. We held hands like we hadn't since we were girls walking the paths of La Luna, skipping and singing. I thought, Oh, speak your thoughts to Sukey, and so I did.

"Oh, Suke," I said. "Now we can skip together again. And we can play."

She said, "Yes."

And I said, "I forgive you," again.

She reached down to her napkin and blew her nose. "Excuse me, everybody." Then she turned to Ricky and said, "I'm sorry, Ricky."

"Oh, Sukey, baby, of course I forgive you."

As she turned to Steve, he was already nodding, and said, "Yes."

Then we all looked at her, and as a group we all said, "Yes, Sukey. Yes."

Sukey laughed through her tears, and said, "Okay, y'all. Let's eat. I labored over this lasagna. And y'all know that I only cook once in a blue moon."

Then Steve asked her, "So what are you going to do for money, Suke?"

"I haven't gotten that quite figured out. I've still got a little to live on, probably a couple months, maybe three if I watch it. And I've been looking for a job. I interviewed for a position at Maison Blanche. There's an opening in the women's shoe department. I also interviewed for a waitress job at Howard Johnson's. Whichever job I get, I'll take."

As we congratulated her, she revealed her long-term plan.

"I'm also planning to go back to school. I want to become a substance abuse counselor. It's going to take me a while because I need to get further along in AA. But they say that nobody makes a better counselor than somebody who's been through a long period of abusing alcohol or drugs themselves. So I figured, that's the job for me. If I can help somebody—some little girl from some small town like La Luna—from drinking and carrying on too much, then I'll be doing a good thing.

"Besides, I just like the way it sounds: 'Sukey, the Counselor.' I think we should put it in big blue Christmas lights. And then when people come for counseling I'll be dressed to the nines. I can get new outfits that simply scream 'Sukey the Counselor!'" She was laughing, and so were we. A laughter of relief.

&

So it was the four of us, together again. And it quickly became the five of us, as Sweet was coming up almost every weekend now. He'd say, "If I'm on land, I'm coming to see you." It was amazing how quickly and easily he had become a part of our group and a part of my life.

Sweet told me, "Now, instead of me trying to cheer up the riggers when we go out, it's the other way around. You were right: a week on the water seems like eternity when you're missing someone you love. And I love you, Calla, and all that love comes with me when I'm away. When I'm in my boat, when I'm out to sea, you are in my heart. I hate being away from you, but even when I am, it's like we are together. I hope I'm not jumping too far ahead with this thing."

I looked at him. "No." I smiled. "You're jumping just far enough."

Chapter 28

1975

There was a spot uptown where Sweet and I loved to walk when he was in town. Between the river levee and the river itself, there was a crescent-shaped plot of land with no trees or buildings on it, called "the Butterfly." Most of it was covered with playing fields for intramural sports. There was also a dock for excursion boats bringing passengers to the zoo. The shape of the pavilion on that dock gave that land its name.

Sweet and I both loved the Mississippi, and we went to the Butterfly because the river makes a crescent bend there, so it's a dramatic place to watch ships go by. You can sit in one spot and watch a ship for more than three-quarters of a mile as it turns with the river.

One day, after we'd been dating six months, Sweet said, "Calla, how about we take the excursion boat today?"

Though it was winter, it was a beautiful day, so I said, "All right, honey."

We got on the boat, and when we were out in the river, Sweet pulled out a little pair of binoculars, which he handed to me. Then he started pointing out ships and barges, telling me what they were carrying and where they came from. Then he said, "Oh, look at those two tugboats."

I did, and I saw the cutest thing. One of the tugboats had a banner along its side reading, "Will You Mary Me?"

I told Sweet, "Oh, look at that poor guy! He misspelled 'Marry.' Either that, or the girl he's asking is *named* Mary, in which case—"

Sweet grabbed the binoculars from me, pressed them to his eyes, and said, "Damnit, Jimbo!" He gave me back the binoculars, and I looked out at the tug again and laughed. When I looked back at him, Sweet was down on one knee, with one hand over his heart and the other holding a little green velvet ring box.

Time stood still as I struggled to understand what I was seeing. Then it sunk in, and I started laughing my head off again. I couldn't help myself and I couldn't stop, much as I hated to ruin the moment for Sweet. He looked confused and maybe even hurt, but then he broke out laughing too. Everyone around us on the boat started clapping and hollering. Finally I caught my breath long enough to say, "Yes, my Sweet! I do, I do!"

One lovely evening a few weeks later, we'd just finished a supper of red snapper and salad, and we were sitting on the sofa together.

I said, "Sweet, I'm a little nervous to say this out loud, but I have this—it's not a plan, it's a dream, really. After I've had enough training, and after I feel like my hands really can handle almost anything that would come up in the beauty business, I want to go back to La Luna. M'Dear always said if I wanted to come back, I could transform her little Crowning Glory into whatever I want, and I have ideas. I want to invite people who have the hardest hair to come to me, and I'll repair it. And I want people to know that they can come to me. I won't just give them a wash, rinse, and a curl, but I'll touch their heads and I'll take from them and give something back.

"I want to do this soon, probably about the time I'm thirty. I don't want to wait until I'm too old. But I want to do this in La Luna. See, I don't want to live in New Orleans forever. Much as I love it here, La Luna is my home."

Sweet looked at me straight in the eyes and said, "I'll have to think about this. I'll have to think about living in such a small town so far away from the Gulf of Mexico, and how in the world I could keep making a living with my boat."

Sweet frowned just a little and continued, "There's something else about marriage I've wanted to talk to you about."

I braced myself for something frightening that I had never guessed at.

"You learn a lot about women when you listen to your sisters," he said. "And I think it's plain silly in this day and age for a woman to have to take her husband's last name when they get married. I don't want to be held responsible for ruining a great name like Calla Lily Ponder."

Then he sat back, smiling a big smile, and said, "You know, it's exciting to imagine starting a new career. Working on the water doesn't get any easier as you age. La Luna. Okay. From what I've seen of that town, I could live there.

"I don't want to live in this rat city forever, either. It's a good place to be for a while, but it's a tough city. And I sure don't want to raise my children here."

Just the sound of him saying "my children" along with "yes" to La Luna! Happiness flooded through me.

"So you wouldn't mind?"

"No, I'd love it. And I know how I could make a living."

"How?"

He said, "I've got two good buddies who already do something like this. They live in Slidell, and they have themselves a situation which I know I could set up in La Luna. They're union fellows who spend two weeks at home and two weeks piloting boats owned by different companies who contract with the oil companies. I wouldn't have to own my own boat."

I said, "But two weeks away?"

He said, "Well, depending on how much money we wanted to make, I could make it one week away and three at home. I could even take a whole month off once in a while if I wanted to."

I couldn't stop smiling for days.

You'd think after that, we'd get married in La Luna. But after much discussion, we decided to have the wedding in New Orleans. Since Sweet's family was in Donaldsonville, just a ways up on the Mississippi, and mine was farther up on the La Luna, we figured we'd sort of meet in the middle.

Father Gerard agreed to come down from La Luna to perform the ceremony. He'd been our priest in La Luna for five or six years. I've always loved Father Gerard. We used to call him "the bicycling priest" because he rode all over the parish on his bike. When Sweet and I went back home for our first pre-Cana counseling session, imagine my surprise when Father Gerard said, "Sweet Chalon! Are you one of the Chalons from Donaldsonville?"

"Yes, I am," Sweet told him.

"I was down there in Donaldsonville for two years. Why, I may have even baptized you. What's your given name?"

"Joseph DeVillierre Chalon."

"Sure enough, I did."

What a lucky coincidence for me and Sweet to get our counseling from a priest who knew both of us and both our worlds.

Because Sweet and I had our differences, that's for sure. For instance, on the weekends, I like to go to the museum or explore different parts of the city, where Sweet would just as soon relax at my apartment and play cards. But Father Gerard said, "Every couple's going to have their differences. What matters is how you deal with them. You got to learn to *roll* with the punches. And you've got to learn how to say you're sorry, even if you feel like the other one's to blame! You hear me, Calla Lily? And you too, Sweet?

"But there's also going to be so much happiness! You're going to bring each other more happiness than you ever knew!"

Next we found the sweetest little house that was in our price range on the other side of St. Charles. It would take a fair amount of work, but that was okay with us. And I'd have a flower garden!

Then I got my wedding dress. Its overall look was kind of 1920s, and it was all ivory and cream. Aunt Helen made it partly out of M'Dear's wedding dress, which had been made out of her own mama's wedding dress. It had a drop waist like Grandmama's, decorated with a lace band and a rosette from the lace of M'Dear's dress. The same lace trimmed the wonderful boatneck collar, threaded through with M'Dear's wedding ribbon. So I was going into my marriage embraced by both Grandmama and M'Dear.

When I told Sukey I was getting married, she said, "Now, don't you dare make me wear one of those peach-colored bridesmaid's gowns that cost a fortune, need eighteen fittings, and then you can never wear them again!"

"Sukey," I said, "I'm not even going to try! You are my maid of honor, so you can wear whatever you want."

I knew that was a dangerous thing to say, but I thought, This is Sukey we're talking about.

We rented the Jasmine Inn for the reception, a bed-and-breakfast on St. Charles Street. I guess you could call it "shabby genteel." It had big verandas on two floors: the beautiful Victorian Lounge, with its antique fireplaces, huge mahogany doors and bar, and stained glass chandeliers; and the peaceful Alberta's Tea Room, which was full of French stained glass. All the rooms had antique beds and furniture.

And there was a ballroom with room for a band and a bar.

Almost all the La Luna gang came for the wedding and stayed at the Jasmine Inn: Papa, Sonny Boy and Will and their wives, Aunt Helen, Renée and Eddie with Calla Rose and Little Eddie, Miz Lizbeth and Uncle Tucker, Nelle, Olivia and Pana LaVergne, and Mister and Mrs. Melonçon from the café, along with other friends from La Luna.

Then there was all of Sweet's family and friends from Donaldsonville. They wouldn't fit into the Jasmine Inn, so we put them at the Corn Stalk, down in the Quarter. It was an old Louisiana-plantation-style home with a grand front hall, gorgeous bedrooms with vaulted ceilings, and that famous wrought-iron fence around it, with bars shaped like cornstalks. Sweet would stay there too, until we were married.

The night before the wedding, I went out on the upstairs porch of the Jasmine Inn. I breathed in the night air and looked up at the sky. There was the moon, and in it I saw the face of the Moon Lady. "M'Dear," I prayed, "please come to me tonight. I need you! I need you to tell me how to be married, how to be a wife, how to be happy and to make Sweet happy, like you did with Papa. On my wedding day, I need you by my side."

I waited, and I could swear, just for a moment, that I saw a cloud pass over the moon. It was like a wink.

I felt that M'Dear was blessing my wedding.

The next day, all of us girls got dressed together. Sweet, in the old tradition, was not allowed to see me. When we gathered in my room at the Jasmine Inn, Sukey brought an ice chest with three bottles of champagne and a couple of Cokes for herself. I like champagne, but I mean, really! I had to get dressed!

For posterity, we took a picture of Renée, who had been drinking little plastic glasses of champagne poured by Sukey, sitting on the commode. Her beautiful pink gown's huge skirt was thrown up in the back behind her, making her look like a little flower coming up out of the toilet.

As for Sukey, well, Sukey was not going to be caught dead wearing pink, but she at least managed a deep lavender that somewhat blended in. And of course the bottom half was a miniskirt.

Somehow we managed to all pile into cars on time and head to the church. The drivers were honking the entire way. As soon as I got out of the car, I got a fanfare! Brass instruments just started blowing. I had no idea what was going to happen when I told Sweet, "You can just take care of the music." And it couldn't have been more beautiful. Everybody was already hugging and kissing and crying before we even got into the church.

We'd asked Father Gerard to give us a Nuptial Blessing, not a High Nuptial Mass, but our service was still Catholic enough to please everybody. Father Gerard's talk got right to the point: "Okay, Calla Lily Ponder, and you, Joseph DeVillierre Chalon, y'all are here to get hooked up forever. And I'm here to bless you. I want to say that there's going to be sadness in your life together, there are going to be tears, and you need to be ready to reach for that Kleenex and cry. Go ahead, cry out the tears. Let the real tears flow—but no fake alligator tears, trying to make the other person feel bad. If you slam the door and call the other one an ignoramus, do your darnedest to come back in and make up and smooch before the day is over. That's where forgiveness comes in.

"And then there's going to be joy. Because just from talking to y'all, I can say that the two of you are about the funniest folks I've ever met. You also have a great capacity to understand each other and for listening. So I say, keep on listening. Because if you want to be together forever, that's going to take a lot of listening. That's why the good Lord gave us ears.

"You will receive the body and blood of Christ. It comes from a broken body. And how appropriate—because we are human. Because we hurt each other and have to ask forgiveness. And there is no better place to learn about forgiveness than in the vessel of marriage. Now, let your love go forth and heal each other and those around you."

Then Father Gerard said, "Do I have a ring-bearer here?"

Then one of Sweet's nephews stepped out of the pew, cute as could be. With his black hair slicked all the way back, he looked like a baby seal. He brought up the ring on a little pillow to Sweet's best man, Antoine, who took the ring and handed it to Sweet. Sweet held the ring while Father Gerard said the vows, which were partly traditional and partly our own.

We exchanged rings, then Father Gerard gave us both the host. "Now, take this body and blood of Christ," he said.

At the end of Mass, Father Gerard said, "Okay, *laissez les bons temps rouler*!"

Antoine's Cajun band kicked in—fiddle, cello, and the horns that had announced our arrival at the church. They played the Mamou Cajun two-step as Sweet and I marched together down the aisle. The whole church broke out in applause and whistling.

We held the reception in the Victorian Room at the Jasmine Inn. Antoine and his combo kicked off the dancing with that sweet Cajun waltz "Little Black Eyes," a slow fiddle melody. Sweet twirled me out onto the dance floor. He held me, and we just moved together, lightly, like we were floating on air, circling the room past our families and all our friends. I thought, *Never have I felt such complete and pure joy.*

Renée kicked off her high heels and was dancing barefoot with her baby, that sweet little boy, on her shoulders. And Eddie, her husband, didn't seem the least bit concerned that the child would fall. He'd torn off his tie and was doing the Twist with Olivia! Papa was dancing with Nelle, who wore a red satin cowgirl shirt and a pleated skirt. At one point Sonny Boy and Will lifted me up on their shoulders and carried me around the room while everyone cheered them on.

The party was still going strong at midnight, when Sweet and I stole away for our first night together as husband and wife.

People always want to go far away for their honeymoons, like Panama Beach or Cancún, Mexico. But I was lucky. I lived right where I wanted to be.

When we left the reception, Sweet brought me to our new home. I'd seen it in different stages of remodeling and had helped pick the colors and curtains and light switches. We decided to keep as much of the original house as we could, including the yellow claw-foot tub and the old gas range, which worked just fine.

Of course, we had to get a new washer and dryer from Sears, since the ones in the house were old and stinky. I got the kind with a glass front, so I could watch the way the clothes swished around. I've always loved just staring into the front of those washers to see clothes swimming, sudsing, and turning, with the water beating against the glass.

When we got to our house, I was so surprised. The porch was all decorated with twinkly lights. Then, when we opened the door so Sweet could carry me over the threshold, rose petals came sprinkling down on us!

Who in the world would do this?

Later, I found out that with Ricky and Sukey's help, Sweet had gotten all our furniture moved in, unpacked, and placed right where it belonged. Even the dishes and silverware were put away. I didn't have to lift a finger.

"Thank you, Sweet," I said. "Thank you, my husband, the man I will love all my life."

And then Sweet carried me in his strong arms to our bedroom, where we made love, deeply and tenderly, for the first time.

When I lay there with Sweet, together in our wedding bed, it was not as though the bed were a rocket ship—like they sing about in the songs—but rather a round bowl of light.

I didn't have a lot of experience, but those girls in high school were right when they named him Sweet. He touched me in places I'd never been touched, hidden places I didn't even know about myself.

"How do you know to touch me there? Like that?" I asked.

"I just know," he said.

Then he kissed my neck and all the way down my spine.

"How did you know to do *that*?"

"I just took a guess," he said, and then he gently rolled me over. I began to feel my legs relax of their own accord. And somehow I felt myself become larger, my hips become wider.

Ohhh! As we started to rock back and forth, it was as though I could smell the La Luna River, the Mississippi River, and then on out to the ocean. All of that, and Sweet—oh, he is a wave. He is a wave that I can hold on to and ride. And we are out to sea and the waves are floating, they are flowing us back and forth and back and forth, coming into us and then back out into the water, and everything that ever held us back is going out to the ocean. Out to the ocean, which M'Dear said can hold anything, and it does hold anything. And I am holding on to my husband and he is holding onto me, until finally, we each break onto shore like a huge wave. And we land on the beach. And by that time, it has been so good and so full that we both start laughing.

We locked and unlocked one another for hours—until we fell asleep in each other's arms, husband and wife. *So this is what lovemaking can be. I see what Renée means when she says, "Calla, sometimes I just feel so wide open, you know, it feels like there's room for anything."*

Afterward, I watched my husband sleep. And I knew why marriage is a sacrament. Why it's sacred. That night our love was sacred, and I vowed that it always would be. At least one thing in life has to remain sacred, or this whole world will fall apart.

At dawn, I woke up and realized: I'm married! I'm a wife! Oh, it was terrifying to have said that big, fat, holy *yes* to Sweet! Marriage is not an escape hatch, not something to escape into so you can run and hide from the world. In fact, I thought that my commitment to loving Sweet was a commitment to loving the world more than ever before.

Oh, I hoped not just that I could let Sweet be a gift to me, but that through our love he would be a better gift to the world and to the people in his life. That I might be a blessing to him. That I might help him find out more about the kind of man he wanted to be. I knew that I'd married a man who had less fear than anyone I'd ever met. I wanted to see the good in Sweet, to keep on seeing it, no matter what happened, and to accept him for who he was, and for who he might become.

And I wanted to heal him, if he needed it. Because I was certainly in need of healing myself. Every time I thought that I was "put together," I realized that we're *always* putting ourselves together, gathering the world in, letting it sift down and form us.

So I prayed, *Moon Lady, M'Dear, let me love Sweet, that he might be healed and be strong. May your purpose for him and for me in the world be helped along in this marriage. May any ghosts in my past be removed. Moon Lady, who wants to give us the Kingdom of Heaven right here, right now, help me so that Sweet can find the Kingdom of Heaven through the love that we've declared to each other, in the sight of God and everyone we know. Moon Lady, M'Dear, thank you for giving me the gift of my husband Sweet.*

Now, please help me stop trembling, so I can get up and make my husband some cinnamon rolls.

Sukey called me late that afternoon. "Good morning!" she said. "We partied until six a.m.! The Jasmine Inn kicked us out on our butts! I stayed sober the whole night, and was the designated driver for at least fourteen of Sweet's relatives." She laughed and was silent for a moment. "And how are you?"

I said, "I'm married. I'm a wife. I'm a very happy wife."

Chapter 29

1975

After I was married, I started to go to La Luna more often. Many times Sweet went with me. One weekend, Sweet and I arrived late in La Luna on a Friday night. We had breakfast with Papa, then I walked over to Renée and Eddie's while Sweet went fishing with Papa.

"What's wrong?" I asked her over coffee and cinnamon rolls. "You're hiding something from me. You haven't met my eyes all morning."

"Nothing," Renée said. "Nothing's wrong."

"I've known you all my life, Renée. You can't hide from me."

She finally met my eyes. "Tuck got married, Calla. In San Francisco. His wife is from there. That's where they're going to live."

I turned away. Tears started to form in my eyes. Renée handed me a tissue. I brushed her away.

"Are you okay?" she asked.

"Oh, of course, I'm okay," I said.

"I've known you all your life, Calla. You can't hide from me."

"It was a long time ago," I said.

"I know," Renée said, and stepped toward me. I stepped forward, and we hugged without speaking.

It was moments like these that M'Dear called "girlfriend moments." When I'd asked her how she came up with that phrase, she'd answered, "Because I witness it all day long. And because I get to have them with Miz Lizbeth and with Renée's mother. 'Girlfriend moments,'" M'Dear had said. "They're a little like 'mama and daughter' moments."

Yesterday was the most beautiful blue-sky Sunday. Sweet made coffee, and then I sat in his lap in my kimono from JoAnn's Vintage Palace, just one of the many clothing items that JoAnn decided I needed. We had our Sunday breakfast of coffee and cheese biscuits.

Then we got dressed and just started out walking. Most everything was in bloom, and there was that spring excitement in the air that just seemed to jump from the flowers right into you. I swore I could smell flowers in my hair and on my skin.

Sweet liked to take things in like I do and not talk too much. But when he did talk, it was to point out things that I would have never even noticed. That day he took me out on his boat, and he just turned off the motor and let us drift. "Feel the river," he told me. And I felt so embraced by her and how her strong, steady current moved us along.

"Everything changed for me when I realized that the La Luna River flowed into the Mississippi," I told Sweet. "If I moved to New Orleans, I would always have a ribbon of connection to home." And oh, I really felt it in my body on the boat with Sweet.

Seeing New Orleans from a boat makes you realize, from a different perspective, that when you live in this city, you are living underwater—the water of the enormous Mississippi River is *above* you. In La Luna we just took for granted that the La Luna River was below us, but here I sometimes feel like I'm living in an exposed place that could get washed away at the drop of a hat. Don't get me wrong, I love New Orleans. But sometimes I worried that we were living in the river's place, and someday she might want it back.

It's part of why, when I thought about making a baby with Sweet, I thought of being back in La Luna.

That evening after our trip on the river, we climbed into bed and made a new and different kind of love. Baby-making love. And afterward, I lay on top of Sweet and fell asleep. We were on the sleeping porch with air cooling our bodies, and it had started to rain. When I woke up, I started to think that something was cooking inside me. Just maybe. In fact, I invited a baby to come on down any time it was ready.

Renée and Eddie had hardly any married time together before they had Calla Rose. I wondered, if I got pregnant, would I still have the same fun and joy and high times making love with Sweet? I hoped so! Renée told me that I should get ready for a happiness that I could never imagine, if I had a baby inside me.

Summer arrived, and it was *hot* in New Orleans—I mean burning up, I mean scalding. I am talking high nineties with 98 percent humidity, and none of those sweet rains that usually come along in the afternoons to cool everything off. Everybody was running their air conditioners on high blow. All we did was slip from our air-conditioned houses to our air-conditioned cars to our air-conditioned work. Sometimes I had to tell the ladies on their way out of the shop, "Y'all, close that door! You're going to let all our cool air out!"

One night Sweet and I woke up from a deep, sweaty sleep. He looked at me, and then got up to check the air-conditioning unit. Sweet told me, "Calla, that thing is deader than a doornail. We're going to have to open up the windows."

"Oh," I said, complaining. "I hate this. I hate sweating. It is so hot."

Sweet got up to fix us two cold Cokes over ice, and he brought mine to me in bed. He took his glass and held it against my cheeks. "Feel, Calla. Feel good?"

"Yeah," I said, grouchily. "It feels good for a minute."

"Okay," he said. And then I could hear him quietly drinking his Coke. I sipped on mine. Soon I could hear my husband set down his glass, take several deep breaths, and then fall back asleep. I tried the same thing myself but I couldn't. I was too angry at the air conditioner.

Why does this kind of thing happen when it's just the hottest, I thought? Why? I'm never going to be able to get to sleep with this heat. And then I began to realize that I heard more without the air conditioner on. I heard the sound of my husband's breath dropping in and out. I heard the sound of my own breath dropping in and out. And I remembered M'Dear talking about breath and gratefulness.

She'd say, "Okay, Calla. When you are most afraid, find things to be grateful for." And so I began to just let myself hear the sounds of the night. I could hear some traffic rumbling by, but not much. Even in the city, I could still hear the insects making their summer sounds, the comforting hum of the refrigerator. If I had a dog, I thought, I would hear it breathing, but a husband is enough. A husband is enough. This house is enough. This life is enough. I do not want what I do not have. I do not want the air conditioner. I do not have it, and so I do not want it. And the more I dropped down into these feelings of gratitude, the sleepier I became. And the less sweaty. I took off the T-shirt that I slept in. The big old T-shirt of Sweet's. I still took that off, and my panties, and lay there nude without even a sheet. The ceiling fan roaring on me. I heard that whirring sound and became thankful for it. Thankfulness flooded me, and then so did sleep.

Chapter 30

1977–1978

I hadn't told but two people that Sweet and I were trying to make a baby. I'd told Renée because I've known her all my life and because she loves making and taking care of babies. Then I told Ricky, but not by choice. Even though I worked side by side with him all day long, I managed to keep quiet. Then one night, Sweet said, "Babe, what do you say if I soak some red beans overnight, cook 'em up in the morning, and then have friends over tomorrow night?"

So we did, and Ricky and Steve came. They all started out with cocktails, but I drank soda water. I'd stopped drinking wine with dinner because it was bad for getting pregnant. I've never been much of a drinker, and that means a lot in New Orleans. Louisiana does happen to be the birthplace of the go-cup and the drive-through daiquiri stand. But I used to drink a beer or two or some wine with shrimp boils or po-boys at parties and get-togethers. So that night Ricky noticed that I wasn't even doing that.

So he cornered me in the shop the next day and got it out of me. "I am appalled," he said, "that my *cousin* and my dear, dearest girlfriend did not care to share this with me."

"We wanted to wait until we had real news," I told him. "Plus, it might be a while in coming. We've been saving our money because having a baby makes you think about every dollar."

Shortly after our talk, a new line of hair products began to stream into the salon. Ricky had turned the shop into a Naturatique salon, where nothing but plant-based products were allowed. He claimed that he'd done it for his health, that eventually all those bad chemicals were going to catch up with him. But Steve told me that the night Ricky heard that Sweet and I were trying to have a baby, he started his research into Naturatique. Ricky did not want me to be exposed to any chemicals that might hurt me or the baby. Once he began to look into it, he became more concerned, because research showed that many of the chemicals cause serious problems in utero.

I couldn't get over the fact that Ricky would do that for me and my baby. A couple of the customers started to gripe, but there were those who still complained about not being able to *smoke* in the salon, for heaven's sake. When they did, I just told them about that beauty shop in Natchez, Mississippi, where a woman lit up a cigarette at the manicure table. Somehow the flame reached the saucer of acetone used to remove false fingernails, and it caught on fire! That woman was lucky to get off with only one side of her hair and both eyebrows singed. Lord knows what could have happened.

When I have my own salon, it will be safe too, I decided. Sweet said that was fine with him. I knew he'd be a real hands-on father. He was already one of the most liberated men I ever knew. He loved to cook and had an ace collection of perfectly sharpened knives. I remembered coming home one day when he was off from work for a week. Sweet was standing there *ironing clothes*, with a pair of boxer shorts on and no shirt! That body of his was so wiry and strong, I could see all the muscles in his stomach. And what was he doing? He was dancing to the song "Barefootin'." Just dancing away while he was ironing. I burst out laughing.

"Hold on, hold on a minute!" Sweet said. "All right now, dance with me, my baby. Dance with me!"

He turned off the iron, and I kicked off my shoes. Then we played that song over and over on that old forty-five record player M'Dear gave me when I was thirteen years old. We just danced and danced, cracking each other up.

Then we wound up making love that afternoon. Afterward, as we lay beside each other, Sweet ran his hand down my belly to my crotch. His hand cupped perfectly around me.

"When that baby comes, I'm gonna help catch him. You got to catch babies when they drop down from heaven."

His hand was warm against my folds, all relaxed from lovemaking.

"You got to catch 'em careful," he continued. "If they're little miracle girls, you got to catch 'em with your right hand." He kept his hand cupped around me.

"If they're boy miracles," he said, switching hands, "you got to catch 'em with your *left* hand."

His finger slipped a little ways into me.

"You got to catch those miracles when they're thrown," Sweet said, then rolled on top of me again.

"Miracles flying through air like curveballs," my husband said, and again he entered me.

"Curveballs," I said, and breathed in deeply. "Curveballs flying through the October sky."

&

Sukey's going back to school inspired me. I knew that if I ever wanted to open up my own shop, I needed more training, so I signed up for business classes at Grassido Community College. Grassido is on City Park Avenue, which is lined with those old live oaks I love, on the fringe of the cemetery zone. New Orleans is so divine and weird at the same time! Fourteen cemeteries all sharing about a square mile of high ground. Sometimes, on the way to Delgado, I stopped by to look at the graves and studied the things people had brought for their loved ones. It always touched me—besides all the flowers, there were lawn chairs for the dead and Xerox portraits of them attached to the gravestones, faded with sun and rain. Once, at a child's grave, I saw a little toy lawn mower. Oh, it made me cry. I stopped and said a prayer.

Maybe one day I'll have a baby. I hope she or he will like to play with little toy lawn mowers and a zillion other toys, and will laugh and let me hold him or her like M'Dear held me.

Most of my classes were in bookkeeping, business law, contracts, and other things a small business owner has to know. But I also signed up for some English classes, because I loved English in high school. Mister Robert Peletier, our teacher, asked us to read the play *Romeo and Juliet*. I'd heard of it, of course, but I'd never read it.

Romeo and Juliet just tore me apart. Those two, they were so young. They were about the age that Tuck and I were—no, they were even younger, like thirteen and fourteen years old—and they loved each other so deeply. Their families had been fighting for centuries. They had been fighting for so long *they* had forgotten what they were fighting about.

I read the whole play in one weekend. I was out on the screened porch, and I couldn't stop crying. Juliet had this plan where it would look like she was dead, but she'd really taken a potion from a monk to put her to sleep.

Romeo came out of hiding to see Juliet and thought she was dead. He didn't know she'd taken a potion and was just asleep. He cried out to her, but she didn't wake up in time. His heart was so broken that he took his dagger out of his belt and stabbed it into his own heart.

When Juliet woke up, finally, and found her Romeo covered in blood, she began to scream. She held him in her lap, with the blood flowing all down her gown. Sometimes I imagined it like Jackie Kennedy's pink fleecy suit, with all the blood on it in the back of that convertible.

The night I finished that play, I was heartbroken. But when I lay down to go to sleep, my sadness lifted. There was something in the beauty of the way the story was told that lifted me up out of my sadness. And I thought, *Mister Robert Peletier is right. Beauty and art are everywhere and can lift us up out of our suffering.*

It was at Grassido that I got my T-shirt that said "Another Hairdresser for Nuclear Disarmament." I got it when my class was called off one day. There I was, with an hour and a half to kill, so I decided to wander around and see if there was something going on on campus.

It turned out that there was a lecture in the auditorium called "Will We Survive Till the Year 2000?"

It had already started when I got there. The woman talking on the stage showed us a screen with one of those detailed diagrams of the human body. I swear, I will never understand why they make those things look so much like a doll with its hair ripped off. I am not kidding, there wasn't a single hair on the entire diagram, when everyone knows that people have got hair *everywhere.*

Anyway, this woman was pointing to different parts of the body and explaining how "rems" would affect each of them. I knew what rems were—radiation. That's what they hit M'Dear with when she got breast cancer. Finally, the woman mentioned the word *hair.* She told us that if a nuclear bomb was to get dropped, people's hair would melt out in *clumps*! Without them smelling anything or tasting anything or knowing what in the world hit them.

I was horrified. I saw M'Dear, propped up on her pillows, in the big bed she and Papa shared. I saw her bald head, only tufts of hair sticking up like a crazed, half-plucked chicken. The sounds she made as she bit back the pain. The burned spots on her body left from the radiation.

I wondered if this lady could be telling the truth. It blasted me to think of millions of radiation-melted heads.

Walking home, I couldn't shake this idea, even with the smell of May in New Orleans, which meant gardenias and magnolias in bloom, their scents almost too sweet. Sweet was napping on the couch when I got home, with the TV on, snoring like a truck stuck in the mud.

I stared at his thick curly black hair and at his lean body, all muscled from working on his boat.

His hair is getting too long, I thought. I am going to have to give him a cut soon. Then suddenly, I saw Sweet's hair start to melt out.

I swear, I was sitting there in our big comfy chair, and I had a vision of Sweet's hair getting soft and falling out. And then his eyebrows and eyelashes melted off, leaving him looking like a painting that somebody went off and didn't finish. His face was smooth, with no male stubble at all—all his whiskers and his mustache gone. And where his denim work shirt sleeves were rolled up, there wasn't any arm hair. Sweet's arms were thin and bare, like a starving child's. They didn't look like Sweet's arms at all.

Then it was all over. Everything went back to normal. All I saw was Sweet asleep there on the couch, with his black hair that always pleased me so much, the way it brushed against my face when he kissed me good-bye in the morning. I got up, leaned over him, gave his hair a tousle, and kissed his cheek.

"Come on, babe, wake up," I whispered. "You know it kills your back if you sleep too long on the couch."

Then we had dinner, watched a little TV, and went to bed. But before I fell asleep, I thought about hair—about babies' soft little tufts, and about how when people get old their hair is like baby hair again. I thought about minds so evil that they could build a bomb that would not only poison every organ of our bodies but melt out our hair as well. Besides, if that bomb ever dropped, I'd be out of business. There wouldn't be any hair left for me to do. Or much of anything to do, come to think of it, for any of us.

The next morning, I sat down and wrote a letter to the president in Washington, D.C.

May 22, 1978
New Orleans, Louisiana

Dear Mister President and Mrs. Rosalynn Carter,

I am a beautician. I work at a salon called Ricky's in New Orleans, Louisiana. I am a happily married woman who pays taxes, even on tips.

Now, Mrs. Carter, you have chosen the perfect cut for your hair type. You especially have lovely hair for a woman your age, and it is very well kept. Mister President, you're thinning on top, so I think you'll strongly relate to what I'm about to say.

I speak as a beautician when I ask you to think, "How would you look as a bald couple?" One nuclear bomb would melt out all your hair. I am a professional in the field of beauty, but I don't know any cures for radiation-melted hair. And as far as I know, no one else does, either.

The human body is not a Styrofoam wig stand. I, for one, will not think you are a ninety-pound weakling if you get rid of the twenty-megaton bomb. I would like to go on waking up and cooking and doing hair and loving my husband.

If nothing else, please: Think of your looks.

Yours Very Sincerely,

Calla Lily Ponder

Chapter 31

1979–1980

Sweet and I had been trying our very best to make a baby. I'd taken my temperature every day to make sure we hit the right window of time. We'd made love in all the positions that the doctor suggested, like being on all fours with Sweet behind me, or practically standing on my head. Afterward, I had put two pillows under my butt and lain down with my feet propped up on the wall for half an hour. But none of it seemed to work.

When I finally missed my period, I was just so happy! I hardly dared to hope that I was finally pregnant. So I waited one more month, and sure enough, I missed another one. Sweet and I were thrilled. We had been trying for three years at this point.

Then I went to the doctor, who examined me and did a bunch of tests. Then he told me, "I'm sorry, but you're not pregnant."

"What?" I said. "I mean, I missed my period for two and a half months! I feel pregnant, like all warm inside and emotional, like before I get my period."

"Well," the doctor said, "these things happen. If you want to get pregnant very badly, your body can fool itself into thinking that you are. These are called 'hysterical pregnancies.'"

"What's wrong with us?" I asked him. "All the tests we've had came back normal. And I'll tell you one thing, Doc: I am *not* hysterical. If you think I'm hysterical, you don't know what hysterical is."

The doctor looked at me like I was the bad student in class. "Many couples are infertile for reasons we can't explain. All you can do is keep trying. And I suggest to you that you learn more about both hysterical pregnancies and hysteria in general."

Then he got up, and walked out of the exam room.

"Hey," I said, when I got home, trying to hide my tears.

"Hey, baby!" Sweet said, sweeping me into his arms and up off the floor, like he often did.

And then I couldn't help it. I started sobbing. Sweet gently set me down and just held me.

"Tighter," I said, and he held me tighter.

I told him what the doctor had said, crying, trying to catch my breath. Sweet began to cry too. I could feel his tears on my face, on the top of my head, his shirt getting wet against my cheek.

"I'm so sorry, Sweet," I told him. "Maybe I could have done something different. I could have had a different kind of diet, or a different kind of—body, or attitude, or—"

Sweet pushed me away just a tiny bit so that he could see my face. He looked down into my eyes. "No, Calla," he said. "It's not you. It's not me. I bet your Moon Lady would say that it's just not yet time for this baby to fall down from her arms into ours."

I looked at him. "You're right," I said. "You reminded me of just what I need to truly hold on to."

And we stood there crying, both of us thinking about the baby we wanted so badly, the one that we really thought had come, the one that was not yet in my womb.

That night, we lay in bed and drank a bottle of wine. Ever since we started trying to make a baby, Sweet had stopped drinking along with me. But that night we had some wine, and neither of us felt like eating. All Sweet wanted was some olives, and all I could eat were some preserved figs that Miz Lizbeth had put up and sent us. I just ate a single fig, very slowly, until my mouth was just holding the stem, which I kept turning around until I'd sucked every bit of sweetness out of it.

After we'd both finished our wine, my fig, and Sweet's olives, we lay in bed and held hands till we fell asleep.

That night, a dream came to me. I saw a naked little baby sitting on her bottom, playing with a ball or a toy. She was about one year old, sitting with her back toward me. She turned her head as though I had just walked into the room, and she smiled. Then, very slowly, she turned around until she was facing me.

She sat with her chubby little legs sticking out in front of her. She leaned down to reach one foot, pulled it up, and began to play with her toes. Then she started laughing—utterly delighted *with her toes*!—and looked up at me and gave the most ecstatic laugh!

She was there to give me a message of some kind, but she didn't have anything to say. All she did was smile and laugh and play with her toes. And I couldn't help it—I began to laugh too, because she had the kind of laugh that you just couldn't resist joining in with. Then I woke up and found that I was still laughing.

Sweet had cracked the window open before we went to sleep. When he did, it hit me that whatever baby spirit had tried to come through me in my "hysterical pregnancy" was now flying out of the window. How sad I would be to see it go! But now I had this new baby, this dream baby, who I bet M'Dear would say looked a lot like me.

Well, my laughter didn't wake Sweet. He just lay there perfectly still, his arms at his sides, looking so peaceful, with no signs of turmoil. I looked at his thick black hair, thankful that he'd listened to me and left it long, especially in the back. He never understood how sexy his hair was. He still didn't understand why the girls in high school named him Sweet. He was so sweet that it rarely occurred to him that others were not.

I looked at Sweet's forehead, his eyes, his nose, and his full lips. God, I loved those lips. I pictured every inch of his body, which I knew so well. I brought my own breath into sync with his, and I pictured his penis inside my vagina. And I pictured that white light that M'Dear taught me about, circling around the two of us, binding us together even as we were bound as individuals. And within that white light, I pictured room for a baby.

I believed that the Moon Lady would know just when it was time for a spirit, for a soul, to come down into a body. I remembered that once, when I was very little, I asked my papa, "Where do babies come from?" I could hear my own little girl voice, and I could hear Papa's answer, "Calla, babies come when an angel blinks her eye. They're like dewdrops from heaven. Babies come when the dewdrop falls on M'Dear and me. Babies come when they are ready."

I had forgotten his words in all my longing for a baby. I had forgotten that, just because I was ready, it didn't mean that a baby was ready. I had started to think of it as *my* baby, as *Sweet's* baby, as *mine and Sweet's* baby, but it wasn't. If I was ever graced with a baby, it still wouldn't be mine. It would belong to the Moon Lady—like I did, like M'Dear did, like Sweet, my husband, did. I'd forgotten that we all are called down, just at the right time, and that every little baby eventually hears its call.

Chapter 32

1980

One fall afternoon, I was doing a coloring job on one of my regulars, Julie, when I saw two men walk in, wearing somber gray suits. They sure didn't look like clients or beauty supply salesmen. They didn't look around, just stayed focused, like they were there on some mission not related to beauty. Out of the side of my eye, I saw Cindy, our receptionist, listening to them. Then she went over to Ricky. He dropped what he had been doing, and went to speak to the suits. I kept on working. Doing hair—that's my job, that's my work. *It could be anything*, I told myself, *all kinds of people come in the shop.*

I put my customer in a chair. "Here's some magazines," I told her. "Look at this *Town and Country*. There's a good piece on Louisville. I've never been to the races there, have you?"

I kept acting like everything was normal, ignoring the men standing by Cindy's desk.

When Ricky turned away from them, he looked so strange. I had never seen him look so—I don't know how to put it—so composed and deliberate looking.

I watched as he walked over to me, faking the whole way. "Calla, sweetie, come back to the kitchen and have a Coke with me. I need a break from the fumes. I swear this colorant will kill me with headaches."

He looked at me carefully as we headed to the kitchen.

"What's up?" I asked him. "Is this about taxes? You can tell me, Ricky. If I'm going to be partners in this salon, you have to let me know what's happening before—"

Ricky opened the refrigerator that had a philodendron on top of it, its vines trailing down the sides. He pulled out a bottle of Coke, snapped off the cap, and handed it to me.

"Let's sit down for a minute, okay?" I nodded yes.

"Calla, sweetie, it's not about taxes," he said. "Something has happened to Sweet."

I stared at the leaves of the plant, which were heart-shaped, and at the vines, marveling at how long they could get.

"Calla." Ricky reached for my hand, I jerked it back. I was studying another plant, an African violet, that had been growing on the back windowsill. It was a virtual jungle in here.

"Calla," Ricky said again. "Honey, please look at me."

"I don't want to look at you," I said. "I've got a color to check." I tried to get up and head back into the salon, where my customer was reading about entertaining during Derby Week. Then Ricky stopped me, his hand on my shoulder. Softly he said, "Calla, honey, there was an offshore explosion this morning. Sweet was killed."

It was like someone came from behind and cut me off at the knees as my mind whirled, *Derby Week brunches, hair color, Sweet, explosion*. Then I went to the ladies' room and I couldn't come out, I wouldn't come out. Somebody knocked on the door. I didn't answer. "Calla?" Ricky said. "Calla, are you okay?" I locked the door. I closed my eyes. Finally he said, "Calla, look, maybe you don't want me to come in. Maybe—Calla, somebody's got to come in there and check on you, okay?" I didn't respond. And finally he said, "How about we have Cindy come in?"

"Get out! Just get away. Nobody is gonna come in here."

Ricky stood at the door, and said, "Calla, I'm just gonna stand here, okay babe, you don't have to talk to me, you don't have to do anything. Just gonna stand here." And he stood there till well after the shop was closed. Until finally I began to feel cold, a kind of cold crept through me, and inside me, going out, down my arms, down my legs. My feet and my hands were so cold I couldn't bear it. Finally I began to shake, and I began to cry. "Ricky? Ricky, I'm so cold. I'm real cold in here. Did you turn on some air conditioning? Please turn off the air conditioning."

"No, Calla," he said, "everything's still the same."

"I'm really cold in here," I told him.

He said, "Why don't you let me come on in there, help warm you up."

I couldn't think anymore. I was so cold. Finally I unlocked the door.

Vaguely, I remembered being in Ricky's car with Steve driving. Then I had a flash of being in the guest room at Ricky and Steve's. By the time I propped myself up in bed—nauseated, too weak to stand—it was dark outside. Later I learned that I'd been out of it for a night and a day.

And then, there in the room with me were Papa and Olivia. At first, I wasn't sure if they were real or an illusion. They reached out for me, but I couldn't lift my arms to touch them. I had the beating heart, the blood flowing in my veins, the breath filling my body, the skin and muscle and hair intact. But my will and spirit of life, which I'd fused with Sweet's, had blown up with him.

I was no stranger to death, but I was a stranger to murder. And that's what the oil company had done to my Sweet. They took him away from me. Ricky and Steve and Sukey and other friends did what they could, but I just couldn't reach down and find what it took to connect with them. I was a skin, bone, and blood machine with working parts, but that was all.

The doctor gave me pills to help me sleep. But even with the pills, I kept dreaming about explosions, body parts flying randomly through the burning air, falling in the burning water, Sweet's body all burned flesh red, and then Sweet's firm, muscled body next to mine. Then in my dream, I was screaming, swimming, trying to reach him. If I could only reach him, if I could get to the boat and stop it from blowing up. I pictured that when I got to Sweet, I'd hold his head on my side and use my scissors kick and swim to shore, no matter how far it was. But I could never swim fast enough, even using my strongest strokes.

Calla Lily, my darling girl, I'm right here with you, holding your hand. Open your heart and let Sweet go, gently and swiftly. Do not hold on. His life was taken so cruelly; help his spirit pass away from this earth to a place where there is no greed that kills. Only full acceptance, full forgiveness.

None of us ever got to see Sweet's body. Whatever remains they could gather were placed in a closed casket. That's what we had at the funeral home. I kissed the coffin, and I stood there until I saw the kiss move through the wood to my husband. My kiss reached his body, then to his heart and then to his soul. Then I broke down crying, and could hardly stand up.

M'Dear's voice came to me then, a faint whisper, saying, "Calla, Calla, you can make it." Then came the night of the Rosary, the night before Sweet's funeral. Sweet's *maman* and papa had been with me at the funeral home the whole time. That night, I reached for their hands and could see that they needed a hug. I hugged Sweet's *maman*, and tears streamed down my face and neck. "Oh," was all she could say. And then we pulled back and she kissed me and said, "Dear Calla, we all grieve together. *Cher*, we all grieve together."

Her husband, Everett Chalon, was reluctant to show his emotions. So I reached up to hug him, and he hugged back. He gave me a big bear hug like Sweet's that lasted a long time. When he stepped back, I looked at him, this man—this father of my beloved—and I could see how hard it was for him. He just held my hand, squeezed it once, and turned away so that I could not see his face.

Then I was with my papa, and my two brothers. They stood close and surrounded me as if I might fall.

Other La Luna folks turned out, some that were close to me, and others who just knew M'Dear and Papa over the years. All of my close friends came, including Renée and Eddie. "Where are the kids?" I said.

"Calla, don't worry," she told me. "My children are just fine. I came to be with you." I could see her sweet face, that blond hair, the sadness in her eyes, and I wanted to take away all that sadness. I thought if I could take away everyone's sadness, then mine would be lessened too, and somehow it would all go away.

Olivia was there with her husband, Pana. Olivia wasn't crying. She was just nodding her head from side to side like this shouldn't have happened. Pana was the one who hugged me. He said, "I hug you for both of us, babe. I don't think Olivia can handle it right now."

I was shocked, so I turned to her and said, "Please, Olivia, give me a hug." She hesitated for a moment, then she gave me the hug that she had all bottled up inside. Oh, how everyone grieved differently.

Ricky was weeping into a starched white cotton handkerchief for his cousin, for his good cousin, who had accepted Ricky when many members of his family hadn't. Sweet had said, "Hey, man, whichever way the bell rings, you just go with it, huh?"

In the midst of his tears, Ricky took my hands, forced a big smile, and said, "You look simply stunning! Stunning. I love you, dear girl," he whispered, and hugged me. "I love you." Oh, it was so odd to laugh and cry at the same time, and that's what he made me do.

Sukey had gone out and bought me a dress on her credit card. It was a plain black dress with just a nipped waist and silk sleeves that were buttoned up high above the wrist. The skirt flared out slightly at the bottom. The dress had a V-neck, nothing too fancy, but it fit perfectly.

"How did you know how perfectly this dress would fit?" I had asked.

"Oh! You could not look more beautiful at a funeral if you were Jackie O," Sukey said, kissing me on the forehead.

Then I felt a tap on my shoulder. When I turned around, I saw Nelle. She looked so solid, somehow so *permanent*. She took me into her strong arms. Without speaking, I stood there, my head on her shoulder, and felt the strength of her love for me.

"I'll be there whenever you need me," she said. "Wherever, whenever. Don't doubt it, you hear me?"

Then it was time for the Rosary. *Hail, Mary, full of grace, the Lord is with thee. Blessed art thou among women and blessed is the fruit of thy womb*, we all said together. I could hear Olivia's voice singing above the others.

As I prayed, I heard the voice of the Moon Lady saying, "Calla, look at me." It was dark outside. "You don't have to see me," she said, "just know that I am here. Light will keep the darkness away, if you let it. You are embraced by those who are alive and by those who have passed on. I am waiting. I am just waiting for your call."

Why didn't you answer Sweet's call when the rig caught fire? Where were you then?

Oh, there was so much anger mixed in with grief. I went back to the Rosary, feeling that the Moon Lady had let me down.

That night, I took the pills again, more than usual to sleep. The next day was Sweet's funeral.

Sukey came over in the morning and said, "How about breakfast?"

"Oh, God, Sukey, no," I told her.

"Just a minute. Hold your horses, Calla." She came back into the room a few minutes later with a small bowl and sat on the edge of the bed. “Here, sweetie,” she said, holding out her hand. In it was a little bowl of cottage cheese and peaches chopped really small, one of my favorite dishes from childhood.

I looked at it, and for the first time since Sweet’s death, I felt a desire for food. “Yes,” I said. “I’ll have just a little bite.” The soft cottage cheese and sweet peaches comforted me. Like baby food.

“It’s the kind of dish that’s good going down,” Sukey said.

She stood up to show me the outfit she picked out for me to wear. “You wore black at the funeral home,” she told me, “so you can’t wear it again. We got you grayish black.”

She unzipped a garment bag and brought out a little charcoal-gray suit. She practically dressed me, right down to my pantyhose and a pair of matching low-heeled pumps. “You look just right, Calla,” she said. “Let’s pull your hair into a very tight bun. Now, for the finishing touch,” she said, and put some little pearl earrings on me. “Remember, accessories make the girl.”

“Sukey, you are one sweetheart of a friend.”

“Well, Calla,” Sukey said, “so are you.”

We drove for an hour or so to Donaldsonville, where Sweet was born and lived until we fell in love. Family and friends from all over Louisiana gathered. The little church was full of big arrangements of flowers—plus one small, clear vase of irises that struck me with its simplicity. There was no card. I didn’t know who sent it, but it was perfect for my Sweet.

Father Gerard, who married us, came to lead the prayer service. He had a Cajun accent, so the service was Cajun Catholic, not “crazy Catholic,” as M’Dear used to say about people who she said were “just a tad bit *too* devout.”

Father Gerard began, “I baptized Joseph DeVillierre Chalon, and then I had the privilege of marrying him to Calla Lily Ponder.” He looked toward me and paused, giving a slight nod. “I never thought that, just a few years later, I would be saying good-bye to him as we knew him here on earth. And even though I'm here as a priest representing Mother Church, I'm also a man, and right now, I'm an awfully sad one.

"His family was in the funeral business, so being a priest, I got to know them pretty well. One thing I remember about Sweet was that when he was out playing as a little boy, and he got hungry, he'd just head to the nearest wake to see what kind of cakes and cookies were laid out. I had to laugh at that. He'd be so happy to see all the cakes and pies brought here today by those who loved him.

"I didn't encounter Joseph, or Sweet, for a few more years. When I did, I was impressed with the man he had become through a lot of hard work as a riverboat pilot, and with the fine lady Calla Lily Ponder."

Father Gerard's voice cracked with emotion, and he paused. He looked out at the riggers who Sweet had piloted back and forth from home. Most of them weren't wearing suits, but they had dressed up the best they could. "Remember that none of us is alone in our grief," Father Gerard said. "All of us, every one of us, is held by God—whatever we think God to be. Whatever Holy Force we might conceive of holding us together is here with us now and will be with us forever. In the name of the Father and the Son and the Holy Spirit, go in peace now, to love and serve the Lord and to bless our brother and our son, Sweet Chalon. And we thank the Lord for his gracing us with Sweet's presence on this earth."

Then Sweet's young nephew, who was a fiddler, said, "This is for my Uncle Sweet, who we'll sure miss." He took a deep breath and then began to play a soft, mournful waltz on the fiddle. It seemed like all of our tears went into those strings, and into that song. And, for a moment, the tightness around my heart eased, and I felt a kind of communion, as if my soul was uniting with so many souls standing there with me. And I felt not so alone.

After the cemetery, we all gathered at Sweet's parents' home, a small wooden house up off the ground. In the back, extra bedrooms were built out from the back porch, and they had opened up the living room and dining room into one big space. Still, there wasn't really enough room for everybody.

Sweet's best friend and best man, Antoine, had come. Oh, he broke my heart. Tears were just streaming down his cheeks. "I'm all torn up, Calla," he said. "I'm sorry, but I just can't control it. If only I could've been on that boat. If Sweet had been carrying me, maybe I could have saved my buddy."

"Antoine," I said, squeezing his hand, "you know how beautiful and strong Sweet was. I feel just the same way. I wish I could have saved him, too. But neither of us could. All we can do is love and remember him." Then I could not breathe, I could not stand. Antoine caught me, and the next thing I knew, Sukey was at my side.

"You can make it, Calla Lily."

For days after we lowered Sweet's casket into mother earth, I was so angry that I swore sometimes as I lay in bed that I would tear the mattress apart, just yank out all the batting and fling it against the wall. I could take a glass of water and just throw it against the door until it crashed into a million pieces. The most that I did to get my anger out, though, was hit my pillows so hard that the feathers exploded like snow all over the bed. I felt my own anger come loose in the feathers that floated down onto me. *Amazing how anger can turn into feathers. If that's possible, then grief can turn into something else, can't it? Can't it?*

What rough God has ridden through my life, like some wild, mean horse—taking away my mother and Tuck, taking my tender teenage trust and bashing it. And now Sweet, my husband. Dear husband who could not give enough, who was always one to make me laugh and to give everything to me. "Calla," he used to say, "you give so much all day long. Let me take care of you. Let me just take care of you." And so finally, after a while, I did sink down and let him take care of me, let his love just flow all over me. And now my Sweet was dead.

I was afraid to open the door of the small closet that Sweet and I shared. You don't get a lot of room in these old shotgun Irish Channel houses. As pretty as we had the house fixed up, we hadn't got around to building another closet, so the rest of our clothes, mainly mine, were out in the hall. I even kept some of my blouses folded up in a drawer in the kitchen.

I'd been taking Sweet's T-shirts out of the drawer in the bedroom, but I hadn't yet opened the closet. The closet and I had been staring each other down. But one day, I realized that I just had to do it.

I put my hand on the old handle, which had turned brown over the years. I looked at my hands on the handle, took a deep breath, and opened the door. And there they were. My husband's shirts, the long-sleeved cotton ones that he always wore with the sleeves rolled up—plaid ones, light blue cotton ones. And his pants, all folded over hangers. But it was the sight of his shoes that did me in. Sweet was a man with small feet, size nine. I could see the way his feet had filled out his shoes, and how wrinkled they were from use, from the pressure of his feet in them. The feet of my beloved, feet that would never again walk the earth.

After that, I fell into a pit. All of my friends and my family tried their best, with all their love, to pull me out of that deep, dark hole. But the gifts they had to give were not the ones I needed. I felt that everything that had protected me had been blown apart. I felt like I did when M'Dear died—alone. Again.

I just lay there in bed—for how many days or weeks, I couldn't say. It didn't matter who came and went. I kept my bedroom door shut. I could hear the sounds of their voices, the smell of food they brought as gifts to feed me. That food they brought! "Take it away, please," I said. It made me ill just to smell it.

One time I thought I heard Renée's voice, thanking someone for their kindness. Another time, it was Nelle. "Set it down on the counter. Oh, Calla has some good friends here in New Orleans." My La Luna friends were here, staying where? Most likely in our little guest room that I'd planned to be a nursery.

I wouldn't let anyone near me except Sukey. Sukey, who knew what it was like to fall into the pit. "Sukey," I'd beg, "hold my hand and squeeze it. Tell me that Sweet and I will get our life back. We'll get it back, right?"

Then we'll sit in the kitchen, and Sweet will be cooking. I'll eat because I'll be so hungry, hungry for everything at the sight of my Sweet. He'll be home with three pounds of shrimp, and we'll boil them with some Zatarain's powder, while I make the cocktail sauce in the blue bowl that M'Dear used for little dips. I'll put the ketchup in and add as many dashes of Tabasco as it tells me it needs, plus a teaspoon of horseradish—got to be careful not to overload it with horseradish. And the Brothers will be playing on the tape deck, and Sweet and I will do a little made-up dance step here and there. We'll dance in the kitchen, like my mother taught me to do. Sweet will pretend to be a shrimp. "Sweet," I'll say, "stop making me laugh so hard—I'll ruin this cocktail sauce."

Oh, my Sweet! With that Cajun skin and dark blue eyes. While we were making love, we never closed our eyes. How could I imagine closing my eyes when he was above me, in me, smiling. "You, Calla," he would say, "sweet Calla, darling Calla, sweet Calla." And then I would feel part of his essence come into me.

Nighttime was the worst. Once I could get out of bed, I walked the city like a zombie. One night I found myself in Audubon Park in the rain. I went from one big oak to the other, feeling the bark, trying to fit my body against the trees. We used to walk under the big live oaks, Sweet and me. But the trees had lost their roots now that my Sweet was dead. I was trying to press my being into the little cracks in the wet bark. Soaked, at 3:00 a.m. in New Orleans, where a woman wandering around is not considered strange unless she's in the Garden District. Unsafe, yes, perhaps, but not strange. I'd thrown on a 1940s house-dress from JoAnn's over my baggy T-shirt, but it was not nearly warm enough. The rainwater ran off my face and down my body. I was surrounded by darkness and shadows. *Take it away*, I prayed. "Please just take it away!" I screamed into the wind-driven sheets of rain. "Take this pain away. Take this anger, loss, longing—take it all away! M'Dear, I miss you, I want you, I need you!" I howled. "Please come back." *Oh, my sweet, sweet Sweet. Come to me, Sweet! Don't leave me here.*

The next day Sukey brought me a long white cotton gown, all crisp and clean. "Sweetie," she said, "come on, let's wash your hair. Then we'll put on the gown."

I didn't understand. I kept saying, "Why? Why, Sukey?"

She turned her head away for a moment, then turned it back and put her hand on her hip, the way she's done since we were little girls. "Why? Because I said so, Calla."

She pulled the covers down slowly, but I didn't get up. Sukey more or less pulled me up, and I sat on the edge of the bed, sobbing. Sukey put an arm around my shoulders. "Come on," she said, "let's stand up and go to the bathroom. I've got it warm in there for you."

Sukey had everything laid out—my razor, shampoo, and conditioner. "Okay," she said, "let me unbraid your hair. We've got to wash your hair."

"No," I said, "I don't want you to take my braid apart."

"Calla, babe, your hair is all dirty, and it's gonna stay dirty if we wash it with that braid keeping your hair so tightly bound."

I sat down in the little chair that Sweet and I kept in the bathroom so that one of us could sit while the other took a bath in the old claw-foot tub. I put my head in my hands.

"Here goes," Sukey said, and she started to unbraid my hair.

"NO!" I screamed. "Sukey, leave my hair alone."

"Come on, Calla. You can't go on like this. You at least have to bathe. You're just so filthy."

"I want to be filthy!" I cried. "Don't touch me."

"Okay, Calla. How about we just shower with your braid like it is, okay?"

"That would be just fine, just fine. With my braid like it is, just fine," I repeated after her, numbly. I looked at the tub but didn't know what to do. Sukey reached over and took off my socks and panties.

"Okay," she said, "let's get your T-shirt off so you can get clean."

"No! Don't you dare touch this T-shirt! This is Sweet's T-shirt."

"Oh, babe," she said, "you've cried all over this T-shirt. It's so dirty."

I raised my hand, just itching to hit Sukey. She grabbed it and held it tight.

"Okay, Calla Lily, let me turn the shower on. We'll shower with Sweet's T-shirt on. He'd get a kick out of that, right?"

"Right," I said. "He would." Then I would not budge.

"Calla, are you getting into the shower or not?"

"No. But I will if you will," I said to Sukey, whose hair and makeup were done perfectly. I just couldn't imagine doing it alone.

Then she started to strip off her clothes. "Okay, we're gonna shower together. Let's go."

Sukey helped me into the shower and sat me on a little bath stool. She poured shampoo onto my head and began to rub it lightly. I could feel the suds running down my braid as Sukey massaged my head on each side of the braid, being careful not to undo it.

"I will not take it apart," Sukey promised. "I'm just going to get some suds into your braid."

"I believe you," I told her. And I realized that I really did believe her, because I knew she loved me. The warm water running over my head and flowing down my body gave me a physical comfort I realized that I had missed.

When I finally let Sukey take off Sweet's T-shirt, I started crying again at the touch of her hands as she washed my back, under my arms, under my breasts, down into my belly button. It didn't feel strange anymore that she was bathing me.

My tears were flowing down the drain to the Mississippi. It felt so good to have my cold tears mix with the hot water. "Oh, I will do this more often," I said to Sukey.

"We'll do this as often as you need," Sukey said. "We'll do this until you can do it yourself."

"All right," I croaked, like a frog, and laughed.

"All right," Sukey croaked back, laughing. "Now, you just stay there till I get a towel."

She dried me as I sat on the stool, starting with my braid, squeezing the water out, then wiping down my shoulders, my back, and my front.

"Okay, girlfriend, let's get you out of the tub and dressed." Sukey wrapped a towel tightly around me, dried my hair, and rubbed my body with lotion.

"All right! 'Spa Sukey's' debut is successful. Now, into your bedroom."

Back on the bed, where the linens had been tidied, lay the gown.

"Do you want to wear the white nightgown I brought you?"

"It's so pretty," I said. "All that lace. Where did you buy that?"

"I didn't buy it. Your aunt Helen made it. Took her a while to get that lace done just like she wanted it."

"Oh, please, I do want to put on Aunt Helen's nightgown."

"That's a girl," she said.

She slipped the nightgown over me. "You know, this is kind of like a gift from your mama, since Aunt Helen is her sister."

"Yes," I said. "Yes, I can see that. I can feel that."

A couple of months after Sweet's funeral, Steve came over. I was lying on the couch, writing notes, when the doorbell rang. I had some coffee already made, and we sat down at the kitchen table where I had sat so many times with Sweet, talking about nothing and everything a million times.

"Calla," he said, "I've looked into Sweet's accident and talked it over at my firm. We think you have a strong personal injury lawsuit. The oil company that owned that oil rig was also responsible for maintaining it, which it did not. To save money, it pulled back on safety measures, in violation of the law. So Sweet's death was what you call a 'wrongful death.'" He took my hands in his. "If you'd like for me to file suit against the company, I will. I can only imagine how hard this must be, Calla. But I suggest that we sue for a really high figure. It might prevent someone else from getting killed."

"I don't want to think about anyone else getting killed," I said. "Go on ahead and file it if you want to."

"In order to file suit, I just need you to sign these papers, sweetie."

"Okay." I signed them and then I said, "Thank you, dear Steve."

"Calla—"

"Sweetie, would you mind leaving me alone now?"

"Absolutely."

I gave him a weak smile.

"You take care now," Steve told me. "Ricky is going to drop by later."

"Fine," I said, lying back down on the couch. "Fine."

My head was spinning. I knew nothing about lawsuits. I only knew that I was lying here, sobbing, and glad that those greedy bastards who killed my husband might at least have to let go of some of their filthy money. I saw Sweet's face, and the faces of the riggers who came to our home for supper, missing their wives and children. I opened my eyes, picked up my pen, and continued writing notes to the families of the other men who had been killed by greed for oil money.

Chapter 33

WINTER 1980–1981

I didn't feel ready to get out of bed, but one night I just couldn't take being in the house anymore. So I got up and threw on a coat over my nightgown. It was an overcast night, but through the cloud cover, I could see the glow of the moon, like a child holding a flashlight under the sheets.

Ahhhh, I thought, *you're here.*

For a while, just staring at that light, I began to feel—I don't know how to put it—some kind of call.

I said to the Moon Lady, "Okay, I can't really see you. But I believe you're up there, behind the clouds. And that you're looking after me as M'Dear said."

I thought of asking her to show herself. But before I got up the nerve, the clouds began to move and the light of the moon grew stronger, until I could just make out her outline: not quite fingernail and not quite half full.

The Moon Lady was revealing herself to me, and she sent a thought into my mind. *I will not give you unnecessary grief.*

That was her gift. That was M'Dear's promise, that suffering would happen in my life, but that even when things seemed their darkest, the suffering would have some kind of meaning.

Then M'Dear's death and Sweet's death began to come together. And I could see that M'Dear, and her death, had taught me to love—and that it had prepared me for loving Sweet.

I whispered, "Calla Lily Ponder, your heart was open, but now it is hinged shut. What will it take to open your heart again?"

It was April in New Orleans again. The azaleas had come and gone, and the Jazz and Louisiana Heritage Festival had begun. Ricky, Steve, and Sukey were going, and they dragged me out with them. I wasn't up for companionship, so once we arrived, I walked around on my own.

I wandered into the gospel tent on the grounds. Though it was a Friday morning, the tent was packed, not with tourists but with God-filled people singing, testifying, and praying.

I sat myself down at the back of the tent next to a black woman. She was wearing a navy blue shirtwaist dress with large white polka dots. The dress was strained over her belly and her huge sagging breasts. On her feet were a pair of tennis shoes that she wore like mules, with the backs of the shoes broken down and her heels hanging out. I knew the *shush* sound those shoes would make when she walked.

It was a sticky-hot morning, and my skin itched because of a rash I had almost all over my body. I wore a light cotton blouse with long, full sleeves to let the air in but hide my rash, and a soft old faded blue skirt. I had no idea what was causing the rashes, and neither did the doctor. All I knew was that I was feeling crazy these days.

I was down to a hundred and ten pounds, which looks pretty scary when you're five-feet-nine. I lived on diet Dr Pepper. I still cried most of the time that I was awake, and in my dreams I screamed. I spent my days napping some and waking up confused. *Call Sukey, call Sukey*, I'd tell myself. Then Sukey would come and help me because I was still having visions of Sweet blown up into so many pieces that we couldn't even tell what was in his casket. She would rub my head and gently massage my neck and shoulders, softly, until I calmed down.

But that day, I stayed in the gospel tent and let the music wash over me—the music and the singing, the testifying and praying. So many voices raised in song. One choir called the Savation Light Choir paraded onto the bleachers. Little children sang with grown-ups. A short black woman with a voice that could curl the clouds sang a verse of "Amazing Grace," which was then taken over by the choir that she led. As I sweated, I could smell my body odor like it had never smelled before, as if something was being leached out of me, leaving me cleaner somehow.

When I went back to the tent on Saturday, I saw the same black woman, wearing a different dress. This one was homemade, white with yellow seersucker stripes and yellow buttons. That homemade dress made me feel calmer. I'd brought a shoulder bag this time, and in it I'd packed a thermos of ice tea, a box of Kleenex, and a bottle of prescription Valium. No food—I still didn't want it, not yet, but I was thirsty.

Again, I took a seat next to the woman. As the music swept over me, I cried—the piano, the snare drum, the bass guitar; the singing voices, the call-and-response of people testifying. These people didn't find it strange for a skinny white girl to sit there all day with a box of Kleenex and an endless flow of tears. When the music was right, when the spirit filled them, a lot of people cried. They rocked their bodies back and forth. They shot their hands up in the air and waved. Sometimes they simply rose to their feet, calling out, "Well, yes!" or "Talk it to me!" or "Amen! Amen, sister!" Certain older women who were feeling the spirit would jump up and wave their hands.

There was room in that tent for my sorrow.

That day, the woman in the yellow-and-white dress sat very close to me—so close that her large brown arm touched mine, and her generous hips crowded my narrow ones. I didn't mind. I just kept losing myself in the music, listening, crying, blowing my nose, sipping a bit of ice tea, and occasionally biting off a small piece of Valium.

Sometime during that afternoon, when the sun was falling in slants on the grass at the side of the tent and the hot air was filled with the smell of sausage jambalaya floating over from the food booths, I started to feel a little dizzy but somehow comforted.

Sunday morning, I took my place in the tent first, and before long, the woman appeared again. As she sat down, her body spread out like a cushion against mine. Normally, I would have edged away to give her a bit more room, but this time, I didn't. I wanted her near me. She sat next to me like a big, soft pillow. There were all those voices singing of pain and sorrow, of faith and longing, of salvation. I continued to cry all day. During the few times when I had to leave to stand in line for the portable toilets, my friend—for I was starting to think of her as a friend—laid her pocketbook on my seat to save it till I got back. I tried to thank her, but when I started to speak, all that came out were tears.

Jazz Fest lasts for two weekends. By the time the next Friday rolled around, I knew where I wanted to be. I returned to the tent, this time with an apple in my daypack, along with the tea and Valium. My friend came as usual, too, and when she nodded to me, I nodded back. What a relief it was to acknowledge and be acknowledged, without having to talk.

This was a big day, when the first gospel choir of children filed in and climbed up the risers, their heads held high, their clothes ironed and starched. The bows on the multiple pigtails of the little girls danced, their colors moving like flags of a young nation. I could not stop a small smile from coming to my lips—the first smile I remembered since that morning Sweet left for work and I kissed him, not knowing it would be for the last time.

The power of the children's singing reached toward the heavens. The tapping of my friend's feet, her head bobbing to the music, and her hands clapping to the rhythm stopped me from going down to that dark place of loss that I'd grown so used to. Sometimes she raised her hands in the air, calling out, "Say yes! Uh-huh, hallelujah!"

She pulled me back from the pit of burying sadness. Without even turning to me, she pulled me from the edge of grief and despair. Seeing the pink flesh on the back of her heels, the gentle reverberation of her ample hips and fleshy arms as they jiggled in jubilation, I thought, *You used to dance like that, Calla. You can come alive again.*

Finally, it was Saturday, the next-to-last day of the festival. That day, I shocked myself by falling asleep in public. When I woke, I was startled to see that it was already dark and that a whole different crowd was now inside the tent. I remember awakening to the scent of hair pomade. That confused me, and at first I thought I was back in La Luna, sitting next to Olivia and M'Dear in the kitchen. Then I realized that, all the time I'd been asleep, my head was leaning against the black woman's shoulder, close enough to smell her hair product.

"I'm sorry," I muttered. "It's kind of warm in here, and I—"

"You tired, that's all," she said.

"Yeah, I am," I replied. "Yeah, I think I am."

Those words were the first we exchanged.

Each day that I'd spent in the gospel tent had left me feeling a little stronger. Each day, I had moved a little further into the land of the living.

That night, I brushed my teeth, I loosened my braid, tried to brush out at least some of the wild tangles, and I washed my hair. I cleaned myself well and let my hair dry freely.

When I woke the next day, I realized that it was Sunday, the last day of the festival. I could feel something in the air, some rare sensation almost touching on magic, the way I imagine birds must feel around certain flowers. Back in the gospel tent, a choir came in, all in blue robes, led by a tall slim black man in his late teens. The children who came in first were some of the youngest I had seen in my days in the gospel tent. Some of those little boys and girls were just five and six years old, not even in first grade, and they behaved better than any child that age I had ever witnessed. Soon four black women in blue skirts and white shirts were buzzing around, helping the little ones, shushing them, hugging the ones who were nervous or crying, helping them get in their right singing places. I couldn't take my eyes off one little girl who smiled from the moment she came in. Just being there was enough to make her happy.

That is how I want to live, I thought, *I can be like that. I have that little girl somewhere inside my skinny, weeping self.*

I'd read about this particular choir. Pastor Tanisse Jackson of the First Evening Star Church held Sunday services in an old filling station where the tanks had been removed. Pastor Tanisse and the First Evening Star Gospel Choir had opened their doors to children, teenagers, and adults—black and white—who needed something to hold them off the streets, and had given them a discipline that came from learning to sing together as a choir as best they could. Sunday mornings, she dished out donated meals of fried chicken, string beans, cornbread, and slices of coconut cake. During these dinners, Pastor Tanisse moved among the tables, greeting family members who had been convinced by their children to come to church. In a city filled with gospel choirs, the *Times-Picayune* wrote, the First Evening Star Gospel Choir rocked the roof like nobody else.

They sure did.

While all the singing I'd heard in that tent had been good, the First Evening Star Gospel Choir took jubilation to new heights. I thought the whole tent would explode, just be blown apart by all that energy and joy. My eyes were as tuned in as my ears, watching the little ones sing with their mouths wide open, totally focused on every movement of Pastor Tanisse's hands. If one of the young ones began to lose focus, the pastor would give her an eye. If one of the teenagers began to slouch, I could see her head nod toward him. My friend sitting next to me began to sway and call out, and I joined her, unable to stop myself. How could my life be unbearable when there was singing like this in the world?

When the First Evening Star Gospel Choir reached its thundering finale, I realized that I would most likely never see, let alone sit next to, my new friend again. While the choir lifted me up, the thought of losing another person in my life brought my tears back. I couldn't bear the thought that I would never again feel her soft wide flesh, her heavy arm, her huge bottom that spread out and touched my hips, just as I would never again feel Sweet's body beside me. I felt naked, terrified, at the thought of being separated from her. Without thinking, I grabbed her hand.

"Oh, don't go, please," I said. "You don't have to leave right away, do you?"

She sat back down, and I felt a wave of relief.

"I do got to be going home soon," she said. "This meetin' just about over."

"But—" I sat next to her, trying to think of what to say.

She took my hand and held it for a moment, looking into my eyes.

"You doin' much better, baby. I think you gonna make it now. We was worried 'bout you at first, but now you okay. You might not know it, but you gone be just fine."

"Thank you," I said.

"You don't need to thank me, baby. Just go on with your praying."

I watched her large chest expand as she took a deep breath. As she exhaled, she reached into her pocketbook and pulled out a flattened cigarette pack that looked empty. It was a green-and-white package of Kools with a book of matches slipped under the cellophane. She pressed it into my hand, and gave me a smile. Then she stood up and walked out of the tent.

I held up the pack to look inside. There was only one cigarette left. Her last smoke.

I was not a smoker, but I fished that crumpled cigarette out of the pack and lit it. I took a long, slow drag, which made me cough. Then I took a deep breath without the help of the cigarette, let it out, and felt my shoulders drop. It was the deepest breath I had taken in ages that did not end up in a sob.

I breathed in and out slowly and fully for the first time since I learned Sweet died. I breathed, watching the smoke from the cigarette in my hand curl up into the air. I watched it burn all the way down, then stubbed it out against the sole of my sandals. It was as though my friend had absorbed my sadness into her large body, shot it up to the Moon Lady, then let it fall back into herself fully cleansed. So the cigarette she gave was an invitation to breathe again, and a temporary memento of the days she sat by my side in a hot gospel tent filled with suffering turned into song and sent to God.

She was doing what M'Dear taught me to do with my hands—absorb the sadness, the grief of others into my own body, send it up to the Moon Lady, then breathe out a fresh breath.

On the way home, I looked up at the sky. "I need you tonight. I need to see you, La Luna," I whispered.

I remembered M'Dear's voice, telling me, "The moon, La Luna, is always there. Her pull is strong, strong enough to move the mighty

Mississippi, Calla. The Moon Lady, La Luna, is your bridge from darkness to light. Trust in her strength."

I caught sight of the moon through the trees, and I prayed. *Oh, Moon Lady, I need your strength. I need some way of just letting this be. I ask you to teach me acceptance. Help me to accept this hard death of Sweet.*

And again M'Dear's voice filled my mind. "Look closely now," she said, "and wait. These are the two most important things I can tell you now. Look closely and wait."

Chapter 34

1981

Steve did some investigation for our case against the oil company. In his research he found out that something had fallen on Sweet during the explosion, and it hit his neck and head. I kept thinking about that, about my husband's bones, his tendons, his muscles. The thought of then holding someone else's head in my hands, well, it was more responsibility than I wanted right now. Just the weight of the skull, encasing the head. The muscles and bones. The top of the spinal column right there at the base of the neck. These precious parts terrified me. What if I hurt someone? It was all too much.

I had to tell Ricky that I couldn't work for a while. When I told him that he should maybe find someone else to replace me, he didn't speak at first. When he did, his voice was kind of husky.

"There *is* no replacing you, Calla."

❧

When M'Dear died, I felt like a big safety net was torn apart. When I married Sweet, I felt that net start to mend. Then Sweet was killed, and the net was blown apart again. Now there was nothing underneath. My life was my high wire, and I had to build my own safety net. Let the Moon Lady weave it out of stronger material than I or anyone could devise.

I took M'Dear's words to heart. I looked closely, and I waited.

I walked, usually one to two hours a day at first, trying to *think* my way to the next step. I walked all around the Garden District until I cleared my mind of everything except the simple act of putting one foot in front of the other.

Then I wrote letters to the folks at home who were worried. They hadn't heard much at all from me since the funeral. Finally, it was time to write.

The best place was our porch in the mid-morning sunlight.

May 5, 1981
New Orleans

Dear Nelle,

I can't thank you enough for coming down to be with me. First of all, to close the rink for a week. Everything you did gave me more hope. Your cooking—even though I know I didn't eat—made our home feel alive again for the first time since Sweet died. The smell of bell peppers and onions being sautéed, the early morning scent of bacon frying, made me remember that life had been good, and that it might be good again.

Our talks in the living room about Golden Princess and Mister Chaz doing well, but getting older. I miss them. This is the longest I've been away from home, and you're right. Maybe I should consider coming back some time soon. Will has offered to actually drive down, pick me up, and drive me to La Luna for the weekend. And drive me back to N.O. He is my sweet, quiet, sensitive brother, and when he plays his fiddle you know what kind of heart he has.

Not now, but maybe down the road, we'll talk more about my coming home and practicing beauty. Isn't it interesting that even though I've lived here in N.O. I still call La Luna my home? You're right, maybe because my roots are there my heart is there. Sweet & I used to talk about it—how we would have one child, or maybe two, and move back. This was before I knew that somehow it wasn't meant to be one of my blessings in this life.

Anyhooo—I've rambled on long enough. I'll sign off for now with much love and gratefulness.

Calla

May 15, 1981
New Orleans

Dear Renée,

Don't worry! Your last letter was nothing but worry. Worry is bad for your soul and for Eddie and the little ones (sounds like the name of a band, huh?), but mainly, worry is bad for your hair! No kidding, it is.

How is Calla Rose? I love the last batch of pictures you sent.

Guess what? I am taking a class in yoga! Now, don't think I've joined a satanic cult or something. It's just a way of exercising that acknowledges the soul. You know I have been interested in the soul ever since M'Dear talked to us about it when we were little girls. Well, I am trying to sort of sew my soul back together.

I've been babysitting Ricky and Steve's little cockapoo named Ginger Rogers. She is so cute and makes me laugh with her silliness.

Sukey and I see each other two or three times a week. She has become another person, Renée. Or maybe the person she always was and just had to uncover.

I've got to go feed Miss Ginger Rogers before she tap-dances across my feet!

Love to you, Eddie, my dear Calla Rose, and Little Eddie,

Calla

Then one morning over breakfast with Ricky, I said, "Ricky, something's changing."

He looked at me over his cup of coffee. We were sitting at our favorite diner, the Bluebird Grill.

"I'm starting to feel different. I'm starting to see the trees again. I heard a bird this morning. Something's widening in me."

"Good, good," he said, smiling. "It's been a while now. All right, let's have some bacon and eggs, huh? How about some bacon and eggs and some good grits, the way you like them, with lots of butter?"

"Ooooh," I moaned. "Ricky, just because I'm starting to feel a little better, don't go pushing that kind of food on me just yet."

"Okay," Ricky said. "How about some grits and toast? Grits and biscuits?"

"Mmm. Maybe just some grits," I said, "just some plain grits. Butter on the side, nothing fancy, okay?"

"Okay," Ricky said, "good."

"I don't want to rush it," I said. "I don't want to rush my mourning. It's mine. Maybe if I take enough time, my heart will just get bigger—big enough to take all this. You know what I mean?"

"Yeah," he said, "I think I do. Sweet was family to me, and to Steve, too."

"I know. Ohhh, bless Steve's heart. He's always the one who says, 'Calla's getting tired now. Let's leave her alone. Let's go home now.'

"And Ricky, you'll be saying, 'No, no, no! We're not leaving Calla alone. We've got *Casablanca* here to watch for the fourteenth time. We've got popcorn and plenty of chocolate!' You know, sometimes, Ricky, how you just don't let up?"

"I know," Ricky said. "It's just my Chalon nature."

It made my heart sad to hear him say that. "Chalon nature"—it's something I'd have loved to see get passed on. I remembered how Sweet and I tried so hard to make a baby—all the crazy things we did that we couldn't tell anybody, like me standing on my head. "Come on, Calla," Sweet would say, "let's do it like the yogis do."

"What do you know about yogis?" I'd say.

"Nothing," he'd say, holding my feet. "I don't know nothing about yogis, but I do know that you sure look good while I'm holding your feet and I get to see what I see."

"Oh, stop it!" I'd say, laughing.

I looked around the Bluebird Grill. It was so smoky—all that bacon and hamburgers and people smoking cigarettes. The smell was comforting and turned my stomach at the same time.

As I looked around, I felt myself somehow move outside of myself, the pain just beginning to let go so that I could finally see something else besides it. I could see where Ricky and I were, sitting in that booth right there on St. Charles Avenue on Skid Row.

I remembered being here at the Grill a few years ago at 2:00 a.m. But who was I with? It wasn't Sweet. So it must've been Sukey and me. I remembered the life I had before Sweet, how wild it was. Probably half of the people at the Grill that night were taxi drivers. I also saw a prom queen, a transvestite, and a police officer, all within fifteen feet of each other.

I chuckled out loud as I recalled that scene, sitting there with Ricky while a plate of grits was set down in front of me. I picked up my fork, inhaled the aroma of the grits, and got very calm.

I looked across at my dear friend, who'd helped pull me through the storm. I smiled and said, "I think I'm ready to start back up at the shop if it's okay."

Ricky smiled back. "Your chair's been waiting."

Chapter 35

DECEMBER 1981

I had been back working at Ricky's for almost six months or so when Steve called and said, "Let me take you to lunch."

"Sure, where do you want to go? Felix's?"

"How about Galatoire's?"

"Uh-huh," I said, laughing. "Yeaaaah, right."

"No, Calla, I'm serious."

"Really?"

The next thing I knew, we were at the glass doors and polished wood of Galatoire's, the grand dame of the oldest and grandest of New Orleans restaurants.

"Oh, wow. Steve, I can't go in there. Look at how I'm dressed!"

"Oh, come on, Calla. It doesn't matter. We can do anything we want."

I stepped in and saw the dining room in all its glory. It has very high ceilings and old mirrors set into the white woodwork. Above the mirrors, all the way to the ceiling, the walls were deep green with a large gold fleur-de-lis pattern.

Galatoire's legendary, graceful waiters have been there thirty, forty, fifty years, and when they retire, their sons inherit their jobs. You can just see that sense of history in the way they move, crisscrossing the dining room with such ease and grace.

"Steve, have you gone a little nuts?" I asked. "Or have you won a huge case, in which case you really should be taking Ricky to celebrate?"

"Well," he said, "I thought I'd take you instead."

"Aw, that's too sweet."

"No," he said. "Nothing's too sweet for you, Calla Lily."

As we sat down I could smell the extraordinary French Creole food that Galatoire's was famous for. A fine meal later, I was halfway through my crème brûlée when Steve took out an envelope.

"Calla, this is a celebration, if a bittersweet one," he told me. "This is for you."

"Well, what is it?" I asked.

"Just go ahead and open it."

I did, and oh, my God, it was a check with my name printed on it, "Calla Lily Ponder." After the dollar sign, there was a five, followed by five zeroes. All those little zeros: zero, zero, zero, zero, zero!

"Steve, this just can't be right!"

"Yes, Calla. It's your settlement. I would have liked more, but hey, this is pretty decent."

"I don't know what to say."

"How about, bring on the champagne!"

Steve signaled one of the waiters, and then for the first time in my life, I said: "Please bring us your very best bottle of French champagne."

After a while I felt so lightheaded that I couldn't think of what to do or say, so I ordered a second dessert, a piece of perfect bread pudding with whipped cream on top.

Then I started crying, crying a flood that wouldn't stop. I lifted my champagne glass one last time and quietly said, "To Sweet." I looked around at all the gold trim and lights and the waiters in their starched uniforms. And at the people who lunched there every day. And I just thought about my Sweet. His thick black hair, olive skin, sturdy body. Always wearing his pants with one leg tucked into his boot, and the other one halfway out. My husband.

Steve looked directly in my eyes for a long moment and then said, "To Sweet."

After all the champagne I drank, I realized that I couldn't go back to work, so I ordered a third dessert for Ricky as a consolation prize. When it arrived, Steve said, "Well, we might as well leave. Your carriage awaits."

Then I walked out the door, and what I saw made me squeal. Right outside the restaurant, there was a carriage pulled by two strong mules, with a liveried driver. I'd never before ridden in one of those carriages, though they are all over the Quarter.

"My carriage *does* await," I told Steve.

We laughed, and I thanked him from the bottom of my heart for the lunch, for the settlement, and for being such a dear friend.

Then I hopped into my carriage and rode it all the way home.

When Sukey got off work, I had her meet me in Audubon Park. The trees there are so beautiful and so ancient. Their roots go so deep into the ground that nothing could rip them up. A hurricane could tear through this place, and those trees would still be standing here.

We set out walking, and it wasn't long before Sukey complained, "Come on, Calla, will you slow down? Your legs are about eight inches longer than mine. I can't keep up with you."

So we stopped and sat down on a park bench. I told Sukey about the settlement, and she said, "Calla! You never have to work again for the rest of your life!"

"It's not that much," I said. "Plus, there are some people I want to share this with. So many who have helped pull me through, including you."

I reached into the deep pockets of my sundress and pulled out an envelope.

"Okay, close your eyes." Then I put the envelope into Sukey's hands. "All right! You can open them now," I said.

"Ahh," Sukey squealed, "Calla, are you nuts!"

"Thanks for sharing so many of your jewels," I said.

And we sat on the bench, and hugged. *Friends for life.* Then I thought of how much fun it would be to share this money with those I loved, and still have more than I had ever thought about.

"Yeah!" Sukey said. "And I could do it with you! Neither one of us would have to work. We could just lie up in the bed and watch movies and eat macaroni and cheese. And then afterwards, we could have big bowls of M&Ms. What do you think?"

"I think you're still fourteen years old."

"I think you're right," Sukey said. "I'm just kidding, of course. I don't ever want to stop working. I love being a counselor, and I'm just getting my practice up and running. Lord knows we've got enough alcoholics in Louisiana to keep me busy until the day I die!"

That night I had a dream so vivid that it woke me up. The moon was so full and bright that I could see my whole bedroom lit up. And I could see La Luna's strength, so powerful that it was driving all sadness out of the room, pushing it out to the Gulf of Mexico, where the vast body of water could handle it.

And as the sadness moved out, a whole new world of light came into me.

Suddenly, I knew what I would do: transform the old Swing 'N Sway into my salon. I could *see* it down to each little detail. It would be more than just a beauty shop.

In my dream, I opened the door of the Swing 'N Sway, a space that had once been a plantation grocery store, then a dance studio, and soon to be a beauty parlor. I saw the doors with their fine handiwork, the floors that were always kept immaculately clean and waxed every year. I saw the floor-to-ceiling mirrors, and the door that opened to the breezeway.

I saw it all, and then I saw an overlay of my shop, the new Crowning Glory, snap into place.

This would be the place where I would practice what M'Dear—and Ricky—helped teach me. I had been reading about reincarnation since Sweet's death, as suggested by my yoga teacher, and suddenly I realized that was true of places as well. The Swing 'N Sway would become the Crowning Glory, *and* dancing would still take place. Oh, yeah, I won't just do someone's hair; I'll invite them to dance! Mothers and daughters will dance together. And mother-daughter clients will always have discounts.

La Luna—I knew I could only do this in La Luna. I'd been planning to return soon, eventually, but when I woke up, I knew now it was time to finally go home.

When I told Ricky the next day, he was excited about my dream but still sad that I would be leaving soon. "Calla, you're so gifted that I'll never manage to replace you. But more than that, you're such a close friend—Steve and I will miss you badly."

"Ricky, I'm leaving what I can't absorb anymore—the noise, the smell, the roaches, the urine, the beer and mildew. I love this city, but I have to leave it. I need my small town."

He was glad that I'd finally gotten a vision of what I wanted to do, and he understood my mission to heal, because he is a healer himself. And it pleased him to see me with my determination back again.

"Calla, you can do anything," he said. "Declare victory *now*. You have gotten through the worst. You're smart, you're talented, and heck, you sure have learned to manage your money better than anybody I know. But most importantly, you have the gift of beauty and healing. Now, *relaxez-vous*!"

Chapter 36

SPRING 1982

The day I was supposed to move, I was slow to get out of bed. Finally, I took a long, deep breath and swung my legs out from under the covers and sat up. It amazed me that not so long ago, I was just lying there, never wanting to get up again.

I knew where I had to go.

When I got to the Butterfly, the spot that Sweet first showed me, the spot where we took the boat out and where he asked me to marry him, I sat for a while to contemplate all that had happened. I watched as the boats went by on the river. You hear those words, "the mighty Mississippi," and they seem like just a cliché. But they're not. This *is* such a wide and powerful river, and my Sweet loved it so much. I needed him, sitting right there by me, watching the ships go by. There was no amount of money that could make up for him being gone.

But I wasn't going to think about that. I was going to think about *this* moment, about this day of leaving, about the part of me that was moving forward. I was going to think about starting my shop and transforming the Swing 'N Sway. I was on my way.

Ricky and Steve came over mid-morning to help me pack.

"Guess whoo?!" Ricky called. "We're here with a bag of beignets and coffee. Where are you? We're here! Your moving men!"

I took a bite and a sip, and I have to admit, life always looks better after a beignet and coffee.

"All right, let's get going," I said.

Ricky was already pulling my clothes out of my drawers and packing them in boxes.

"Calla," he said, "we're going to set you up with a little 'three-day emergency pack' of clothes that you can wear till we get up to La Luna with the U-Haul. You'll be so busy you probably won't even notice."

"That's a good idea," I said. "And I'm going to take all the most special wedding gifts in the car with me. Every single thing that people gave us has a meaning—every fork, every spoon."

So very carefully, we packed all my wedding gifts in newspaper. With each object we touched, I got a little flash of memory. Especially the big, round Coca-Cola zippered thermos container.

"Why, Calla," Sweet had said to me, "that looks a whole lot more like a wig-carrying case than a thermos! Let's keep it in case you get some really hot wigs you need to cool off." We laughed so much about that. The two of us had actually ended up rolling around on the floor. I thought about how absolutely silly the two of us could be.

Ricky saw me looking sad and said, "Let's go get some nourishment. I could go for a po-boy right now."

"I'll stay here and keep packing," Steve offered. "But pick one up for me, too."

So Ricky and I headed out to Delucia's. Edna was behind the counter as usual.

"I think I'll have an oyster po-boy," I told her, "with as much sauce as you want to put on it."

"You got it."

"I'm sure going to miss you, Edna."

"Calla, I can't believe that you're really moving back home," she said. "Not a lot of people can leave New Orleans. You know, once you get down here, the gravity of this place can hold you tight."

"Oh, I know! The pull is strong," I said. "But going home has been a longtime dream for me."

Edna wrapped up our po-boys and put them in a bag.

"Could you give us three soda fountain Cokes, too?" I asked. "Not bottled or canned but real soda fountain Cokes with a lot of ice, please. And a big bag of Doritos."

We brought the food home and sat out on the glassed-in porch to eat. Ricky and I sat on the swing where Sweet and I had spent so much time.

"I'm gonna miss these tomatoes on the po-boys, and how the bread gets soft from the sauce," I said.

"Yum," Ricky agreed. "But don't you worry. You're going to have plenty of good food in La Luna, too."

Steve came out and joined us. "Are you going to miss Ginger Rogers, too?" he asked, unwrapping his po-boy.

"Yes, I am," I said, thinking of that crazy little dancing dog they had.

We finished our po-boys and the entire bag of Doritos. Then Ricky said, "Y'all can lounge around here as long as you want, but *I* am getting back to work. Lazy butts, lazy butts! How do you ever expect to get packed?"

"Just let me finish my Coke," I said.

Ricky and Steve went into the house, and I took a few minutes to enjoy my Coke and think about my move. The idea of it both thrilled and scared me to death. Then I opened the porch door and heard a tippy-tap sound, like Sukey in high heels. "Hey, Suke?" I called out.

But it wasn't Sukey. Instead a little creature with wonderful blond and white hair, big eyes, and long floppy ears came tip-tapping out from the kitchen. *I must be dreaming*, I thought.

Then Ricky and Steve appeared in the kitchen doorway, both of them grinning. Ricky said, "Now you know why Steve wanted to stay here while we went for po-boys. Calla, honey, this little guy is a stand-in for the two of us. He'll be with you to keep us on your mind."

"Oh, how adorable," I said as I picked up the little dog, who was just the right size to hold and pet in your lap.

"He's a cockapoo, just like Miss Ginger," Ricky told me.

I set the little dog down, and wouldn't you know it? He just started tip-tapping in this little backward dance on the wooden floor.

"What are you going to call him?" Steve asked.

"There's only one name I could give him," I said. "Why, he's Fred Astaire!"

Finally, there was nothing left to pack but Sweet's clothes. Ricky and Steve had offered to box them up and take them to the thrift store. But that just didn't feel right to me. I wasn't ready to have every trace of my husband scattered to the winds as his body was. I didn't want strangers—who didn't even know that he always wore the sleeves of his shirts rolled up—to have more of Sweet than I did.

"Let me look these clothes over and think," I told them.

So they left me alone as I opened Sweet's dresser drawers and flung open the door to the closet. I wanted to feel the fullness of his presence.

"Sweet," I said, "I believe in the kingdom of heaven, and I know that while you were here on earth, you earned a just reward by bringing people joy. Your joy, your spirit, is still in these clothes. Help me figure out where they belong."

And then it came to me, just what I needed to do. I called Ricky and Steve back into the bedroom.

"Let's box them up," I said. "I'm going to take them all with me."

So we did. When we were all through, I walked through the empty house. I looked at the floors, remembering how we'd stripped off coats and coats of paint and then sanded and oiled them—Sweet was so good at that.

"I hope the people moving in will treat these floors as nice as we have," I told Ricky and Steve.

"They'd better," Ricky said, "or they'll have us to contend with."

As we walked down the front steps I said, "Y'all, wait a minute. Hold Fred Astaire for me. There's just one last little thing I need to do inside."

And I went back in. I kissed the door handle of our bedroom, and I looked around the room and thought of all the times we'd made sweet love in there. Then I went in the kitchen and I kissed the stove, thanking it for all the pots of red beans and rice we'd cooked on top of it, and all the gumbos. I looked around the kitchen and then stood on the back porch, and finally, the front porch. As I walked down the steps for the last time, I turned around and gathered it all in my hands, pulling it into my heart. And then—*whoooshhhh*! With a whoosh, I let it go.

Chapter 37

1982

After kissing our house good-bye, I climbed into my Mustang, and drove away from New Orleans, my home for over ten years—the place where I'd found the love of my life, the city where I'd made a home. I felt kind of relieved that it would be a few days before Ricky and Steve arrived with the U-Haul. I needed to feel myself at home again in La Luna.

So it was just me and Fred Astaire, heading out on the highway. He was a good little traveler, curling up on the front seat and sleeping the whole way. I had Stevie Wonder on the tape deck. I love Stevie Wonder. His music has often comforted me. It's made me laugh and cry and dance and sing.

Pretty soon, trees and fields, sky and water, took the place of buildings. I saw a wide flat horizon with billowy white thunderheads coming up from the south. I knew I'd better get on home before those thunderstorms hit.

Living in New Orleans, it had been easy to forget how beautiful the home soil of rural Louisiana was. Fertile fields and farms and bayous whizzed by as I made my way along the red-earthed low flatlands. Gradually the road drifted away from the river delta into prairielike land that wasn't farmed as much as the rich soil next to the river. The road climbed just a bit, and the two-lane highway began to split patches of piney woods and stands of hardwood trees. There was just the occasional white clapboard farmhouse now and then, and white egrets standing motionless in the fields that opened up between forests.

I began to breathe a little easier and deeper, and I turned my thoughts to La Luna.

Papa still taught a class or two, and the first Saturday of the month still found everybody dancing and playing music, starting at nine in the morning. The Swing 'N Sway had been constantly in my thoughts, with its floor-to-ceiling mirrors and its rich history, in my vision for the Crowning Glory.

I could not wait to get into that studio and make it even more beautiful than it was. Soon I came upon the last rural stretch of the parish before Claiborne, where the curved edges of the fields and the unexpected stands of trees made me think of the old European landscape paintings I'd seen in the museum in New Orleans. As I got off the main road and took a detour to avoid going through Claiborne, I came to the bridge that crossed over the slow moving, red-brown water of the La Luna River.

And then I was home! La Luna was about a mile square, bounded by the river on one side and farm fields and woods on the other three. I got off the bridge and drove toward the town center about a block in. There was a small black AME Baptist church at the edge of town, then

Our Lady of the River church, then the high-steepled white Southern Baptist church. I smiled as I drove by Nelle's Shop, Snack 'N Skate. Nelle, I'll see you soon!

Our home was downriver from the bridge, a few sleepy blocks away. And indeed, all was quiet as I pulled into our gravel driveway. I turned off the ignition and leaned back in my seat for a while. My window was open, and I listened to the silence and the soft sounds of the river. I let the shadows of the live oaks and magnolias settle down upon me.

I'd already talked to Papa about converting the dance studio into my salon. On my last visit to La Luna, I'd brought him and my brothers some of my settlement money. Papa said, "Calla, honey, this money will let me do what I've wanted to do for a long time—move out of the house, start out fresh, and make new memories. I've been wanting to scale back on my teaching and play more with my combo. So if you want the house, it's yours. I'd love to move up to my fishing camp full time."

"Oh, Papa, I don't want to kick you out of the home where you've lived forever."

"I've been holding on to this place for you," he said, "like your M'Dear told me to. I knew you'd be back someday." Then Papa grinned. "And I got catfish with my name on them!" He laughed, and I joined in.

"Oh, Papa!" I said, then I hugged him tight. It felt wonderful to laugh together.

The next morning I stood at the front entrance to the Swing 'N Sway. There I was looking at an old dance studio to renovate into a salon—plus a house to make my own for me and Fred Astaire. I prayed, *Oh, Moon Lady and M'Dear, I need your help to step over this threshold and claim this place as my Crowning Glory.* Then I felt a slight nudge, and the next thing I knew, I was standing in the studio with brand-new eyes.

I had a vision of just where I wanted the shampoo sink and the special, comfortable leaning-back chair—just one, because I'm going to be one-on-one with all my customers, hoping that healing will come with my touch for all of them. I'll find someone to handle manicures and pedicures.

I'll use M'Dear's antique vanity for my rollers and perm rods and scissors. And I'll get some kind of rolling unit made out of lightweight wood. I don't want anything cold and plastic in my salon.

I can see it now. I'll expand the old dance studio porch and get a new swing with pretty cushions on it. Then I'll paint up our old wicker chairs and table, so clients can sit there and read magazines while sipping on real lemonade and ice tea. I'll make my salon so inviting and beautiful that just walking in will make clients feel relaxed. So my vision for the Crowning Glory was emerging, and I had the Moon Lady and M'Dear to thank for it.

Oh, it was so wonderful to be back home! I wanted to keep the house more or less the way M'Dear had it, the way it had been for years. I'll leave M'Dear and Papa's room the way it was for the time being, but I'll redo my room with a new paint color—a lavender that makes me feel both calm and alive.

And the kitchen—I *loved* that old kitchen! The walls were an old rich buttery yellow, and it had old green-and-white tile countertops, a painted wood floor, and all the wooden cabinetry originally built by my grandfather. The cabinetry was painted white when I was little, but then M'Dear painted it all a fabulous deep scarlet. Using that color in the kitchen was just unheard of in La Luna, or *anywhere* as far as I was concerned. But that was M'Dear for you. That kitchen with all its color always felt like a party.

The house still had ceiling fans in every room, which we used all year round. In winter, I loved how the blades moved counterclockwise, to push the hot air down to warm us.

How I loved this house that was once shared by the five of us. Now it would be home to me and Fred Astaire—and who knows, possibly someone else someday.

It was such a comfort to me to have Sweet's clothes with me as I settled in, but I knew it was time to give them away.

One day I saw Olivia's husband, Pana, riding by on his bicycle. So I called out, "Pana! Hello! I've got something for you."

"Are you cooking?" he asked.

"No, it's not food." Then I gave him Sweet's nylon windbreaker jacket, which was gray with black and purple diagonal stripes.

"Try it on," I told him. "Go on in and look at yourself in the mirror."

"Oh, this nice, this real nice. Thank you, Miss Calla. It so nice to have you in the house. I look out at night and see your lights. Since your daddy spend so much time up to the camp, this old house so lonely, be like you could just feel how lonely it was. You need anything done around here, you just call. I be watching over you all the time."

Since the jacket fit Pana so well, I gave him some of Sweet's shirts and pants too. I tied them up in a bundle with string.

"Are you sure you can carry all that on your bike?" I asked. "I can bring it to you later."

"No, no, I carry lots of things on my bike."

Then he was off, slowly pedaling the bike across the road, wearing Sweet's jacket.

Little by little, I gave Sweet's clothes away to people I knew. Then I piled up the rest and drove them to the black Baptist church. After that the strangest thing would happen. Every once in a while, I'd spot Sweet's clothes on the back of someone heading out to pick pecans, on someone walking to the mailbox, on the school bus driver, on a man going to church. I even saw some women wearing Sweet's shirts. At first, that threw me. I'd catch a glimpse of a certain plaid shirt, for instance, and would think it was Sweet. I'd have to stop the car and take a big, deep breath to calm myself down.

Then I started to love seeing Sweet's clothes being worn by people in La Luna. They were like little pieces of Sweet still moving, a reminder that he really was still there—not so I could touch him, but in the way that red birds flit past on a cold winter day. You can't touch them, but they are there, giving a bit more color to the world.

The one thing of Sweet's that I kept for myself was his T-shirts. I'd loved sleeping in them when he was alive, and I still did now that he was gone. Sometimes, I'd lift the soft cotton of the T-shirt to my nose and imagine that I could still smell his smell. That was such a comfort.

Once I let Sonny Boy know that I had to decided to convert the dance studio into my Crowning Glory salon, it seemed like everybody started calling and showing up, wanting to do something for me. I couldn't believe it. I didn't even have to ask most of the time. Somehow, I had forgotten how people in a small town just pitch in and help to "*get it done!*"

The first thing I discussed with Sonny Boy, who now had his own construction company, Sonny Boy Building, was how to divide the space so we could continue the first-Saturday-of-the-month dances and cook-ups that had been a tradition in La Luna since we were kids. I told him I only needed a third of the old dance studio for my salon.

He helped me with everything, making sure that those floors got resanded and then putting a good coat of varnish on them. He sketched a plan for putting French doors in at the entrance.

"I want to get that whole front section open for you," he told me, "so that the light and a view of the river can come in. I think two, maybe even three sets of French doors. I've found you some good old brick out by the Bennett plantation, so I can make you a patio with a fountain. Will is on board to design everything. I want your ladies to look out there and see the river and be able to hear it. And you can plant all kinds of flowers around the patio and have an awning and little tables and lounge chairs where the customers can sit and relax."

Aunt Helen, of course, offered to do anything involving sewing. We decided to drape gold tulle around the edges of the mirror where I would do hair. It had been the mirror that sat on top of M'Dear's antique dresser, and it had these wonderful 1920s ornate rosettes and curlicues on the edges, plus two little drawers on the side where I could keep my instruments. I wanted to start with the mirror because it would be the first thing clients would see. I wanted the salon to feel like an old drawing room in the South, homey and a little mysterious.

As for the rest, Renée found me some gorgeous old wooden cabinetry and helped me paint it a glossy black with gold accents. And I found a comfortable plump chair that was red with tiny little gold specks.

Ricky and Steve arrived early Saturday morning for the weekend, and worked with Will and me to choose my color scheme. We decided that the walls should be painted mauve. Steve took control of having the paint mixed just right. Then we all went to work painting. By the time Ricky and Steve headed back to New Orleans late Sunday night, Ricky was saying, "My back is killing me. I shudder to think what the hairdos I come up with tomorrow will look like."

The next weekend they came back, bringing Sukey along, too, to start focusing on all the accents for the salon. Ricky was particularly good with lighting. Ricky said, "Now, we need to start working with your aunt's chiffon fabric. I'd like to be a little more careful in the relationship between the lights and the chiffon. We do have everything on dimmers, is that correct?"

"Exactly, Ricky."

"I couldn't take it if it wasn't. Now—"

"Ricky, come over here. I want to show you this little area that I'm calling 'the parlor.' We're going to have lamps in there, too."

"Very good. The more lamps, the better. Remember, everyone looks better in a pink light."

"Ricky, I know—but I want people to leave here looking like they will in the real world."

"Calla, I ask you, what is more healing? To see yourself as you want to see yourself, or to see yourself as you think others will see you?"

I said, "Well, to see yourself as you want to see yourself."

"I rest my case," Ricky said. "Everyone looks better in *pink* light."

I had to laugh, but that silly conversation made me think. *He's right. This whole place is about healing. It's about healing myself and healing anyone who comes in.* Then I walked Ricky out to the porch.

"Papa's redoing the porch with Pana's help. They're putting in new screens and making sturdy new steps. I'm asking them to paint them periwinkle, along with the interior of the porch. So when my customers enter the Crowning Glory, they will know they're entering a different kind of a place. And I'll be having music playing that you can hear from out here, music that makes your hair feel good."

"Perfecto," Ricky said. "Yes, Calla, relaxation is everything."

"This space," I said, "which has healed for years, will continue its magic!"

That evening, Ricky, Steve, Sukey, and I cooked dinner and had a lovely, lively visit together before they had to head back to New Orleans. I missed them terribly as they drove off, but I was excited that the Crowning Glory was really coming together.

Miz Lizbeth was the one who gave me the rug for the parlor at the salon. The day I'd gone to visit and update her about all my plans for the salon, she said, "Why, Calla, I've got a rug here that has been rolled up forever that would be perfect."

It *was* perfect and so beautiful, an old-fashioned shade of light blue with a wine-colored pattern.

"Are you sure you want to give this away?" I asked.

"Absolutely. We've had that rug rolled up ever since my sister passed. That was about the time you and Tucker started going together."

I stopped for a minute and looked at her.

"Ohhh," she said, "I haven't forgotten those times. It sure is good to have you back in town." Then she pulled a photo album off the bookcase.

"There are a bunch of memories of you and Tuck in here. I thought you might like to go through it after all these years."

She opened the album and set it in my lap, leaving it to me to turn the pages. And there we were: me and Tuck when he first got to La Luna and I hated him, then the two of us after we got to be best friends, and finally as a couple during the summer when we fell in love.

By the time I got to the prom pages, my whole body was hot! I felt nauseated.

"Well," I said, "it's just been lovely to look at these pictures." I closed the album. "Will you excuse me, please? I need to go to the bathroom."

I went upstairs, because the Tuckers never did put in a bathroom downstairs in their old house. The bathroom was just as I remembered it, with its big old claw-foot tub. I grabbed one of the washcloths, and I wet it and put it on my forehead. "Don't get mascara all down your face," I told myself, "or else Miz Lizbeth will know something's wrong."

I squeezed my eyes tight. You can do that, you know—squeeze your eyes so tight that the tears don't come. Then I looked in the mirror, took a deep breath, and walked back downstairs.

Luckily, Miz Lizbeth didn't have a clue. "You know how well Tucker's doing?" she said. "I mean, that law firm of his, it's one of the finer ones in San Francisco. And Mimi, his wife, is so beautiful. Her father's one of the founding partners in that firm, and Tuck is getting real close to being a full partner himself. Not because of the father-in-law, mind you. No, he's earned it. He's been working sixty to seventy hours a week since he started. Tuck's come out just twice, and both times by himself. Well, he's so busy at the law firm. And you know, she's got all her charities and society parties and all. I probably shouldn't be telling you this, but last time Tuck called, it sounded like they were having marital problems."

Then Miz Lizbeth took a clean handkerchief from inside the cuff of her blouse and swiped a tear from her eyes. "It makes me so sad, Calla. I always dreamed that you and Tuck would be together." She looked at me, and I looked away.

"Yes, ma'am," I said, in a voice that wasn't really mine. "Thank you so much for the rug, Miz Lizbeth."

I mumbled an excuse and started to back toward the door.

"Anyway!" she said, "I'm so glad you came by, Calla. I'll have that rug carried over to the Crowning Glory. And if there's anything you need, you know you can call on us—we're right next door. I'm an old lady, but you just call me, okay?"

"Thank you," I said. Then I left, and I walked the path that Tuck and I had used hundreds of times, going back and forth through the pine trees. I could walk it in my sleep.

When I got back home, I called Sukey and told her I had just come back from the Tuckers'.

"What's wrong?" she asked.

"Well, nothing, really, except that—oh, Suke! I thought I didn't care anything about Tuck anymore. It's been so *long*, you know? I loved Sweet so much, and my heart is still so full of love for him. I don't understand why I should be so upset when Miz Lizbeth talks about Tuck and how well he's doing." I paused. "You know, Suke, I think about our senior year in high school, when Renée and Eddie were already ahead of us, announcing their engagement. Tuck wouldn't even look me in the eyes when they did. He knew then, didn't he? He knew he wasn't coming back. Why didn't I know? Why was I so *stupid*?"

Sukey said, "Snap out of it, Calla. You've got a wonderful new life there in La Luna. You're building a business, your Crowning Glory. Believe me, it's going to be a place where everybody wants to be. You have fulfilled your dream, Calla. You wanted to come to New Orleans. You wanted to get trained. You wanted to become a really good beautician. And now you're back in La Luna like you wanted to be. With your own shop."

"Yeah," I said. "Only I found what I wanted, and then I lost it."

"I know," Sukey said. "I think about Sweet, too, and about how funny he was. I mean, that Sweet could have you on the floor."

That made me laugh, and then I started to cry while I was laughing.

"Calla," Sukey said, "why don't I come tomorrow and spend the night? We'll eat pizza, and I'll bring you some good beer from New Orleans. How does that sound?"

"No, Suke, no. You can't—no—don't bring beer!"

"Ha-ha-ha! Gotcha," Sukey laughed. "You know I wouldn't touch a beer with a ten-foot pole."

"Okay, you got me," I said, with a sigh of relief. "But really, I'm fine, Suke. You don't need to come."

"You promise?" Sukey asked.

"I promise."

"Cross your heart and hope to die?"

"Yes, cross my heart and hope to die."

"Stick a needle in your eye?"

I started laughing. "Stick a needle in my eye."

"I love you," Sukey said.

"I love you too, Suke. Love you like a cuke."

I hung up the phone and just sat on the couch, stroking Fred Astaire in my lap. Sometimes, I can't tell how long it is that I just sit. Quiet. Time just melts away.

Chapter 38

1983

The whole town had pitched in. It was like a Shaker barn-raising. So we were able to open the Crowning Glory in six months! Of course, everyone who had been involved in any way with the renovation wanted to put in their two cents' worth about the grand opening. At first, the only thing everyone could agree on was that there should be a grand opening and that it should be a very big deal. I just listened and noted everyone's suggestions. The one thing I knew was that I wanted to hold the opening on a night with a full moon. March's full moon happened to fall on a Saturday night.

Joseph Moreau, my neighbor down the road, had volunteered to groom the grounds all around the salon. He pruned the trees and pulled old pecan branches and brambles out of the tall grass before cutting it. He even uncovered a forgotten fig tree. Our place was really beginning to shine again. One evening, I brought out a pitcher of lemonade and thanked him for all of his hard work. He just brushed it off, saying, "Y'all's place always felt like a park to me when we were growing up. I was shy back then, and you and your mama were always kind to me. Fixing the grounds seemed the best way to honor her memory and welcome you back."

I was thinking of how to respond when Joseph gave me a shy smile and got back to work. As I walked back to the house, it struck me—not for the first time—how many lives in this little community M'Dear had deeply touched and how many people cared that I'd returned.

Joseph's family's place was on the other side of Gum Swamp. It wasn't a big farm, but being so close to the river, it had excellent soil. "Ice cream dirt" is what Pana called that kind of land. Joseph had badgered his daddy and brother into switching to organic farming. At first, the rest of the farmers in town shunned the Moreaus and made jokes about them, considering them to be somewhere between hippies and communists. But then they noticed that the Moreaus were getting a good price for their crops, while a lot of other small farms were going under. Any way you cut it, farming is hard work. Anybody who can make a go of it earns respect. Eventually all those farmers' wives, along with the rest of the town, started showing up at the Moreaus' roadside produce stand to buy honey and vegetables.

When Ricky and Steve moved me back to La Luna, I took them to the Moreaus' stand to load up on goodies for the weekend's meals. I was surprised by Ricky's reaction to Joseph's sign. It was bright yellow with thick hand-painted red letters: "Home-grown, Hand-picked, Fresh as You Can Get."

Ricky just stared at it and then quietly said, "That is a poem. That is just a perfect Zen poem."

Those words embodied what my life had become since I came home to La Luna: "Home-grown, Hand-picked, Fresh as You Can Get."

One weekend Sukey came home to stay with Sally. Helping me paint a dining room chair that we'd made comfy with colorful pillows, she looked up from painting for a moment.

"Calla, I'm lonely for La Luna. I didn't know it until I started coming home so frequently, watching how everyone cares about each other, how they all remember me so well. They don't know how I lived my life in New Orleans, but even if they did, they'd still love me. Do you think I'm right?"

I put down the glue gun I'd been using on one of the cosmetic carts. "Yes," I said to my friend, "you got it right."

"Well, then," she said, "I'm going to wrap up things in New Orleans, and move back to La Luna."

I have to admit that my jaw dropped before I gave her a hug. I hadn't known how lonely I was for Sukey. "Welcome home," I said.

So Sukey moved back a couple months after I did. "Hey, there are alcoholics everywhere," she said. "Especially in small towns. And then, of course, there's Claiborne."

On the afternoon of the Crowning Glory's grand opening I happily walked the grounds. Everything was so beautiful that I spread my arms wide to the river and sky, inviting everything—birds, angels, lost souls, friends old and new, friends not yet met, babies not yet born—to join me in celebrating the Crowning Glory.

I was halfway up the path to the house when I ran into Ricky and Steve. Talk about boys who knew how to dress up for a party! Steve wore a vertical-striped vest with a pink satin bow tie, and Ricky was decked out in a light linen jacket over elegant pale gray, pleated gabardine slacks. I squealed when I saw them, and we hugged and kissed.

Then Ricky handed me a small parcel.

"Calla, this was left on the porch of the shop. There's no name on it, but it has to be for you."

"Oh, come on, you guys, I know you too well—"

"No, Calla, it isn't from us," Steve said firmly.

The parcel was wrapped in old-fashioned, shiny, brittle brown paper and tied with a length of brown string. I turned it over and shook it a few times before pulling the paper off. Soon I was looking at the back of an old, beautifully carved, Art Nouveau picture frame. When I flipped it over to see the front, I got a little chill. The frame held a faded but still quite beautiful picture of a Victorian woman in a flowing white gown sitting in the curve of a cutout moon. Her arms reached slightly downward toward a little painted hamlet beneath her bare feet.

"I have no idea who this is from," I said, unable to take my eyes off the picture. I decided to think about it later.

Then I walked back to the salon alone and stood before a black-and-white photo of M'Dear, draped in a mist of silk gauze, with a group of young girls in leotards and tights (one of them was me). *M'Dear*— I smiled—*be with me tonight as we celebrate. And thank you.* Then I pressed my finger to my lips and kissed M'Dear's image.

Outside, car doors were already slamming, so I walked out onto the porch. Folks started streaming in with casseroles and side dishes. Miz Lizbeth directed the flow as if she were a seasoned traffic cop. Ricky said, "Well, my protégée, I'd say the gala has begun."

So many people hugged and kissed me as they arrived that I lost count after ten minutes. When the sun set, the children were finally allowed to light the luminaria lining the paths from the road to the house and to the pier. Sonny Boy and Will took charge of the lanterns they'd placed overhead in the trees. The heavenly smells of gumbo and barbecue—Louisiana ambrosia—wafted through the gathering crowd. Nelle was camped in a wicker chair, telling whoever was in earshot, "They all done a real fine job fixing up this place." Everybody was amazed at how Sonny Boy's crew had renovated the studio. Outside in the fading light, people happily mixing together in the patio were saying how it was magic that I had so many fireflies around when it was too early to find them everywhere else.

Then came the unmistakable ringing sound of a dinner knife hitting a glass, signaling that it was time for a toast. The crowd gradually quieted down, and in the warm center of the big room, Papa was saying, "I'd like to raise a glass to my Calla Lily. Where are you, sweetie?"

Everyone started to clap and holler as I made my way to Papa's side. His eyes were wet, and he glanced up at the ceiling to try to keep the tears from rolling down his cheeks.

"I was gonna say," Papa began, "that the only thing missing from this evening is our Lenora, Calla's M'Dear. But you know what? I think she *is* here—all over this place, but mainly in my daughter, who has the hands, the healing touch, of her mother." Then Papa gave me a hug, and said, "You want to say a few words, babe?"

I looked out at the gathering. "Thank you," I said, "for welcoming me home—for your love and your labor in transforming the Swing 'N Sway into the Crowning Glory. I'm gonna wash, color, and cut your hair. I'm gonna massage your bodies—if you'll let me! And all along, I'm going to try to make this place as much fun as it was when M'Dear danced with Papa. Now—*laissez les bons temps rouler*!"

Ned and Jolie, a local couple who played a guitar and fiddle, were providing the music. Two of their cousins from Evangeline Parish had joined them on the bass fiddle and squeeze-box accordion. The accordion player started out with a solo that led into a full-tilt boogie Cajun dance tune that got everyone up and moving, and the old folk tapping their feet. After a few tunes, Will and Papa and the La Lunatics sat in, too. I worked my way back through the crowd to the open French doors of the salon. I stepped out into the courtyard, where the night sky was so bright and the scent of jasmine from the garden was deliciously strong. I sat down on a garden bench and simply enjoyed the sweetness of this evening. Nelle snuck up behind me and, sitting down next to me, she asked, "So, Calla, sweetie, could you have hoped for better than this?"

"No," I said. "This is just perfect. Thank you, Nelle. For your encouragement and support."

"I told you, Calla Lily, didn't I? You built yourself a career just like we talked about all those years ago. Now look at you! I love you—and don't you forget it!"

We put our arms around each other, and I kissed her on the cheek. "I owe you most of this, Nelle."

Nelle said, "Ha! We both know better. Your mama had a lot to do with this. And Ricky. But mainly you. Now, don't stay up too late now, you hear me? You got to do my hair day after tomorrow."

Almost all the older people were making their good-byes now, leaving the dancing to the younger folks. Will took me back out to the porch with a big bowl of gumbo and some warm French bread. "Hey, sis, you sit down now and eat. You been on your feet for hours."

As I ate the good food, Sonny Boy and Papa came out to join us, and the four of us sat there in the light of the grand, full moon. Papa got up after a time and leaned down and kissed me on my forehead. He said in my ear, "You made your papa proud tonight. More than that, you made your papa happy. And your M'Dear, too. Love you up to the sky, daughter of mine." I took out my hankie to wipe my tears and half-jokingly offered it to Papa. He looked at it and said, "Isn't that M'Dear's lavender hankie?"

All I could do was nod. He squeezed my hand, then he hugged my brothers and headed out to his truck, giving a wave over his shoulder. He paused for a moment in the shimmering moonlight, and waltzed a few steps as though his partner was fully there. He gave a little bow, then turned and walked back to his truck. In the glow of the moon, he looked like a much younger man, a man in love with someone he'd dance with forever.

Will offered me his arm and said, "Hey, sugar, care for a dance?"

"I'd love to, Will. Yes, I would. I am ready to dance!"

So I danced and I danced. I danced with JoAnn and I danced with Aunt Helen. I danced with Will, with Sonny—and then in a trio with Ricky and Steve. I even danced with Fred Astaire, who had appointed himself my mascot for the night. With the little handmade tuxedo Aunt Helen made for Mister Astaire, he was quite the canine gentleman.

A few minutes before midnight, the band wrapped up with a rousing swamp-pop number. Then Ricky announced that everyone was supposed to go down to the pier at twelve o'clock sharp. Folks looked at me to see what was going on. "I have no idea," I told them. "This is news to me."

There were only about twenty of us left, and we all wandered down the path toward the pier. Some of the luminaria had burned out, and a few others were flickering. But the bright moonlight helped us to make our way.

As we got to the pier, we could see lanterns being lit on a small boat drifting toward us, silhouetting two passengers. As the boat drew closer, we could see a man who was rowing and a woman wearing a large, loose-flowing dress that was falling off one shoulder. The woman took two long objects, one in each hand, and touched their tips to the six lanterns on the bow, setting off a shower of light on each. She then flung her arms out to her sides, which revealed the objects to be two large, pale fans, now fully open, with sparklers extending from the ribs. In the white light of the sputtering sparklers, we could see that the figure was Sukey, moving her fans in a slow dreamy dance.

Our small crowd stood silent as the sparklers burned out and the boat slipped back into the darkness. Then Renée broke the spell by whispering, "Oh, Sukey, you always did have—" Then we finished the sentence together: "*Jewels* in your purse!"

Renée called out, "The La Lunettes live eternal!"

Then we all let go with whoops and hollers. What a night! What a magical, overflowing night.

As I walked back to the house with Ricky and Steve, I asked them, "Y'all know a lot of painters down in New Orleans, don't you?"

"Sure, we do," Steve replied. "Why do you ask?"

"Well, I'd love to get someone to paint a scene of the moon over the river and Sukey in the boat. I want to hang it in a place of honor in the Crowning Glory. I want art all over the place. I want the whole place itself to be a work of art."

When we reached the back door, I told Ricky and Steve, "Y'all go on in. I'll join you in a minute."

I looked up at the moon and I thought of something M'Dear told me on one of the afternoons when we talked about her dying: "Look up and throw me a kiss, baby, and I'll send one back to you. Think about the stars, Calla, think about the moon."

Through happy, teary eyes, I threw kiss after kiss after kiss up to M'Dear and the Moon Lady, and the friends who had helped carry me this far.

Chapter 39

SPRING 1983

As soon as the Crowning Glory was open for business and I got my schedule down, I was able to go out to St. Mary's Home one afternoon a week to do the old people's hair. I took Fred Astaire with me because the old folks just loved to pet him. Sometimes Nelle would come with me just to visit with the folks and try and cheer them up. With Bertha and Cleveland at the Shop, Snack 'N Skate, she had more time to herself. We made a point to ride at least twice a week, and I was in love with her horse, Mister Chaz.

We both enjoyed our time at St. Mary's.

St. Mary's used to have a staff beautician, but she insisted on smoking because it was her constitutional right. According to Nelle, who heard everything, Sister Claire told her, "You go exercise your constitutional right somewhere else."

When word got around that I was back in La Luna, Sister Claire asked me to take over the position of in-house hairdresser. But I told her that I was up to my ears in my own practice.

"Oh, my," she said. "I suppose we should pray to Mary Magdalene, patron saint of hairdressers."

I was so surprised that she knew that. But, of course, nuns know exactly how to get their way.

"Tell you what, Sister," I said. "I'll come every Wednesday afternoon as a volunteer. It'll be my donation, okay?"

Between my volunteer work and the salon, I was busy as a Mexican jumping bean. I started getting clients from Claiborne. Beth Owens was one of them. The first time she arrived she was dressed chic as the day was long, with a French manicure, which I appreciated because I was exhausted with all the foot-long fake scarlet-colored nails I'd been seeing.

"My daughters have raved about you," she said. "And I just had to see who was giving them such smart cuts."

"That would be me," I replied.

She smiled and started admiring the art on my walls, including the new painting of Sukey on the boat I'd just hung.

"That other painting, the one of the woman with long red hair," I said, pointing to it, "it was done by a woman who lives in the French Quarter. She's never had any formal art training. She just loves to paint people that most folks don't consider saints—not yet anyway."

Underneath the painting, I'd put a plaque reading "Saint Mary Magdalene, Patron Saint of Hairdressers."

"You do know about Mary Magdalene, don't you?" I asked her.

"Well, yes, I mean, she was a sinner. I know that," Beth replied.

"Indeed she was!" I said. "History's most famous reformed harlot. I am devoted to her. I mean, any woman who washed Christ's feet with her tears, dried them with her hair, anointed his toes with perfume, and also enjoyed sex has my vote! She's the one who was with Christ when he died, and she helped bury Him—not to mention she was the first witness to the Resurrection. Saint Luke wrote, 'Her sins, which are many, are forgiven, for she loved much.'"

I caught myself and slapped my hand over my mouth. "What a way to welcome a new client! I'm standing here acting like this is catechism class."

Beth said, laughing, "Lord knows, I need forgiveness, for I have sinned a helluva lot myself."

I laughed. "Oh, I think you might be a daughter of Mary Mag."

"Mary Mag! That's hysterical. And to think I've spent my whole life trying to be a good daughter of the other Mary."

Suddenly, my new client burst into tears.

"I'm awfully sorry," she said, "I *must*, I just can't seem to—you must think I'm deranged."

"Who isn't deranged one way or the other? It's how we dance with the derangement," I said, leading her to the massage chair.

"Now, before I wash my clients' hair, I like to give them a scalp and neck massage. How's that sound to you, Beth?"

"Delicious."

"Then just lean back, and let your head rest in the cradle. You've had massages before, right?"

"Yes," she said. "But not as much as I crave them."

"Okay, now, just breathe."

"I'm not good at just breathing," she told me. "My mind is always too busy."

"Well, pretend this is your to-do list for the afternoon: (1) Breathe in. (2) Breathe out. (3) Breathe in. (4) Breathe out. Count up to a hundred that way and see what happens. Let me do the rest."

Then I took a deep breath myself and began to massage her scalp, rubbing circles around her temples. I remembered watching my mother do this with Mrs. Gaudet, years ago, when the woman was grieving for her husband.

Beth's head was heavy in my hands. I moved down to the base of her skull, rubbing every little point in her ears. She breathed more deeply, exhaling little puffs of tension. As I massaged the different points, I felt her fear. *We all have our fears, some that are known, and others that are unknown*. I let her fear come into me, as the large black lady in the gospel tent did for me.

I massaged the crown of her head and then the sides. Slowly, I worked my way to her shoulders. That's when I heard her heave a huge sigh of relief. I kept kneading her shoulders, but not too hard. Her shoulders sank and relaxed.

I finished the massage by placing both of my hands on top of her head, holding them there for a moment. I waited a beat. "Okay," I asked, "are you ready for your wash? Come on and get up, slowly."

I led her over to the part of the shop where the sink and shampoo were, and leaned her back in the chair. I carefully lifted her neck to put a rolled-up towel underneath it.

"Your neck feel okay?" I asked.

"Fine," she said. "I'm still floating from the massage. You could do anything to me."

"Well, for now I'll give you a wash and a good conditioner, and then we'll talk about a cut."

When I was done shampooing, I took Beth over and sat her in the beauty chair and pumped it up so that I could work comfortably.

"What do you think?" I asked.

"I'm in your hands, Calla Lily," she said.

"Then I'm going to sneak up on you and just give you a little trim. Texturize a tiny bit in the front, take a little off the back, but keep it feminine. Nothing big this time. Okay?"

"That sounds perfect."

I began snipping carefully on her hair. I studied the lines of her face to see what would accentuate her eyes. "So, what brings you to La Luna?" I asked.

"My oldest recently got married, and my younger daughter flew in from New York, where she lives. The entire time she was here, she kept pointing out all the Claiborne ladies who she thought were really *très élégante*, and she found out they all got their hair cut by you.

"I couldn't believe your shop was in La Luna." She laughed. "I mean, I hadn't crossed the bridge for years. I loved the name of your salon. Anyway I called the Crowning Glory, and I was shocked to hear that it took weeks to get an appointment. But then you said, 'Once you're in, you're in.' And here I am!"

I stopped trimming and asked, "Do you have any special hair concerns?"

"My natural blond hair," she said, "which, of course, has absolutely nothing natural about it. It's so thin that I'm scared people can see my scalp."

"But what wonderful hair you have, so soft," I told her. "And your complexion, oh girl, peaches and cream, peaches and cream! You're so lucky."

"Really? Tell me, is Calla Lily your real name?"

"Yes, ma'am. My mother and father loved calla lilies, and they named me for them."

"Well, it suits you beautifully."

I pulled her hair up to weigh it, and then I snipped some more.

When I was finished, I spun her around to face the mirror and said, "What do you think?"

"Ooh, you make me feel like I 'clean up good,'" she said, beaming. "I love it, especially the bangs being a tad bit uneven."

Oh, I do feel good! I realized, as Beth left, that she had never explained why she burst into tears. But I knew she had left here feeling a little bit healed anyway.

Every Friday since I opened, Miz Lizbeth and Aunt Helen came to the Crowning Glory to get their hair done. They'd show up together around eleven.

First I'd give Aunt Helen her massage and wash, set her hair with brush rollers on the top and on the sides around her face, then blow it dry.

Miz Lizbeth preferred an old-style bubble dryer I kept in the salon for my older clients. The older clients also loved their Aqua Net. No self-respecting Louisiana woman of a certain age felt that her hair was truly "done" without a good shellacking of Aqua Net.

Then Aunt Helen would insist on helping to clean the shop, and Miz Lizbeth and I would go out on the patio. Since she had the best garden in La Luna, Miz Lizbeth would go around checking on all the flowers in the beautiful wooden planters that Sonny Boy made me. She'd tell me, "These coleus should get less sun," or "I'm going to pull those little weed shoots out of your planter of pink calla lilies."

When we were done reviewing the garden, we'd wash our hands and set the table for lunch, which Miz Lizbeth always brought. Some days it would be cold fried chicken with cornbread and tomato salad. Other times it might be ham sandwiches on Miz Lizbeth's homemade bread. But whatever she brought—even her tuna fish salad, which had some of her homemade sweet pickle relish mixed in with just enough Miracle Whip—it was delicious. And, of course, Miz Lizbeth was never one to skimp on dessert, so there was always a special treat—like her pecan tarts or her pineapple cake or her fudgy peanut butter brownies—to end the meal.

Those Fridays with Miz Lizbeth and Aunt Helen were just so loving and warm. I was glad to have the chance to give something back to these two women who, along with Olivia and Nelle, had been second mothers to me. Of course, M'Dear had given me a good foundation for learning how to become a woman, but all of them had shown me how to grow up and become myself.

Chapter 40

1984

How I love October in Louisiana! It is, hands down, the most beautiful time of year. Even though we know that another week or so of heat can still sneak in and blast us, in October, a happiness breezes in. The cotton is being harvested—you can see the combines in the fields—and the big cotton trucks leave a scattering of bolls that looks like white snow along the roadside. Some people get angry as all get-out when they get stuck behind a cotton truck, but I don't. If a fluff of cotton falls onto my Mustang, I consider it a sign of good luck. When M'Dear was still alive, we'd gather up bolls of cotton, glue them to thin pieces of rope, and hang them around the dance studio, strung with Christmas lights. M'Dear said, "Bébé, you got to celebrate every season, not just Christmas and Easter. There's beauty in every day of the year."

People who think that Mardi Gras is Louisiana's only celebration—

well, little do they know! Almost every small town in Louisiana sponsors an annual festival dedicated to its best product or favorite pastime or dish. Louisianans love to party and look for any excuse to sing and dance, invite friends to spend the weekend, and celebrate with good food and drink.

Of course, the best festival themes are snatched up by the towns that are the most publicity-minded. Sometimes I can't believe that there are actually *two* crawfish festivals, one on each side of the Atchafalaya Spillway. There are celebrations of jambalaya, frogs, swine, rice, gumbo, strawberries, and more. I guess you'd have to say that the annual Shrimp and Petroleum Festival in Morgan City is in a category all by itself.

In La Luna, naturally, we have our moon festival. During the festival parade the queen gets to sit on a little bench carved into a crescent moon painted violet blue with tiny silver stars. The queen and the moon get carried through the streets on the back of a flatbed truck decorated with pastel-color Kleenex flowers.

But my favorite festival is held in the little town of Opelousas, which celebrates the harvest of its big local crop with the Yambilee on the last weekend of October. I love it because the ugly heat of summer is pretty much over. And because Tuck brought me here.

Events are held at the Yamatorium, and the festival's royalty are named King Will-Yam and Queen Sweet Potato. In addition to the usual cooking and eating contests and a parade, there is a fun street festival and an auction of sweet potato products. Children get to do a Yamimals contest in which they create characters, in Mister Potato Head style, out of construction paper, toothpicks—and of course, yams.

I hadn't been to Yambilee since Tuck took me in high school, so when Sukey and I saw it advertised in the paper, we decided to go. We asked Ricky and Steve to come up and make a weekend of the festival. We packed up a big cooler with sandwiches, chips, cookies, and Cokes and then put four lawn chairs in the trunk of my Mustang. When we got to Opelousas and were looking for a spot to sit and view the parade, I was shocked. The town had changed!

"Wow!" I said to Ricky and Steve. "I was planning to play tour guide for you, but I can't believe that there's a chain motel here now, and even a Burger King."

It turned out that the motel was where the festival queen and her royal court were staying. "Let's set up our lawn chairs near the motel," Sukey said. "That way, we can get a look at them when they're fresh at the start of the parade."

We didn't have to sit there long before the queen and her attendants came out, all decked out in ball gowns with skirts inflated by crinolines and hoops. "Oh, my God," Ricky said. "Will you look at those dresses?! I think I'm having a flashback to the 1950s!"

"Oh, Ricky," I scolded, "don't suck all the beauty out of those girls! You have no idea of what they have to suffer."

"Yeah, like those hairdos!"

I had to admit that they all had hair that was teased and shellacked within an inch of its life. "That's the style I call 'Cajun Girl Stir-Fry!' " I told him. "But think about it. All of us want to be kings and queens of something."

The parade was an interesting combination of white Cajun and local black culture, and worked a few indignities on its royalty. Opelousas is a town of fewer than 10,000 people, so convertibles are in short supply.

"Looks like only the queen herself is getting to perch above the back seat of a top-down car," Steve said.

"Yeah," Ricky raved, "her twelve less-lucky attendants look like they've had to settle for any transportation they could get. Look at them precariously seated on sunroofs, their legs inside the car and their skirts pouffed out around them. It makes them look like doilies with heads!"

Others had to contend with actual car hoods.

"My goodness, y'all," I said, "those girls risk slipping off, in slick taffeta gowns, and being crushed under the wheels!"

"I bet those hoods are hot!" Sukey said, then took a big sip of Diet Coke.

"Oh, my God!" Ricky said, "look at them! Those poor girls are having to rock from side to side, trying to cool off the right cheek while they lean to the left. That is just butt torture."

"That takes skill, y'all," Sukey said.

"No kidding," I added. "I've heard one year an attendant's pantyhose melted—actually fused to the hood of the car. Think of what *that* did to her behind."

We all started laughing hysterically, holding on to the arms of our lawn chairs. "There's a lawsuit somewhere in there," Steve said, barely able to talk.

As the festival royalty passed, the folks who were lined up on the sidewalk flung candy at them. A man walking in Earth Shoes picked up some of the candy and pretended to feed it to the statue of the Infant of Prague that he was carrying in a basket.

"Uh-oh, I hope the baby Jesus doesn't get a case of the chewdaloos-kas," Sukey said. That's what her mama used to tell us we'd get if we ate too much candy.

Of course, that set the four of us off into more fits of laughter. Then we watched the parade for another hour, and headed to the Yamato-rium.

As we walked down the residential streets off the main parade route, there was a nip in the air. Sweater weather. Enough to make you feel alive with a new season.

All of a sudden, I ached to have Tuck next to me, holding my hand as we walked. I remembered when he'd taken me to this festival all those years ago. It had been the day after he'd made two touchdowns for La Luna High. I can still remember the crowd yelling, "Go Snake Boy! Bite 'em, Snake Boy!"

The memory of that made me giggle a bit. My friends turned to me. "Do you know a secret that we don't?" Ricky asked.

"No," I said. "Still thinking of the parade. Why don't the three of y'all head on over to the Yamatorium, and I'll meet you there."

"But Calla," Steve said, "you'll never find us. Not with this massive crowd of yam fans."

"Oh, leave her alone," Sukey said and looked at me. "Meet us back at the car, Calla. It's easy enough to find."

Then I walked along the streets by myself, with the memory of Tuck's hand in mine. The smell of his leather letter jacket, the way we'd stop and kiss every ten or twelve steps. All that we'd already been through at such a young age made something like a yam festival silly, fun, and precious.

I stopped abruptly for a moment at the sound of a distant car horn. It pulled me out of my reverie, and I felt such a complex weave of grief, guilt, love, and longing that I could barely stand. I found the nearest place where I could sit on a curb.

I'm sorry, Sweet. I miss you, I want you, I would give anything if you were still alive. Forgive me for this longing that I still carry like a stone in a beautiful basket. I still want him. I still want Tuck. How does that feel to you, now that you are on the other side?

I stood up and resumed my walking. It felt good to move my body, to feel its muscles and bones work together. I felt myself moving into a dance. *Du plus profond de mon coeur*, from the bottom of my heart. I was in my own world when I heard a little boy say, "What is she doing?" I opened my eyes to see a towheaded five-year-old wearing very small cowboy boots. His hair was blond and curly. A combination, I thought, of what Tuck's and Sweet's hair might be if they were combined. And that longing for a baby rose back up in me so strongly I had to wrap my arms around my waist as I forced a smile toward his mother.

Had I lost my chance to have a child? Would I ever love someone in that way again? I watched as the mother and her little boy walked off, the sight of his small cowboy boots staying in my mind.

I'm sorry, Sweet, but I know now that I'm still alive and I still want. And the one I want I may never ever see again. But at least now I have admitted it to myself, and to you.

Chapter 41

NOVEMBER 1984

Olivia was the one who found him. Though she was in her seventies, she still came over to prepare meals for Miz Lizbeth and him. She told me later that the chickens were flapping around him on the ground, like they were trying to wake him up. The doctor said that Uncle Tucker had died of a heart attack.

Tuck never got a chance to see his grandfather one last time before he died.

Within an hour, the news of Bernard Tucker's death was all over La Luna. Businesses closed, and people came in from the fields to be together and mourn. That's how beloved Uncle Tucker was. When I called the fishing camp to tell Papa, he broke down in tears.

"Calla," he said, "I have lost my friend. You don't get another one like Tucker. Only one in your life. And now he's gone."

Papa asked me to come and pick him up, since he didn't trust himself to drive. On the way, I thought about how Papa and I had lost M'Dear, how I had lost Sweet, how Papa had lost his closest buddy, and how Miz Lizbeth had lost Uncle Tucker.

I'm sure I'm not the only person to notice that the most segregated hours of the week are Sunday mornings, when black and white worshippers head off to different churches. It was true in La Luna as well, where the pews at Our Lady of the River usually held a sea of white faces. But on the day of Uncle Tucker's funeral, at least a third of those faces were dark—all sitting at the back of the church, like they always did when they came to a white church. Many of them worked at the La Luna cotton gin that Uncle Tucker owned. They'd picked cotton, starting probably when they were six or seven years old, and as they grew up, they worked on the tractors, then in the combines—running the gin, alongside Uncle Tucker.

My papa was invited to sit up front to bid his old friend good-bye. Aunt Helen was sitting next to Uncle Richard, who came out for the occasion. Sonny Boy and Will and their families were sitting all in one row, near the confession booths with Eddie and Renée and their kids. Sukey and her mama sat across the aisle.

I deliberately chose to sit next to Olivia and Pana. The two of them had loved Uncle Tucker so much, and taken care of him for so many years, and yet no one had thought to ask them to sit up front. M'Dear did not like the custom of black people sitting in the back, and neither did I.

In addition to grieving for the old man they loved, the church was buzzing over the fact that Tuck had returned to La Luna for the funeral. Tuck the big-time lawyer, pride of La Luna, now coming home for the first time in years. I'd heard from Eddie that Tuck had flown into Claiborne, rented a car, and driven to La Luna. Eddie also told me that Tuck was recently divorced. I was truly sorry to hear that.

And then, there he was. Marching right past me down the center aisle, staring straight ahead. He took his place in the front pew with Uncle Tucker's other surviving relatives. We all noted that Tuck's mother, Charlotte, was not there. Nobody knew what had become of her.

I must have flushed bright red when I saw Tuck, because Olivia reached over and placed her hand on my arm. Sukey and Renée kept turning around to look at me. Renée shot me her famous one-eyed stare. This could mean anything from "Watch yourself," when she turned it on Eddie or the kids, to warm encouragement, which is what I was getting. Sukey kept making faces at me, but subtly, so as not to disrespect Uncle Tucker.

Throughout the Mass, Tuck faced his grandfather's coffin. Now and then, he bowed his head to bury his face in his hands. Then, after the sermon, Father Gerard asked Tuck to come to the podium to deliver the eulogy. When he stood up to talk, I gasped and covered my face with my handkerchief.

I'd dearly loved Uncle Tucker. He was like a grandfather to me and like a second father to Papa. I don't know what would have happened to my father after M'Dear's death if Uncle Tucker hadn't been around. I'd cried long and hard for Uncle Tucker, but now I also had to hide my emotions at seeing Tuck for the first time in a decade. His face hadn't changed much at all. It was more angular, with cheekbones more pronounced than when he was in his teens. His thick blond hair was shorter and more carefully shaped than when I knew him. Definitely an urban professional cut.

His tailored suit hung well on his tall, lanky body. But the language of his body contradicted his sophisticated image. My body immediately responded to his, a deep animal identification with what he must have been going through. He held his arms behind his back. *I feel the shaking of your hands.* He dropped his head and took a deep breath. *I can feel the tightness in your shoulders.* A hush fell over the church as

Tuck paused to compose himself, with the discipline of a well-trained lawyer. Then he looked up and took in the different faces around the church.

"Thank you all for coming here today to say good-bye to my grandfather, Bernard Tucker," he began. "He was 'Uncle Tucker' to many of you, and he was a true papa to me. I know you all might think I broke his heart by not coming back to La Luna. I can tell you that it was done out of love, between Papa Tucker and me, a love which maybe only one or two other people might understand. Finishing college and law school was a dream for me, for my mother, Charlotte Tucker LeBlanc, and for all my family. All I can say is that I'm speaking for Papa Tucker at his own request, delivered through Father Gerard. My mother isn't here today. But I'd like to think that I'm representing her as well.

"Papa would appreciate y'all being here because he loved La Luna. And he earned your love in return. As you know, he was a man who gave a lot and didn't keep score."

Tuck closed his eyes for a split second. *I feel the tears being held back. I know.*

"Papa was born and raised here. He met and fell in love with my grandmother, Miz Lizbeth. The two of them were always the greatest of companions. My mother, Charlotte, was their only child. She left La Luna when she was eighteen. I left La Luna when I was eighteen. Both of us went looking for something better, but a lot of what we found was simply harder."

Tuck seemed so vulnerable and wounded that I could sense my body leaning toward his, willing him to go on. I could feel a ripple pass through Olivia beside me, acknowledging Tuck's frailty. It was as if the two of us had become a silent chorus for him.

"Papa and Miz Lizbeth took me in with open arms when things were not good—not good at all—with my parents."

I guessed that Tuck didn't even want to mention his father.

"They fed me good food from the La Luna earth, put me in the fields, loved me, and managed to make sure that I still had plenty of time to ride horses, play football, make friends, and enjoy high school. Papa Tucker taught me to hunt and fish at his beloved 'Camp David,' where at night a lot of y'all here would cook duck gumbo and play cards. Y'all were what made Papa's life such a rich one. And mine too, back then. It was the first time in my life that I'd ever been among generous men who actually loved each other and who were willing to welcome in a confused young man. I can't say that I've seen much of that since I left La Luna."

Some of the older men in the audience, mostly in their seventies and eighties, squirmed in their pews. A few were trying to stay poker-faced, others nodded in agreement, and even more were blowing their noses and dabbing their eyes. My papa was one who let tears roll down his face.

"But it wasn't just hunting and fishing that Papa taught me about being a man. He taught me that kindness is more important than anything—that what you do and how you treat people means more than what your last name is. That's a lesson I've had to keep on learning. And he taught me a tough lesson: that the largest part of kindness is to ask for it when you need it, and to give it whenever you can. And he taught me an even tougher lesson in the end—that the highest form of kindness is to ask forgiveness and—"

Tucker's voice broke in a sob. He covered his eyes with his hands. For a moment, the whole gathering held its breath.

He looked back out and continued. "He taught me that true kindness includes the ability to ask for forgiveness, and to forgive."

I watched Miz Lizbeth as she ever so slightly touched her short widow's veil.

"As a boy growing up, I did my best to listen to Papa. I trusted him. He always wanted the best for me—no matter what it cost."

I couldn't tell if I was imagining it, but it seemed that Tuck was now staring straight at me.

"It took me a while to understand Papa's lessons on being a *man* in the truest sense. He raised loving a woman to an art form. I'm seeing that the way he treated my grandmother—so different from the way my own mother was treated—was *gallant*, a word Papa Tucker would never have used himself."

Olivia, who'd been getting worked up in her seat, called out, "Amen!"

The attendants, most all of them white, were not used to shouting in church, and a good number of people crooked their heads around. I figured there would be some sore necks in La Luna the next day.

"Thank you, Olivia," Tucker said, and smiled.

"My grandfather knew most everyone, and most everyone knew him. Sitting up here is Will Ponder. While Will is easily twenty years his junior, their friendship was solid and true.

"The man who Papa Tucker was closest to is sitting in the back—'Pana,' Papa Tucker's name for him when Papa was around four years old. We white people just kept on calling him that. James LaVergne is his given name and he is as fine a man as I've been honored to meet. And he's patient enough with us to let us keep calling him Pana."

Tuck looked out at us, and with what sounded like forced cheerfulness, said, "I'll end by saying that I was lucky to have been loved by Papa Tucker. And by you, Miz Lizbeth. And by you, La Luna." He smiled. "How about we say a silent prayer, then head on over to the Ponders', where I hear there is a *cochon de lait* waiting for us."

We bowed our heads in prayer, eyes closed. But I couldn't resist keeping mine open. I guess I thought I might have a chance to see Tuck when he didn't know I was looking at him. Opening my eyes, though, I saw his eyes glance quickly at the back door of the church, where a woman in a blue skirt was quickly exiting. The look on his face was one of such pain and longing that it made me feel ill to witness it.

I knew who it was. I had wondered if she would come. *I feel the pull toward your mother. All pulls toward the mother have something in common.* I watched him. What could he do? Run down the aisle to try and stop her before she could get away? But he did not run, and instead stood solemnly at the podium.

The look on Tuck's face: loss, longing, letting go. I know what these are. These years of good-bye. These times of good-byes. I thought of Sweet's funeral. It hurts to hold on to anger. And I realized that I could no longer be angry at Tuck. In the presence of his grief, my anger turned back into love.

After we left the church, when we were all at Uncle Tucker's graveside and Father Gerard was commending him to the earth, Tuck kept staring at me. I noticed he was clutching a small, clear vase of irises, and I wondered where he had gotten them. It was well past the season for them, and—

I stifled a gasp as I suddenly recalled another bouquet of irises at Sweet's funeral.

When we all took a handful of dirt and tossed it into Uncle Tucker's grave, Tuck's hand brushed against mine. The contact was electrifying. I stared mutely at my hand, and when Tuck removed the irises from the vase and dropped them carefully onto the coffin, it sent a shiver through my whole body.

I told myself, "We're celebrating Uncle Tucker, as Tuck well knows. We cannot be thinking about each other."

When the ceremony was done, I got into my old Mustang with Sukey and her mother. Sukey, as usual, asked, "Okay, Calla, what's up?"

"Nothing," I said.

"Come on, I could feel the vibrations between you and Tuck."

"That's just your imagination."

"Bull," Sukey started. But thankfully, her mother told her, "Sukey, have some respect and leave the girl alone."

When we got home, I changed out of my black funeral dress and into the charcoal gray outfit that Sukey had bought me back in New Orleans.

And I began to pray, this time to Sweet. *Sweet, my beloved, my husband, my heart is going out to this man who I no longer know. Oh, Sweet, give me guidance if you can.*

I keep seeing you and me eating leftover gumbo and laughing. You, in your clean brown pants and your sleeves rolled up, with your face all tanned and kind. Bless your sweet soul, bless how you told me, "I'll love you, Calla Lily Ponder, in each and every way, each and every day, until the day I die." You did that, my love. So how can I open up my heart to the past?

Then I felt a sense of peace flow through me, like a blessing. Dear Sweet had always filled me with calm and certainty, along with passionate desire. Never with the wild adolescent confusion that I'd felt with Tuck. I had never doubted that Sweet deserved love and trust. But Tuck had betrayed me—how much, I wasn't sure—and in some ways that were profound.

The sense of peace faded, and I took it as a sign that my Sweet, my beloved riverboat pilot, was telling me to chart my own course.

In most of the United States, roasting a pig outdoors on a spit is not your usual approach for cooking funeral food. Where I come from in Louisiana, a *cochon de lait,* a pig roast gathering, is expected. M'Dear and Miz Lizbeth weren't born in La Luna, but Papa Tucker was. He could never rest in peace without the traditional farewell.

My papa said he would host it at our family's home. Since it was my house now, I was more or less expected to help out, so I did. Besides, it had been years since I'd been part of a *cochon de lait.*

Pana slaughtered the pig, something he rarely ever did anymore. Butchering was hard work, and he was in his eighties. Besides, the older he got, the less he liked to see blood. He no longer even raised chickens to eat, he just raised them for the eggs. But on the day that Uncle Tucker passed, Pana let it be known that he would honor his oldest friend by personally slaughtering the pig.

Two days before Uncle Tucker's funeral, Pana and my papa sat in lawn chairs out behind the house and helped coach Pana's grandsons and Sonny Boy and Will through all the steps of the old-time ritual. Pana was very specific about how things should be done. My father, who had learned from Pana, followed the old ways to the letter.

After Pana slaughtered the hundred-pound pig, they prepared it for seasoning. Inside and out were salt and pepper, and dozens of cloves of garlic that had been dipped in a seasoning, the recipe for which had been passed down in Pana's family for ages. Then the marinade took some cooking up, with no shortcuts. Finally, they shot the secret marinade into the pig before it was packed on ice. No one knew what was in that marinade, but one major ingredient was hot sauce—and not one you could buy at the store.

The day before the funeral, they dug a big fire pit in my backyard, filling it with pecan wood and sugarcane. They drove the heavy spit supports into the ground and stuck the spit through the pig to roast.

At three in the morning, the smell of smoke from the fire pit woke me up. By then the coals were ready, and soon the aroma of roasting pig came drifting in. I wondered if Tuck was sleeping, or if he too was awakened by the smell. He was just next door, and if the bedroom window was even slightly cracked, he must be breathing in the tantalizing aroma, a Louisiana scent that he'd never smell in San Francisco, no matter how many fine chefs might cook in that city.

By the time we got back from the cemetery, the smell of that pig tickling your nose was so good that your mouth couldn't stop watering, even in our sadness.

Everyone was told to gather at my place at three. Pana and Olivia's daughter, Bertha, had stayed at the house to receive dropped-off food.

Coleslaw and potato salad; green-bean-and-onion and spinach casseroles; succotash; carrot and raisin and three-bean salads; different Jell-O molds made with mandarin oranges, cottage cheese, and pineapple; plus good, crusty French bread with cheese.

Then there were the desserts—all kinds of pies, including pecan, banana, and coconut cream; and carrot, lemon, poppy seed, and sour cream pound cakes.

What a feast!

My stomach had felt a bit churned up, but when Papa made me up a plate of pork, the tantalizing aroma woke up my appetite. The skin of the pig was perfectly crisp, and the inside well done and spiced.

"Papa," I said, "never in my life have I eaten anything so wonderful."

"Well," Papa said with tears in his eyes, "there's nothing like the true old ways."

Cochon de lait is just one of the old ways of my homeland, Louisiana, which makes us a world unto ourselves, and maybe not like the rest of America—and maybe not like the modern world. I sometimes feel that way myself.

Chapter 42

NOVEMBER 1984

The postfuneral *cochon de lait* was filled with good food, good drink, old friends, and lots of stories about Uncle Tucker. Underneath one of the old live oaks, Miz Lizbeth sat in a chair made of old cypress that Uncle Tucker had made for her. The chair was outfitted with the most comfortable of cushions, and it was from there that she received condolences and hugs. What always touched me about her generation is how often they hold one another's hands. I watched as that happened all afternoon and into the evening, to the soft music that Will played on his fiddle, then on his guitar.

When the last of the pork had been wrapped in aluminum foil and put in paper sacks for people to take home, along with pieces of pie and leftover casserole put in containers that circulated around town over and over till nobody knew whose was whose, and nobody cared; when the old folks had already been seen to their cars or driven home; when Bertha,

Sally, and Aunt Helen had all but swept the rug clean from under us to turn my home back into shape; there were just a few of us left.

One was Tuck.

And one was me.

I would have preferred that the crowd had stayed a little longer. I didn't know if I was ready to face him. Or if I'd even have to.

Sonny Boy had already taken our father to his house. It had been a hard day for Papa. But no matter how tired he and Pana were, they wanted to make sure that their old friend had been celebrated properly.

As people started to drift away, there was less and less of a buffer between Tuck and me. Finally, it was just Renée and Eddie.

"Would it be okay if I stayed just a little longer?" Tuck asked.

"Sure," I said, in a voice that was a couple of notes too high.

Renée, who was rounding up her kids to leave, shot me another one-eyed stare. This one definitely meant, "Watch yourself." She gave me a kiss on the cheek and said, "We love you," then she, Eddie, and their kids went out to the car.

Then it was just Tuck and me.

My heart was beating so loudly that I could almost hear it. I had to force myself to take deep breaths. I wondered if Tuck knew how nervous I was.

He looked at me. I thought I could feel the heat coming off his body.

"Well," I said, looking around. "Good night. I have to finish up some dishes." I turned in the direction of the kitchen.

"Can I stay and help?" he asked and stepped toward me.

"No, no," I said, backing up, wishing I had a tray or something to hold between us, and wishing I were in his arms. "Thank you for your offer, but no, no, but thank you very, very much." How much more idiotic could I sound?

"Okay. Well," he said, "thank you for being so gracious with the *cochon de lait.*"

I looked at him and thought how I saw some of his grandfather's face in his.

"You're welcome. It's the way things are still done here. One of the old ways that still makes the community."

"Well, 'bye, Calla," he said, and it sounded old-fashioned or something and made me want to kiss him. He turned, went out, and closed the door behind him.

I stood in the kitchen and beat myself on the head with a dish towel. Was I really that scared? Was I really that *scarred*? Couldn't I just wash dishes with the man, for goodness sake!

My mind was an arcade of thoughts and emotions. With all these memories flooding back, I realized the only thing that could possibly console me now was Golden Princess.

Running up the stairs to my room felt good. My body needed to move. In a second, I ripped off the funeral pantyhose, pulled on some jeans and a sweatshirt, and ran down the stairs and out the back door. But not before putting my hair back in a braid. I didn't like my hair flying all around my face, especially when I was in the barn.

Ah, it felt good to be outdoors.

I felt invigorated by the comfortable air of the unseasonably warm November night. One of the things that I loved about returning to La Luna after those years in New Orleans was how easy it was to see stars. Lots of them.

I walked into the barn and was immediately struck by that intoxicating smell of the horses, the sweet hay—and even the manure, sweet in its own way from the grass and feed. The smell of horses is one I love so much, and a comfort to me in so many ways. It was Nelle who taught me to ride, and thoughts of us riding together always came with caring for the horses. This old wooden barn was full of these scents, and I filled my lungs. I closed my eyes the way I do when I smell something good, and let it fill me up. I went over and stroked Golden Princess's mane. "Hey Golden Princess, hey girlfriend," I whispered as I nuzzled my face into the soft folds of her neck. I breathed in again, and immediately sensed another presence. Not Sable Star. And not Mister Chaz, Nelle's gelding.

This smell was human. Tuck. I didn't know if I had thought his name or whispered it or shouted it, but it could have been anything because I was just so shocked.

There Tuck was in the shadows, down by the dark brown gelding's stall, talking to him softly, feeding him sugar cubes from his blue jean pocket. Tuck had changed clothes since the party, and was now wearing almost the same outfit he used to wear when we were teenagers. In fact, it looked as though he might have just reached back into his old closet and put on the rumpled white oxford cloth shirt and jeans, his look that I'd always loved. Both still fit him perfectly.

Had I not noticed him when he came in? Was he already there, and I hadn't been aware?

I walked over and touched his horse's mane, and my hand brushed his.

"Calla," he said.

I took a step into him.

"Tuck."

We each knew the other remembered that day in the hot morning sun, two teenagers drenched by sweat and rain and something that could have been love—that kiss, that morning, that touching.

We kissed in the near dark this time, the horses' smell all around us, the same horses making their own tired sounds as they shuffled and sighed in their stalls. Our bodies remembered that summer. And now, the same horses bore witness as we kissed. The inside of my mouth became the inside of his, until we didn't know the difference.

I pulled back, in shock. The moment was over. I tried to breathe.

"We just seem to do that in here, don't we?" I joked, stepping away nervously.

"Yeah, Calla," he said, and looked at my jeans. "Those the same ones you had on a few years back?"

"You trying to talk like a La Luna boy?"

"I *am* a La Luna boy."

"'Scuse me, I have to go finish cleaning up." I needed to get out of there. I patted my horse, then flicked off the light.

"It's getting late," Tuck said, following me out. "How about I give you a hand?"

I knew my way back home with my eyes closed. Tuck stumbled twice. I didn't reach out to help him.

"I can clean up by myself," I said.

"Why don't you just treat me nice?"

"Who says I have to treat you nice?"

I walked up the kitchen steps, opened the door, then let it slam. He followed me in anyway.

"Well, help if you want," I said, and turned to the sink. I filled the sink with soapy water and started washing the dishes. Tuck grabbed a towel, and pretty soon, we had a rhythm going. I'd wash the plates, the silverware, and glasses, then hand them one by one to Tuck, who dipped them in the rinse water and dried them. Whenever my hand brushed Tuck's, I couldn't help but shiver. I didn't trust myself to say a word.

I washed the dishes in silence, feeling the hot soapy water, the soft scent of the mild detergent wafting up. We worked side by side without talking. The sound of the water splashing, the light clinking of silverware, the swoosh of the rinsing, the placing of the dishes in the drainboard rack.

Then, without looking at me, Tuck said softly, "Calla, I'm sorry."

At first I thought I'd imagined it. I waited a while, kept washing. "'Scuse me, did you—did you just say something?"

Tuck stopped rinsing dishes. "I'm sorry, Calla."

"Could you please look me in the face and say that again?"

Tuck closed his eyes for a moment. When he opened them, tears were gathering.

"I'm sorry for hurting you, Calla Lily Ponder," he said, his voice rough. "I'm sorry I left."

Our eyes locked on each other.

"It was a bad decision, Calla," he said. "I never stopped loving you. I was young, I was stupid, and I was scared."

We were both silent for a moment.

"Can you forgive me?" he asked.

I turned. It was his eyes. The words were important. But it was his eyes.

My hands were shaking. I kept on scrubbing at some crust stuck on a pie plate. Words were running around my head: *honey, peaches, white flour, sugar . . . Run, run, danger, danger!*

I wanted to touch his cheek and assure him that I forgave him everything. I wanted to make him crawl across the desert on his knees.

Could I forgive him? Had I already forgiven him? I must have, on some level, or I wouldn't be standing there next to him washing the dishes after his grandfather's funeral.

When I had nothing left to scrub, I passed a final clean plate to Tuck. Our fingers brushed once more. He set the plate in the drainer and covered my hand with his. Achingly, I remembered everything about his hands: their size, their color, their texture, his long elegant fingers, the strong grace. And how those same hands once knew how to please every inch of my young body.

"Calla," he said. "Calla Lily."

I stared at his hand on top of mine.

Tears streamed down my face. Longing shot through me like a cramp. I lifted my eyes to look at Tuck. His were filled with tears again.

I turned my hand over so our palms touched. Slowly, our fingers began a smooth dance of touching, turning over to feel the back of each other's hand, then palms. Then his thumb pressed hard in the center of my palm, and it was all I could do to swallow. It had been so long since I had been touched. *Don't stop touching me, Tuck. Please don't stop. Oh, God, stop now. I cannot bear for you to hurt me again.*

He stepped behind me, and slowly, he lifted my hair and kissed one spot, one particular spot, and with that, my heart and my body began to open. At that sink, on that night, I was sixteen years old again. I was being given a second chance. What I thought could only be fantasy was actually becoming real.

"Your hair," Tuck breathed. "Oh, that lavender-vanilla smell . . ."

He turned his head and gently kissed the side of my neck, and all the vulnerable places that I touch on so many people.

His hand came around so that his palm was cupping my cheek. I turned around to face him and gently moved Tuck's hand from my cheek to my lips. He did the same with my palm. I could now feel his lips on my palm, feel his breath on my skin. I began to kiss the palm of his hand. I kissed his life line, his love line, then the center of his palm. He sighed, and with the exhale let out a trembling sound. Each of us closed our eyes. The world met at two points: where our lips met our palms.

I opened my eyes and looked into his. Then my head dropped forward slightly and I gave a soft little moan. He heard my consent.

I listened as he deeply inhaled the smell of my hair. *Tuck next to me riding Sable Star. Early morning storm rolling in. Hot summer morning. Freshly cut hay. The scent of leather.* I began to have trouble standing up. I reached out to hold on to the counter.

"Calla," Tuck softly asked, "you want something to hold on to?"

I could not believe he was saying this. I breathed deeply for a while before I answered. *Once I answer, it's all over; I'm gone.*

"Yes," I murmured.

"Calla?" he whispered, his voice a soft puff.

"Yes," I said, "I do."

"You do what?" Tuck asked.

"I do want something," I said.

"What do you want, Calla?"

I knew he was both teasing me and checking with me every baby step of the way.

"I want something to hold on to, Tuck."

"So do I," he said.

"Then hold on to me," I said, facing the sink and looking at my reflection in the kitchen window. I moved my thick braid to the front and pulled off the little elastic band at the bottom. As my fingers began to loosen the strands of hair from each other, I turned and looked up at Tuck in invitation. He took my braid from my hands, wrapped his arms around me, and gently finished loosening my braid. Then slowly he pulled his fingers through my hair.

In front of me was the wooden carpenter's table that my grandpa had built, with its warm, gleaming surface. Most of it was covered with open Tupperware containers of leftovers: spinach casserole, shrimp succotash, and crawfish étouffée. Tuck lifted me and set me down on the table's edge. His hands went to my hips. They were trembling as he bent to kiss me.

My legs wrapped around his waist and pulled him slightly forward. I lifted my lips so they were right next to his. For a while our lips almost, but not quite, touched. He moved a tiny bit closer. I moved a little closer, and then our lips definitely touched. Full smooth lips. No tongues just yet. He was waiting for my subtle signal. I gave it, and then our kisses began.

I touched the very tip of my tongue to his. Tuck's tongue came a little ways into my mouth. I let my tongue trace the inside of his lips slowly. There was a whole world inside Tuck's mouth. Then, just when my tongue was coming back to the front, his lips closed on it and began to suck on it softly.

Find me, kiss every little place. Worlds slowly fell away. World of loss, world of anger, world of buying, world of selling, world of loudness, world of cars and asphalt, world of clocks, world of scarcity, world of thinking, all fell away. Only lips and tongues, all energy focused on small intersections.

My legs closed tighter around Tuck. Our kisses took us further and further down the road we were walking. He did nothing without my permission. Finally, he pulled away and looked at me, tilting his head to the side in question. I laughed, and tilted my head back as if to say, *You may, oh yes, you may.* Tuck gave me a big smile. He reached his hand down and began to touch me. With each touch he gave a little groan of arousal, a little groan of recognition. He leaned in and put his face close to mine and breathed in my scent.

"Oh God," he said. "Oh sweet Jesus Lord."

Then the scent of old floors polished with lemon oil, and I am lying on the old four-poster bed, the soft chenille bedspread underneath my back, Tuck's body on top of me. Then my body on top of his. Then side by side. I loved him in ways he'd never been loved, because I myself had been well-loved in a good marriage. I did things I'd dreamed about doing but never had, not even in all those years of marriage. I also let myself do things I had never thought of before. All those teenage years of yearning were the best aphrodisiac possible. He gave me more than any of my fantasies had.

Our stamina was fueled by the memory of our teenage arousal. Slow dancing to "When a Man Loves a Woman" on the gym floor, our bodies touching, Tuck's head bent, his lips grazing my shoulder, our hips swaying. *Oh, God. How can it be that I am sixteen again?* Again and again we entered and explored and pleased, and there was so much moaning that at one point we both started laughing at the same time, and it was soon after that we finally stopped to rest.

Later we climbed into the big old tub, and Tuck said, "Lean back." He reached out for my bottle of baby shampoo.

For a moment, I froze. Strangely, after all the intimacies we'd just shared, it just felt too intimate to have Tuck wash my hair. I wasn't ready to have him hold the weight of my head in his hands.

"Come on, this won't even sting your eyes," Tuck assured me.

"Okay," I said, and leaned back to wet my hair. When Tuck began to rub the shampoo into it, I felt so unprotected. But the time for that fear had gone. As Tuck massaged around my temples, the day and night began to catch up with me. I began to drift off.

I floated deeper into the doze, and pictured myself in the river on whose banks La Luna rested. I pictured myself being held in M'Dear's hands.

To wake me, Tuck gently rocked my head. He climbed out of the tub, filled an old pitcher, and began to rinse my hair.

"You're pretty good for an amateur," I told him.

"That was kind of intense, wasn't it?" Tuck asked. "I mean, when I was holding your head in my hands, I could have done anything to you. At the salon, when you wash people's hair, do you feel that?"

"Yes, sometimes. Most of the time. But I feel all sorts of other things, too."

After rinsing my hair, Tuck smoothed it down my back. "Calla, I can't believe that you still have such long hair. It's been years since I've even met a woman whose hair wasn't gelled or sprayed to death."

"Hey, let's don't knock styling," I said, joking.

"I just mean, in the world I lived in, a woman over twenty-eight with a long, full mane of hair pulled back into a braid was pretty rare."

Then we went back into the bedroom and climbed under the covers, breathing in the scent of old line-dried cotton sheets and clean bodies.

Before we drifted off, I whispered, "In high school, I dreamed of having you inside me."

"I dreamed of it in high school and ever since." Tuck hugged me tightly to him.

"Have you been loved enough?" I asked.

"Tonight? You've got to be kidding."

"No, I mean, have you been loved enough, period?"

He frowned, and turned away from me. I waited, remembering the young boy with his beat-up suitcase, getting off the bus in La Luna.

"No, Calla," Tuck said, turning back to me. "I don't think I have."

I closed my eyes and breathed. I knew there was more to say, but now was not the time.

Our breathing filled the room, joining with the sound of the river.

"Calla," he said, "you awake?"

"Yes," I said. "Are you?"

"Barely. I want to talk to you, though. I want to tell you about my grandfather. What I said in his eulogy today: that he wanted what was good for me, no matter what the cost? Well," he said, his voice shaky, "you were the biggest cost. I don't blame him. But he was blind. And I was blind."

"What do you mean?" I said, propping up on one elbow.

"I'll tell you. Do you remember how we promised we'd write each other every day?"

I was silent for a long moment.

"Did you ever write any letters?" I asked.

"I did. They're in a box that I found late last night in Papa Tucker's study with a letter to me," he said. I stared at Tuck as he continued. "I read late into the night until I couldn't take it anymore. I brought the box over here this morning, to give to you, if you wanted it. If you cared about the letters."

"Where is it?"

"I asked Sonny Boy to put it in his old room for me."

"Well?"

"Do you want to see it?"

"I'm not sure. Maybe I've had enough surprises tonight." I sat up, pulling my hair into a loose bun. "All right. Go get it."

He slipped his jeans back on, and I could hear the floorboards creak in Sonny Boy's old room as my mind raced.

When he returned, he was carrying an old leather-bound box. We sat on the floor and opened it. Inside were a stack of letters. As I picked them up, the image of the girl I once was felt so strong it was like she was in the room with us.

Tuck held one of the letters up. "I read them yesterday after reading the letter from my grandfather. He explained what he had done. Actionable. It makes me sick. And it could only have happened in a small town where a man like Papa Tucker could actually intercept mail. Can you imagine it? He threatened Jean Randolph, the postmistress—said if she didn't hand over every one of our letters, he would fire her husband, who worked at the cotton gin." He paused. "He said he wanted me to have a fresh start, to leave La Luna behind. He loved you, Calla, but he said he loved me more.

"He wasn't a demon, Calla, although part of me still feels that way. Remember that day our senior year, when I went off with my mother and drunken father in his truck?"

"I remember it clearly."

"Well, my father pulled out a pistol and threatened to kill me if I ever tried to get my mother out of that horrible drunken marriage.

"Papa Tucker was there. And his reasoning afterwards—or as he put it to me—was that there was no way that he could keep me safe as long as I was in the state of Louisiana—that he could keep me away from them, but he could never keep them away from me."

"God," I said. "I feel physically ill." I reached over and took a drink of water.

"You wrote me," I said, looking through the letters.

"I wrote to you almost every day, Calla. I let myself wait until 1972, the new year. No letters came—"

"But why didn't you take my calls at the dorm?"

"I never got your messages. Believe me, Calla."

"Tuck, this is almost too much to grasp."

He squeezed my hand.

"Oh, no," I said. "My letters. That I rushed to the post office each day to make the afternoon pickup."

A few minutes of silence went by as I tried to take it in. Then I picked up a letter I had written him and we read it together.

Dear Tuck,

Why have you stopped loving me? What have I done wrong? Please tell me. You can tell me anything, you know you can. So tell me please, why have you stopped loving me?

We were both crying.

"I remember the day I wrote that letter. I was in the café after bussing all my tables at Melonçons'. I sat down with a Coke and put my feet up. My feet hurt bad because I had forgotten where I'd left my innersoles." I couldn't continue speaking, so I picked up a letter from Tuck from the stack.

Nov. 2, 1971
Palo Alto, California

Dear Calla,

When will I hear from you? Papa Tucker tells me you're dating a fellow from Claiborne. Someone you met at the café. You might have told me yourself, Calla. Our vows on the pier, don't they mean anything?

I love you, Calla. Please give me one sign that you love me.

I will wait until the holiday. Then if I don't hear from you, I won't come home. It would hurt too much. Maybe it's like Papa Tucker says—"It's just a teenage romance."

Please, Calla, tell me he's wrong.

I love you,

Tuck

"Tuck, this is too big to take in all at once."

She must have known, too. There is no way Miz Lizbeth could not have known. All the time—my God—my family's oldest, dearest friend—"Uncle Tucker"—and Sonny Boy's godfather. All the time!

As if reading my mind, he said then, "Miz Lizbeth—she wasn't a part of this." Then he tenderly put his hand on my shoulder. After a moment he helped me up off the floor, and we got into bed.

We held hands under the covers and rested.

"Calla, do you think we could have a second chance?" Tuck asked.

I lay there, surprised at how calm I felt in the face of all this.

"Let's see what tomorrow brings," I said.

"Thank you, Calla. If there's a chance, I'll wait."

"Let's rest," I said, fluffing my pillow and turning off the bedside lamp. We were quiet for a long time, just breathing.

"He's at rest up there at last, I imagine," I said.

Tuck sighed. "Miz Lenora is resting too. And your Sweet. Now all three of them are up there."

"Hmmm," I murmured softly.

We grew silent again.

Then I said, "Maybe they're not resting at all. Maybe they're all up there playing Bourrée."

Tuck laughed softly.

It was as if we were saying little prayers through these simple sentences.

"May I roll over and hold you?" Tuck asked.

"That would be a very good thing to do," I said, turning to my side, feeling his body spoon against mine, his face near my neck, his knees in the crook of my knees. I liked the way he asked my permission, the way he took no gesture for granted.

We slept this way until a few hours later, when we woke, each of us having grown used to sleeping alone.

Tuck turned to me.

"God, you are so lovely," he said softly.

"Umm," I said, in the most languorous tone I'd heard come out of my body in years.

Then he pulled me to him and hugged me tightly. Our bodies, no longer young, were relaxed and open. I could feel little endorphin-angels flying rapturously around the bedroom at the sight of us, our armor dropped. We had both lost enough in our lives to know that such perfect bliss does not last. But we also knew enough to surrender to this one glorious moment.

Once Tuck was asleep again, I got up. I was tired, but my body needed its daily morning swim. Quietly I put on my vintage kimono and left the house. Walking down to the pier felt good, my muscles stretching. My arms swinging at my side. I felt happy at the prospect of a swim. I walked through the backyard toward the river, thanking everything. Everything needed thanking, deserved to be thanked, and I felt I hadn't done it in far too long.

Just as I reached the pier, the sun was rising. I stood there, not moving for a moment. Then my long-legged body that weathered every storm began a slow easy dance. With my mother. A private dance, just the two of us. Then I opened out to the sun, to embrace the fiery star that brings us life. In the year since I moved back to La Luna, I'd frequently felt tiny sparks inside my body. Today I danced, welcoming a new little white spark inside me that was glowing. Welcome, little spark, to this body. Sun, moon, male, female, old, young, death, birth. I opened my arms to everything.

At the end of the pier, I dropped my kimono and dove into the La Luna River.

The waters were still warm, after the long months of scorching heat. I slowly swam the crawl, letting my neck roll lazily from side to side as I breathed in. Legs doing strong flutter kicks, arms cutting into the water smoothly with hardly a splash. I switched to the breaststroke, my arms reaching in front, my legs cutting a sharp scissors kick.

Then I smoothly rolled over onto my back. I could hear the sound and feel of my love-tired body rolling over in native waters. Lifting my arms up above my head, and then back down, I pressed my body forward with strength. After swimming for a while, I stopped kicking and let myself float, just let the La Luna hold me up. I could feel the waters of my mother's womb when she carried me; I could feel the waters of my own womb.

As I lay on my back, a gate opened inside me, and forgiveness began to flow through my body. The words of the old spiritual—*Will the circle be unbroken, by and by, Lord, by and by*—came to me. As the tune thrummed through me, I forgave M'Dear for dying. I forgave myself for wanting Tuck while I was married to Sweet. I began to forgive Uncle Tucker for betraying me, for robbing Tuck and me of years of love. The hardest to forgive was the oil company whose greed killed my precious husband at the same time that it was killing my homeland. This is one I'll forgive, but not forget. This is one I'll keep score on.

Mainly, I forgave Tuck. He meant no pain. And now he was offering love.

I looked up at the sky. The old longing to see myself reflected in M'Dear's eyes began to dissolve, as if the river's current were washing it away. I blinked, and then I was no longer looking for her eyes as I had been, without knowing it, for so many years. Instead I was looking clearly at an early morning blue sky. I no longer needed my mother's eyes to reflect me. I could do it myself.

"Hey Calla!" I heard Tuck call from the dock.

I began to tread water as I looked in his direction. He stood barefoot, wearing a pair of ancient jeans, a T-shirt, and a sweatshirt flung around his shoulders.

"I want to marry you, Calla Lily Ponder!" he said.

"You're crazy!" I laughed.

"Okay," he said, holding up a red plaid thermos he pulled out of a canvas bag. "Then how about a cup of coffee?"

"That's more like it." *For now*, I thought, swimming toward him.

"Bet you don't remember how I like it," I said, pulling myself up onto the pier. I could feel him gazing at my naked body. Leaning over, I squeezed water out of my long hair, so thick it took some muscle.

"Are you cold?" he asked.

I nodded.

Then Tuck slipped his old sweatshirt over my head. The gentle touch of his hands made it hard to keep standing. He handed me a pair of sweatpants to slip into, then poured some coffee from the thermos.

Taking the cup of hot chicory coffee, I warmed my hands on it for a moment before I took a sip. It was perfect. Cream and two sugars, the way I've liked it my whole life.

"You remembered," I said, sitting at the edge of the pier.

"Yeah, Calla Lily," he said, sitting next to me. "I did." The warmth ofhis body next to mine brought both comfort and arousal. *I could get used to this.*

I looked out at the waters of the La Luna River, at the blue Louisiana sky, and at the man at my side. And all I could do was give a prayer of thanks. All I could do was sip my coffee, kick my legs in the water, and think, *Yum, yum, yum.*

EPILOGUE

Moon Lady

The breaths of my daughters and sons are the notes that sew their songs together. If I could enfold my children in a soft silk cloth and play lullabies to them from a harp of gold, I would. But there are pastures for them to ride, to plant, to tend. There are streets to be crossed, friendships to cement, hearts to be broken and healed, and hairdos to create! If I could, I would lift them from their bodies and let them fly, free of fear, in a wide open sky. But they would miss the lyrics of being human: the dance in the kitchen; the touch of bodies in bed; the near-mad grief at the loss of a dear one; friendship with a dog; the laughter of friends over good food; the gift of a cool breeze out of nowhere on the face while walking on the levee in mid-June in La Luna. If I could, do you think I would spare my babies from the pain and love and suffering of the body from the first breath drawn? If I could, I would spill a silk sack of secrets down, like fireflies in the hot magic air. But my dear ones might not be ready. They might just swat those sacred secrets away like mosquitoes. If I could, do you think I would use my lunar power to rob them of their beautiful, poignant, soulful earth opera?

I must hold these questions and ponder them in my beating heart and accept that there may be no answers, only the mystery, the great mystery of it all.

I too must know what it is to wane, to grow thin and disappear. After I have grown my fullest and lit every tiny leaf, I must love them as I leave them in my slow fade to black for a while. I must hide so they will seek me as they touch the woman on the corner who is ever so slightly crazy and has hidden it well. They must touch the crazy one inside themselves. They must touch the lonely one, the lost one, the wanting one, the motherless one. They must touch their own brokenness as if it were a pearl of great value, then use it as the key to that which most needs to be unlocked. No matter how great their brokenness, there are still dove gray clouds and blazing suns and music too old for the radio; the old wooden floors and green blue earth they dance on with its pecan orchards and old live oaks; its tender soil, its rivers and tributaries flowing out to the mighty oceans. They must know that they have only this moment and all the time in the world. They must take the world into themselves, then harvest their very selves into themselves.

"All the time in the world" is the song of the blue fescue grass. "Only this moment" sings the air as the mallard duck drops down onto the marsh water.

I am with you while you sleep, I am the dream of world peace that dances like the little angels on the bedstand lampshade. I am the ballerina on the pillowcase that touches your cheek. I wait with you, my babies, I wait with you when you lie down on the old single cot and fall back, finally, into my arms.

I am there with you while you sit on the steps of the back porch and hear the screen door slam. I am the peach you saved—"Don't eat that one yet! I'm waiting until it is just ripe." I am with you until you hear the message the jasmine sends to the noon day sun. I am with you while you work, read, study, hold hands, touch and receive the touches from other bodies.

See? It is not what you thought. You are not alone. As I hold you in my arms, the body's weight drops away. As the heaviness of the body falls away, you grow light.

I see that somewhere in La Luna, a baby cries out, announcing its ar-

rival on the planet. Soul will roll down into an infant girl. I hear tears of joy shed. Oh, at moments like these, I want to reach down and scoop up the little human baby child for just one second, to hold her against my breast. Oh yes, the heavens long for the earth as the earth longs for the heavens. And the sheath that separates us is so fine that never in eternity will we comprehend where earth ends and the heavens begin.

Oh, I know the moon and the moon knows me. I am the Moon Lady. I am the moon and the moon is me. I am La Luna. I watch my children on the banks of a river in the heart of Louisiana. There is one particular daughter there named for a flower. Her mother Lenora makes sure I keep special watch over her.

I am the Moon Lady. I watch my darling children in the beating heart of Louisiana, in the lovely soul of the world.

ACKNOWLEDGMENTS

With special thanks to the following:

TOM SCHWORER JR., my husband and helpmate. His name should appear on the cover next to mine. *The Crowning Glory of Calla Lily Ponder* should have his name on it because he did just about everything but put the words on the page.

STEVE COENEN, whom we lost this year. Louisiana singer, dancer, landscape architect, and one-of-a-kind friend. Thank you for inspiring this book. Now please teach us how to be in New Orleans without you, *dah*lin'.

KIM WITHERSPOON and DAVID FORRER, whose agenting includes deep wisdom, compassion, intelligence, and humor as they, in many cases, save me from myself. With the rest of the staff at Inkwell, they make the business part of book-making as easy as it gets.

HARPERCOLLINS, for the fearlessness it takes to keep love of books intact.

SALLY KIM, my editor at HarperCollins, whose clarity, swiftness, and ability to cut to the quick has won me over.

JONATHAN BURNHAM, and his whole team at Harper.

MARY HELEN CLARKE, Southern Woman of Letters. Just knowing she is there makes me want to write.

JENNIFER HAGER, who showed up, and with her quiet way, revealed eyes to see and ears to hear, with as strong a poetic sensibility as a writer could hope for in a literary assistant.

WAYNE RICHARDSON-HARP, Louisiana storyteller extraordinaire, whose research sharpness helped when my Louisiana memories grew dull.

And to these essential people and places:

Lodi, my home soil; my sweet hometown, Alexandria, right there in the heart of the state; Louisiana, my home state, drenched with soul; Julia McSherry, for sharing her CENLA memories; M. Burke Walker, who held my hand; Jacque and Ed Caplan, Sherrie Holmes, Susan Ronn, Wendy Best and the entire Best family, Donna Lambdin, Tami and Connie Mahnken, Mark Lovejoy, Jan Constantine, Keith Heinzelman, Judie Elfendahl, Patty and Neill Raymond, JoAnn Clevenger, Cindy Harrison, Tom Wells, Mark Lawless, M. Cain, T. Gibson, Maurine Holbert, D. Tauben, Lynn Chadd, Meilynn and Steve Smith, S. Harris, Dave Koehmstedt, Jordan Fischer Smith, Amy Tan, Debby Evans, my mother, Sister Jordan Wells, and my siblings, Tom Wells, Anna Elizabeth Wells, and Dru Wells, who pulled me back on the dance floor; Tom and Barbara Schworer, Sally and John Renn, Susan

Wiggs, Danielle Harden, Curt Pool, John Pizzo, Miranda Ottewell, Marta and David Maxwell, Mary Stien, Linda Huggins, Trish and Paul King, Jon Kabat-Zinn, whose work inspires me daily, Willie Mae Lowe and family, whose love is always there; Pat Smith and the Lyme Disease Association, all those in the Lyme community: the medical practitioners, brave soldiers on the frontlines; Lyme support groups; Lyme patients—I tell you: *There is hope*. You will get better. Hold on to the indestructible ring of hope; those Lyme patients who have written to me—you are not alone, and this book comes with prayers; Brenda Stacey, ya-ya.com Web Hostess, and the divine Ya-Ya communities all over the world, including online, I invite you all to come in and join the fun.

If I've missed anyone, please forgive me and accept my gratitude.

If you enjoyed this novel, why not try . . .

YA-YAS IN BLOOM

Rebecca Wells

Ya-Yas everywhere rejoice – the incomparable Sisterhood is back, busting with life, funnier and more charming than ever before.

When four year old Teensy Whitman stuffs a pecan up her nose, she sets off the chain of events that lead her to become true sister-friends with Caro, Vivi and Necie – the original Ya-Ya Sisterhood.

Now they're back, in love, and at war with convention. Discover the roots of the Ya-Ya's friendship, and roar through sixty years of marriage, child-raising and hair-raising family secrets.